The Lost Books of Benjamin
3 Benjamin 2:1–85

Beyond the d'Arc

Novel 2 of 12 in the 3rd Book of Benjamin

B. Albertill

Beyond the d'Arc, Published June, 2024
Editorial and proofreading services: Taylor Morris, Katie Barger
Interior layout and cover design: Howard Johnson
Cover image: by Ruth Angulo-Cruz
Interior images: by Ruth Angulo-Cruz

 **SDP Publishing**

Published by SDP Publishing, an imprint of SDP Publishing Solutions, LLC.

ISBN-13 (print): 979-8-9882715-8-1

ISBN-13 (e-book): 979-8-9882715-9-8

Library of Congress Control Number: 2024900062

Printed in the United States of America

Children (Great Grand) of our Children
(Grand) of our Children, inclusively

You all are the most precious of our bright stars.
Our skies would be darker without you.

Not unto us, O LORD, not unto us, but unto thy name give glory, for thy mercy, and for thy truth's sake.

—Psalms 115:1

Acknowledgments

*B*eyond the d'Arc, the second novel in the Third Book of Benjamin (3 Benj. 2:1-85) within the Lost Books of Benjamin (LBoB) series, could not exist without the support of so many people. Hence, sincere gratitude must be given to many, including my family who provided insights and commentary on those rough early reads. A special tipping of the hat must go to the Lorelei, who helped me shape and hone characters, served as my plot sounding board, and (with go bag in hand) traveled with me throughout France along the Joan of Arc trail—the northern arm (to Rouen) and the southern arm (to Chinon), visiting all the way stops Joan made in the 15th century; to Steve and Hilda, who helped me photograph and document the castle at Vaucouleurs; to Letitia and Thierry (along with Noa) in Péronne who brilliantly hosted us—the LBoB gang—numerous times for dinner at *Le Bistrot d'Antoine* and lodging in *La Porte de Bretagne*. To my creative editor and contributing author, Cathleen Salsburg-Pfund, who has been there to shine and polish the novel's creative delivery. To my developmental editor, Taylor Morris, who provided timely sagacious guidance for novel depth and structure. To my primary illustrator, Ruth Angulo Cruz, who, with her brilliant art, worked tirelessly to make constructs leap from the pages. To Emersyn Pfund who provided the research, modeling, and formatting for Loni's childhood art. To my interior layout and cover design guru, Howard Johnson, who provided me the mallet and chisel to release my literary work in aesthetically sound hard copy. To my publisher, Lisa Akoury-Ross at SDP Publishing, who very early believed in the beauty of this book and the series and has patiently allowed me the pacing to make an idea tangible to the masses. Also, I must give thanks to my triune God who has blessed us and kept us in His hands, as well as being the inspiration for all things done in this novel and throughout the LBoB series.

Table of Contents

Prologue

*K**ill Him! Give us Barabbas!*
    One can't change the lives of historical people. However, can past historical personalities change lives in the present? Mickey and Loni Peronne want to know. Reeling in the aftermath of the Leaning Tower affair, they opt for much-needed downtime. A proposed trip to the French historical region of the Vermandois holds the promise of fine food, wine, chocolates, and relaxation. More importantly, Mickey may trek a bit farther to visit his namesake town of Péronne, where he can research the origins of his family's lineage.

True to form, both Mickey and Loni hold hidden agendas for the journey. For Mickey, he plans a reunion with an old Templar friend. Loni hopes to secretly meet with her DIA colleague. All converge on the town's most prominent attraction, Péronne Castle. What could go wrong?

Since evil rarely takes a vacation, hidden dangers await our heroes at inconvenient times and unexpected places. The Peronnes must use the knowledge gained from the Leaning Tower affair to help guide them through challenges which engage and potentially supersede their professional skillsets. How will they do? No different than you or me, they must reach deep inside for strength. They must shore up personal flaws by borrowing from unexpected faces in unaccustomed places.

1

Yesterday's Terror Today

Château de Péronne
Péronne, France
Current day

Am I to become one of the rising body count?

Mickey spit blood onto the ground. The world as Mickey knew it faded in and out—he lost all control of reality. The only thing he positively knew was that he was belly down on a cobblestone walkway, and he did not have enough strength to physically lift himself up. Mickey wanted to move, but his blood-matted hair glued his head to the walkway of the castle courtyard where he lay among the bodies of the wounded and dying. The cold cobblestones sucked the heat from his battered body. Blood trickled in between his lips but, with so much carnage, he couldn't even be sure the blood was his. The thought made Mickey flush hot as nausea rose within him.

Minutes ago, casually dressed, Mickey Peronne and his wife, Loni, were pleasantly chatting while striding up to the famous Château de Péronne museum in the Vermandois to meet Mickey's desert friend, the Palestinian Asaad, a visiting museum curator and current presenter of the Staff of Moses. The French city of Péronne was honored to display Asaad's prize exhibit from the Istanbul Museum. Short of Dr. Loni Peronne, no one had done more intelligence research on the Rods of Power than Asaad Baghbah al Bethany and Loni's Defense Intelligence Agency colleague, Douglas Coletrane. For years, the three had collaborated on studies involving either the Staff of Moses or the Rod of Aaron—collectively known as the Rods of Power. They knew the historical significance of these two art pieces and of the hostile Amalekites' interest in them.

It had been a pleasant day as Mickey—tall, in his mid-fifties, with olive skin and a salt-and-pepper-colored military haircut—walked joyfully, supporting his fatigued but contented pregnant wife. Even at eight months of pregnancy, the fair-skinned Loni glowed brilliantly. From her dark, shoulder-length hair to each of her soft pink painted nails, she depicted a smoldering beauty blessed with a rather significant belly bump.

In a blink, peacefulness morphed into sheer pandemonium. Masked men fired weapons. The air filled with smoke, bullets, and screams. People trampled others as they tried to escape the frenzy. Others just dropped in place either from fear, gunshot wounds, or hasty attempts at self-preservation. The fifty-foot stretch of walkway that connected the arching castle entrance to the castle museum became splattered with ripped flesh and human blood.

Mickey had no idea if he had been bumped, shot, or if he was just overwhelmed by the event. He closed his eyes. *Maybe if the sirens would stop wailing and everyone would stop screaming, I could assess myself and then start looking for Loni. . . .*

The day's events flickered in his mind—a fast-forwarding film strip. The last contact he remembered with her was just outside the museum—her hands playfully looped through his arm. She was trying to be so very careful not to injure his splinted and bandaged right hand.

There was no one in the world that Mickey had ever loved more than Loni. To lose her would create a vacuum so great within him that he would emotionally implode. He knew she felt the same about him. *Where is she? Is she looking for me?*

Maybe she went into her Defense Intelligence Agency work mode? No, a DIA analyst wouldn't be much help subduing armed gunmen in a shootout, and an eight-month pregnancy belly would make it difficult to fire a weapon out of a tuck-and-roll maneuver. Loni's expertise revolves around knowledge about a weapon like the Rods of Power—not how to wield them. But maybe that's very reason that these gunmen made the strike.

Mickey knew that the Amalekites, historic follower of Amalek and current follower of Haman, had a personal interest in the Rods of Power long since biblical times. If today was indeed an Amalekite terrorist strike, the sacred Staff of Moses—as well as Asaad and Loni—would all be valid targets of interest.

Mickey's acuity began to cloud again as his desperation rose. *If Loni is collateral damage, then there is much more at stake than the loss of my precious wife.* In her work, Loni had accumulated years of expertise in understanding Amalekite terror methods and practices. In a flash, all this would go with her if she was impaired, injured, captured, or dead. Additionally, there was something recent that Loni had mentioned discovering which was very specific to the power of the Staff of Moses, and she had wanted to get this information to Asaad today. Mickey didn't exactly know what the information was. However, he was quite sure that Asaad would understand its full value. Mickey sensed that until this information was shared, his wife might be the only legitimate source that could lock up the grinding wheels of terror that Haman, the Amalekite leader, had apparently set in motion today.

For a myriad of reasons, Mickey needed to know Loni was alive and well. However, he also knew that if she was out of commission, there was only one face she needed to see right now. *It's not mine . . . or even Asaad's.* Mickey nodded. *Oh yeah, it's Douglas Coletrane's.*

2

Rendezvous Unkept

Château de Péronne
Péronne, France
Current day

I can't keep the blackness away much longer.

Loni Peronne panted. Lying no more than thirty feet from her husband, Mickey, she took a brief check of her wooziness. Loni knew that if she succumbed to the blackness, the implications could be disastrous. *I must stay focused. I must make sense of this spinning whirlwind of scenes in my head.*

Loni had always believed that at the end of a person's life there exists an instant replay of sorts which recaps the entire person's life history in a flash. But that did not seem to be what was happening to her now. *Either I am not at the end of my life . . . or I'm at the beginning of someone else's life. Either way, I'm losing me.*

Loni touched her aching head. Her fingers drew away hot and tacky. *That explains why this isn't my usual headache. What's spinning my vision? Something's not right.* She tried to shake her head to clear her mind, but it just made her nauseous. The scene playing in her head was garbled—the snippets of lives and locations which passed by her view were familiar, but really didn't belong to her.

Despite the slipperiness of the visual bursts teasing away any grip of meaningful understanding from her mind, in her heart, Loni fully connected. She embraced the beautiful places she saw, even though she couldn't recall having ever personally been to them. The plush green forests of western Europe yielded to the rocky hills of the Balkans. Middle Eastern desert oases faded into the crashing English Channel shorelines of Brittany. Loni struggled hard to understand this, but even if she could make some sense of the places and the people, the timeline didn't jive. The correct association of person, place, and time was very badly skewed.

Instead of seeing images of her husband Mickey, mother Monique, father Monty, or sister Jillian, an odd parade of characters in bizarre locations appeared. Loni didn't remember reading, studying, or learning about most of these people or places. The people she saw reflected time periods from fourteenth-century

17

France to the recent past: emperors, queens, cardinals, bishops, doctors, soldiers, scientists, thespians, philatelists, and professional people of all time periods, each of whom correlated well with each other but connected poorly with her existence in the twenty-first century. It appeared that somehow, world history had strangely become intertwined with her personal history. *Could it be that in all the years I chased after my doctoral degree, those historical faces and places are now my life's story—or is mine theirs? What is this?*

Loni wanted so much to be able to take the time to study the places and faces that flashed in and out of her vision. But just as she reached a brink of understanding of yesteryear's snapshots, she was uncontrollably catapulted back into the present. Momentarily, Loni was in the present, then the past, then back to the present. It was a cruel space-time continuum roller coaster.

Tossed into this tumultuous mix was the image of the Staff of Moses—wielded by the only man to have seen the presence of God. The vision of the staff triggered Loni to physically capture and hold on to the present. As she did, her eyes searched frantically for Douglas.

She and Douglas had made a secret plan to meet with Asaad today. *Please, God, let Douglas be here. Let him be safe.* Knowing that the present time wouldn't remain long, Loni's eyes scanned the decimated world around her. Sweat-ladened first responders, panicked visitors, and flotsam and jetsam floating on or through a smokey haze all tilted sideways as she lay on her back, injured, making observations only with the uncoordinated movements of her failing eyes.

For a fleeting instant, Loni thought she could see Douglas through the number of people crouching all around her, prodding her in French. She wished the crouchers would all go away and leave her alone. It was their well-meaning, but obstructive, presence that was preventing her from laying eyes on the one person she needed to see. No matter how hard she tried, Loni couldn't seem to find him. *He's here. He must be. What I have to say, he needs to hear. . . .*

3

Faces and Places

Château de Péronne
Péronne, France
Current day

The road to hell is paved with good intentions.

Loni wiped the blood from her fingers onto her shirt hem. *I should have seen the signposts marking the way, but I didn't.* Amidst the surrounding clamor, she groaned trying to shift positions. *The idea of this trip was never mine. This is all Mickey, and now look what has happened. What we needed was a good threat assessment. Too late now.*

Today was to be a casual, relaxing day filled with joy and frolic while traveling from Germany to France. Mickey was wearing his favorite tan Australian bush hat and his safari jacket, across which was slung the strap of his leather under-arm wallet and phone holster. Loni liked to call his European bag a manssiere, but he cared only for its convenience. It freed up all his other pockets to hold their various travel needs. Loni was dressed in less of a safari mode in dark casual slacks, patterned maternity top, and Cordoba flats, desiring only to be comfortable in the later stages of pregnancy.

Loni struggled to turn to her side on the cobblestone walkway. The weight of her belly was far too much to have pressing down on her. She slowly caressed her belly, in part to reassure the twins within as well as herself that her existential multiplicity was a force multiplier for the positive. In all actions, she would choose prudence over the cavalier. Satisfied in this thinking, Loni tried to put her thoughts elsewhere—away from her discomfort, and yet still in the present. *The drive, yes, think about the drive.* She bent one knee to prepare to rotate her hips. *Miles and miles of Mickey and history.* She took a breath and propped her elbow on the ground. *History about his family . . . history about this place.* She rotated her hips and rolled her weighty upper body over to the ground. *Maybe that is where these flashing faces and places are coming from.* Her exertion drained her—reality faded away. *Oh my, it's that face again.*

19

A crowned, bearded face appeared with greater and greater frequency. It was a horrible face, by far the worst of all of them. Every time Loni saw it, she looked into his haunting eyes and felt pain, sadness, and a deep-seeded, disgusted guilt. *What could have happened to him? Why is he so wretched?*

Loni's knowledge of European history might have helped her to better understand, but every time she reached for her prior knowledge the sad, bearded face faded from view, and she returned to the physical pain of the present day. The numerous cobblestones pressed against her body, and the taste of blood was becoming her only present reality. *I can and will endure this if doing so helps me find Douglas.* She grasped at the present with all her mental acuity and held on as tightly as she could.

The nearby crouching masses of triaging first responders around her finally began to move away, and Loni had a sterling opportunity to look for Douglas. Some people still blocked her view back toward the twin tower entrance; nevertheless, she struggled to look.

The entrance she and Mickey had taken into the castle courtyard had been through the portal of the twin bastions. The second-story archway, which spanned the width of the walkway into the castle, cast a shadow over a huddled crowd as they seemed intent on surrounding another injured victim. *No doubt if there is an injury over there, even with his injured and splinted hand, Mickey will be there helping. After all, he is an army physician.*

She tried to home in on the people moving about from body to body, searching for a familiar bush hat or safari vest. She could not hold the gaze for long before she had to rest. Then her eyes landed upon a familiar face. This face was the only one in the crowd under the archway that was not in a tilted side view.

She could see directly into this man's face. Like hers, his bandaged head also lay on the cool cobblestones, but unlike her, his eyes were closed. Loni spasmed as she came to the realization that she was staring into the bloodied face of Douglas Coletrane. *Wait, something isn't right about the turn of the nose and the contour of the chin.* Loni squeezed her eyes tightly, blinked hard, and looked again. Before she could release a breath of relief, she sucked it back in. *It isn't Douglas. It's Mickey.* Loni's eyes scanned down to his hand to confirm her worst fears. The hand was indeed wearing the splint that was placed on it this morning. She fought hard to stay with Mickey's face, but like a shawl, blackness draped around her. No matter how much she resisted, the crowned bearded face filled the entire expanse of her vision. *Not you.... Please, not you.... Anyone else but you.*

4

Unforgivable

Château de Beauté-sur-Marne
Paris, France
14th century

The poisons we make ourselves are far worse than the poisons we're given by others.
    King Charles V arched in pain. Only in the dead silence of the night can the human body feel the moment-by-moment liquefying of its own joints and tissues. Fifteen days ago, the king knew that this was coming. He knew it when he saw the festering sore on his arm dry and disappear. Those who didn't know that this apparent healing was a bad thing jubilantly rejoiced for His Highness. In reality, a poison was moving from the skin surface into the deeper tissues of the body. Eventually, these toxins would reach the blood. *It races into the deep, dark places where only the agony dwells.*
    "What have I done to deserve this, Lord?" King Charles cried out into the blackness. Tormented, he raked his hands through his straggled beard. He already knew the answer. *Of the many sins committed in a lifetime, there are some more difficult to forgive than others.* The king's mind tumbled back to one significant day that occurred five years ago in the same place where he now stood.

✠ ✠ ✠

It was a day of critical issues; so many that he needed to have his soul absolved. For the matter of private confession, the king sent for the highest clergy in France, the archbishop of Paris. The pair stayed locked in the king's private confessional for several hours before the mission was completed. Once finished, the men exited, and their reddened faces reflected the session's intensity. Mopping the sweat from his face, the archbishop was first to break the long silence.
    "Sire, may I have your permission to speak?"
    "Speak, my dear Archbishop."
    "Unrestricted with full liberty?"

"Of course, Counselor. I will temporarily stay the hangman's noose. Speak your peace."

"Highness, in your confessed words I have seen evidence of all seven deadly sins. I saw envy, gluttony, greed, lust—" Before the archbishop could finish listing, the king interrupted.

"—pride, sloth, and wrath. Archbishop, I am not proud of these thoughts and actions. I strive to eliminate them from my daily life and from my dealings with everyone."

"As your spiritual counselor, Highness, there is one sin above all the others that gives me my greatest concern for your soul."

"You are talking of the one for which I lack remorse, Counselor?"

"Yes, Majesty, we live our lives burdened with the curse from Adam and Eve. We sin. We then confess these sins before God and pray for forgiveness. . . ."

"Yes, Counselor, then we sin again. The cycle repeats itself for time on end."

"Nevertheless, Majesty, you lack any indication of repentance for that one sin. Without repentance there is no forgiveness."

"Would you rather that I lie to you, Counselor? Wouldn't that just add more sticks to the fire?"

"I would rather that you felt sorry for the action."

"Maybe in this one case, you will have to feel sorry for the both of us."

"I'm not sure I understand. . . ."

"Let me help you to see things from my seat. Close your eyes, Archbishop."

"Majesty, please . . . I don't want. . . ."

"Close them, Your Reverence. Your king commands it!"

The archbishop's eyes reluctantly closed. His breathing began to slow into a steady rhythm while King Charles drew in a deep breath. The king began to speak in a hypnotic tone, moving steadily through his own memories of the day.

"Imagine being at home alone at a time late in the afternoon. Workdays have become strung together beyond counting. The quality and quantity of today's workload has made you tense all day long. No matter how hard you've toiled, your mind fixates on the fact that you've been left to face everything all alone.

"The table before you is domed with scrolls and documents. They are to be worked, but nonetheless lie untouched—virtually scorned by your hand throughout the workday. You look at the gilded cage that surrounds you. Although beautifully crafted precious stones and metals adorn the fixtures all about you, they cannot provide you a comforting touch or one gentle word. The heart that God has given you serves only as the vessel to collect the rising levels of your soul's pain.

"To take your mind off this oppressiveness, you then pause to look out your window. There you see strong, barebacked field workers lying coolly in the shade under your great elms. These great trees exist because you and your fathers before you have earned the money to have them placed there. These workers splash their bare feet in the cool waters of a bubbling brook. They lie there in the fresh, clean air as you suck in the staleness of your golden, prison-like workroom.

"You notice that the workers' comfort is disturbed only by the hot meal and cold drinks brought to them in their moment of utmost relaxation. Each basket is carried by the milky hands of fair young maidens so sweet of essence that the honey-breath they exhale seasons the food and drink to an elevated level of dining ecstasy. The fairest of these maidens you know. You know her well. She is an apprentice to the royal court recorder. You have heard her laugh and have seen that smile, but mostly from afar. She is as skilled with the luncheon baskets in the field as she is with each of the court documents of human misery she has placed upon your desk.

"As you look at the outdoor scene, your insides cramp and rumble mercilessly. You are so famished that your stomach thinks that your throat has been slashed. It is true that meals have been brought to you throughout the day. But because of your toil and responsibilities, that mountain of food sits spoiling on the far table providing a haven for flying and burrowing insects alike.

"You own the world outside the windowpanes as well as inside. However, what you have built with the sweat of your brow escapes your touch. The pleasures that mere field workers experience are beyond your reach even though you are the master of this domain. Like a volcano, a burning rage builds within you.

"And then it happens. . . ."

"What happens, Majesty?" the archbishop croaked in a gasp.

"You hear a rap-rap-rap on the library door."

The archbishop shifted uncomfortably and leaned forward in his chair producing an eerie squeak.

"As the door opens you see her, the fairest of the basket carriers from the fields, the one that you know. Here she stands; the very one from beyond the windowpane who—just moments ago—you saw with a smile on her lips, exuding grace with every touch. She stands before you quietly with her head and eyes slightly bowed. Her skin glistens lightly with a thin sheet of perspiration. Your nostrils are filled with her rich pungency. It is an intoxicating fragrance of youthful femininity. She isn't smiling now. She isn't laughing now. She stands without joy, almost motionless, holding out to you in that fair extremity another cluster of wretched documents like those which already fill your desk to vile, repulsive proportions.

"You reach for the scrolls, jerking them from her hand. You throw the rolled papers across the room, scattering the insects from the food. The momentum doesn't stop there. Your hand grips her skin, imprinting them with your fingernails. You then pull at her smock which tears away, falling to her feet. Standing half naked before you, her head raises. You then see in her eyes that look of fearful dismay when this maiden knows what is about to happen."

The archbishop interrupted, "Sire, please don't . . . I understand better now—"

"Silence, Archbishop. You dared to counsel me on deadly sins and regrets. You dared to tell me how I should feel remorse when every fiber within me feels a vicious hatred of pent-up frustration. You sit now. Ears open. Mouth shut."

"Sire . . . I . . ."

"I said closed! Where was your smug wisdom when my queen couldn't find an escape from her sadness in the leisure environment which I created for her in this very castle? What were you doing while I watched my beloved queen grow sadder until death took her? Neither religion nor medicine provided her a blessed reprieve. I lost my beautiful queen to her depression, Archbishop, along with my little daughters Marie and Isabella in twelve months. That's right, Your Reverence, three dear hearts in one accursed year."

"Highness, I may have miscommunicated my message. I am the one person responsible for your spiritual well-being. Inasmuch, it is my solemn duty to counsel the king regarding the sins of the flesh."

"I got your message, Archbishop. Are you getting mine?"

The archbishop started to speak but as he looked at the intensity on the king's face, he rolled his lips inward and remained mute.

"I have admitted to you and confessed to God that I took full physical liberties with the blossoming young court apprentice. I consumed her youth as I would a ripened fruit, rich and succulent. And I did so against her will atop a pile of court documents on this very table again and again until she accepted the spewing of my royal seed. For this I have no remorse to you or to God that this maiden walked into my chambers and left no longer chaste. I do, however, regret that I was the hand that lessened the dignity of another human being. It is shameful for any system that society has created which allows any king—nay, any person—to have such unabashed power over any subject, be they male or female. She did not deserve the physical expression of my rage and frustration."

"Highness, I don't know what to say."

"Say nothing, Your Reverence. Just pray that when you stand before God, you can say that you had done all you could do to save the soul of a king. On that day I will, in turn, pray for the failings of a societal system, an archbishop, a court physician with inadequate skills, and the unfortunate maiden. Her name still escapes me and yet, in that moment, I hesitated not in locking her softness against me and bending her to my will. Mind you, this maid-no-more erred only by being in my presence in the wrong place at the wrong time."

✠ ✠ ✠

King Charles pressed his palms to his ears, trying to block the words and the guilt that they carried from his memory, but he could not stop them just like he could not stop the rising morning sun. In the coming of the new day there would, at least, be a distraction from the never-ending supply of physical agony. As the sun prepared to rise, the king squeezed his eyes shut and braced himself for the next wave of cramping.

In the silence, the clicking of the door latch pricked the royal ears. *Who would dare violate the sanctity of the royal bedchamber at this hour in the morning?* The door slowly crept inward as the wave of the king's pain rose toward its peak. *Could it be an assassin? Oh, how I wish it would be. Then again, how can one kill a man who is already dead?* As the door fully opened, King Charles strained forward in the dark to see the identity of the dawn intruder. His eyes seemed to behold a silhouette of an angelic figure framed by the doorway. Her robes were dark and gently swished as she moved. She came closer. Her shadowed face appeared soft and kind. In her mouth, she seemed to be holding a flower. No face he could remember was more heavenly. *Indeed, the time to leave earth is rapidly approaching.*

Collapsing back into his bed, clenching his teeth, he allowed the cramping of his joints to reach its excruciating climax. As the pain began to temporarily subside, his breath slowly eased and his face relaxed. *Who could this be? This is no assassin. An assassin would have certainly killed me by now. This is no angel either. An angel would have already lifted me from my misery.* He tried to focus his eyes on the darkness before the dawn.

"Wait." His hoarse whisper was barely audible. "I know you, dark angel. I do. You are her—the weight on my soul. Where are your damning scrolls? You are what I must carry to judgment. Are you here to witness my earthly wretchedness and gloat? If so, get on with it, there isn't much time left. Otherwise, pity me as you depart."

5

A Rocky Start

Château de Péronne
Péronne, France
Current day

The smell of gunfire began to slowly fade and most of the smoke haze had lifted as well. The urgent heightened exchanges between French emergency personnel seemed to have lessened but nonetheless were still present. Mickey felt so very tired. He was glad his headache had abated. However, now his right hand seemed to be the focus of his discomfort. He glared at the splint and his bloodstained fingers.

✠ ✠ ✠

Several days earlier, inside x-ray room number one on the first floor at the United States Army Hospital in Heidelberg, Mickey sat aggravated by his role as unfortunate patient. He was typically on the other side of the clipboard, so to speak. He looked around at the walls which surrounded him and at all the radiographic equipment currently being used to image his right hand. He wondered about all the patients who had stared at these same walls since the hospital was first used by American forces at the end of the war in 1945. *Back then, these walls probably surrounded patient rooms since x-ray facilities were still being developed commercially,* he mused. *I wonder who sat here? Waited for good or bad news here? Died here?* The throbbing in his right hand snapped him back from his historic reverie.

Mickey, who had just recently been promoted to army colonel, knew that his hand was broken at the very moment he fell over the table at home. He could feel the way the broken bone painfully flipped every time he opened and closed his dominant right hand. Incorrigibly playful indoors, Mickey was titled the biggest kid in the Peronne home. However, he felt this title should have been exclusively reserved for their pups: Domino, their Dalmatian of seven years now, and the newest addition to the household, a Jack Russell terrier–Chihuahua mix named Pepi-Roni.

26

Heidelberg to Péronne

Musing on titles, Mickey recalled how his wife, Dr. Loni Meriwether Peronne, called herself the *real doctor* of the house. He knew this was a valid claim because her terminal degree was a doctorate in special education from the field-based program at Nova University. Mickey and his medical colleagues had been frequently reminded by her that the title *doctor* meant teacher while *physician* meant practitioner of the physical and natural. As such, sporting an education doctorate made Loni the only real doctor among Mickey's medical friends, colleagues, and acquaintances, except for the metaphysician Douglas Coletrane who often taught his clientele through alternative medicine techniques.

Mickey inspected his injured hand. Except for some pinpoint bruising in his palm, it felt far worse than it looked. He shook his head. *All for a stupid game of chase.* Why he spontaneously thought it was a rational idea to make a maniacal lunge over a kitchen table to catch two scurrying canines was beyond reason.

"It seemed the best course of action at the time." Mickey again recited his own pitiful defense. Then he recalled Loni's face after it happened. "She could have pretended to care," he whispered to himself.

The fact was that Loni had no sympathy for his carelessness, even if it did result in a broken hand. She was eight months pregnant, and this was the time when she needed him most. Mickey grimaced. *This is going to jack up the trip—our last one before the twins are born.* He further understood that she just couldn't yet come to terms with the fact that he had also broken the table she had painstakingly sanded, finished, buffed, and shellacked.

One would think that promotion to full-bird colonel and pinning on US Army eagles might have taught me something. Being a bird colonel doesn't mean I can fly.

"As you know, Dr. Peronne," said the radiograph technician, nodding her head, "your x-ray will be reviewed upstairs in Orthopedics. They will let us know shortly if they need more pictures of your hand. Until then, you can go back to the waiting room. I believe your wife is there waiting." The radiographic technician smiled, pulling her red hair back with one hand while pointing up the small hallway with the other. There, in the patient waiting area, Mickey saw a very pregnant Loni angrily crocheting.

"So, Michael Philip, are you still going to be able to drive?" Loni asked curtly. "We have the whole Joan of Arc trail to negotiate today with the deadline of meeting with Suzanne Coletrane in Paris by nightfall." She put down her crochet piece and then began vigorously sliding the pendant crucifix on her necklace repeatedly up and down with a noise that emulated fingernails on a blackboard.

"Remember, Mickey, it was your idea, thank you very much, to use this time to visit the town of Péronne to research the family name—which is no small task," she began, "*and* its deviation from the original, Piérronne le Bretonne, which, in essence, doubles the work! On top of that we must meet with Asaad at the art exhibition at the museum in Péronne. All this ahead and we are still here in Heidelberg delayed because of your flying antics with the pups."

Gritting his teeth from the skin-crawling noise of the necklace, Mickey rubbed his sore hand, which longed to be cradled back in its splint. Reaching over to stay Loni's hand from further chalkboard-like scratching, he replied, "Too easy, honey, it's a piece of cake. In fact," Mickey continued in a most upbeat manner, "Suzanne said she would get a ride from Charles de Gaulle Airport, which will save us a bit of driving in Paris. Furthermore, we can just visit with Asaad at the art exhibition. We can always drop the family heritage research if time becomes crunched. We can always defer the academic portion of the trip till next time. From what I hear, France is not going away any time soon."

Mickey forced a smile through the increasing pain in his hand. Loni returned none; she simply resumed her crocheting and pursed her lips tightly. Mickey could smile because he knew something that Loni didn't know.

Loni's parents, Harmon and Monique Meriwether, were secretly coming from the United States to surprise their daughter in her last phase of the pregnancy. They were to meet in or around Paris at a place to be later confirmed and then later join the return trip back to Heidelberg. As the Republic of Germany permitted visitors to stay for ninety days, the timing would be perfect for some grandparenting help with the newly born twins.

Mickey considered telling Loni that her parents were planning the surprise visit. However, after much internal debate, punctuated by the relentless clicking of crochet hooks, he conceded to himself that the secret needed to be kept. The reveal might cheer her up now, but it would not be seen as a positive thing later. The Meriwethers would ultimately view this as an act of disrespect since they wanted greatly to surprise their younger daughter on her joyous occasion. Looking at Loni's unhappy face, Mickey was quite certain that right now she was in no mood to hear anything about withheld secrets.

Reviewing his own x-ray, Mickey confirmed that a fracture truly existed just behind his fist knuckle. It was broken clean through the bone. He knew all too well what this meant. His hand would have to remain immobilized until the swelling dropped and, later, be surgically pinned. This meant that he still had some unfinished business here at Heidelberg Hospital, going to orthopedics for a twenty-minute stop before his final patient release. In the ortho cast room, the broken hand bone would be splinted for better immobilization.

With this diagnosis percolating in his brain, Mickey subsequently escorted Loni out of the Radiology Department toward the central hospital elevator. As they exited the Radiology Department and turned right into the long hallway, they passed a beautiful photographic memorial to General Patton which decorated the wall on the left side of the department's entrance. Having hardly noticed the pictorial tribute to the famous man, Old Blood and Guts, Mickey now realized that he had never given it its due respect. Although he was distracted, with his attention split between his pulsating hand and his eight-month gravid wife, the memorial to General Patton nevertheless stirred up a memory of an almost forgotten ghost of Christmas past.

6

Of Christmas Past

Route to Neckarstadt
Rhine Valley, Germany
1945

Along the road, stretching away from the castle fortress, a Cadillac convertible hummed. The windblown passengers knew that a day trip to Mannheim could be finished in just half a day's effort. Along the passenger side of the car, the sign for the town of Neckarstadt clipped by quickly, informing the morning travelers that the center city of Käfertal was just around the bend. The crispness of the winter air did not seem to bother the two occupants in the rear seat, nor the driver for that matter. A day filled with pleasure hunting was foremost on their minds. In the back seat, George and his faithful chief of staff, Hap, were discussing the intricacies of fine bird hunting. Both knew that this day would not end until each of them had met their quota of game birds.

In the shadows of Schloss Strahlenburg, dueling pheasants battled in the early light. Strutting and gesturing, the birds boasted their claim on both preferred turf and promised mate. Although there would be no death in the dueling, there was an ominous sign of death in the west wind as it blew cool and steady toward the Oldenwald Mountains of the German Rhine Valley. On this early December day in 1945, the wind was not strong enough to blow away the lingering morning haze.

Though today seemed filled with ill winds, they hoped that Lady Luck would change all that as she presented herself. However, whether she did, it made no matter. The bottom line was that the hunting for birds had to be today. Tomorrow was not an option, at least not for George. He was already on the airplane manifest, scheduled to take the long trip back home to America where his family waited for their soldier to return.

The peacefulness and serenity of the morning drive was suddenly broken. Directly in front of them, out of the fog, a large hulk of shape appeared. It was the forebodingly large silhouette of a military cargo truck filled to the brim with its maximum two-and-a-half tons carrying capacity. Stretching ominously across the full width of the road, the truck looked to be stalled in midturn across the direct path of the rapidly approaching Cadillac.

The screeching emanating from the locked wheels of the convertible heralded the severe impact to follow. There was nothing on God's green earth that would prevent the thunderous collision and profane intertwining of crafted vehicular metals. Silence followed the resounding echo of the metal-on-metal fusion. Game pheasants fluttered in the wake of the crash.

Many hours later, in the Heidelberg hospital bed propped on his side, George lay motionless. He was totally numb from the neck down. He didn't remember anything beyond the crisp morning air and the hope of hunting. *Where is that nagging leg pain, my constant companion and reminder of past battles fought?* Ironically, his desire to lose the pain of his old gunshot wound finally played out but not in a way he had ever imagined. Never in this life did he experience such a situation as now he faced—physically paralyzed and living in a world fueled with constant motion.

Lying motionless in what would someday become x-ray room number one permitted George to think. He reflected upon the troubles which ebbed and flowed between him and his immediate supervisor, Dwight. George had known Dwight for many years and even remembered the time that Dwight, as a junior upstart, wished to learn under George's professional mentorship. As it turned out, even without George's guidance, Dwight moved up the ladder of success with great speed. Eventually, Dwight surpassed George. Despite George's seniority, he was relegated to the lower ladder rungs as a subordinate ranking officer, fostering an ever-brewing basis for discontent between the men. Unfortunately for both, George was always the painful thorn in the lion's paw. As such, George knew that because of this well-published professional conflict, there would be those who might see this vehicle accident as sabotage. *No one, not even Dwight, deserves that kind of cheap accusation. But eventually it will surface. It always does.*

In his career as a professional soldier and military governor, George had seen thousands, if not tens of thousands, of other poor hospitalized unfortunates in various degrees of paralysis. Some were military. Some were war-torn civilians. However, in his wildest vision, he never saw himself as one of them. Now he understood the look they had in their eyes—fear, shock, disconnection, anger. He understood it all.

He stared into the hospital bedside mirror. He saw the helplessness to which he had evolved, coming to the sober realization that he might not be able to walk into his family's Christmas morning celebration which lay just sixteen days away. The potential of this reality was impossible for him to fathom. Never since his days as a toddler had walking ever been an issue for him. That was almost sixty years ago.

Moving his eyes from his reflection in the mirror to the bedside table, George's eyes spied a deck of fifty-two playing cards. *Is this someone's idea of a bad joke? Here I am, staring at playing cards—unable to fan and hold them in my bruised and swollen hands.* He resented the irony that life had dealt him. It was a difficult hand upon which he had no ability to play. Looking at the top card, which just happened to be face-up on the deck, he glanced into the eye of the mustached Jack of Hearts. *Finally, here is an old friend I know well.* Except in the world of the author Lewis Carroll, to most Americans the Jack of Hearts had little significance. However, to George and the French, the Jack of Hearts was much more than an *Alice in Wonderland* "tart thief." The Jack of Hearts was known as the great French Knight, Étienne "La Hire" de Vignolles. Focusing through the cloud of medicines coursing within him, George looked at the Jack of Hearts and spoke aloud to his old French friend and compatriot in arms.

"So, look at us, my knighted friend. Here we both lie, unable to do anything except to blankly stare at each other." George blinked at the moisture building in his eyes. "I understand, Monsieur. I don't feel much like conversing either. After all, what more is there to say? In this war, all the battles have been fought and won. Now begins the painful march to the rear. That is, for those who still can feel their feet. Eh?"

George remembered quite well that the Jack of Hearts was the French military commander who marched with Joan of Arc, the Maid of Lorraine, throughout the war campaigns of 1429. His service to Joan was significant at Orléans and most notable at the Battle of Patay.

"So, when was it that we last crossed shadows, Monsieur La Hire?" George's eyes followed the contour of the card's face hoping, in vain, for any lip movement.

"If memory serves me better than my arms and legs, we embraced after the rescue of Orléans from the Godon English in 1429." La Hire winked and smiled but remained silent.

"The Maid never looked more daunting. Would you agree?" As the Jack of Hearts began to respond, the screeching of a hallway gurney muted the reply. George pushed on.

"Yes, my friend," said George, "once Orléans had been relieved from English control and the city was saved, we French realized the next mission. The bridge over the Loire River had been destroyed during the fighting. So, it was incumbent upon Joan and you, my dear Monsieur La Hire, to regain tactical and strategic command of the other bridges, thus initiating what the world would come to know as the Loire River Campaign of 1429." The Jack of Hearts rolled outward his lower lip and nodded but said nothing. George paused for a breath, searching around the room for a cool drink but found none.

"Though you may not know it, Monsieur, it was not the lifting of the siege at the Battle of Orléans that made you great. It was at the Battle of Patay where you made your mark for all time." George saw the Jack of Hearts smile broadly and nod—they both remembered the battle as if it had just been yesterday.

George's mouth was parched dry as desert sand; he closed his eyes and swallowed hard. Monsieur La Hire took the floor, speaking with a heavy French accent. "It is quite true. Our defeat had always been at the hand of the

Godon English long bowmen. Like mobile artillery these archers cut down our heavy armored cavalry at a coward's distance long before our decisive ability for mounted battle shock—"

"True, but at Agincourt our vulnerabilities were more complex," said George. "The English were further aided by the fact that the ground was soft and pliable. The weight of our heavy battle armor slowed our French knights and mired them down in the mud. Those fortunate few who made it through the quagmire were then impaled on long stakes. The resulting defeat for France was astounding." Replaying the graphic imagery in his head, George's croaky voice trailed into an uncomfortable silence until he again heard La Hire speak.

"Agincourt was a bad day for France, Monsieur, but God did not let it end there. It was English overconfidence that led the English to defeat. At Patay they formed up just like they did at Agincourt. However, God was watching and so sent a white stag on to the battlefield."

"*Oui*, Monsieur La Hire, I remember it well. The English archers, being hunters by trade, frantically scurried after the hapless stag. They wanted its honored presence at their victory table. What they didn't know was that a small assembly of our French cavalry quietly stood in the wood line."

"You are being most modest, my dear Jean," La Hire chastised kindly.

"Modest, La Hire?" George asked. "Rarely anyone considers me modest."

"Yes modest, Jean. You are being modest. It was you," La Hire's voice rang with great authority, "one Jean Poton de Xaintrailles, despite battle wounds from Orléans, who was the leader of the cavalry. Was that not you, Jean?"

George, in turn, responded with great reverence, "Yes, Monsieur La Hire. It was me, Jean Poton, that day . . . but I did nothing more than any soldier would do when duty called."

"Agreed, Jean. It was duty that brought you with me to the edge of the forest. However, it was that keen military mind of yours that understood the immense tactical advantage. You knew that with the passing of another moment, the stag would no longer distract the English. You spurred us on to decisive victory."

"Monsieur La Hire, you are too kind to think all this keenness of mine belonged only to me. You forget that Arthur was there with us."

"*Oui*. I remember. Arthur III de Richemont was there with us at Patay as he was with us at Agincourt."

"Yes, Arthur stood with me in agreement to attack even though our full ranks had not arrived."

La Hire's tone changed to grateful indebtedness. "Yes, my friend, together both you and Arthur urged me to attack at that moment, armed only with courage and the minimal shock force at hand. History would see it as either great courage or great foolishness."

"There is always a fine line that separates courage from foolhardiness."

"For France on that day, history saw unbridled courage," La Hire iterated. "Without further hesitation, together with the Maid of Lorraine, we quickly eliminated the English advantage. By the time the remainder of the full French and English armies had marshaled for combat, the battle was essentially over. The one key advantage that the English held ran away on the hooves of a wild French stag and the brilliant engagement of carpe diem. I had never seen the Maid of Lorraine more ecstatic—the victory cost so few French lives." La Hire's voice trailed, and astute silence again followed.

George closed his eyes on the gratefully smiling Jack of Hearts on the top of the deck. In his memory, he reviewed just how many times, both before and after the Battle of Patay, he had unhesitatingly opted for speed and shock while fighting and how that method often turned a disadvantage into a blazing victory. Battling as an Israelite against the Amalekites in Sinai, as a Carthaginian at Cannae, and as an American in the Ardennes Forest, George remembered and appreciated the fact that although he had been dealt many bad hands, he always managed to taste victory more often than defeat. He felt that soon, very soon, he would have to change seats to keep playing the game. He opened his eyes to see La Hire, as the Jack of Hearts, blankly staring back at him.

"Take care, old friend. Take the best care. We will meet again in another place on another battlefield. We always have."

George looked around the hospital room as if he would find answers to his plight painted somewhere on the walls or ceiling. *A new and better seat at another table—in another place and in another body.* He took solace in the thought of such continuity. Until the next game, however, George lay motionless. He wondered if Beatrice, his wife, would recognize, or even remember, him when he came back. *It may be a long time before our souls meet again—years, decades, scores, or even centuries—but we will. We always have. Christine in the fourteenth century. Jusztina in the fifteenth. Anne-Angélique in the nineteenth century. And even Monique in the twentieth. Ours is a passion unbounded by time.*

With the reverence of an altar boy, although unable to kneel before his Holy Father, he prayed that God with his infinite mercy might grant him at least one last holiday with his beautiful Beatrice. He felt the answer deep in his core and knew he had to depart without his last wish granted. He was to go to a place where he was destined to rectify the wrongs of others in the way only a timeless warrior could do. Liquid salt streamed from the tear ducts of his eyes, and George couldn't even reach up to wipe them away. Imbibing this heartbreaking scene, the Jack of Hearts could do no more than stare through empty space at the hospital room ceiling.

Mickey recalled missing the yearly ceremony held for General George S. Patton, whose soul passed from his body in what is now x-ray room number one, four days before Christmas in 1945. Mickey wished he had taken the time more often to honor the governor general. It was never for lack of interest. There just never seemed to be enough time.

It was good that today Mickey, as Dr. Peronne, was able to jump to the head of every patient line because even as their tires rolled out of the Heidelberg Hospital caserne, Loni's parents were just leaving Charles de Gaulle Airport in Paris.

Mickey looked over at Loni and tried out a dashing smile. "First stop, Joan of Arc's birthplace."

"Yeah," Loni stared out the window, "in three and a half hours." She stretched her neck, rubbed her temples, and then slouched down in her seat as best as her belly would allow.

Mickey turned his eyes to the road and clamped his mouth shut, giving time for mutual healing.

7

The Archbishop's Play

Notre-Dame de Paris
Paris, France
14th century

The archbishop watched as his dutiful secretary locked the small breadbox-sized trunk then looped a small chain through the handles and secured it with yet another lock. Finally, he placed the small trunk in a red velvet cloth bag and tugged several knots tightly on the drawstring.

"Have you secured it well, Jacques?" the archbishop asked. "I need to know, beyond all doubt, that it is safe from any hint of danger."

"Yes, Excellency, I have it secured and will guard it with my very life."

"All as God wills it."

Silently Jacques crossed himself in the manner of Catholics. The archbishop cautioned, "Mark my words, Jacques, if for any reason we are waylaid by brigands or ruffians, stow it into the secret compartment in the coach seat. It must not fall into hands outside the royal family or the Church. You know what you must do."

"But of course, Excellency. I promise that it will remain safe until it reaches the royal hands of His Highness the King."

Both men nodded their acceptance of the importance of the assigned mission. A six-kilometer journey by horse-drawn coach does not take long. However, despite the short journey from the grand cathedral in Paris to the king's castle near Vincennes, time was the enemy. Because of this, the archbishop of Paris—His Reverence William de Baufet—and Jacques had to leave Notre Dame at daybreak. The first stop from the grand cathedral was at the small, nearby chapel of La Sainte-Chapelle. It was a necessary delay. There, into the horse-drawn carriage, Jacques quickly and secretly secured another special package which was doubly locked for safekeeping. In minutes, both the cathedral and the small chapel on the Île de la Cité were dots on the distant horizon. Silence was the oppressive traveler both inside and outside of the coach until they arrived at the central city market of Paris.

The noisy market vendors had the narrow alleys and byways annoyingly clogged with their wagons and kiosks. On these sparkling cobblestones they were permitted to display their specialty wares. Their sweat-lathered horses munched on breakfast, having been working hard since well before light, but the archbishop had no time for breakfast. He only had time to twist again and again on the smooth beads of his mother-of-pearl rosary. His lips moved quietly with each word of the Hail Mary.

A screeching of a wagon wheel against the slippery curb interrupted the gloom of the travelers. The noise caused the archbishop's horses to bolt and the coach to lurch momentarily. Then as quickly as things had roused, they settled. The coach resumed its steady pace into the streaming light of the rising sun. Time seemed to be of the utmost essence as the message that came from the Lord de la Rivière this morning was quite concise, clear, and most urgent. The archbishop's stomach growled loudly as he again read the written words on the parchment he held in his hand.

> Archbishop of Paris: Go to the royal chapel and bring the Holy Crown of La Sainte-Chapelle to Château de Beauté-sur-Marne near Vincennes. His Highness King Charles V wills it now.

"I'm not sure I like being addressed in such an irreverent manner by Lord de la Rivière. I'm learned enough to know where Château de Beauté sits. I am not a choirboy, you know," the archbishop grumbled aloud as he straightened out the folds of his sacred robes. *Had the command not originated from the king himself, I would certainly not be the vehicle of this routine transport. It is far too menial of a task for one of such importance as me—the chief clergyman of the city of Paris.* He looked directly at Jacques expecting to hear the confirmation of his internal opinion.

Jacques sat, looking beyond the ruddy features of the miffed archbishop, and focused on what he knew was the heart of a great man.

"Your Reverence," Jacques began, "only a simpleton or fool would doubt your greatness. Lord de la Rivière is not a fool by any stretch. Wouldn't you agree that the very crown of our Blessed Savior should never be transported outside its haven at La Sainte-Chapelle? If so commanded, only the esteemed clergy of the highest order like yourself could be trusted to escort the crown."

Jacques watched as the archbishop cleared his throat and grunted. "Yes, Jacques, this crown of thorns once sat on the head of Jesus Christ himself. The responsibility of transporting it far exceeds that of a lowly messenger. I guess that points the finger of responsibility to greatness. And so, it points directly back to me."

"Absolutely, Your Reverence. There is no one else worthy."

"I pray that we arrive in time, Jacques." Reviewing the words on the parchment note, there was no doubt in the archbishop's mind that the health of the king was failing.

"Is it that urgent?"

"I don't know, so I fear the worst. The royal court physician, Dr. Pizan, said that there would be a sign which would start a fifteen-day countdown to death."

"What is the sign?"

"Dr. Pizan said that the blemish on the king's arm would change in appearance."

"Your Reverence, I'm confused. What I saw on His Highness's arm was a wet, festering sore, quite disgusting to see. I have prayed and prayed for it to go away so that the king could have his health return."

"You heart is in the right place, Jacques, but your prayers were misplaced. I have spoken at length regarding this subject with all the court physicians and most specifically to Chief Physician Doctor Thomas de Pizan himself. They all agree that the healing of the skin on the arm will mean that the poison in the wound has left the surface of the skin. The poison will then move internally."

"I am so sorry, Your Reverence. I have accidently brought more illness down upon His Highness. What would appear to all to be a most joyful occasion is not, in fact. What have I done? Could bloodletting or some other treatment from the royal physicians undo the damage that I have done?"

"First, Jacques, it is not your fault. Second, regretfully, nothing can be done. I asked. The physicians assured me that no degree of medicinal bloodletting would be sufficient to reduce the level of the vile impurities that will be eating away at his muscles and bones. Depending upon when the sore dried, His Majesty doesn't have much more than fifteen days—a fortnight at best. I can only wonder just how much of those fifteen days of life remains for His Highness."

Biting the inside of his lip while pondering His Majesty's health, the transport of the Savior's crown, and the necessity of upper-level clergy involvement, the archbishop resigned himself to believe that time was, indeed, his enemy. He needed to be in the presence of the king to assure that the Crown of Christ was delivered into the royal hands. Meanwhile, the royal coach whisked beyond the noisy din of the city and passed into the peaceful countryside eastward toward the River Marne.

As the silhouette of the Vincennes city skyline came into view, the archbishop's eyes fixed on the Château de Vincennes. He pondered an interesting parallel while his lips mouthed the words, *Doctor of Stone.*

Sitting across from His Reverence, Jacques spoke aloud what the archbishop was obviously thinking. "The Doctor of Stone, Monsieur Pierre de Montreuil, built this castle, *oui?*"

"Yes, Jacques. There are times in one's life when one knows that one is standing in the presence of greatness. Do you remember all the discussions revolving around the architectural problems with the pillars and crossbeams at Notre-Dame de Paris?"

"Yes, Your Reverence. There were some serious structural concerns. It was agreed that the work that had to be done needed the touch of a master architect. There were many names discussed."

"Yes, but who better to do the work than the Doctor of Stone?"

"Honestly, Your Reverence, he had my vote from the onset since I had the pleasure of seeing his work in King Saint Louis's La Sainte-Chapelle."

"La Sainte-Chapelle is a masterpiece in stone. I think Christ himself would be pleased to know that his holy relic has been housed in a structure made by the greatest architect of our time."

Even as this conversation ended, the magnificent castle passed by in a blur of street sounds and images. In the minds of both men, the same thought lingered. It was unfortunate that the Doctor of Stone could not heal the king's sickness—crafting health instead of stone with enduring, resolute beauty. Soon, Vincennes and the talented architect were mere wisps of ponderings trailing behind the lathered horses and the ever-pressing royal coach.

In a few moments more, a two-story tower appeared on the crest of a hill. Château de Beauté-sur-Marne nestled quaintly at the end of the great forest around Vincennes. King Charles V much preferred this castle to the hubbub of the royal palace pulsating in the heart of Paris. Just five years ago, Château de Beauté was transformed by being the site of the depressed queen's escape from her worries.

"Did the queen find this residence as peaceful as the king had hoped, Your Reverence?"

"No, Jacques, the queen suffered badly from doldrums that began eight years ago. It was hoped that Château de Beauté could help Her Majesty recover from a condition of unwellness which followed the birth of Louis. This malady changed into a sadness so significant, Her Highness plunged into an invisible blackness. None of the castle's beauty was ever realized, as the queen was not in a mindset to enjoy such splendor."

"How long did she live in the castle?"

"Three years. Again, experiencing a blackness after childbirth, her spirit of life departed. This time it was with the birth of Catherine."

"Did she leave the castle since it failed to heal her?"

"Yes, in a matter of speaking . . . the queen died that same year. So, without the need for a queenly residence, great attention was given to the castle to meet the needs of our deeply religious, but nonetheless depressed, king."

"The king turned to God in his darkest hour?"

"As do we all. However, the king went far beyond changing the happy nature of the castle. It has become a memorial to the religion of man. You will see this in the great fountain which is a solemn tribute to the religious nature of a saddened, widowed king."

The horse-drawn coach passed by well-armed sentries as it traveled over the wooden slats of the drawbridge. Heralded by the sounds of leather straps and jingling metals, the coach finally stopped in the circle by the great garden fountain. A welcoming group, consisting of everyone from horse handlers to housekeepers, ensured that the passengers were minimally delayed. The archbishop and his secretary spent little time dismounting the coach and entering the main castle entrance. Jacques, as the humble secretary, unpacked the precious cargo and then took his leave of the archbishop near the entrance on the ground floor.

The main floor of Château de Beauté was primarily an open space. Except for one doorway leading into the library on the far side, this large room was essentially a common area with completely open access. However, in these days filled with the king's ill health, an area at the far end of the room had been cordoned off to form a massive bed chamber hidden by a screen of curtains. The king had asked that this makeshift bedroom be kept adjacent to his library and work study. It was here, just next to the library door, that the archbishop caught a glimpse a figure twisted and awkwardly propped up on an overstuffed couch set in front of the curtain which hid the ornate footboard of the king's massive bed.

It had been less than a month, but the change in the king's appearance reflected the grips of his failing health. Afraid to immediately engage the debilitated monarch, the archbishop gravitated to the side of Lord de la Rivière, the sender of the summoning letter, who also stood next to the library door at the far edge of the curtain, just outside the makeshift bedchamber.

Peeking around the bedchamber's curtain, the archbishop spoke to the Lord de la Rivière in a labored whisper. "King Charles looks more dead than alive, my lord. He wears a hideous mask of pain."

"Indeed, Your Reverence. The previous fourteen days have been long and agonizing. I am glad that some of the pleasant surroundings here at the castle provided a degree of distraction for His Highness."

"I can't imagine him waking each day only to find pain and misery tugging at his elbow."

"As bad as the days have been, the worst of it settles upon him once night falls. He has said so himself. In the silent dark, there is nothing to ease his mind from the excruciating extraction of life from his body."

As the two men spoke in hushed conversation, the king was carefully moved from the couch to the privacy of his bed behind the curtains. Grunts and groans accompanied each labored step. Many minutes of adjustment passed before the king finally settled.

"May I go in and see him now?"

"With his time growing short, make each minute count." Lord de la Rivière lifted the curtain and gave the archbishop a curt nod. With great trepidation, the archbishop passed though the drapes and entered the royal bedchamber. He emotionally braced himself in anticipation of the scene he was about to see. It didn't help. He thought he would be seeing the wretched, failing monarch Charles V in his final clutch. He saw something much, much worse. In horror, he stood speechless.

8

The Abbot's Trump

Château de Beauté-sur-Marne

Paris, France

14th century

"How can such a travesty exist?" said the archbishop, balling his fists until the knuckles grew white. The Doctor of Stone could have sculpted no better statue than the archbishop of Paris as he stood rigid in absolute shock at the king's bedside. The archbishop's eyes had long left the shriveled frame of King Charles V and instead bored holes through Guy de Monceau, a lowly abbot of Saint-Denis who dared to stand ahead of him in the presence of the monarch. Smoldering from rage and embarrassment, the archbishop's mind searched through every protocol to justify why the junior abbot of the Basilique Cathédrale Saint-Denis was permitted to be with the Royal Highness in his absence. There was absolutely none.

Before the archbishop could utter a syllable of condemnation, the king spoke haltingly in his direction. "Counselor," the king rasped, "I am glad you have made the trip from Paris." The archbishop bowed low but then returned his steely glare to the abbot. The king continued, "It was at my insistence that Abbot Guy be atypically permitted to tend to me in your esteemed absence. I know that this command egregiously breeches every clerical protocol. No insult to you was intended. However, because my time remaining is short, I truly needed him to stand in until you had safely arrived."

"I have arrived, Majesty. I have done as you have asked. Will the abbot's services be further required at this time?" His glare returned to Abbot Guy, who fixed his gaze squarely on the king.

"I am afraid so, my dear Archbishop." The king winced a pain-contorted nod. "I want to explain but I need to rest a moment. Abbot, will you tell him what he needs to know?" Having spoken these words, the king slunk back, panting.

The archbishop leaned toward the lowly abbot. His voice was frosted with disdain. "God's blessing, Holy Abbot. What brings you to accept a task which should have been appropriately deferred by you to the level of your senior?"

After kissing the ring of the archbishop, the abbot spoke with an unexpected absence of timidity. "Like you, Your Reverence, I have come at the urgent request of His Highness. I mean you no inkling of disrespect."

"I have no qualm with the issue that you were summoned along with me. What concerns me is that your presence trumps me in the presence of the king."

"I did only what I was asked to do. I am quite sure Your Reverence would not have disrespected the order of His Highness had you been in my situation."

"Again, that is not the issue. You continue to remain with His Highness clearly after having received the knowledge that I had arrived. Did you not hear my horses and coach announce my presence? Did you not hear my title announced as I broke the door's threshold? I am concerned that arrogance and self-importance may be a resident visitor in this house even as I speak."

"No truer words have been spoken, Your Reverence. However, that is between God and the one filled with arrogance and self-importance. I can only pray for the soul."

As the archbishop momentarily paused, the abbot hastened to continue. "Just as you, Archbishop, I have been asked to urgently provide the king that which he desires here in his last hours of life."

"Yes, but I have been asked to bring the one sacred thorny crown of our Savior, Jesus Christ. What manner of *trinket* could you have been asked to bring which could rival?"

"I bring nothing that could rival the crown of thorns worn by Jesus as he hung on the cross. I bring only the one item that all abbots of Saint-Denis have been charged to secure and protect."

The archbishop looked to what the abbot held in his hands. His eyes fixed upon the glittering, embedded jewels of the king's royal crown. He now remembered that Saint Denis himself was the first bishop of Paris and that the highly esteemed abbey of Saint-Denis was charged to hold and protect the royal regalia, including the king's earthly crown. The archbishop begrudgingly bestowed a respectful nod toward the lowly abbot while the king was returned to the couch. Helping hands quickly tidied the king's pillows and bedcovers while others tied back the curtains at the corner bedposts. Once everyone settled, the king nodded.

"Your Reverences, the time has come." Lord de la Rivière spoke the words that terminated the standoff between the two clergymen. He continued, "I need to have the Crown of Jesus Christ." The archbishop then bowed and passed the crown he had carried from Paris to the kneeling Lord de la Rivière.

"Tell me quickly, Archbishop," Lord de la Rivière quickly whispered. "Do you have any information of the missing thorns from this crown? The legend states—"

"The Legend of the Missing Thorns is nothing but folklore, my Lord," whispered the archbishop dismissively. "There is no miracle or chance of an alternate outcome in the offing here today."

"Then the answer to my question is no. Fine." Lord de la Rivière quickly rose and approached the king on the couch, then knelt and handed the king the thorny crown.

While the statues of Saint Matthew, Saint Mark, Saint Luke, and Saint John stood at the corners of the room regarding the proceedings with stern solemnity, all mortal eyes in the room pointed toward the king. Protected by the four corners of over-watching evangelists, a miracle occurred.

There, framed by the curtains and giant bedposts, stood an unrecognizable royal stranger holding the Crown of Christ. It was His Majesty the King, but it wasn't. The king stood upright, portraying a strength which had been hidden from all in these last two weeks. Even his voice had lost its sick tremble. In the background, on the wall above the headboard of the bed, were two large wooden rods which touched end-to-end forming a peak pointing upward to heaven. Enclosed within this pyramidal frame, the ruler of all France stood as a re-invigorated Charles V instead of the whisper of the man he had been moments before.

"Behold, the Savior's crown from Paris," said King Charles. In his voice a confidence of great substance dwelled. The king then looked directly at Lord de la Rivière who listened and reverently obeyed. "Stand here by my side. Take and hold this thorny crown high above my head, but do not let it touch one hair of my head for I am not worthy." Tears rolled down the cheeks of the archbishop as he recalled the morning transport of the crown by *his* hand—a hand even less worthy. Lord de la Rivière obeyed. All listened as the king spoke again.

"Abbot, take the crown you have brought me and place it on the ground at my feet."

"But Sire," the abbot hesitated, "are you sure that the floor is the correct place for your royal crown?"

With kindness in his voice, Charles again iterated his request—unmoved by the challenge of the lowly clergyman. The abbot respectfully complied. Having his royal crown positioned so, King Charles V then spoke to all the people in the room.

"Behold the Thorny Crown of God and the Golden Crown of Man have now taken their proper places. I ask the Lord God to please forgive me if it any time I have switched their importance. To all of you who have endured the failing of your king, I beg your forgiveness. In these past two weeks, you have so patiently waited upon me as I have weakened from this horrific malady. I have heard no word of complaint or cynicism from any of you. I thank you for your kindness. Last, but of no less importance, I must ask forgiveness from the dear hearts and young souls who found me in my darkest days of despair. To the maiden who accepted the pinnacle of my wrath, before God and his four saints, I thank you for absolving me with angelic mercy. As God be my witness, in the frustration of my gloom I meant you no harm. God has His reasons for the timing of our life and death. He must often smile at us as we try to steer our own course."

The silence was broken by an occasional sobbing from the room's occupants. The king tried again to speak. His body staggered back to a seated position on the couch. His breathing labored and his voice grew faint. He now spoke only to Lord de la Rivière, the one nearest to him.

"Please help me to lie down. I wish to have my final rituals in time for my meeting with God on his most holy day of the week."

Lord de la Rivière hastily retired the crown he held and fetched the rods from the wall behind the headboard. With their aid, King Charles V carefully lifted himself from the couch and edged beyond the fringes of his bed curtain to the repose of the royal bed. Once he arrived at the bedside, the king released the poles. They hit the floor with a clatter that resounded off the walls amidst the stunned silence that still reigned in the room. The archbishop of Paris and the abbot of Saint-Denis rushed into their respective roles in the issuance of last rites and final unction to the quickly waning monarch. The curtains were hastily closed behind them.

The archbishop's words could be heard behind the curtain. "Majesty, are you penitent for all your sins?"

In a loud whisper the king could be heard to reply, "All and especially one, Archbishop, all . . . and. . . ."

From the adjacent library, amidst the Irish wood with cypress inlay, a sliver of a young woman's face peered into the scene from a door left ajar. Her face was marked with streams of tears bisecting the rose coloration of her freckled cheeks. The woman was present merely to visit her uncle, the court physician, and she knew that the scenario which had just played out before her was not intended for her eyes.

But, as a former apprentice recorder, she also knew what had to be done— what should be done. In her hands, she held a piece of parchment filled with the scribbling of her notes. While alternating the wiping of each eye with the back of her wrist, she was able to record the final words of the dying king. Once the writing was finished, she gave one final glance into the royal bed chamber where the king lay surrounded by his solemn clergy. His days on earth were quietly coming to an end. With tears still streaming down her face, she wrapped the page around the smooth core of a scroll and tied it off with leather straps. She then carefully pushed away the pole which had rolled toward her and lodged itself in the doorway. She tugged steadily on the heavy library door until the latch responded with an almost inaudible click.

9

Basilica and the Pucelle

Basilique du Bois-Chenu
Domrémy-la-Pucelle, France
Current day

"Driving can be therapeutic for fractures?" said Mickey, arching an eyebrow.

"Why are you talking medicine when we are surrounded by these beautiful statues in this lovely garden?" Loni's eyes never riveted off the marble.

"Sorry, Loni, it's just that—" Mickey tapped at his gauzed forearm splint. The pulsating pain in Mickey's hand had lessened. He glanced over at Loni. *I can't say the same for you, darling.* As the trip from the hospital across western Germany melted into eastern France, Mickey noted how Loni had become increasingly agitated with a brewing headache. *Thank goodness this was a short trip.* Only a few hours after getting on the road, their black sport utility vehicle rolled into the small French town where Joan of Arc was born.

Domrémy-la-Pucelle, the village of the girl, was a precious little town in France known for being the location of Joan of Arc's home and her village church. Right before reaching the village's welcome sign, prominently perched on a hillside stood a basilica with a well-manicured sloped garden where Joan first saw her angelic visions of Saints Margaret, Catherine, and Michael. It was midafternoon and Loni and Mickey had time to take a rest at the foot of the Basilique du Bois-Chenu and its statue garden before heading onward into the center of Domrémy. The Peronnes reveled in the time they spent outdoors with the beautiful statues of the angels in front of the basilica.

"You know, Loni." Mickey hid a smile. "If you don't start moving soon, busloads of tourists are going to include your photo along with these statues." Mickey's chortle tapered into silence. Ignoring any attempt at humor, Loni's eyes slid through the swirls of the marble grooves of the sculpted stone. Her fin-

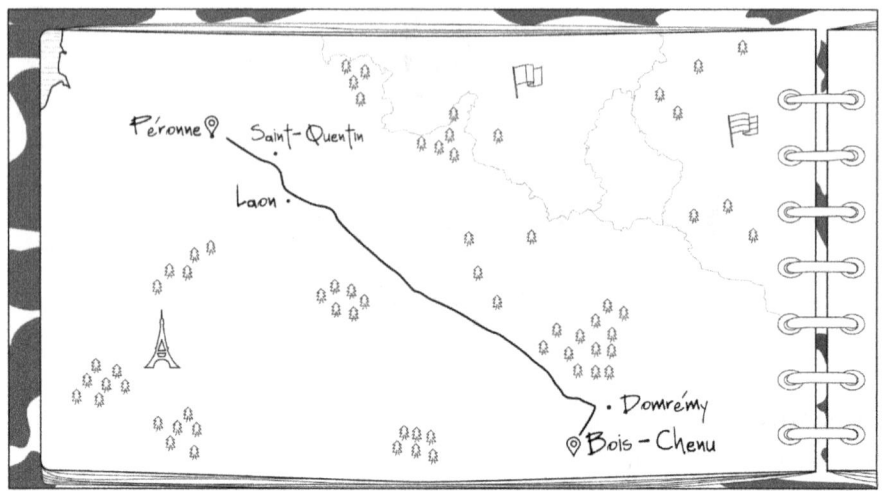

Bois-Chenu to Péronne

gertips delicately traced curved patterns across her belly, subconsciously trans-
lating the chiaroscuro she sensed around her to the babies within her. Finally,
she leaned into Mickey while he gently massaged her neck as best he could with
his un-splinted hand.

Ever the physician, Mickey had been watching as his wife repeatedly
stretched her neck and shoulders during the drive, and he hoped that the
therapeutic massage could better help her to enjoy the value of the day. *For
now, it seems her pain is manageable. Maybe, just maybe, we can stave off some headache
side effects.*

"Who were the angels that spoke to Joan and what did they say?" Loni asked
as she absorbed the radiant beauty emanating from within the statue of Saint
Margaret.

"You asked me that the last time we were here."

"I know, but I get so distracted when I come here. It's like I lose myself and
become one with the statues."

"Saint Margaret, patron saint of pregnancy, is the one with the helmet."
He indicated with his splinted hand. "Saint Catherine, patron saint of female
scholars, holds the sword over there. And that's Saint Michael, the armored
archangel—essentially God's chief of staff. They told twelve-year-old Joan that
her mission in life was to drive out the English soldiers from France and restore
the French monarch to the throne at Reims."

"It's incredible that a twelve-year-old girl would be entrusted with such an
important mission, Mickey."

"Ah, but was she really twelve?"

"Are you saying she wasn't?"

"I am saying that although her death date is recorded in history virtually right down to the hour, the birth of Joan of Arc is the real unknown."

"Is it important to know the exact day she came into the world? That seems trivial, Mickey."

"Not the day, but the year is important because it leads to a better understanding of the world she knew and the people alive at the time who influenced her. Joan herself did not know how old she was."

"What are you getting at?" said Loni, rubbing at her temples again.

"Maybe nothing. Maybe something. It lends some historical questions as to her lineage." Mickey saw the pain of the headache rearing in Loni's squinting eyes and diverted. "We'll leave the issue moot for now, and for argument's sake we'll say she was twelve."

"She was twelve," parroted Loni rubbing at her temples.

"Yes, but she would have been a twelve-year-old girl with some serious advisors in the form of the archangel, who also visited Abraham, and two of the fourteen so-called helper angels to assist her with scholarly issues such as her trials for heresy and to guide her in protecting her chastity. She was picked to fulfill a prophecy that France would be resurrected by a 'Maid from Lorraine.' Who better to help this maid than two of the three holy maids, the martyrs, Margaret and Catherine?"

"I remember the fourteen helpers," Loni began. "They were honored in the church in Bad Staffelstein just north of Bamberg—the Vierzehnheiligen Basilica. Remember, when you were the commander of the Bamberg Health Clinic? We went there with Edith and Friedrich Mauder for a day of porcelain shopping at Kaiser Porcelain."

"I remember you kept reciting the prayer about the fourteen angels; how does it go, Loni? 'Now I lay me down to sleep, fourteen angels . . . my soul do keep. Two my head are guarding; two my feet are guiding. Two upon my right hand, two upon my left hand. Two who warmly cover, two who o'er me hover. Two to whom 'tis given to guide my steps to heaven."

"For the most part correct, Mickey."

"Most part? I don't think so. I nailed it." He gave her a boyish grin.

"Well, the opening is incorrect."

"I opened with, 'When at night I go to sleep, fourteen angels watch do keep.' Isn't that correct?"

"Yes, *that* is correct, but that's not what you originally said."

"I was close," Mickey replied.

"Close is for horseshoes and hand grenades. You've said that a million times to me, Mickey." She chuckled for a moment, then became serious. "When it comes to our children, you must know it exactly right. Remember, I want each of us to hold a baby and we must recite it in unison perfectly each time." Looking up at Saint Margaret, Loni continued, "I wonder how many times Joan prayed to the *Vierzehn Heiligen*—the 'fourteen angels'? She was a blessed child with such a strong name. Listen, it's even better in French—Jehanne d'Arc." Loni pronounced the name, seeming to savor each sound. "The name carries such strength . . . like an arrow flying through the air and then hitting its target."

Mickey smiled at his wife's penchant for sounds and the emotions tied to them. *Part of her work in special education, no doubt, seeing meaning in what the rest of us take for granted or what we don't understand.* "Du Lys was the name that her family was granted because of her deeds."

"As in fleur-de-lys?"

"Yes, the flower of France. I imagine that Joan, also a flower of France, prayed often since the war and pestilence, primarily the Black Death and the bubonic plague, were still fresh in the minds of the survivors in medieval France. These helper saints were invoked time on end to help protect the miserable populace from so many troublesome issues." Mickey watched as Loni unconsciously rubbed at her temples. "Let's get out of the sun and go on into the basilica."

"Mickey, could I get you to—" Loni reached into her purse and opened the lid on a jar of soothing balm.

"Yes, darling, but not here . . . not now." Mickey tapped her purse. "You've been standing a while in this heat. Let's get you indoors."

"Fine." Loni frowned while tightening the lid on the jar of balm. Returning it to her purse, she then gave a forlorn parting glance to the statues. She and Mickey turned left and crossed the parking lot to access the front steps of the beautiful basilica. Loni's shuffled pregnancy gait was coupled with Mickey's gimpy stride. Echoing off the stone walls, the sound of Mickey's steps distinctly mimicked the *lub teh-dupp* heart sound that physicians call an S3 gallop. Mickey's John Wayne walk served as testament to his heroic war act that resulted in a damaged leg nerve that no Purple Heart could ever repair. However, this was an egalitarian place where a limp, shuffle, or even a stomp and drag would not be thwarted. There was unquenchable strength here in the granite arms of the church which honored Saint Joan of Arc.

Although noticeable from the exterior, a comprehensive understanding of the depth of beauty inside the basilica was merely a tongue wagging in the empty air. Once inside, Mickey and Loni experienced an immense pummeling of human emotion as they crossed the doorframe at the entrance. The basilica's interior was a monumental icon to every aspect of holiness ever applied to the nineteen-year-old saint. On the ground-floor entrance, behind a floor-to-ceiling glass shield, was a spectacular shrine. Within it and upon its walls were portrait after portrait of Joan which demanded deep homage and respect from all who entered.

"There are so many beautiful artistic interpretations of Joan here," said Loni. "Each a veritable treasure."

"I know," mused Mickey. "We paid handsomely for our Dani Lachuk *Exultation of Joan* oil on canvas."

"How do you place monetary value on such beauty?" Loni whispered back. "It's an original art piece done to utmost historic accuracy. At least that is what Dani said to me when we discussed the purchase."

"True enough. I asked Dani if she was attempting to capture, in art, Joan just after the Battle of Patay. With the French victory at that battle being so swift, and with so few lives lost, that would give historic substance to the exultation."

"What did she say?"

"She said that she had not tried to capture a point in time but more so the depth of human emotion."

"So, then the Battle of Patay wins by default."

"Indeed."

"Mickey, all historical accuracy aside, I love it just because out of all the paintings of Joan I've seen it was the only one that showed her expressing great joy."

"Agreed. People forget that, albeit Joan was a spirit-filled child, she was just as human as the rest of us."

"I am also glad you love Joan as much as I do. You are the most incredible man in the world, and I love you beyond life."

"Me too you, Loni."

Mickey took Loni's hand, leading her beyond the entrance room and up the spiral marble steps to the rear access of the body of the church. There, in heart-pounding magnificence, postured the most brilliant panoramic mural adorning the entire expanse of the north and south walls. Vividly portrayed was a daunting Joan of Arc in the heat of battle with her army at Patay. In front of the charging French cavalry, Joan rides a full horse length ahead. Without any weapon unsheathed, she brandishes only her banner scripted with the names JHESUS MARIA to spur the cavalry forward. The presence of the great soldiers like La Hire de Vignolles, known to the world today as the Jack of Hearts, Jean Poton de Xaintrailles, and the daunting Sir Arthur III de Richemont, a famous Breton and Marshal of France, all paled in the passionate depiction of the Maid of Lorraine. Even the most stoic of visitors could be moved to an unbridled display of emotion. The usual lighting of the candles, praying for souls, and genuflection in respect to the heavenly spirits which resided within the basilica were reverently performed as the pair slowly migrated back to the exterior of the church, this time from the upper-south exit.

The exit opened into a pleasant breezeway. As they made their way down the stairs, a cool wind blew past them, causing the long hair of a passing adolescent schoolgirl to whip up like tentacles about her head. She was dressed in a plaid uniform jumper which spoke of Catholic matriculation in a nearby parochial school. Neither the *pucelle* girl nor the Peronnes spoke in their passing of one another on the steps. No words dared infringe on these moments of blessed personal reflection. But Mickey did glance back at her. As he did, he noticed beyond her the jagged tombstones which, like broken teeth, marked the grassy hillside behind the basilica. He could not help but think of Joan, marching off to certain death, her hair whipped up in flames. The image of youth and death in such proximity stayed with him until the bottom of the stairs.

"Do you want to stop at the Beast before we go on to the gift shop?" Mickey asked cautiously as they approached the oversized-for-Europe black truck. The size of the family's sport utility vehicle gave rise to the nickname. The fact that Loni always named her car Beauty served as a further link to plausible justification. Mickey wondered briefly if he ever told Loni about Operation Beauty and the Beast at the Esso station last year. *Kind of funny now that I think of it.*

"I don't think I'm up to visiting the gift shop today." Loni's voice hinted of a combination of pain and fatigue.

"What? All right, who are you, and what have you done with my wife?" Mickey teased.

Loni forced a smile.

"Honey, you *always* want to go browse. Who will meticulously comb through every print, every knickknack, every statuette, every charm, if Loni Peronne fails to report for tourist duty?"

"I know, Mickey. Humor me this one time. Let's spend my waning pregnancy-taxed energy by covering more outdoor roadways than indoor aisleways."

Shaking his head in legitimate disbelief, Mickey conceded. They boarded the vehicle and endured an extended period of pensive silence as the Beast proceeded a mile or so northward to the Joan of Arc home, Maison Natale de Jeanne d'Arc, and the local church. The tall poplar trees that lined the road whispered Joan's name. With his splinted right hand, Mickey clumsily executed the half-right turn following the simple signage toward their destination. Then, after only a brief drive farther, Joan's odd-shaped home appeared on their left. The Peronnes reverently disembarked the Beast and quietly stood looking at the home which consumed the entire expanse to their immediate front.

From left to right, the roof was in a downward slant over the top of a stone house reminding the onlooker that a rear portion of the yellow house was markedly absent. Seeming to be awkwardly placed by a drunken Picasso were windows varying in size, shape, and position. The shadow of the doorway was almost tunnel-like as the actual door was deeply recessed or maybe actually ajar. A hint of a church steeple peeked over the house's roofline with a strange sense of curiosity. Mickey spoke about the neighbored pair of structures, reminding his one-person audience of the piety of a young Joan who spent much of her days praising God.

Mickey guided Loni through the verdant archway made of neatly manicured hedges, bushes, and trees. They strolled across the lawn only to saunter up to a sign which read, *MERCI DE NE PAS MARCHER SUR LA PELOUSE.* They stood for a moment trying to translate the French.

"I am guessing that doesn't say, 'It's okay to lead your pregnant wife across this lawn.'"

"Nope, I'd have to say not." Scanning around guiltily, Mickey looked back at the sign and translated it word for word. "'Please do not march' or walk 'upon the grass.' It really doesn't address the physical state of pregnancy." Loni elbowed a shot to his ribs.

"Are we going into Joan's house or not?" Loni chuckled.

"That depends."

"Depends on what?"

"Well, for one thing, if the authorities don't arrest us for violating the rules."

"Since when have the French been worried about rules?"

"That, my little frog, is a fact. Whereas the Germans would never break any rule, the French laugh loudest at those who feel compelled to abide by them. Come, let's get hopping."

Loni smiled as Mickey took her by the arm and guided her across the lawn. Within seconds they had arrived at the gravel clearing that led to a patchwork of irregular-sized stone squares. A sidewalk of sorts led the traveler to the eastern entrance doorway of Joan's house. They noticed that the door was, indeed, ajar. Mickey felt a firm squeeze on his left hand. He surmised that his excited wife knew that just inside, Joan waited for them.

10

Beyond the d'Arc

Maison Natale de Jeanne d'Arc
Domrémy-la-Pucelle, France
Current day

Loni started to break the threshold when she felt Mickey abruptly pause to take in the ambience of the outside façade of the doorway. She felt his hand lift hers as he marveled at the embedded art. Directly centered high above the door was a stone statue in a framed inset. The statue was a figure of a person dressed in armor and pantaloons. No doubt, it was a tribute to Joan as a warrior. Beneath the statue's inset and above the top of the doorjamb was a decorative carving of three shields with the fleur-de-lis.

Hand in hand with Mickey, dreamily, Loni spoke. "Youthful girl backed by a powerful but naive prince. Are you truly here with us today? You were born to save a nation of people. There were those who believed you to be a living symbol of strength for all. There were those who would never know or could never understand the secrets you had. Where did you find your path to God? Did God beacon his path for you?"

"You read all that in *those* stone carvings?" Mickey replied, astonished.

"What carvings? I was just listening to what the house was saying as it was speaking to me."

"Why would it say *those words* to *you*?"

"I dunno. Maybe it knows me better than I do."

Leaving Mickey stupefied outside on the walkway, Loni released his hand and plunged into the shadow which veiled the door. After many moments of listening for anything that the house might say to him, Mickey followed onward through the doorway. Hearing no movement inside, he went over to Loni, who stood in front of a statue of Joan. It took him a moment to determine which was made of stone.

In the space of what was once a living room, the statue of Joan was positioned to the left of the marble fireplace which was centered in the tall south

54

wall. The mantel framed the upward-pointing, pentagon-shaped furnace, and it looked to be a part of the existing stone thrust out of the earth solely by the commands of a warrior goddess.

Resting upon a marble pedestal stood a quietly imposing Jehanne d'Arc dressed in soldier's armor, her arms crossed upon her breast. In her right arm she clutched a sword. Her gaze was downward—not in defeat or despair, but in humble solitude.

"Why is Joan always depicted as sad or reflective?"

"Well, Dani Lachuk didn't take that angle in our painting, did she?" said Mickey. "I still think that the Joan on our canvas is portrayed just at the end of Battle of Patay."

"I agree. Her armor is pristine which lends credibility of the swiftness of battle. Coming out of a battle as clean as I went in would certainly make me happy." Loni tilted her head in thoughtful observation of the statue.

"Maybe. Then again, maybe Joan was just happy to be on a Lipizzaner war stallion."

"Could it be both?" Loni smiled at Mickey.

"Ask the house. It speaks to you, not me."

"Ahhh," she cast her eyes around the nearly empty room, "the house says that a sparkling clean, bloodless battle sword embodies joy."

"She does hold the sword of heaven—that is a joy all by itself." Mickey looked at his wife, awaiting the expected follow-up question but Loni didn't stir. He continued, "The sword of heaven was the sword of Charles Martel."

"What?"

"Loni, that was not just a causal weapon. That sword gave Charles Martel the title Hammer of God which he used to defeat his enemies." Mickey paused for a response. He heard none.

Gently, Mickey turned Loni to face him. Like sculpted stone, Loni stood statuesque. Her expression mirrored the statue of Joan's with one variance. Like the weeping woman statue back home, tears flowed on Loni's marble cheeks. He kissed dry her salty flesh.

"Loni," said Mickey, lightly rocking her shoulders, "are you okay, honey?"

"Don't you sense it?" Loni snuffled. "This house is troubled."

"Houses can't be troubled. They're just houses."

"The house is very troubled, Mickey. I feel it."

Silently, Loni passed Mickey and moved to the north wall of the room. Mickey's eyebrows contracted, observing his wife's odd behavior with increasing concern. As she moved past two recessed niches in the wall, Loni let her hand trail across the base of each as she entered the nearest of the paired doorways at the far corner of the room.

Once inside the room she paused by the stone mantelpiece, touching it gently. She looked down to where a fireplace should be, though there was none. Mickey followed her into the room with rising trepidation. As he came in, she moved to the faded stained-glass window and wiped the tears from her eyes. Mickey took her in the cradle of his good arm.

"Why do you do this to yourself every time it involves Joan, Loni?"

"I can't say." She turned her face toward his chest and closed her eyes. "I just feel like I have a connection here in Joan's home. I know this house, but it has long drifted away."

"Honey, how could that be? It's beyond credibility."

"Is it?" She broke away from his arms. "Then tell me—why do I remember singing songs right here? I can vividly see the loops of flax and yarn around my arms while the flickering of the fireplace dances off the walls."

"Hollywood."

"Hollywood?"

"Sure, the spectra of Hollywood movies add so many unexpected dimensions to our waking lives. When a dark cloud suddenly obstructs a sunny day, my mind immediately goes to Hollywood's depiction of Thermopylae, a battleground that I never have seen and certainly not when an abundance of attacking Persian arrows blotted out the Greek sun." Mickey scoffed. "Hollywood gives us memories."

"Maybe so." Loni drew a deep breath. "I want to go, Mickey. My heart feels heavy. Joan's home drains me."

"As always, Loni," reminded Mickey gingerly, "and yet you feel the need to return."

"I didn't mean it in a bad way. The fatigue I feel is from deep within. It is an ever-present exhaustion of a tired soul like . . . like the *Bird Girl of Savannah*."

"The statue in our backyard?"

"Yes, that one. She holds yesterday in one bird feeder dish and tomorrow in the other."

"What does that mean?"

"I don't know. I don't know," Loni sobbed. "Despite the physical taxation, I seek a deeper understanding of Joan for selfish, self-serving reasons."

"Learning is not selfish, Loni. It benefits all."

"Mickey, the learning of this one far exceeds the learning of the many. I firmly believe that the key to knowing myself lies with what I learn about Joan. Because I am the sole recipient of the knowledge, I must confess that I, Loni Peronne, am selfish. Can God forgive me for being thus?"

Recalling the many past Joan-related interactions, Mickey knew that any further dialogue would be diatribe and quite pointless. He guided his wife out of the house, maintaining silence until they had arrived back at the Beast. Loni broke the silence first, continuing the conversation which began back at the basilica.

"Mickey, what part of the Joan of Arc trail will we visit this time?"

"Like I told you before, we should visit the significant places in Joan's life which lie north of here."

"That's right. Last time we were here we took the southern arm from here to Tours, Sainte-Catherine-de-Fierbois, Blois, Orléans, and then to Chinon."

"That adventure was filled with many unforgettable events."

"We could go back and experience them again. . . ."

"Wait a minute. You are the one who always says that one can never go back."

"Yes, it's true. One can't. But maybe two can. . . ." Loni blew her nose, and an infectious smile spread across her face.

"Do you really want to?" Mickey stepped carefully, not wanting to spoil the more pleasant mood Loni had resurrected.

"Not really, but you decide." With that said, Loni accepted Mickey's help into the passenger's seat. Mickey climbed back into the truck and began the first leg of their journey. He pointed the truck northward out of Domrémy toward Greux, Vouthon, and ultimately in the direction of Vaucouleurs.

"Which way this time?" Loni again asked.

"Since Asaad awaits us, I decided to stick to the original plan and head us always north and west from here toward Champagne, Compiègne, Reims, Soissons, Saint-Quentin, into the Vermandois, through Beaurevoir, and finally to Péronne." Mickey's voice was firm and convincing.

Loni was quite relieved at the decision. Like Mickey, she had already made additional tentative plans in Péronne. She decided she would deal with that issue once she and Mickey arrived at Péronne in the historic region of the Vermandois.

"Will we ever get to the cities of Arras and Rouen?" Loni's voice was accented by the sharp sound of metal on metal as her hands worried at her necklace.

"Maybe in the next trip we'll get to Arras and Rouen. Mind you, you *are* pregnant and in your eighth month. I don't want your ankles to swell up so much they burst."

"They can't do that, can they?" Mickey's ears were homing in on the metallic serenade of her chain. "Okay, forget Arras and Rouen," she continued. "As you have seen, I am not at my tip-top best today anyway. After Péronne we will meet with Suzanne."

Mickey lovingly glanced at his gravid wife and smiled. Loni persevered in her ponderings.

"What is it in us that seeks to follow in the footsteps of—"

"—Joan of Arc?" Mickey interrupted.

"Yes, Joan, among others. I was thinking more so about veterans of war— Normandy, Saint-Lô, Bastogne, Anzio, Pearl Harbor. People make pilgrimages to special locales. Sometimes soldiers retrace their own footsteps from decades earlier, wars long since passed. Descendants follow where their family members were, or where they went, during times of war, upheaval, or displacement. Then there are all the religious pilgrimages. Muslims do a haj to Mecca. Christians and Jews go to the Holy Land. Templars go to Scotland's Rosslyn Chapel, Tomar's Convent of Christ in Portugal, Jerusalem's Temple Mount in Israel, and—"

"—the Newport Tower in Rhode Island. Maybe we pilgrims do it for closure."

"Yes, closure for pilgrims is logical, they have a connection with the place they seek. But Mickey, why do you and I do it? Sure, we go to historically or religiously significant places and pay witness or homage. But we have no earthly connection with Joan of Arc, yet we follow her path."

She paused for a moment as her words hung in the air. "Funny . . . I say that, but I don't believe it. I've always had a connection with her, even when I didn't want one. What is it about her that burns so deep? Why do I feel the need to seek her?" As she spoke, Loni resumed the nervous grating of the pendant on her chain.

"Loni, I'm confused. You profess to want to understand Joan, but you fail to deliberately study her. You revisit her special sites time on end, yet you seem to remember nothing. Where are your notes, journals, charts, and spreadsheets? When one wants to learn more, there is a process." He looked at his wife, sensed her mood, and put on a comical exasperated pedagogical scowl. "Shame on you, Loni," he teased. "You have a terminal degree in education. I don't see you engaging any structured learning processes. Why is that?"

She propped her elbow on the door, chin in palm, looked out the window, and answered matter-of-factly, "GiGi's apple pie."

"Your great grandma's dessert. That is your answer?"

"Yes, Mickey, I can't reproduce the pie. Neither can Mother or Grandma Meeley."

"I don't understand."

"Of course you don't. You think that understanding is a summation of all facts. As an educationist, I'm here to say that no matter how much Mother and I have learned the recipe, the sum of all the ingredients does not produce GiGi's apple pie."

"You're talking about intangibles."

"Yes, intangibles like sensations, feelings, vibrations, textures, shadows. . . ."

"Maybe you haven't studied enough, Loni. Maybe you haven't put enough effort into memorization."

"Maybe you aren't listening, darling. I think I need to learn this using my heart and not my brain. Agree?"

"I'm not sure I can answer that for you." Mickey's voice drifted into silence like the peals of the church bells whose steeples dotted the ridgelines en route to Vaucouleurs in the Lorraine. Mickey seemed to have become immune to the grating sound from Loni's pendant—possibly due to the increasing pain in his right hand. Mickey thoughtfully stroked his chin while Loni rubbed hard on the necklace and then harder on her temples. With all the flexing and surging of emotions, today's sojourn was shaping up to be the basis for the mother, grand-mother, and great-grandmother of all headaches for them both.

11
Over the Big Pond

Route to Paris
Current day

The airplane ride toward Paris to meet with Mickey and Loni was about as smooth as Suzanne Coletrane had ever enjoyed. Nevertheless, she chewed at the tip of her blonde ponytail and tapped her foot nervously. She scowled, and her hint of Asian features added intensity to what were already penetratingly green eyes. Over the last year, she had flown tactically in multiple military aircraft undergoing one urgent mission or another. Today she was glad to have the cozy comforts of a commercial airliner. The hope that she would have sufficient time to spend walking the footsteps of her lifetime idol, the medieval poet and early feminist Christine de Pizan, in Poissy managed to keep her in her seat . . . barely. Flying and Suzanne were like oil and water. Her ears perked at every announcement coming from the speaker system. She just *knew* there would be instructions given to assume the position for a crash landing. If not that, there would be an explanation of why an emergency landing had to be made into the blue Atlantic. However, hearing none of this, she eased a bit in her seat . . . but only a bit. She leaned forward again, feeling for the leading lip of the life vest which was most assuredly stowed beneath her seat.

This was the first lengthy vacation that army Colonel Dr. Suzanne Niles Coletrane had since her taking over the Chemical Casualty Care Division at the US Army Medical Research Institute of Chemical Defense in Maryland. Her boss, Colonel Sampson Blythe, the commander of the Institute of Chemical Defense, was a stickler for the healthy use of passes, liberties, and personal leave.

Suzanne was always dangerously close to being in trouble with the commander because of her unwillingness to take leave. She had assumed responsibility for the division about a year ago after the death of her former boss, Joachim "Yogi" Wunschmann, had a reported laboratory accident in Tegernsee, Germany. She was surprised to be considered for the vacated chair as she was the first to acknowledge that either of her two colleagues, Mickey Peronne or Russell Lange, was better suited for the position.

The fact that Mickey and Russell were better choices, and the fact that Suzanne herself had killed her boss, the former division chair, were probably reason enough not to select her. Regarding that incident, Suzanne had some serious explaining to do when she returned from Germany. Fortunately, the justification of Suzanne's actions was well documented in the after-action report of the Leaning Tower affair. The report filed by Judge Dagmar Harehorse vindicated Suzanne Coletrane, finding her actions to be in self-defense and appropriately in the best support of mission. Even though she was not charged for any wrongdoing, Suzanne still was cautioned in her use of deadly force as part of her exhibited rules of engagement.

The other people involved in the Leaning Tower affair were also investigated in the hearing which had followed. Represented in those formal hearing records by the accomplished defense attorney Margaret Custis, one by one they were acquitted for malfeasance. Dr. Loni Peronne, the chief Defense Intelligence Agency planner who had mission oversight, was given a verbal reprimand for continuing to act on an officially closed mission. Army medicine colleagues, Mickey Peronne and Russell Lange, who had joined Suzanne in the ground phase of the operation, were chastised for using government property without full authorization. Whereas this amounted to no more than a wrist slap, it was certainly enough to keep them out of the running for the coveted position of division chair.

On the plus side, because Suzanne, Mickey, and Russell were under Loni's DIA-sanctioned ground operations, they had surfaced the evasive lost chapters within the Second Book of Benjamin, and all the mission's transgressions were buried in a blaze of glory. So, in the final count when all things were considered, despite the fact that Suzanne executed the mission heavy handedly, the pros still outweighed the cons. She still remained, head and shoulders, above the better qualified candidates. And what sane selection committee would say no to Suzanne Coletrane—a valid competitor against any blindfolded carnival knife thrower at the Double Wheel of Death sideshow?

Suzanne shifted in her first-class seat. With a little more than two hours of flight time, she rechecked the oxygen mask compartment door. She strained to see anything out the airplane window, but it was still too dark to make out details. Suzanne's thoughts went back to Mickey, Loni, and Russell. Her mind sifted through their lives in the aftermath of the Leaning Tower affair.

Suzanne recalled that Mickey was now Deputy Commander Peronne of the European Medical Command, working directly for Brigadier General Oliver D. Framingham in Heidelberg, Germany. This was the same general who directed him to conduct the ground phase of operations in the Leaning Tower affair under Loni's Defense Intelligence Agency directives. Loni had returned to her DIA analyst duties in remote viewing. Apparently, she had kept up a reasonable pace for a while, until pregnancy began slowing down her game in the third trimester.

Suzanne's other colleague, Russell, was on fire. He accepted his second stint as Joint Task Force East Command surgeon at Mihail Kogalniceanu Air Base in Romania. The first stint at MK had displayed incredible success in the Proof of

Principle phase. Enough promise was demonstrated using credible tactical operations between the American, Romanian, and Bulgarian militaries that regular rotations of brigade-sized troops would soon begin visiting eastern Romania and Bulgaria at a secret top gun base near the Black Sea.

Suzanne knew that Russell's success in standing up the first US Army medical clinic in Romania and Bulgaria was not necessarily directly responsible for this assignment back to Romania. In fact, just like with Mickey and her, it was his part in the Leaning Tower affair that gave him the leeway to have first pick of any assignment he wanted—except for Suzanne's job. Suzanne had watched as, without a blink of hesitation, Russell again chose to be the command surgeon for the Joint Task Force East which guaranteed his return to his beloved Romanian-Bulgarian jewels of the east.

Going back is always a double-edged sword. On the upside, the return to familiar faces and places is calming. On the downside, repeat assignments are not seen favorably by promotion boards. Russell already had enough barriers ahead of him in making the next rank. With this move, Russell's chance of pinning on the eagle as full colonel became a definite uncertainty. There were other issues as well. Only time would tell if these shortfalls would be enough to keep him from getting promoted. But Suzanne knew him well. She knew that in his heart of hearts, Russell could live without the eagle. Rank never defined Russell. Success for him was defined by who he was and what he believed—not the shape and size of a piece of shiny metal pinned to his clothing.

Suzanne knew that his choice of returning to MK Air Base would make him smile. Then again, she wondered how much smiling there would be since there were so many changes brewing on the Romanian assignment's horizon. *Going back is always tough—it is never the same. It can't be. Things will be different somehow, someway.* She wondered how Russell was managing because his boss in Romania, Colonel Milton Sandhurst, was recently brought up under investigation for his practices as the Joint Task Force East commander. Russell could soon be dragged into a snarling sea of drama.

Sandhurst's shenanigans involved heavy drinking, womanizing, and abuse of authority. These vices apparently had finally set him up for what he really deserved. When the errant colonel's wife found out that he had special commander's sessions with no less than three of his *special staff*, the ensuing divorce stripped him of property as well as professional respect.

Presently, Sandhurst held his title only while the bulk of command decisions fell to his deputy, Mr. Holman Cates. Cates was more beloved, and he was called, with the greatest respect, Wild Bill. Suzanne always heard Russell comment that all the real work that was done at MK Air Base had always been at the hands of Holman Ireland Cates. His leadership style meshed kindness with a firm sense of fairness, and that was something that Russell could admire and respect. Suzanne smiled knowing that Russell had at least one friendly face back in Romania.

Solitude was yet another issue that made Suzanne worry about her dear rascal. Russell was at the top of the medical totem pole as the clinic commander and command surgeon. As such he would not be able to engage in personal friendships. *That old army adage is again, quite true. As a leader, it is always lonely at the top.*

A sudden staccato snoring sound to Suzanne's right disrupted her thoughts. Pressing her head back against the headrest, she surveyed the overhead devices which could effectively silence the offender. *Flash of light or blast of air?* Suzanne cracked her knuckles as she contemplated. Neither was necessary, as a passing flight attendant gently shook the adjacent passenger, releasing a short burst of snorts, snarls, and then welcomed silence.

Suzanne turned back to the window and nodded her head as she came to the realization that it was all good. The Leaning Tower affair was the best thing that could have happened to Loni, Mickey, Russell, and her. For Mickey and Loni, it was the ability to remain in the army's big green machine. For Russell, it was a return to his beloved Black Sea. For her, she wasn't in jail, and she had even received a promotion to a higher position. *Not too bad at all, really.*

When the overhead speaker squawked that the Boeing 787 aircraft flight attendants would now begin serving breakfast before the final approach into Paris and the Charles De Gaulle Airport, Suzanne made one more check of her life vest and oxygen mask before leaning back in her seat and clamping her eyes closed. Amidst the din of awakening passengers, she tried to put her mind on the reason why she was going through all this. After all, there are reunions and there are reunions.

It really is a shame that I haven't seen Mickey and Loni since last year. Maryland isn't so far from Europe. But now that I'm here . . . or almost here . . . maybe I can also make time to see tower keepers Jude and Justice James in Britain. Then there's my one-on-one time with Christine de Pizan at Poissy . . . been looking forward to that. Russell. . . .

She felt her face flush as she remembered being with Russell at Niles, Illinois, the home of the only leaning tower in the United States. In fact, they were literally in the shadow of the Leaning Tower of Niles when Russell received word that he had gotten his first choice on assignments and would be returning to Romania. He danced with her on the polished bricks until she felt her legs would fall off.

There's only a snowball's chance of getting to see Russell this time around. No matter.

He had emailed her that he was in a unique phase of operations and that a furlough from his duty might be a little difficult for him at this time. Nonetheless, he was going to try to get away even if it meant meeting her at a quasi-halfway point like Brno, Bratislava, Dubrovnik, or Budapest. All in all, Suzanne firmly believed that—unlike her last experience in Europe—this was shaping up to be a quiet, restful escape where life would be held at a comfortable, more manageable pace.

12

Reflection Connection

Northern Joan of Arc trail

Meuse River Valley, France

Current day

Just like most Americans, Mickey hated the way the French drove. No matter what they did on the road, it was always your fault. *The French are a people who have mastered the art of enjoying life,* he thought to himself. *And God forbid that on the highway, should you ever be the one to hinder their right to enjoy.* This being the case, Mickey's foot was a little heavier than normal and the twelve miles to the town of Vaucouleurs passed almost in a blink. It was only a few heartbeats beyond that when the small town of Vaucouleurs melted into the east. Silence pervaded the truck's interior while Saint-Dizier introduced Vitry-le-François followed by the signage which heralded Châlons-en-Champagne. The trip northward from Domrémy-la-Pucelle to Péronne, to meet Asaad, was passing quickly and quietly.

Mickey tried to stir up some pleasant interaction. "Remember the fulfilling of our eponym in the little bed and breakfast? Having a glass of champagne in Champagne is the only way to drink sparkling wine."

"Every zing else eez juss water, no Monsieur?" Loni boasted in a thick French accent. This brought about a combined chuckle from them both; the first thus far on the trip. Loni's version of speaking "fluent French" had always been speaking English in an overly exaggerated French accent.

But Mickey's smile immediately dimmed as he saw Loni's face grow stern again.

"What's troubling you, darling?"

"Mickey, when I asked you why we do pilgrimages, I wanted to be sure that I understood the underlying intent of our actions."

"When it comes to anything that concerns Joan, our dear *pucelle*, what dark motives do you think lurks in this heart and mind?"

"Are you doing this pilgrimage for me because of my love of the *pucelle* or is this to satisfy that longing to better understand your family heritage?"

"Yes, Loni."

"Yes to which?"

"Yes, it is for me to unlock the mysteries of my past, but I thought this was, more importantly, something you really wanted to do."

"I do . . . I did . . . I do. . . ."

"Which is it, Loni?"

"Both, I guess. You are on a noble quest to better understand your family heritage. I admire that. Meanwhile, I am on a selfish quest just to find me. This ignobility seems to have been ongoing my whole life. For example, I remember when I was in fifth grade. We were stationed at the Presidio overlooking the Pacific and San Francisco Bay. One day we went as a family to LA to visit the Saint Joan of Arc School. I just remember walking hand in hand with Jillian in the hallways mesmerized as I looked at all the artistic representations that the other children made of Saint Joan of Arc."

"As a future artist, your sister Jillian must have reveled in that experience."

"She did. We could both see how Joan's passion inflamed something deep within each child artist. Using pencil, oil, or chalk on canvas, they created a whirlwind of emotions deep within Jillian and me. Two years later, my heart broke because Jillian, filled with an artist's passion, left and went to Canada to create for Aunt Louise her greatest selling ceramic piece—*Saint Joan*. Right now, I feel that same intensity from so many years ago."

"Was that when you first felt connected to Joan?"

"Yes, it was. You had to admit that you felt that Joan of Arc flame too that day when we ended up at Sainte-Catherine-de-Fierbois."

"The village which once housed Joan's famous sword from heaven? Yes, I admit it," Mickey held his injured hand up yieldingly. "I remember that I had no intention to go to the small church at Sainte-Catherine-de-Fierbois once time got away from us. Based on my poor calculations, we didn't have enough daylight to walk the grounds of the Grande Salle in the castle ruins at Chinon with that delay."

"Yes, but God and Joan laughed at us."

"So it seemed. After all the miscues and wrong turns, we ended up at the sign marking the way to the church in Sainte-Catherine-de-Fierbois."

"The church was beautiful. Joan's statue was beautiful. Her banner was beyond words, awe inspiring. In my mind, I could see the sword of heaven being removed from beneath the altar there."

"The location of that sword was told to Joan by her angelic helper Saint Catherine. You saw Joan clutching it to her chest in the likeness at her home. Charles Martel's heavenly sword from Sainte-Catherine-de-Fierbois replaced the one given to Joan by Robert de Baudricourt at Vaucouleurs. That's like exchanging mere glass for a shiny diamond."

Loni went quiet and remained silent for many miles. Reims, the coronation city for French monarchs, came into view. The statue of Joan of Arc atop her steed in front of the cathedral, Notre-Dame de Reims, was breathtaking even in a moment's glance from the truck's window. Mickey could tell that statue spawned another thought which took Loni's mind's eye back to the church at Sainte-Catherine-de-Fierbois. Watching the pivoting of her eyes, Mickey followed her train of thought.

Breaking the silence with a whispered yearning, she queried, "Tell me again about the sword that was found at the chapel in Sainte-Catherine-de-Fierbois. You mentioned it when we stood in the east room of Joan's house. Sorry, I wasn't paying attention. Joan carried my thoughts elsewhere. Please, Mickey, tell me again."

Mickey sucked in a deep draught of air which hissed through his teeth and began the story of Joan that most people never knew.

"When Joan was at Tours being fitted for her suit of war armor, it was revealed to her by the voice of Saint Catherine that in the church at Sainte-Catherine-de-Fierbois, behind the altar, was a sword buried in the ground. It would be recognized because imprinted upon it were five crosses."

"What was distinctive of the five crosses?"

"This was an indication that it was a very special historical sword."

"How special?" Loni asked.

"I am getting to that."

"Hurry up about it," chided Loni with a poke to his ribs.

"During *Joan's inquisition*," goaded Mickey, returning a playful nudge to Loni's ribs, "she was asked about Charles Martel's heavenly Fierbois sword."

"Hey! My questions are not an inquisition." A big smile lit up her face. Mickey returned the smile. He could sense she was feeling better.

"The inquisitors, churchmen all, were accusatory. They asked if she had blessed the sword or if it had imparted special powers to her."

"What did she say?"

"Honey, you act as if I've never told you this story before."

"Chalk it up to a smoldering headache affecting my long-term memory trace and your riveting ability to spin a yarn. What did she say?"

"Actually, Joan became very indignant as she knew that they were trying to trap her into confessing a practice of witchcraft."

"Yeah, but, what did she—"

"She said, Ms. Impatient, that she neither blessed it, nor had it blessed."

"Hmmm. Such a clever response from an uneducated teenage farm girl. She is truly the daughter of God."

"An opinion made by many. My favorite Joan of Arc response, however, was at Rouen when she was asked if she was in God's grace. It was a question which was designed to be a trap along the lines of 'Did you kick your dog today?'"

"What did she say?"

"She said, 'If I am not in God's grace, may God place me there; if I am, may God so keep me. I should be the saddest in all the world if I knew that I were not in the grace of God.'"

"Brilliant!" Loni pumped her fist then clapped.

"She shoots! She scores!" Mickey reverberated. "I can think of no better reply."

"Laon."

"What?"

"The town, Laon, we are passing it. Can we stop? My feet ache, my head hurts, and I really must do that which nature best intended."

"Laying on a stop at the Templar town of Laon," promised Mickey as he exited for a pit stop. "I think we need to give you an extra lap in the fresh air. You look like you could use the break."

Loni nodded. "I really do need to take a knee. I think I am beginning to see three of you."

Mickey stroked his chin with mild concern. "It's fine, darling, just keep talking to the handsome one in the middle."

13

The Church, the Cat, and Christine

Pedestrian plaza
Poissy, France
Current day

*I*s it coincidence or do all the people in Poissy just happen to be walking in the same direction and to the same destination as me?* Even on vacation, Suzanne worried about such matters.

Having left the Paris airport, she kept checking her rearview mirror obsessively hoping not to see the mint-green duck car that followed her through Germany and France like a second shadow. Even though she knew her fears about this vehicle were no longer relevant, she checked the mirror anyway. When she had successfully fought the maddening modern-day traffic from Charles de Gaulle all the way to the tranquility which abounded in ancient Poissy, twenty miles west of central Paris, she allowed herself to take a deep, calming breath.

Staying at Poissy had nothing to do with convenience, comfort, or anything which usually brought visitors into Paris or its suburbs. Suzanne wished only to be in the same environment as her mentor, the fourteenth-century trailblazer, Christine de Pizan. Christine's inspiration fed from the beautiful surroundings in this riverside community. Suzanne preferred to be inspired as well, however *without* being followed. Suzanne had learned to accept the fact that in her world of government service, she was always a potential target, even when on vacation.

Suzanne's first stop in Poissy was the boulangerie and patisserie which were the weaknesses she accepted in her character, though she still occasionally had to talk herself through it. *We all have vices. One must decide whether to own the vice or be owned by it. My vice is European pastries. I know it, and so that's okay.* The pastries were not overpoweringly sweet like American bakery sweets. Instead, the emphasis was on taste and, of course, smell. The aroma that filled the

67

cobblestoned streets of Poissy this morning was mind-altering. In the clutches of such a rich fragrance, she could understand the intensity of what her former husband, Douglas Coletrane, always called the therapeutic value of the senses. Breathing in deeply, Suzanne scoffed slightly. *What other statement would you expect from a certified aroma therapist and metaphysician?*

The next short jaunt carried Suzanne to the dark-stoned Collégiale Notre-Dame de Poissy. In front of the church, she stood beneath the statue of Louis IX, a French monarch who was born in this sleepy town and in his lifetime became venerated as a saint of the Catholic Church. At King Saint Louis's marble feet, Suzanne tarried only a moment before she quickly entered the church to pray where her mentor Christine must have knelt and prayed six hundred years before.

Suzanne idolized Christine de Pizan for many reasons. First, Madame Pizan was historically documented as the first successful, world-renowned feminist back in the late 1300s. The fact that Christine was self-taught, self-trained, and self-polished made her misogynistic fight an incredible feat. Suzanne believed that Pizan should be venerated by every freethinking person alive but, in essence, she has fallen to obscurity in modern society. Even in the town of Poissy, only the very few and very educated knew the significance of her name.

"How tragic for you, my dear, dear beloved Christine," Suzanne mused aloud.

Inside the coolness of the darkened church, Suzanne walked the perimeter, going from chapel to chapel and paying homage to the selected saints of each. Included among them were John the Baptist, Bartholomew the Apostle, and Erembert the Bishop of Toulouse. Saint Margaret of Antioch, the ancient city, was revered there as well in a chapel portraying her with a serpent as was part of her legend of survival. Most auspicious was the indoor statue of a young Saint Louis, king of France. *He went to the crusades and successfully brought back Jesus's crown of thorns as well as the Legend of the Missing Thorns.*

Suzanne carefully listened to her own footfalls as they echoed within the confines of the stone walls. She also paused now and then to make note of any echoes that did not belong to her. True, she was in the arms of God in his holy church, but nonetheless, she kept reminding herself of the people, like the sinister Jean Dalton, who took advantage of these quiet surroundings to produce harm for personal gain. Satisfied that all was well, she continued in and out of the chapels' shadows. After she lit a votive candle, she sat in the second pew from the altar, open-eyed, and whispering her private words to Jesus.

Upon completion, she recited aloud what most people call the Jesus Prayer: "Lord Jesus Christ, Son of God, have mercy on me, a sinner."

Suzanne struggled in her violation of the tenth commandment. In her unhappiness, she always coveted. She seemed to covet the low-hanging forbidden fruit just outside her reach.

"Lord Jesus Christ, Son of God, have mercy on me, a sinner."

This coveting ruined her marriage with Douglas leading to its dissolution. Suzanne hated history, especially her own—she loathed it.

"Lord Jesus Christ, Son of God, have mercy on me, a sinner."

Having recited her prayer thrice, Suzanne cautiously looked left and right then departed the church. She went across the street and up the far sidewalk to the Musée de Jouet, a toy museum. She held to the belief that the first prayer given at a never-before-visited church warrants God's granting of the prayerful wish. As her heels clacked loudly on the cobblestone, her wish today centered on the personage of a man performing medical support operations in a place not all that far away.

Suzanne really had no personal interest in the museum, although its historical collection accurately displayed hundreds of years of children's diversions and toys, and it wouldn't open until nine. However, the view of the abbey grounds from the upper loft of the museum was spectacular. It was this loft that acted as the top of the entrance archway into the abbey itself.

The stone archway that connected the left and right sides of the museum served as more than the entrance portal of the abbey enclave. Today, as she entered the archway, Suzanne's lateral vision captured the movements of a determined stalker. Suzanne's fist clenched as she involuntarily sucked in a deep breath of the cool morning air. She watched as a gray tabby moved in and out of her morning shadow. Seeing the local cat ignore her, Suzanne exhaled steadily into a growing smile. Her thoughts immediately raced back across the Atlantic Ocean to her precious Tobermory, a cat of uncommon intelligence. A feline with an ability to listen and talk would make him a "beyond-cat" as defined by the author with the penname Saki. There was one difference in his Tobermory than hers—Suzanne's cat, unlike the Hector Hugh Munro's cat in his story, could not speak human language.

Suzanne smiled as she knew that her Toby would also be prowling the shrubbery in her Maryland backyard, pausing only to look at the fishermen or birds which were bountiful back home in the head of the Chesapeake at this time of year. When she was away from it, she always missed her stone mansion on Plumb Point Loop at Aberdeen Proving Ground. Being here at Poissy, and soon to be checked into the Maison d'Etrangers, would be an adequate compensation for the beauty lost. Looking through the rear archway, Suzanne could see that the abbey complex had long since disappeared but, nevertheless, an ambience still lingered. She paused as the tabby closed in on her, occasionally brushing by her ankle. She kneeled and stroked the feline's fur along its stripes.

"I can imagine that in richer times your hunting grounds were filled with hidden prey," said Suzanne, recalling her research about the countless parks and gardens that once existed in the ancient town. The cat blinked as it scanned the abbey grounds while Suzanne stood and removed the hairband which held her hair in a ponytail. Shaking her head, Suzanne's yellow hair dusted her shoulders briskly before resting over her high-boned cheeks. She brushed her hair vigorously with her hands all the while locking her gaze on her feline friend. The cat looked back at her with feigned interest but made no effort to speak.

Suzanne knew that on the abbey's grounds, some parks still existed but these were a shallow inhalation of the profound respirations that existed in

Christine's time. She and the tabby proceeded through the portal and then through the gate of the Musée de Jouet. Suzanne and the cat turned left. They found a small park and an unreserved stone bench where they comfortably sat to drink in the peacefulness of the surroundings. It was early morning and the *Maison d'Etrangers* was visible—just across the duck pond, past the hedge, and down the cobblestone alley.

"Well, Kitty, we can check in at lodging now if you prefer." Suzanne chuckled softly. "But look at what we'd be missing." Suzanne pulled out a period sketch of Christine in a long-sleeved flowing blue dress. An arch of white lace collar adorned her chest right below the neckline above which was a pendant cross. A white scarf cascaded over twin peaks covering her hair as a headdress. "How can we keep such a fine lady waiting?" Suzanne smiled, closed her eyes, and slowed her breathing, trying hard to let her guard down, if only just a little. The cat deferred to some morning grooming. After several moments of peaceful reflection, Suzanne opened her eyes then froze. There, on the cobblestone pathway, a blue-clad figure eased toward her.

Suzanne remained statuesque, hardly blinking. An image of Christine, in full fourteenth-century apparel, approached, smiled, and then quietly sat next to the cat.

Is this a hallucination? Suzanne rubbed her eyes, but the image persisted. She cast a wary glance around the garden. *Is it a projection? A holograph?* Suzanne resisted the strong urge to touch the vision next to her—whatever it was—and instead focused her energy on slowing her rapid heart and breathing rates. The image reached out and began petting the cat's fur, and in response the cat leaned into the stroking. Christine stared at the pond for a long time before speaking.

"I remember, as a child," the image began, "asking my father to allow me to visit my friends at the abbey. Many of the palace's female royalty had been sent here. I never understood why my family, people of common birth, would have been afforded this privilege. I just assumed that Father's influence as chief physician to King Charles V had to be the basis. Later in life, after the death of my husband, Étienne de Castel, the privilege was accepted by my family. I sent my only daughter, Marie, to this priory as an escort to the king's daughter by the same Christian name. Marie and Princess Marie passed through that stone archway together. I can hear Marie's voice now . . . I remember it perfectly.

"'Mother,' she said to me, 'why do I have to be sent away?'

"I told her, 'Marie, darling, life is so very hard.'

"'But Mother, you said life in the royal court is an island of softness in a world filled with hardness.'

"'Life's difficulties come in many forms,' I said to her. 'Both your father and mine have been taken from us. Even the king mourns with us as he has lost the service of both his chief physician and his chief secretary almost at once.'

"'Grandpa was the best doctor there was,' she said to me. 'I am sad he and Father had to be taken from us and the king.'"

Christine's figure rose and moved to the edge of the pond as she continued speaking. Suzanne watched a duck on the pond create shimmering ripples in the water as it paddled through Christine's image.

"My father and husband both died in the service of the king. When the king himself died, this meant that I no longer had the ability to come visit Poissy. To make matters worse, I didn't even have the income or the wherewithal to properly raise my own two boys. To guarantee success, my sons had to be sent away for professional grooming. Before this happened, my elder son died. I was devastated. The kind-hearted Earl of Salisbury took pity on me and became the sponsoring patron for my younger boy, Jean. Then, I was able to send my daughter here, to the safety of this abbey."

Christine turned away from the pond with her hands clasped behind her. Her gaze searched in the direction of the entrance arch.

"And yet now, things at court are changing. I fear that the earl is falling out of favor. My children need a patron, a sponsor. There is only so much I am allowed to do as a widow—even with my current influence. But at least Marie is safe at the abbey now. Safe from so many dangers."

Christine leaned over and straightened the pleats in her dress. Then, holding out her hand toward Suzanne, she began to count on each transparent finger.

14

Behind Abbey Walls

Abbey grounds
Poissy, France
Current day

"First and foremost, the high walls physically protect Marie from harm in ways the palace grounds never could." Christine paced near the bench, her dress swaying close to the cat, causing the animal to arch its back slightly and reposition itself. Suzanne tentatively reached out to the startled feline, and after a couple of strokes on its fur, he settled down and began licking his paws.

"Second, Marie's virginity can be fostered in a safe environment. As a society, it seems that males—particularly in the palace—are free to take from females without permission or hesitation. I am troubled and grieved when men argue that many women want to be raped. Such men say that it does not bother women at all to be abused as such, even when the women verbally protest. Rest assured: Chaste ladies who live honestly take absolutely no pleasure in such assault. Indeed, for women, rape is the greatest possible sorrow and violation.

"I remember when I was eleven. Rumors on the palace grounds spread that many of the girls were being raped. No names were ever given, probably because of the shame it would bring to the girl's family. Tongues even wagged about the possibility that any girl who was raped by royalty could carry within her the seed of a potential contender to the throne of France, bastard no matter. Father, as the chief surgeon, was obligated to intervene on behalf of these girls' families. Working through his connections at the royal priory and abbey at Poissy, he would often arrange a place where the girls could be taken to safety. I am sad to say that very early on I lost confidence in the safeness of the royal grounds which I had been led to believe was an unquestionable place of protection and a locale of flawless personal security. I knew my daughter needed to be spared from the actual reality." Christine paused near Suzanne and then with hands shaking in agitation, tugged harshly at the folds in her fourteenth-century dress. Suzanne drew in a jagged breath and bit her lip.

"The third reason for Marie to reside at this abbey is for a greater opportunity for learning. Wherever I go in my travels for the king I am introduced as the royal court scribe or the king's secretary. Occasionally, reservedly, I am called Cupid's secretary by those seeking advice on the status of women in our time. I'm not sure if this is praise or the intent to brand me an over-educated female shrew. No matter, I use any of the titles in behest of the king despite the fact I am female. I want Marie to understand that a woman need not fear promoting herself as educated; being a woman in a man's world is already a strike against her, and being educated cannot bring her lower, only raise her up." Christine gathered her dress as she sat down next to Suzanne on the bench. Licking her dry lips with her dry tongue, Suzanne turned cautiously toward her while edging back a bit. *Is this flight or fright? Whichever, I hope the sound of my pounding heart does not make Christine go away.* Steadily, the image never wavered.

"Marie's demonstrated brilliance as an apprentice scribe whispers a chance for future success. The fortitude of strong women like Marie has the potential to champion the cause against our society's repression of women. However, Marie needs a nurturing environment which promotes the learning necessary for strong women leaders. Further, I want her to be close enough to me, her mother and mentor, so I can ensure that her training develops in the proper manner."

Christine used the space on the bench between herself and Suzanne to draw an imaginary map. Her finger traced lines as she continued speaking. "You can see the road to Poissy from Paris runs along the river here. This is a mere day trip. With Marie here at the abbey, I am close enough to influence the mind and heart of my church-protected daughter. Additionally, because I have replaced my deceased husband as the king's secretary, I have the full freedom and authority to go hither and yon to the most distant marches in the land. Therefore, I can quite easily place myself in proximity to continue the mentoring of Marie on any trip that takes me through the abbey at Poissy."

Christine again stood. This time she came and kneeled in front of Suzanne, placing her elbows on Suzanne's knees. Suzanne inhaled sharply, expecting to feel weight, but instead only a breath of pressure grazed her legs, and with it came a curiously warm tingling sensation. Christine motioned for Suzanne to come closer, and then she placed her chin on her hands which she folded in prayer. Trembling, Suzanne leaned her head forward, tilting her ear toward Christine and pulling back her dangling hair until it curled tightly behind her ear. The air seemed to crackle.

"Last and most important," Christine whispered urgently, "I learned something that I never shared with anyone." The image of Christine looked right, left, and then continued. "Even as a child I always believed that I would be a key piece in the fulfillment of a prophecy. Father had always said that the throne of France would be lost by a queen but regained by a maid from the Lorraine. Father told me one day I would understand how. Just recently, Suzanne, my feet were placed on that path to discovery."

Suzanne jerked her head back reactively at hearing this image speak her name. Her brow furrowed. *This is really happening. This spirit or whatever knows me.*

Christine paused and nodded as if to affirm Suzanne's silent thoughts. Suzanne's eyes grew wide. Christine buried her nose and mouth in her hands. She drew in a deep breath through her fingers. Then as before, she folded her hands in prayerlike fashion, tucking them under her chin. Suzanne leaned in toward the apparition.

"I know I am not worthy, but I am blessed with thoughts placed in my mind by God through the Holy Spirit. Each day I begin with the same plea. 'Father God, mantle me with the Holy Spirit so that I know that the thoughts in my mind come from you. Help me to understand these thoughts so that I may execute your bidding.' Suzanne, I was given the answer to my daily prayer."

Suzanne shifted her body to the ground and kneeled so that she could be face-to-face with Christine. Christine turned so that both women were eye to eye.

"A day came when I was tasked to quietly investigate an irregularity that involved Poissy. Using palace resources and acting as the royal scribe, I began probing a past rumored instance of royal rape which involved the king, my father, and the abbey at Poissy. Blessed be me among earthly women. Despite Charles V and Father's passing, God saw that I would obtain help from inside the abbey." Dolefully Suzanne shook her head and lowered her eyes. She pressed one of her fists into her other palm until the knuckles crackled. As she glanced back up, Christine smiled warmly.

"You don't see it, do you, Suzanne? What are the chances that three events of significant importance to me converged at one spot on the earth? I believe that through His infinite wisdom, God has placed me at Poissy where I can perform a vital mission for the crown, try to uncover the mystery of my dear, dear cousin's disappearance, and bask in the warm love of my daughter, Marie. There are no accidents when it comes to God. You are here too, Suzanne; you must know the reason." Christine winked and smiled warmly. The image of Christine rose, gave one last passing stroke to the cat, and strolled down the long cobblestone pathway, dissolving as it moved farther away. Tears welled up in Suzanne's eyes. Still kneeling, she placed her head and arms on the bench, allowing herself to freely cry with only a cat to witness.

She wasn't exactly sure why she was crying. Was it the sheer magnitude of the encounter? Was it stress? Fear? Whatever it was, she let it come; she let it flow through her. When the emotional tidal wave had ebbed, Suzanne turned her head to the side and watched the cat lounging in the sunlight, seemingly unimpressed with the proceedings. She took a steadying breath.

She felt an uncertainty rising in her where before there was solid, reassuring fact. It was true that she had studied Christine all her life. Every word published by Christine de Pizan had been read and reread by Suzanne. There was very little she didn't know about her—except everything which Christine had just divulged to her.

Suzanne sat on the bench and frowned. *With God, all things are possible.* She nodded to herself then scooped up the cat and looked deeply into its eyes. *Let's look for some answers.*

"Why am I here, Sir Tabby?" Like the wide-eyed cat, Suzanne fought off any desire to blink. "I came to feel the presence of Christine, right? Is there something else, some ulterior motive of mine? Or an ulterior motive of hers? Suzanne cocked her head synchronously with the Tabby's. "What else was it that Christine felt I should know? Why would it matter that I know that God placed Christine in Poissy? Come on, Tabby, say something." Suzanne leaned back onto the bench and held the limp tabby high in the air above her.

"I'll bet you've seen Christine before." Suzanne rested the cat on her belly and petted it. "Of course you have. What clues did she give you?" The cat looked around, blinked, and rested its head.

"Did Christine ever tell you she was heartbroken at an early age? Yes, it's true. Christine grew up with a cousin who was closer than any sister could be—two halves of the same heart, they were. Siamese twin sisters could not be closer. Did she tell you that her heart was torn from her chest when life's good deed became a punishment?"

The cat looked back at her blandly.

"That's right. Christine's dearest, favorite cousin received the right to join the female ranks at Poissy. What a blessed opportunity ... right? Christine was so happy . . . at first. And why shouldn't she be? There was no envy or jealousy between them. Then solitude set in. As a cat, I don't think you fully understand the concept of loneliness, do you?" Suzanne stroked the cat.

"Anyway, as weeks went by, the absence of her sister cousin at home in the royal palace soured the joy she once felt. Weeks stretched into months as our Christine sucked loneliness from even the rich food and velvet drinks she was given. Did she tell you that she missed her dear cousin so much it incapacitated her? Nothing could slake her misery save their brief reunions where Christine felt the touch of her cousin's laugh on her ear and the warmth of her cousin's hand in her own. Regrettably, after only a couple of visits to Poissy, her cousin inexplicably disappeared. The hole in Christine's soul reached new fathoms.

"We people are different than you cats. We depend on having others in our lives. For you, company is optional. Isn't it? Because of her longings, youthful Christine's connection to Poissy pained her heart greatly.

"As you know, my dear tabby, life can hold joy in one hand and cruelty in the other. I'm sure Christine told you that love escaped her for many years. One day there came a time when she met the king's scribe, a loving man who respected her as a person and a woman. Lust for life returned. This man's love for her attenuated the forlorn longing she had for her dear cousin. Upon her marriage to him, Christine initiated the repair of a saddened and lonely heart. In the years that followed, children were born, and her life became even less settled. We both know that even when life is heaped with affection and responsibilities, there remains a smoldering desire to receive explanations not offered to us as children." The tabby yawned, blinked, and licked his paws in not-so-excited anticipation.

"So, here, in this place, she fostered her present hope in her daughter, researched her past, and did her duty to king and country. That's a lot for one day, and tomorrows are never guaranteed, Sir Tabby." Suzanne sat up, allowing the cat to move into the cool shade under the bench.

As the last wisp of Christine's holographic image faded into the dark orchard in the distance, Suzanne's eyes fixed on the ducks in the pond. On the surface, they seemed calm and unfettered, but a closer look showed their little feet churning the waters beneath. *Hmmm, just like Poissy.*

15

The Abbey's Secrets

Abbey grounds
Poissy, France
Current Day

Sir Tabby, why does it seem like everyone is staring at me?
Still reclining on the stone bench, Suzanne patted herself down to confirm that she had not worn her underwear over her clothes. *Maybe there is some breakfast baguette with cream cheese stuck to my top lip.* She mocked playfully. Finding these not to be the case, she tried to subdue her recently acquired edginess, reminding herself that she was, after all, on vacation.

Shifting gears, Suzanne focused on the beauty of the spring day and wondered if it was like any day upon which Christine traveled to Poissy in the 1400s to see her daughter all those many years ago. But now, like the ducks on the pond and the water beneath them, Suzanne could no longer lose herself in the factual, reassuring calm that was the history she knew. Her mind dredged up ponderings about what else Christine was doing on her frequent visits to the abbey.

✠ ✠ ✠

The coach picked up Christine at L'Hôtel Saint-Paul in Paris. She was going to see her daughter, Marie, at the abbey in Poissy. Christine mulled over the additional agenda which would be better fleshed out once she was able to talk to her daughter. She entered the coach as the king's scribe in her tenth year as a widow. She had taken the position out of financial necessity and not of loyalty or sheer ability.

The coach moved quickly this day, and Christine hardly noticed the splendor of the winding Seine which usually played the strings of her poetic heart. A multitude of brilliantly colored flowers dotted the pastoral scenery. Farmers and animal herders could be seen taking time from their workday to stitch together floral garlands for a love gained or love yet to be conquered. The intermittent cry of a nightingale stirred no inkling of the usual emotions within her. None of this fazed Christine, not on this day. Her mind was exclusively focused on the conversation ahead of her.

Christine catalogued the brief roundtrips to Poissy over the past three years. These sojourns were an anthology of joyful meetings and tearful partings. Christine had watched Marie grow from a nineteen-year-old assistant scribe to a maturing holy bride of Christ at the nunnery. In Marie's carriage, bearing, and confidence, the transition was amazing. *Marie floats in and out of a room on a cloud, despite the stark paucity of her environs.* Sister Marie lived a life of meagerness among the abbey's plush richness of flora and fauna.

The nuns at the abbey lived life like prisoners in a gilded cage. In an environment of earthly temptation, they held to a discipline which stressed being without comfort. *She lives in a paradise which she is not permitted to sample. Few have the fortitude of mind and spirit for such a life.* Christine knew well the difference between how the nuns treated guests and how they treated themselves. The meals the nuns served to Christine at the feasting table were an endless banquet of delicious foods served on gold and silver dishes. But her daughter knew none of that pleasure. The guest beds in the abbey were plush and lavish. Marie, instead, slept on wooden slats. The visitor's schedule was liberal and casual, but, for the nuns, tardiness was an unacceptable thought. Marie suffered beatings if she arrived late to vespers, prayers, or even scheduled meals. With such a dichotomy in coexistence, Christine often wondered how was it that the sisters of the abbey found their rigorous life fulfilling. *Perhaps freedom does not always equate to fulfillment.*

✠ ✠ ✠

Suzanne sat up on the stone bench, which probably had existed as long as the park had been a park, stretched her arms over her head, and then looked at her watch. The Musée de Jouet would soon open as the church tower struck nine. She decided that she would do as Christine always did and check into her lodging—the enclave which used to be the abbey was now a hotel—then change out of her travel clothing. *At least I have a water closet inside the abbey walls. Christine probably had to use the facilities outside in the town.* A thought massaged her brain as it had so many times when she worked, like the character Secret Squirrel on highly classified material in a bunker which didn't exist behind a high voltage electrified fence. *Are the high walls and barred windows of security to keep people out of the abbey or to keep secrets in? After all, there are secrets, and then there are* secrets.

What is really going on at the Abbey of Poissy? Christine mused as she jostled along in the coach. Some people of the town believed that the abbey held lepers. When asked the question, Christine emphatically denied that the female inhabitants within were mutant, marred, or horrid in appearance. Poissy was not a place where society's rejects were protected from an abusive world. The spiritually committed women of the abbey were disciplined followers of a martinet regimentation. Indeed, they preferred a strict, imposing order over the absence of boundaries which lay rampant outside the enclave walls. Christine found it interesting to note that her daughter found a freedom of spirit in such seclusion that she never found in the previous nineteen years spent in an elegant royal court.

Marie had now been with the sisters of Poissy's Dominican community for three years. Marie, along with Princess Marie, had both become venerated nuns which guaranteed them a safe future within the arms of the church. Marie's position within the abbey walls had, thus far, allowed Christine to gain some insights and intelligence on an issue that had plagued her soul for twenty-five years.

Christine felt that today there would finally be some answers. She knew it. An intensity she sequestered long ago had been steadily gaining force over the last few years, and now it was surging from within her soul. She stood on the brink of revelation, and she felt dizzy at the height of it. *It must be today that I learn of the disappearance of my dear cousin.* Christine's lips articulated the name. She then looked down to her lap as her finger scripted the cousin's name on her dress; her once-steady hands were shaking. *So many years of secrets have passed over these palms . . . or perhaps it is just vibrations from the road.* She shook out her hands and placed them together, rested her chin upon them, and began to pray.

16

Sword of Heaven

Northern Joan of Arc trail

Aisne River Valley, France

Current day

After a brief respite at Laon, Mickey and Loni's trip resumed. The silence stretched on for many miles. That is, until Loni reeled in the closing comments of the previous dialogue.

"What about the sword of Charles Martel? In fact, who was Charles Martel?"

Mickey was rapidly shifting his vision from the left side-view mirror to the rearview mirror to the right side-view mirror.

"Are you okay? What's up, Mickey?"

"Oh, just crazy drivers on the highway. I was thinking I might have made one of them mad with my snail-like American-style driving, and that he might be in pursuit of me."

"Is he? We certainly don't need to be dealing with a French version of road rage."

"I am seeing a car, but I'm not sensing that there is any aggression. I'll just keep an eye in the rearview mirrors. What were the questions? Wait a minute, I recall them. Answering your second question first, Charles Martel is one of the reasons we currently are not part of the Islamic nation. Regarding his sword, it was a symbol of power in Christianity in the eighth century."

"You once said that Charles Martel preceded Joan by seven centuries. That would mean that his sword—"

"—would have been at least seven hundred years old when it was found it in the church."

"Amazingly, yes."

"Here is where the story becomes so very interesting," said Mickey, his pulse rising with the anticipation of pursuing this tale. A quick glance into his rearview mirror gave him sufficient information that there was no road rage issue at hand—at least for now.

"After being told of the location of the sword by the Archangel Michael, a local armorer from Tours went to the church to retrieve the Fierbois sword of Charles Martel. When the sword was found, it was blanketed just beneath the surface behind the altar. As soon as it was found, the priests of the church touched the seven-hundred-year-old blade, and the rust upon it melted into dust. The priests of Fierbois knew that what they held was divinely revealed. The five crosses shone brightly, completely untarnished."

"What would be the metal that would behave so? They must have had to take special precautions to protect such a valuable sword," Loni mused.

"Chemically the sword would have to have had a chromium matrix which would essentially make it stainless steel. The problem is that the technology of using chromium didn't exist when the sword was forged. The only other explanation would be that it came from heaven."

"God sent it?"

"Yes, in a manner of speaking. It could have come from the metallic component of an iron- and nickel-rich meteorite. Remember the church at Nördlingen, near Rothenburg ob der Tauber?"

"I do, Mickey. Nördlingen is that little town that was built with the city walls on the edge of the meteor crater. All roads in Nördlingen lead down to the very bottom of the crater where the church sits on the remanent core of the meteor."

"That's right," said Mickey. "If the metal in the meteor was melted down and forged into a sword, then the hand that wielded the blade would, in essence, have a weapon from the heavens and essentially from God himself.

"Wherever it originated, when it was found at Fierbois, the sword had to be regally prepared for transport. To protect such a sword, the priests constructed a scabbard made of crimson velvet. When the sword reached Joan, she understood it to be, in every way, the sword of Charles Martel. The people of Tours, for love of Joan and with deep respect for the sword which saved Christendom at the Battle of Tours-Poitiers, made yet another royal scabbard, this one being of a rich golden cloth."

"It was a nice thought but doesn't really pass the good sense test," said Loni, shaking her head slowly. "Knowing the potential for the sword to see battle again, Joan would probably have had something more practical made for battle, right?"

"Correct," Mickey said, "and indeed she did. She commanded that yet a third, more functional scabbard, be made of very strong leather. It was in this casing that the sword of Charles Martel once again saw battle."

"With or without this sword," Loni said, "Charles Martel had to be a great warrior."

"Yes," reaffirmed Mickey. "He was a military genius. Eventually, all of Europe that was once held by Islam was then returned to the realm of Christendom, by the power of the arm and the sword, the Hammer of God, wielded by Charles Martel."

"Saint-Quentin lies ahead," commented Loni as she copiloted and read road signs. "Can we take another break?" She rolled down her window to draw in some fresher air.

Mickey arched his neck upward toward the sunroof.

"They're gone," said Loni.

"What's gone?"

"The horse and rider shapes that were within the clouds. I lost them after you turned away from Soissons and Compiègne. I figured that was why you changed our route."

"You saw the horse and rider in the sky?"

"Of course. I followed your eyes as you were looking in the clouds," said Loni. "Then I saw her."

"Her?"

"Joan."

"Why didn't you say something?"

"Why didn't you?"

"I didn't want you to think I was bringing my imagination into high gear while cloud painting," Mickey confessed.

"In the clouds, I clearly saw a rider leaning forward on what appeared to be a head and neck of a horse. The horse and rider were riding from left to right."

"Yes, when I saw it and I knew it was Joan, the question in my mind was why now and why here? So I took the right-hand road although it took us away from Soissons."

"Why does Joan want us to go this way?"

"Why indeed, my dear Watson? That would be the key question of the moment."

17

Dr. Pizan

Château de Beauté-sur-Marne
Paris, France
14th century

As the coach pulled away from King Charles V's mournful royal residence, Dr. Thomas de Pizan and a hooded, cloaked woman sat facing each other in silence. With great concentration, Dr. Pizan held to his eye a tasseled gold-trimmed red velvet pouch containing an exceptional treasure. Unbelievably it now belonged to him—the gift of a now-deceased monarch. Interrupting this scrutiny, the woman's familiar voice whispered from beneath the shadow of the hood.

"Is it precious, Uncle?" The woman noted how the good doctor cupped it with great reverence.

"This? It's something the king thought I should have."

"Do you know what it is?"

"Not really." Dr. Pizan twisted his lips. "I've held it in my hand, turned it on end, and thoughtfully studied it top to bottom, front to back. Honestly, I don't fully understand its importance. His Highness said it was more valuable than all the lavishness surrounding him, stone and mortar included." Dr. Pizan looked into the eyes of his darkly cloaked niece and then again at the cloth pouch. He thought about how he had arrived at this place in his life where God willed that he was able to receive such a thing. His niece asked aloud the very question he silently thought to himself.

"Why do you think His Highness gave it to you, Uncle?"

"Maybe he was appreciative of the doctoring I did for him." Dr. Pizan recalled his work for King Charles V and contrasted it from his humble beginning at his home in Pizzano, Italy, where, as a boy, he dreamed of one day studying medicine at the great university in Bologna.

"You know, the study of medicine is not easy, my dear niece."

"I remember seeing you use medicinal leeches and do bloodletting." The niece visibly shivered.

"Leeches are not my favorite part of medicine. Nevertheless, those and heavy metal tinctures are all appropriate tools and therapy that we use these days."

"Did you ever think you would receive royal gifts when you began practicing medicine in Bologna?"

"No, dear. However, King Charles has been so kind to us. He gave us the property in the forest at Fountainebleau near the Château de Beauté; the Château de Memorant; and the Tour Barbeau in Paris near the royal residence." Dr. Pizan smiled and patted his niece's arm. "It has been a hard row to hoe. My work is no easy task. However, to be together with my family, it is worth it." He leaned back against the carriage seat and closed his eyes for a moment.

He remembered King Charles V's wife, Queen Joanna de Bourbon, and how she had so much difficulty with her health of mind and body. *She was a frail woman plagued with difficult pregnancies and frail children. Despite my best medicine, I have only watched a tragic tale unravel.* He had almost constantly tended to the needs of the queen and the royal family while his daughter Christine and her favorite sister cousin played in the royal court. The Pizan children's brilliance drew them to the royal library where, for hours, they pored through the world's greatest center of knowledge. *I never realized that the mere playing would lead the children to an interest in what those books had to offer them—discipline for life-long learning.* Christine and her beloved sister cousin became court recorder apprentices, demonstrating the abilities girls possess when given an opportunity.

Dr. Pizan opened his eyes and looked down at the king's gift. He felt the soft velvet case and thought about how its contents would be passed through his heirs. There was Christine, whom he rarely saw these days. She was married and busy with her own life, managing the last child remaining at home. Her only daughter, Marie, worked at Vincennes in the castle doing various administrative errands. It was Christine's hope that one day Marie would be enclaved at the abbey at Poissy. That was yet to be decided.

"I am sorry I couldn't attend to your presence earlier, Niece. You caught me at the worst moment possible."

"Believe me, Uncle, I knew you were quite busy with the king. My message did reach you, then?"

"Yes, but I didn't know if was from you. '*A family member needs your presence. She will meet you on the first floor.*' Such a vague message indeed. When did you arrive, Niece?"

"I arrived very late the evening before. Seeking quiet and solitude, I became a mouse in the library. I peeked in on His Highness as the night waned and witnessed firsthand the agony that consumed him. I have never seen a human body undergo such torment."

"I'm sorry you had to see that. As a physician, I see things no one should ever have to see. I'm sorry you had to witness such firsthand." He ran his hands over his face and rubbed his eyes. "I am glad you saw me before I did you, my dear niece. I'm not sure these old eyes would have recognized you—the last time we were together was when we left the royal palace on the way to the abbey." Dr. Pizan smiled and, despite the situations behind and ahead of him, he let the joy of being in the presence of his favorite niece be a balm to his soul.

He looked again at the regal gift and wondered if, where they were going, it could be of more help than he himself could. Whichever way God willed would determine the potential the gift had to bring health back to his family. Dr. Pizan consoled himself. *There is no more I can do for a dead king, but there is still great need for me elsewhere.*

Briefed by the niece about a sickly child needing his care, Dr. Pizan pondered deeply while the coach lurched toward Vouthon in the Lorraine region. As he mulled over the patient information, the doctor put the royal gift in his satchel knowing it would go with him into the Lorraine, but it might not return with him. *As God wills it. What best to do with the most precious of gifts? Give the gift to the person who will exact the greatest joy from it.*

The coach ride was bumpy and, in some ways, reminiscent of a mother rocking her baby to sleep. Dr. Pizan's eyes became heavy lidded. Over the course of many miles, his body grew increasingly relaxed until he finally tilted over in a dead fast sleep. Neither he, nor his dozing niece, saw the satchel tip over. From the velvet pouch, out spat the royal gift, sliding into the recesses of the coach floor where only the forgotten dwell.

18
Making of a Piglet

Vouthon, Meuse River Valley
Lorraine region, France
14th century

It seemed to Dr. Pizan that these days the Grim Reaper hovered in a circling pattern over Vouthon. Twenty years earlier it was disease and pestilence stealing the health of the people. Now, raiding parties destroyed homes and families—killing and maiming the unfortunate inhabitants.

In Vouthon, which was his destination, he had been briefed by his niece that a mother grieved because her five-year-old child, Isabella, could not overcome sickness. He imagined the forlorn mother clutching her adopted daughter to her chest, hoping that a mother's love alone had curative powers, though she knew differently.

As a favor to his niece, Dr. Pizan brought his knowledge of medicine to the girl, hoping he might be of more help to her than he was to King Charles V several hours before. Upon arriving, the exasperated mother, through sobs of concern, updated him regarding the girl's weakening strength over the past days, weeks full of fevers, and her increasing refusal to eat or drink. He nodded as she spoke, taking a quick account of her health as well.

"I understand. Please go lie down and rest. I am here now, and I will do all that I can."

"I can't. I must fetch more water for her, Doctor."

"If you must go, then take my riding cloak," Sister Sibyl offered. "It might be a bit dusty from the ride in, but at least it will keep the brisk air off your neck and shoulders."

Father Jean Minet adjusted the cloak's hood on the worried mother, echoing the physician's concerns.

"I am quite happy to fetch the water for you. Afterall, an exhausted mother can be of no help to a sick child. I'd rather you go rest as the doctor suggests. We'll keep watch on Isabella."

The parish nun, Sister Sibyl, hummed softly and rocked her godchild, Isabella, with the great love and affection.

"You see," Father Minet said to the mother, "she is safe in the arms of the Church."

Nonetheless, the door slammed, and the mother's footsteps faded into silence.

Rifling through a cornucopia of pharmaceutical combinations Dr. Pizan had memorized, he walked to-and-fro in his minilab situated in the kitchen area of the family's meager home. The doctor agonized through the child's symptoms and compared them to the symptoms he knew all too well. His medical training guided him to make two working lists in his head. The first list was the possibilities of what the sickness might be. The second list was the possibilities of what he could not afford to miss or rule out. Outside children were playing and chanting.

"Ring around the rosies, pocket full of posies!"

Children have the potential to have sicknesses which resolve themselves safely.

"Upstairs, downstairs!"

But there are those diseases that mimic benign pathology only to later wreak havoc and even death.

"We all fall down!"

In his mind, he went through the first of the two lists—the most common childhood sicknesses—in the order that he learned them. *The first disease presents with a three-day, red-spotted rash which has a bluish-white spot with a red halo in the mouth on the inside cheek and tongue. Red eyes; red, runny nose; and a cough. The second disease presents with a dewdrop-on-a-rose-petal rash which forms crusts on the skin. The third disease presents with a five-day version of the first disease. The mouth spots are different—usually just red and on the soft part of the roof of the mouth. The fourth disease makes the children have a rash with painful jowls on one side of the face or both. The fifth disease presents with a slapped-cheek appearance.*

"These are all manageable," Dr. Pizan muttered. "They come, they go, and life is fully spared." He began the recitation of the second list—the sicknesses he hoped it wasn't but couldn't afford to miss. One topped the chart—the Great Pestilence. He remembered it well from his practice in Venice. The Black Death manifested with swollen bumps over the entire body and eventually the darkening of the skin as the body's tissues began to liquefy. He remained hopeful since there were no visibly open sores on the child's skin nor history of bloody exudates or excrements. Dr. Pizan prayed that this child's sickness was housed in the first list.

Inspecting the child in the nun's arms, he used his trained senses to gather data. He listened to, smelled, and felt the natural and physical state of the child's body. With his ear against her body, he listened to her breathing and the sounds from her chest and belly. He smelled the quality of her breath and the bouquet of scents which emanated from her body. He touched gently and then deeply the areas which often change in sickness, palpating for any atypical presence and mentally recording the turgor and pull of the skin. As he inspected the subtle groove resting behind the jawline of the face, the sleeping child winced. He repeated the maneuver, and the child winced and moved away, repositioning herself in the sister's arms with a grunt.

Dr. Pizan released a big sigh and nodded knowingly. *List two has been eliminated. This child will evolve in the manner of the first list.* Smiling, he patted the head of the sleeping child and then searched for a corner to nurse his own weariness.

The nun didn't ask what he had learned, but quietly exalted in the knowledge that the physician's features had eased, his tension and worry seemed to be quelled. She looked over at a busy Father Minet pouring the freshly drawn water into cauldrons for heating. Meanwhile the still-hooded and cloaked mother dozed limply on a stool in the far corner.

As the doctor settled down to rest, he listened to the singsong chanting from the children outside and their numerous playful giggles. If he was right, some of these children would eventually succumb to the same sickness as the little girl. However, he would inform the townspeople that time, rest, fluids, nursing, and prayer would bring health back to their precious little ones. *Yes, upstairs and downstairs they might temporarily fall, but in God's grace they will again rise in restored health.* His eyes searched for holes in his eyelids as he drifted off to the diminishing chanting of the children at play.

19

The Precious and the Piglets

Vouthon, Meuse River Valley
Lorraine region, France
14th century

The next day began with a cock's crowing. Dr. Pizan saw a sleepy-eyed, two-legged piglet standing in front of him pulling at his frock. The sounds of her mother carrying morning dishware from the kitchen to the table lent a sense of calm and normalcy to the home where before there had been fear and worry.

Sister Sibyl called for little Isabella, and the piglet walked to the nun then pulled herself up using the habit's belt, dangling crucifix, and other of the available uniform accessories. Little Isabella took her goblet of drink, looking over the rim at the smiling doctor. Sister Sibyl held up her godchild and kissed both the girl's eyelids, then kissed her again lightly on her messy lips. Dr. Pizan smiled at the sister's devotion to the child.

Looking directly into the child's eyes appraisingly, her cheeks still puffed like a pig's from her illness, the physician spoke, "Good morning, sunshine. How is the little piglet today?"

Sister Sibyl answered, "Sorry, Doctor, my friend Isabella here isn't talking much this morning." The sister knew the child was more interested in breakfast than chatter.

"She is a beautiful little piglet today, isn't she?" The doctor began to drink some cool honey mead, this morning sustenance which the child's mother had brought for him.

Sister Sibyl began to probe. "I am assuming that you knew that her cheeks would puff out in this manner?"

"Yes, from the puffiness of her cheeks, I deduced her sickness, the mumps, as still somewhat early in its presentation."

"I have not seen this before. How will the sickness progress?"

"I can answer that one," offered the sweaty red-faced mother as she paused in her shuffling to and from the kitchen. "She may have a little rash, but the fevers will stop. After a time, her puffy cheeks will shrink down back to her normal pretty little face."

"Very good! I concur with Dr. Mother," reaffirmed the increasingly waking physician. "Isabella will need only water from the well and not from fruit or vegetable as the sourness might pain her swollen cheeks. Time, prayer, and lots of love will be the only things additionally needed."

"Will she need to be kept indoors and away from the other children?"

"Most likely, yes, Sister. However, don't be surprised if we have other community piglets or semi-piglets arising from full or partial facial swelling."

"What about Paris?" asked Sister Sibyl, knitting her brow. "Is this disease prevalent there?"

"It is, and there is so much more."

"Like what? Please tell us of Paris and the things that have transpired since the king's illness took a turn for the worst," asked Sister Sibyl gravely.

A deeper voice then chimed in unexpectedly. "How will the church be affected in the loss of the king?" Father Jean Minet asked as he peered in from the frame of a window behind the startled physician.

"That I cannot say," began Dr. Pizan. "But when I left the king last night there was nothing more I could do for him; I expect that he died shortly afterward. It has been fifteen days since the disease moved internally. We will most likely hear news of his death today. Even though I told no one of the fifteen-day countdown, the court can smell blood like sharks in the sea. As the king's health began to fail rapidly, the long-brewing storm began to break. The prince, sixteen-year-old Charles VI, has never demonstrated the regal strength or wisdom of his father, Charles V. Even before his death, the king's family was subtly fighting within for the reins of power in France. One of the uncles drinks the milk of the English to fuel his aspirations."

"Maybe a new queen needs to provide a calm hand to steady the hearts and souls of the restless," posed the priest in the window.

"Maybe a queen is the last thing that is needed," warned Dr. Pizan. "Remember the words of the legend. . . ."

"'The kingdom of France will be lost by a queen only to be saved by a maid from Lorraine,'" recited Sister Sibyl.

"Thus far, there is no queen on the horizon for the future King Charles VI, at least not now. This is not to say that the queen consort, whoever she may be, will be the one to fulfill that prophecy," reminded the doctor.

"All happens as God wills it." A tone of finality rang in the priest's voice.

"Indeed." All shook their heads in reverent agreement.

"However, God works through his believers," Dr. Pizan added. "If the kingdom of France will be lost by a queen but saved by a maid from Lorraine, then it is incumbent upon us to ensure our maidens here in the Lorraine are healthy and strong in mind, body, and spirit. As it is my lot in life to help with the body, I will see to the health of the flock. God has granted me that skill."

"It is my obligation to ensure that *this* maid has a sound, strong mind and body," boasted the mother as she held up a basket of fresh eggs in one hand and a pitcher of milk in the other.

"It is up to the church to reinforce her spirituality," spoke Father Minet and he received a confirmatory head nod from Sister Sibyl.

Dr. Pizan smiled at the group, knowing that the time was right to begin his departure actions. His work was almost done. He walked over to the child and stroked her curls as he looked deeply into her eyes.

"When this maid becomes of age, I want you to give her a gift which was passed to me from someone very special." Dr. Pizan spoke in a most fatherly tone. "It will help to solidify her spirituality."

He went over to his satchel and searched its contents. A quick rifling of his frock pockets also came up empty. Dr. Pizan stood motionless, deep in thought, trying to remember the last time he saw the king's gift secured. He then remembered. He started to bolt for the coach when a voice halted him.

"I am guessing," said Father Minet, "that I may know something of your missing gift, if indeed that is what is happening here."

Dr. Pizan smiled at the priest with relief then nodded his appreciation. He approached the window and held his hand out in anticipation of receiving the gold silk-trimmed red velvet package bound by a soft, braided tasseled string. Father Minet didn't move.

"I'm sorry, Doctor. I don't have it."

"I thought you said you did, Father." The doctor's voice was tinged with anxiety. "What did you do with it once you found it?"

"I didn't find it, Doctor. A child brought it to me. She said that she and her friends were chanting and playing games over by your coach when a voice in her head told her to open your coach and search the floor under the seats."

"A voice? What kind of voice?"

"Does it matter, Doctor? The voice directed her to search the crevices in the floor for something that was to be brought to the house of a mother with a sick child."

"Did she open the gift?"

"No. She said that the gift lay separate from a red pouch. The voice told her to place the gift into the pouch. As I was making my way here, this child brought to me a neatly bound blue handkerchief weighted by the gift within."

"Then you do have it."

"No," said Father Minet, holding his palms outwardly. "I no longer have it."

"Well, then . . . who?" Dr. Pizan looked at the mother. She held her hands upward and outward, indicating the gift did not reside with her. Dr. Pizan's eyebrows bristled, and his gaze shot back to Father Minet.

"I gave the gift to Sister Sibyl," said the priest, pointing. "I instructed her to give it to whoever first asks for it."

"And so I shall," said Sister Sibyl. "I confess, Doctor, I have it. Forgive me for not coming forth before now. We've both been a bit busy." Sister Sibyl broadly smiled and produced into view the red velvet pouch that she had held only briefly and passed it to the doctor. "Once I saw what was within the kerchief, I would have given it to you even if you had not asked, Doctor. I felt in my soul that the contents were precious."

"I understand, Sister. Indeed, you are correct, it is most precious." Dr. Pizan looked at her and gave a knowing nod. "Did you remove the gift?"

"No, it was not my lot to do so," Sister Sibyl said.

"Yes. That falls to me." Dr. Pizan puffed his lips and nodded. *This gift must go to whom God intended.* He silently prayed for guidance as he unwrapped the gift from its silk, velvet, and braided bindings. He held the object in his hands, looking at the mother and then at the sister. With affirmation, the doctor placed the unwrapped gift into the hands of the nun. He spoke to both ladies.

"Right now, the one person who needs to hold the gift must be this bride of Christ, a mere nun, who may have the responsibility of the fate of France in her hands." Dr. Pizan placed his hands on Sister Sibyl's shoulders. "From regal hands to mine, the gift's trip began. Even when lost, through children and priestly hands it found its way back. Its journey is shrouded in the divine. We'll keep it there."

"As God wills it," said the two ladies almost in perfect unison.

Sister Sibyl gazed into her hands at a pendant crucifix. It was small, fitting neatly into the palm of her hand. The workmanship was refined and elegant. It was the most unusual pendant she had ever seen. Sister Sibyl dragged her eyes across the features of the cross itself.

The cross was wood, but its front was black and accented with silver. Its vertical and horizontal crossbars were equal in length, and the ends of each arm flared abruptly. In each of the four quadrants formed by the central cross were tiny, smooth, symmetrical silver crosses. *A symmetrical five-cross cluster? How strange*, she thought. Centered upon this base, a metal figure of crucified Jesus was mounted to the polished silver surface.

She turned the pendant over in her hand. On the reverse side there was a word etched into the cross. A tear rolled down Sister Sibyl's cheek as she read the word *Jerusalem* in Latin.

With a moment's more scrutinization, she noticed another oddity, but this was neither the time nor place to investigate it. Taking in a deep breath, she closed her fingers around the pendant and thrust it into one of the folds of her stately garment. Pulling out a blue handkerchief from another fold, she blew her nose and directed her question to Dr. Pizan.

"How will I know the right time to give this to the child?"

Before the doctor could answer, Dr. Mother spoke kindly, "I believe you will know. God always tells us. We fail to listen."

Father Minet added, "God will make it obvious when our piglet is strong and has become a maid worthy of the title. You will see. God has never yet let me down."

"Nor has he done so to me, and I am unworthy—as evidenced by my poor stewardship of this gift," reaffirmed Dr. Pizan. "Nevertheless, I must begin my return journey to Paris, but I will come back to check on the child within a month's time. It is good that you have guardianship of this gift, Sister, because it is most safe with you. The king's work keeps me in faraway lands as I execute service to His Majesty. There are never any guarantees to my schedule."

"I thank you for your trust in me. I will strive to be a worthy stewardess."

"It is God who trusts in you most, Sister. Will you remain, or do you wish to ride with me as I go east from here? I must stop at Domrémy before going back. Will you need a transportation that I can provide?" Before the nun could respond, Father Minet chimed in.

"I will take a ride back," said the father. "There is work for many though we clergy have few hands. So, the sooner that I can return, the more work can be done."

"Then you'll need me to go as well, Father. However, I really would like to continue tending to this piglet so that her mother can do those things most pressing."

Seeing the look in the nun's eyes, the priest laughed and replied, "Let the hands of God be yours here in Vouthon today, Sister. There are probably a few more piglets and piglet mothers in the area who can also benefit from your recent medical education. The work that awaits you in Domrémy can wait one more day. In your stead, I will take your charge as best I can, Sister, if you trust that these hands won't fail you so badly."

The nun smiled her appreciation and the father nodded. He leaned back from the window's edge. "I will plan to see you on the morrow or the day after, Sister Sibyl. For now, Domrémy remains on your eastern horizon."

Father Minet turned from the window and made his way toward the coach. At the thought of all the uncertain violence that had consumed the Lorraine recently, the good priest's smile turned into a saddened frown. Deep inside him he hoped that Domrémy still safely sat just off the horizon to the east. With the English and Burgundian renegades, there were no absolute guarantees from one day to the next.

20

The Prince, the Prayers, and Péronne

Northern Joan of Arc trail

Somme River Valley, France

Current day

L oni looked out the vehicle window wondering if the blurriness in her vision was due to the headache, the speed of travel, or maybe a combination of both. Soon the hazy city of Saint-Quentin disappeared in the rearview mirror as the Vermandois opened, enveloping the two travelers. Closing her eyes, Loni conjured up a vision of the sword of Charles Martel. The image in her mind was crisp, clear, and devoid of any fuzziness. Loni concluded that her external eyes were victims of smoldering trouble. She held the image of the sword in her internal vision, and it seemed to her that perhaps Mickey could sense her focus because the sword became his burning topic of conversation during the ensuing miles.

"The finding of the five-crossed sword of Charles Martel which, mind you, lay hidden for seven centuries, was a miracle and gave credibility to the Maid of Lorraine," Mickey resumed.

"This begs the question of why Charles Martel would have placed the sword there in the first place," posed Loni.

"Legend states that after the Battle of Tours in AD 732, Charles Martel founded the church at Sainte-Catherine-de-Fierbois. There, he secretly buried his sword to be found by the next person God chose to act as the savior of Christendom. This secret location of the sacred sword was passed from Frankish king to Frankish king."

"Is this where Charlemagne comes in?"

"Yes, Charlemagne was the grandson of Charles Martel. Charlemagne's great-great-great-grandson, Charles III, who was called Charles the Simple, was alleged to reveal the secret of the sword to his jailor Rudolph of Burgundy in none other than the Château de Péronne—the 'Péronne Castle' to which we travel today."

"Why was Charles called simple? Was he daft?"

"Actually, no. He was called simple because he was straightforward and not complicated."

"Like you, Mickey the Simple, straightforward and uncomplicated."

"Well, yes . . . er . . . well, no. . . . Okay, I concede. I really have a hard time seeing his title as very flattering."

"What did Duke Rudolph of Burgundy do with the information from his imprisoned royalty?"

"He had a scribe document the information so that he would have a chip to play against the ruling Frankish kings. Rudolph himself, however, was so consumed with battle plan after battle plan that he never got to exact that leverage. Rumor of the document's existence eventually got back to the Capetian line of the French monarchy to King Philip II, known also as Philippe Augustus."

"Did he get the sword?"

"No, not per se. Under the guise of building up Péronne Castle to a fortress, he searched and searched the foundations until he found the lost document wrapped around a pair of sticks."

"It was a scroll?"

"History doesn't mention a scroll—only a large piece of parchment affixed to two sticks."

"Sounds very scrollish to me."

"True. I guess it would depend on the size of the sticks and the parchment."

"Specifically, where was the document—be it scroll or not?"

"History doesn't say. However, once found, Philip II ensured that the secret document made it back to Paris, and some say it went to the castle at Vincennes where it again disappeared until a pair of scribe apprentices found it."

Swiftly but silently, Loni moved her hands to her face, covering her eyes, and leaned back in her seat.

"Are you okay?"

"I really think we need to stop." Loni rocked her head. "I just need a break from riding . . . the way the sunlight flashes through the trees. It's wearing me out."

"Perfect timing. Next stop, Antoine's Bistro for sustenance and the Péronne Castle for the exhibition at its museum."

"Mickey, I'm failing. I'm not sure I have the energy for a long visit with Asaad."

"Darling, I know the discussion on his Staff of Moses is what you both want. However, we can make it short or even postpone it a bit. You can rest here in the truck or, if you like, we can check into a hotel for some rest on a bed with your feet elevated. It's really up to you."

Loni appreciated her husband's modification of the city of Péronne visit for her. As concerned as she was regarding her waning energy and its effect on her ability to meet with Asaad at the exhibition, she worried more about her other meeting with Douglas. She drew in a deep breath and forced a smile as she began accessing what little energy reserves she had while deciding how they needed to be distributed.

"I can make it to Péronne," she said. *I must.*

The Beast pulled into a parking space in the center of Péronne. Within minutes, the pair passed Église Saint-Jean-Baptiste and the statue of Marie Foure, heroine of Péronne. Loni listened as Mickey prattled incessantly regarding the historical significance of Marie, also known as Mary Catherine of Poix, and her patriotic deed to save Péronne. As they rounded the corner to Antoine's, the full magnanimous view of the paired bastions of Péronne Castle came proudly into view. They were a rather odd-looking pair of oblong-shaped battlement towers.

"How do you feel? Are you leaning toward dinner or dessert?" Mickey playfully challenged.

"Actually, for my part, I really want to see Péronne Castle first."

"Really?"

"Really, silly," said Loni as she clutched Mickey's arm. "Look, if that elderly lady up ahead can make it, so can I."

"Yes, but she has a walking stick."

"I have you—the best walking stick ever."

"Are you sure?"

"Really, Mickey. The walking did me good. I feel a bit better. I say let's push on a bit farther with the castle museum exhibition and then have no obligations after dinner except rest."

"Overruled. I think we should, at a minimum, have some fluids to rehydrate."

"Always on duty, huh?"

"Yes, and you are my favorite patient, or should I say patients." With his bandaged hand, Mickey stroked her rotund belly.

They went into Antoine's and sat next to the window on the far side of the register island. The corner was secluded and allowed them to enjoy the view of the street without interruption by either the traffic of the street or passersby within the bistro.

Once they were comfortably seated with her water and his Cybele-brand fruity white wine, their reinvigoration began. Mickey took in the view of the castle directly to his front, and after a few moments he leaned over his side of the table and began speaking to Loni in almost in a whisper.

"So, on All Saints' Day, the outcast Charles VII, the Dauphin of France, prayed to God for three things. He told no one about the prayer or that for which he prayed. These three things were known only to him and God. Then, when he met Joan in Chinon, she told him the three things that he had prayed for. Joan knew his prayer and, additionally, she showed him two things which utterly convinced him that she was truly sent by God and therefore was the Maid of Lorraine. Mind you, at this point, she herself was not convinced she was the Maid of Lorraine and even told him so."

"What did she tell him?" Loni asked as she took a sideways glance at the castle. Her gaze lingered there as Mickey spoke.

"No one knows for certain, and she never told anyone. When inquisitors pressed her, she said that if they wanted to know then they would have to ask King Charles VII himself. The only thing she *would* say about the meeting was that what transpired 'was beautiful, honorable and good, and the richest that there can be.'"

"Well, then, what did she show him?"

"She showed him the sword of Charles Martel. It had the legendary five stars upon it."

"Wait," Loni's eyes snapped back to Mickey and away from the view, "before you said it had five crosses."

"Yes."

"Which is it? Crosses or stars?"

Mickey smiled mischievously and scratched his chin. "Well, they were not truly stars . . . in reality, the in-folding of the Damascus steel created five distinct fleur-de-lys."

"Crosses, stars, and or fleur-de-lys? I don't believe it," Loni whispered conspiratorially. "How did she know this was the one and only sword belonging to Charles Martel?"

"How indeed? History doesn't say. History can't even really tell us if it was crosses, stars, and or fleur-de-lys."

"Okay, I yield. It's all conjecture. What was the second thing she showed him?"

"Again, honey—"

"Wait, let me guess. . . . History doesn't say."

Mickey tapped his nose and smiled. "Remember though, whatever it was, it had to be beautiful, honorable, good, and nothing could be richer."

"What could a peasant girl possess and display to the king of France that met these criteria?" Loni shifted in her seat as her focus was pulled, yet again, back to the castle. "I would imagine in his treasury he had things that were of the same caliber."

"For that answer, you would have to ask Joan herself," beamed Mickey, knowing that the world would never really know anything beyond the records that had already been kept and studied for generations on end.

"I'll just do that!" Loni boasted as she turned back to the table. She murmured questions in a series of whispers and clicks into the pendant which she wore around her neck, alternately holding it against her ear for answers.

"*L'addition, s'il vous plaît.*" Mickey asked the bistro staff for the bill, and he shook his head at his playful wife. He seemed to remember that the crucifix was a private wedding gift from her grandmother, and for some reason, Loni had always associated it with Joan of Arc.

The brief break seemed to accomplish its task. Loni and Mickey left the bistro and, with greater energy, strolled across the pedestrian walkway to the twin towers which guarded the entrance of Péronne Castle. The cobblestones made Loni's gait a little unsteady but the strong, unbroken left hand of her husband more than adequately compensated.

Loni looked down as her husband's hand patted her arm, then she turned backward and looked upward as Mickey and she passed under the arch. She was about to comment on the medieval architecture when suddenly she felt a forceful blow on her back ribs. A groan emanated from deep within her. She lost the sensation of Mickey's touch. The world was blacking out. As the margins of her visual screen closed in and her body swayed, two thoughts crossed her mind. Two names. *Mickey. Douglas.* Her world faded to black. Loni saw no more.

21

A Time to Sprint

Château de Péronne

Péronne, France

Current day

Mickey was pushed from behind, knocked into another fleeing person. Bending forward, he struggled for his next breath. A shoulder rammed into his solar plexus and his world moved into the realm of slow motion. He could see himself falling—he grew hypersensitive in his swirling surroundings. He heard the popping of rounds being fired and smelled the accompanying gunpowder smoke. In his drop to the ground, his cockeyed peripheral vision caught the shadow and shape of an unrecognized person passing over him in criminal flight carrying a wrapped tubular object. Mickey's ears cultivated a cacophony of scuffling which swam in a matrix of increased distant shouting. People were falling or diving all around him, and the cobblestones were being splattered with blood. He fought to regain his breathing, but his respirations remained a spastic laboring and kept him crippled on the ground. He lurched forward attempting to rise, but his head began to spin uncontrollably. He felt himself collapsing on something or someone directly in front of him. He couldn't see or feel Loni and wanted to know that she was safe. The blood trickling into what remained of his vision hindered his search.

He heaved himself to his knees and, through ragged gasps, he clumsily steadied himself into a reasonable posture to focus on his search for Loni. He realized that he was propped up on a crumpled body which wasn't moving. *It's human. That is, it was human. Thank God it's not Loni.* He craned his neck with great effort. *Where is she? I can't see her.* His eyes looked down and finally captured a face with a familiar form. In a twisted contortion beneath him, the face who wasn't Loni looked vaguely familiar. *Asaad? Is that you?* It was indeed Asaad Baghbah al Bethany. However, it was not the man he remembered in their last interaction at the Bavarian castle. To his widening eyes, Asaad's face became bordered within a quivering haze—his skin bloodstained, pale, and flaccid. Mickey wanted to help him, but he felt himself slowly losing consciousness.

Despite his objection, the world became a blurred, visual carousel of stone, steel, and the underside of the portal framed against the cloudy sky. Approaching from his left, a set of parapet stone stairs closed in on him as the sharp acrid smell of smoked almonds, freshly spent firecrackers, and stale tobacco started to fill his nostrils. Mickey's visual fields became filled with a multiplicity of hands and faces which faded quickly into a grayness of sight and sound. Yielding to the gray, he submitted to vertigo, allowing himself to be carried into a silent blackness.

✠ ✠ ✠

Mickey's eyes suddenly reopened to an upright world of strange colors and sounds. In front of him, many people were moving his arms and arm brace. Behind them were uniformed people pushing gurneys of medical equipment with a great sense of urgency; his eyes focused rapidly, capturing fleeting images of nametags reading *Boucher, Dubois, Sadlier,* and even an *LT B. Braille.* Although there was a mild ache in his ribs, his breathing had now returned with relative ease. Hungrily he consumed his immediate surroundings. He had been moved to a seated posture against the inner side of the Péronne Castle gateway. His vision was partially blocked with a head bandage that someone placed on him. With his good hand, he removed all evidence of this mummy-like medical aid. Now, less hindered, Mickey eased himself up on the stone pavement; then pushing off from his knees, he forced himself into an upright stance and tried to steady his rubber-band legs. In front of him, he saw a lifeless Asaad lying on the cobblestone walkway. In the distance, he located his precious Loni on the parapet stone way with caring people attending to her medically within the triage area. Now, and for the next few seconds of immobility, he was dependent on the kindness of strangers. He moved toward the triage area and his dear wife.

Relegated to be a mere spectator at the triage station, Mickey bit hard on his lower lip. To him, it did not matter that he had been first inadvertently knocked over by Asaad and then bowled over by an escaping ruffian thief, nor did it matter that he could have done nothing to prevent what happened. *I didn't protect her. Now, I can't even help her. I didn't even see her fall. She has a head injury. Oh, God.*

The ambulances and patient transporters buzzing around him were consumed with the task of evacuating the masses of badly wounded casualties—many of them women and children. Mickey shuddered involuntarily at the sight of a child's bloodied angelic face which framed unseeing eyes, her body garbed in what was once a green-and-white pinstriped pinafore, now darkly stained. *Is this child's blindness pre-existent or post-traumatic?* Mickey rubbed his eyes hard with his good hand and strained his ears to understand the rapid French being spoken around him. *Sounds like all the gunshot victims and everyone severely injured is heading to Saint-Quentin. Loni must have passed the triage evaluation—so, she's not a gunshot victim.*

As his head became clearer by the second, Mickey came to a sobering realization. Being an injured American doctor in this scenario offered him no way to help Loni inside the triaged area. He was standing on the wrong side of the triage cordon and there was nothing he could do about it. He couldn't even protest in intelligible French. However, he could make critical observations with a clinical eye and move to assist her when the opportunity arose.

Since it appeared that Loni, though pregnant, had been triaged at the low end of urgency, he—and only he—would be the transportation method to take her from Péronne to the maternity emergency center they had passed on their way here. Mentally, Mickey calculated his route: the maternity hospital sat high on the hill overlooking the city center in Saint-Quentin. *Forty minutes without ambulance traffic.* Mickey turned away from the triage area and bolted for his vehicle.

He gritted his teeth and ran as he never had before. He got to the Beast and began negotiating it through the crowd to get as close as possible to Loni. Moments later, and again with the help and kindness of strangers, Loni was released from triage and assisted into the waiting vehicle, engine idling.

With his truck's emergency flashers blinking, Mickey and Loni initially followed on the tailwind of the screaming ambulances toward the closest trauma center in the Vermandois. Mickey prayed aloud as he then maniacally passed ambulances and patient transporters through the flatlands of the Vermandois. He frequently cast sideways glances at the intermittently conscious, but unbroken, Loni. It took everything for Mickey to keep both hands on the steering wheel.

It would be easy to blame the melee on the castle for all Loni's current instability of consciousness, but Mickey knew that not to be the total truth. The tragic event at the Péronne Castle just contributed to her current neurological condition—but his complacency was the real villain. *I missed, or ignored, all the neurological signs that she gave me from the very onset. What good is it to be a physician when you lose the ability to help your most beloved ones in their moments of intense medical need?*

22

Garden Whispers

Abbey grounds

Poissy, France

15th century

A rustle caught Christine's attention as she was walking among the apple and pear trees in the abbey's orchard. She froze in her footsteps as she surveyed her surroundings. With some mild neck-craning, she saw a three-legged fox pause, look dead into her eyes, blink twice, lick its snout, blink twice again, then scuttle through the base of the far hedge. *Is his freedom real or imagined, I wonder? Was it bought by chewing his leg free from a hunter's trap?* She cast her eyes about the trees. *Hmmm, I haven't seen the stray cat recently. Maybe he was the basis for the snout licking of the fearless fox.* Before she arrived at an answer, Christine caught a glimpse of another movement followed by yet another rustle.

The sound behind her was different and evoked no sense of danger. It was as gentle as the fanning of a peacock's tail feathers. Nevertheless, it caused her to turn in recognized anticipation. In the soft grass, wearing a nun's cowl, Marie knelt to receive her mother's kiss. The pair then walked hand-in-hand throughout the abbey grounds, the church, the parks, and the gardens where a long-awaited conversation began.

"I've missed you, Mother," Marie confessed.

"No more than I have missed you; that I can promise you."

"How are things for you at the palace?"

"Mostly well," said Christine, brushing her fingers lightly over a manicured bush. "There are those who love my writings and there are those who don't. Men must come to terms with the fact that women have abilities, a voice, and a position in this world other than that which men assign them."

"Where do men learn this domination? Is it that the women are taught to yield the power to them?"

"Honey," said Christine as she pivoted herself in front of Marie. Christine clutched her daughter's shoulders. "If a woman does not have respect for herself as a woman, then she will have no confidence in herself as a person. She will then yield to the basic dominating nature of the man. I believe it is the man who has the responsibility to see a woman as a person before he sees her for whatever other role she plays in his life. I have tried to instill this into Jean."

"Jean?" said Marie, as she resumed the previous leisurely pace. "How is my brother?" Marie asked.

"Your brother is still with Monsieur John Montague."

"The third Earl of Salisbury, yes?"

"Yes. Jean relates that these are troubled times for the earl. I don't know what I will do for Jean if the earl falls out of favor with the king. Jean would lose his sponsorship, his money, position, and prestige."

Stopping abruptly, Marie frowned. Christine bit her lip pensively. *Maybe it would have been better not to share this information. Why burden her with that which she cannot change? Too late now. Words that leave the mouth have no possibility of retrieval from the ear.* Before Marie could resume walking, Christine squared off in front of her daughter.

"Darling, it is in God's hands." Holding Marie's face in her hands, Christine continued in a softer, soothing voice. "No matter what happens, it will always turn out for the best."

Marie's calm smile took Christine back to memories of happier days when she and Marie played endlessly on the palace grounds. However, those grounds were far away, and now there was a mission here that had to begin.

"Marie, how has your research progressed? Quite some time has passed, and some details certainly must have availed themselves. I can honestly tell you, darling, the pains of not knowing what happened to my dear cousin—"

The moment was interrupted by another figure whose presence demanded total attention and wanton respect. Marie de Bourbon, head abbess and the chief of the abbey at Poissy, approached the pair. Christine and Sister Marie bowed in reverence. Abbess Marie de Bourbon greeted Christine, exchanged brief formalities, and soon escorted her, but not her daughter, to an exquisitely elegant lunch to be served immediately.

With each morsel of her meal, Christine plotted how best to re-engage her daughter. *Surely by now Marie has research findings.* Christine ruminated on each bite. The abbey food was painfully delicious but, the leisurely meal was so very slow to culminate.

Only after the final gratuities were given to the serving hands was Christine able to steal away with her daughter in the guise of visiting the dormitory, the library, and the church. Once out into the gardens, a majestic pine tree caught her attention. Taking Marie by the hand and chatting about general topics, she led them into its shade. Nearby a beautiful fountain splashed merrily, supplying fresh, clean water to all parts of the abbey grounds, and it also served to mask their voices as they spoke.

"What has your research found?" whispered Christine with a hint of a nervous tremor in her voice.

"You are talking about Sibylle and where she has gone, yes, Mother?"

"Indeed. Is it a secret?"

"Behind these walls are many secrets, Mother. Sibylle's visit here at the abbey was long ago, and the priory records are vague in many critical places."

"I am sure. I know she came here in my eleventh year, Marie. She would have been about fifteen."

"The records in the library document that Sibylle came here to the abbey in the year of our Lord 1375. At that time the abbey was expanding their library and research room to include a—"

"That's nice, dear," Christine patted Marie's hand lovingly. "I know that Sibylle could not have stayed very long behind these walls. Where did she go?"

"As I was saying, Mother, when the decision was made to expand the library, it was also decided that the librarian here could be better used as an administrator's assistant in one of the churches in the Lorraine. It seemed that throughout that region, there was a dismal accounting of the simplest things such as birth, marriage, and death records."

"Are you saying Sibylle was a librarian here?"

"No, I am saying the records here show that she was an assistant to the librarian. She was a recorder of important life events."

"What did she do after the librarian left?"

"The records do not indicate that the librarian ever left."

"Darling Marie, I am so sure that all this is making sense in your head with librarians, recorders, and building expansions, but for this weary heart my aim is simple and focused. What has become of my dear Sibylle?"

The convent's demanding dinner bell sounded, and the sisters of the abbey had to say goodbye to their guests, family, and friends.

"I must go to the refectory, lest I miss the meal." Marie held her mother's hand. "I promise you the answers to ease your heart."

Christine nodded. "I will return as soon as the cloister reopens after dinner." She squeezed her daughter's hand and turned to part ways.

Christine left the abbey enclave through the same stone archway she had earlier entered and immediately stepped back into the city walls of Poissy. Once across the threshold, she looked for the tabby she had seen on previous visits but couldn't find it. She hoped and prayed that it found its way home or, at least, to a nice warm spot to spend the evening. Her mind conjured up the image of the three-legged fox and a shudder ran through her spine. *Surely four feet can outrun a set of three.*

Christine homed in on a small, noisy tavern located nearby, but she was unable to eat, both because of the lavish abbey meal and the information she had obtained thus far. Still, to pass the time she ordered a small meal of hard bread with warmed cheese. With each tiny bite and meager sip of stale cider she carefully listened for the church clock which would announce the time for her to receive answers which had evaded her for the past twenty-five years. She strained her ears to hear over some locals engaged in a new card game, called La Prime. They were heatedly debating the rules for winning. Apparently three of a kind beat two pair. Christine immediately thought of the abbey cat and the three-legged fox. She hoped the belligerent card players were wrong.

23

Lorraine on the Horizon

Abbey grounds
Poissy, France
15th century

With great angst, Christine's footsteps clicked in synchronization with the chimes of the clock. She reached the abbey arch and the door creaked inward. A cat darted from somewhere behind her into the dark crevice that slowly widened. She smiled with relief, but then a sudden sadness consumed her as she thought about the poor, hungry three-legged fox. Hopefully he found the food she had left in the garden by the pine trees. As Christine's attention drew back to the door, she wondered which face waited behind it. If it wasn't Marie's, she wondered how long she would have to wait. As it turned out, the face that was framed by the archway was Marie's. *A bright smile to brighten the setting day.*

"I never knew time could move so slowly," exhaled Christine.

"For me, time is something that exists only in your presence, Mother. When I know you are near, God must grant me patience, for I fear I have lost it all."

Marie led Christine through the portal, then to the left where stone benches sat next to a lily pond. The frogs there tried to intimidate ducks from infringing on their pads. Acknowledging the hunger for information in her mother's eyes, Marie rapidly began where she last left off. Her eyes constantly shifted to a manicured hedge and the abbey building beyond as she spoke.

"The librarian didn't want to go to the Lorraine. She was well versed and quite set in her ways. She posed to the prioress that Sibylle, her competent assistant, be allowed to make a fresh start in a church which needed to be revamped."

"A fresh start? Why would Sibylle need a fresh start? Was she unable to embrace the life here in Poissy? This is foolishness. Who is this saucy librarian? Why, I'd box her ears if she—"

Someone shuffled nearby.

Christine was about to repeat her queries when a nun of the sisterhood ambled in, squatted, and began skimming the edge of the pond water with the back of her fingers. Marie shot her mother a look and pointed to the nun with a pursing of her lips.

"The expansion of the library will increase the capability of records documentation both for the priory and the royal palace," Marie redirected.

Noting the cleverly cloaked new tone in which Marie had shifted the conversation, Christine didn't miss a beat and continued in the same vein. "True, honey, and that is what the Royal Library in Paris was hoping. However, unless my calculations are incorrect, an expansion of this library hasn't occurred for the past twenty-five years. I can talk to the royal treasurer if money is an issue, but mind you, I pose no guarantee of funding in the absence of a reasonable plan for expansion."

The nun at the pond wiped her hands of the residual moisture and moved back into the darkness from whence she first came.

"Mother, there are secrets and there are *secrets*."

"So, I see."

"Sibylle was sent away so that she and her baby could have a new beginning in a place far away."

Christine pulled away in shock. "You must be mistaken. Sibylle was unmarried, and . . . oh my God, she was with child?" Christine's horror flickered to anger then immediately to grieving sympathy, all in the space of minutes. Marie sat silently watching the fluctuating emotions flood her mother's face.

"Why didn't Father tell me? Maybe he didn't know . . . maybe he knew something but was afraid I couldn't keep it secret. Maybe. . . ."

"I am thinking he knew and didn't know how to tell you, Mother. I can understand this because I didn't either."

"I thought these walls were safe," Christine whispered hoarsely. She clutched her daughter's hands tightly. "I thought you were safe here. How could this happen here?"

"Mother, it didn't happen here."

"You're not saying it happened in Paris? Was my family involved? Was Father involved?" Christine's voice ratcheted up.

"Mother, shhh. Please." She moved her hands to her mother's face and looked steadily into her eyes. "The records here do not say. The only thing I know for sure is that whoever was involved, Sibylle had to be taken away and protected at the Abbey of Poissy in secret. She then had to be moved and was done so as a sister administrator to a church in the Lorraine."

The firm hands of her daughter were like anchors holding Christine to earth while her mind spun out into the cosmos. She drew in a steadying breath. "Where in the Lorraine?"

"The place is called Vouthon."

"The child, what was the child? What happened to the child?"

"There is no reference of a name. Her baby was a female infant. The record keeper of the area would probably have a written document with the child's appearance, and such a document may be in the town of Vouthon or maybe at the church at Vaucouleurs or Domrémy."

Christine's mind began to wrap around the idea that the lost cousin she loved was no longer lost. *Not yet found, but no longer lost.* In mere minutes, Marie had revived a hope that had been smoldering in Christine's heart for over two decades.

She pulled her daughter into a tight hug and whispered into her ear, "Thank you, blessed daughter, for closing a chapter in my life which has spanned twenty-five years of emptiness." She released the embrace and held Marie's shoulders. "I think that now my work will take me to the Lorraine. Thanks to you I now have firm footing upon which my hope can grow."

"Mother, before you go, there is one more thing you should know. It is probably no more than anecdotal but it is rumored that the father was—"

Bustling in with girlish squeals and great strides, the chief prioress appeared with the previously seen nun. Both nuns seemed consumed with excitement. Christine rose at their appearance and walked to meet them.

The prioress handed Christine a glass container filled with sugar-preserved apples and pears. "Madame Scribe," she said, "I have heard whisperings of the potential of some royal funding for our research archives. I truly believe this is an endeavor worth championing."

"There are secrets and there are *secrets*, Your Grace. Are you able to keep a secret?" Christine challenged.

"Of course, my lady." The prioress spoke with sincere intent while nodding vigorously in unison with the accompanying nun.

"And so must I. Please, develop your plans for expansion and I will conduct some research. I believe my path from here lies in the Lorraine."

"The Lorraine?"

Christine smiled at the prioress and the nosey nun, then blew a kiss off the back of her knuckles in the direction of her daughter. "I will see you when I return from the Lorraine."

"Mother?"

"Have faith, darling. There are some secrets that must remain." Christine moved back toward Marie. Setting down the preserves, she took her child's face in her hands and kissed her gently on both eyelids and then lightly on her lips.

"I love you, dear daughter."

Nodding her understanding, Marie gently kissed her mother goodbye.

"I love you so much, Mother. Hurry back."

As the priory door closed behind her, Christine slumped against the stone archway and let the emotions she had been withholding wash over her. She wept in waves for all those she had lost. In her mind a list of names from yesteryear passed. Knowing Marie lived safely in the arms of the Church brought some degree of comfort. Knowing now that Sibylle was potentially close, and reachable, made Christine's melancholy abate for a moment. She thought of the baby girl who, in all reality, was presently a woman in her own right. *There are secrets and there are* secrets. *But this secret has an end point, and I will find it.*

Far off in the Lorraine, two dedicated clergy from the parish church at Domrémy worked long into the night to help the many refugees to recover from the ever-present disease and violence that churned chaos. In the still of the night, the Burgundians, with help from the English, had taken what they wanted when they wanted it. The towns of Vouthon and Greux lay in devastation. All available clergy, including Father Minet and Sister Sibyl, moved what wasn't destroyed or looted from the shells of survivors' homes in the valley towns into temporary residences near the parish church of Domrémy. For those who could not be moved, crosses were firmly affixed to their graves.

24

Insanity Unleashed

Domrémy-la-Pucelle, Meuse River Valley

Lorraine region, France

14th century

The royal coach roared through Vouthon while Dr. Thomas de Pizan remained pensive, on edge even. Three days ago, word had reached him in Paris that his services were again needed in the Lorraine.

Has it been seven years since I left the little piglet? He did some quick calculations. *It is 1387. She was five when I promised to return within a month. . . . How can it be that seven years have gone so fast?*

Unbeknownst to him, during those years Isabella had blossomed into a beautiful adolescent with the brightest eyes and a kind smile. However, he did know that the Burgundians had recently abducted her on one of their foraging raids. Only by the grace of God had she managed to return home alive a few days ago. He feared that she might be just barely holding on to life.

As the coach stopped in front of the church, Father Minet, looking stern and serious, and the distraught looking Sister Sibyl, came into view.

"I'm glad to see you, Dr. Pizan," greeted Father Minet as he helped the weary physician from the coach. "It has been many winters since we last sat face-to-face."

"Have I arrived too late?"

"Yes and no. There is nothing we could do. Please follow us. This way, Doctor."

The three of them passed the front of the church and went directly into the d'Arc home where Isabella lay in a rearward bedroom. The light filtering through the slit of a window fell upon the very young, very pregnant girl. Dr. Pizan's eyes grew wide.

"I know it is a shock, Doctor," Sister Sibyl whispered, "but unless I'm wrong, this child is due to birth twins within the day."

He turned his dazed face to the nun and mumbled, "She's not but thirteen. Why . . . why had no one told me?"

"She needs you now, Doctor. We need you now."

Dr. Pizan shook his head to clear his mind. He nodded firmly, resolutely. He and the ever-present Sister Sibyl got right to work—she to restore the girl's strong heart and mind, and he to return her to a strong body.

"Why has God allowed this to happen?" Dr. Pizan asked himself aloud after the twins had been birthed. *Have I given away the king's gift errantly?* It now crossed his mind that Isabella was not, and would never become, the Maid of Lorraine.

"God didn't allow this to happen," responded the nun. "He has always given man volition. Man chooses what will happen to man. God is always there to give strength in times of weakness for those who ask. Please, Doctor, know that God's plan always works even if we can't see it as it unfurls."

"I'm sorry, Sister. Right now, I really can't see it."

"It is not for us to see. It is only for us to competently keep to the part in life He has prepared us. For me, it is to be here in Domrémy. I will follow the children of Isabella the way I followed her, in God's light. Our king and France may one day behold the work we do here in the Lorraine. I may never live to know. I just know that I am responsible for a small piece of God's plan, and I will ensure that it gets done to the best of my ability."

"As will I," a fatigued Dr. Pizan conceded as he collapsed into a chair. "Some days it's easier to see God's plan than in others. These are dark times for me."

"It shouldn't be, Doctor," reminded the sister. "As long as there's life, there's hope. According to my understanding of mathematics, we presently have two times the hope."

The sister's smile infused life into the weary physician's bones. He knew she was right, but he also harbored much trepidation. He knew of the true situation at the royal palace in Paris, the mental fragility of the king, and how it engendered instability throughout France. *It is hard to see blue heavens when the skies are filled with dark clouds reaching far beyond the horizon.*

"His Highness seems to be having increasing fits of madness," began Dr. Pizan. "Even at my last visit, I saw early indications. I had hoped I was wrong."

"What kind of madness?" asked Father Minet, almost in disbelief.

"Sometimes he becomes disoriented and knows not who we are. My fear is that one day he will see us, his staff, like the enemy and will attack us with the intent of killing or maiming us."

"How horrible!"

"If that was only the worst of it, there would be hope. The king has lost his sense of presence. He sometimes passes many days unwashed. If left to his own schedule, I fear that one day he would become unkempt like a woodwose—"

"—that hairy beast of the forest which originates from lands far away?"

"Yes, Father. I have always known that the potential was there as his mother, Queen Joanna, had so much mental variance, even to the point of mental collapse. Before she died in the effort of childbirth at Château de Beauté, she was only a shell of her former emotional self."

"The new queen, Isabeau, will she be able to provide for France if the king is not mentally healthy?" the priest asked.

"She is our only hope, I fear. If she fails, France will fail. If France fails, then we will all be speaking English. Can any thought be more horrid?"

"Dr. Pizan, I must ask you a question of personal importance," interrupted the nun.

"I know your question already, Sister, and wondered why you haven't asked it before now."

Seeing that the conversation was moving into the realm of personal and private, Father Minet quietly excused himself to address pressing matters of the Church elsewhere.

25

Choices

Domrémy-la-Pucelle, Meuse River Valley

Lorraine region, France

14th century

As the priest's shuffling became a faint echo, Sister Sibyl continued, "How is my cousin? Does she ever ask about me?"

"Christine is doing well," the doctor said as he moved closer to his niece. "Her husband, Étienne de Castel, is the official royal court recorder. Christine helps him as a transcriber. I think that ne'er a day passes when her thoughts don't either begin or end with you."

"I knew the days we spent together in the Royal Library would lead her to a profession as a scribe or recorder. She is so bright. Does she have children?"

"She has three children now."

"Three? What are their names?"

"I will leave those things for you all to discuss when you reunite."

"Does she know yet what happened with me? I mean the king, the child, all of it?"

"Not by my mouth," said Dr. Pizan as he stroked his beard. "Since she has little contact with the abbey at Poissy I believe that she does not know."

Sister Sibyl shifted a bit closer and began whispering even though they were alone.

"When I returned to Château de Beauté on the day the king died," she began, "I came to see you. However, there were so many important things going on, I felt it wrong to satisfy my personal wishes. I wanted very much to see Christine, but I knew that it was not the time to do so. It was good that I was there that day. I was able to see the king privately and forgive him for what he did to me."

"That had to be very difficult to do." He looked into the nun's eyes with great sympathy. "He took from you your flower, your maidenhood, the future you expected—"

"Yes," Sister Sibyl interrupted. She paused a moment and then continued. "I understand now that it was not lust that drove him. It took much prayer and time, but with the grace of God I came to know that it was not me he sought to harm. He was a man sick with a terrible loss. I appeared at the wrong place at the wrong time."

"That does not excuse him," her uncle replied, his emotions rising. "Certainly you cannot believe that the king is absolved of all wrongdoing just by his station. I cannot believe what I am hearing, Sister!"

"I never said he didn't do wrong, Doctor," she said, her voice rising to match his. Then, regaining her composure, Sister Sibyl continued. "I said I forgave him for what he did wrong to me. He took away my dignity. He used me like an animal—not for pleasure but to release his own demons. What he did was wrong, and I forgave him for that."

"I'm not sure that if I were in your place, I could ever do it." He took her hands in his, resting his forehead upon them.

"I didn't think I would be able to either. It took me many months at the abbey to arrive at a clear vision of understanding. God placed me in the king's presence at that time with a greater purpose."

He looked up abruptly. "Are you saying God knew that this would happen to you and did nothing to prevent it?"

"No, I am saying that God placed His Highness and me in the same place at the same time. Each of us had choices to make. He had to make the choice in his mind whether to take advantage of me. In his sickness, he chose to do so. He made the wrong choice. I had to make the choice of whether to run or fight when I saw what was about to happen. I chose not to."

"You chose *not* to run away? *Not* to fight? How can that be? I would have thought—"

"I didn't want it to happen!" She pulled her hands away from her uncle, fire in her eyes.

She saw the sorrow in his face, the apology forming on his lips. She inhaled deeply, pressed her palms to her face and then dragged them down with her exhalation until they rested prayerlike at her chin.

"Uncle, we are all taught to do what royalty ask of us. I didn't want him to rape me, but he was the king." She paused and looked toward the door where Isabella lay. "I chose not to run. I chose not to fight. I have paid dearly for that choice. But," she continued with conviction, "I have grown from the experience of that poor choice. For some reason, God has given me and Christine a set of hardships to endure so that we can learn from them. He gave us an education so we could take what lessons we learned and instill them into the generations that follow. Because of what has happened to me, there can be the substance which could forge the basis for a Maid of Lorraine."

"Your Isabella has no chance to be this Maid of Lorraine. What hope can you have?"

"Yes, I know it is not her. Truer words have never been spoken. However, I believe that all I have experienced in life will not go to waste. I have been given this life to nurture Isabella, and now her children, in case one of them becomes the Maid."

"You have learned much from that day, Sister."

"Yes, Doctor. I have gained much life experience from that single act on that day and from every day after. For that, I forgave the king. I went to Paris and got help for my little piglet. I kept the records from the day of the king's death so that the information could be used to verify the basis of Isabella's royal lineage."

"I often wondered what you did with the documents, Sister."

"They remain wrapped around their poles like a scroll. For the royalty of France this scroll must remain 'lost' a bit longer. God will tell me when to bring them to light."

He gave her a genuine smile. "You were always my favorite niece, and now I know why."

"Why, Uncle?"

"Because Sibylle, you are like my precious Christine. Both of you cut from the same frame and both of you walking in God's light. I pray for the day that you two can meet again. I feel that together you will travel your paths as you did when you were young maidens."

"That is a prayer I have had for many a year. I truly regret not going to see Christine on the day of the king's death. I love her so. I was so close, yet not."

"I know how you must have felt."

"It was torture to my soul."

"There will be a time and a place when you will again meet." The sincerity and conviction in his voice soothed Sister Sibyl, and she raised her eyes to his face as he spoke. "With the start that you two had in each other's lives, there is no doubt that God has a plan for the both of you. The future intertwining of your paths has long been known by Him though we may not see it. The mission is for you to continue to do His will. She will serve in His light as well. When the two missions align, you will be together again in God's light. We foolishly try to plan how our life will go and yet," he motioned toward the sleeping Isabella, "in the end, we are diverted by the actions of others—but always to the benefit of His ends, if we have kept Him first in our lives."

Sister Sibyl smiled faintly. "I remember the king saying such words during the last of his days."

"As do I," recalled the physician.

"So, Dr. Pizan, you appear not to be the same troubled man I first met on the road today. It seems our roles have reversed."

"Only for the moment, dear Sibylle, only for the moment. I am quite sure that as my coach closes in on Paris, the worries of my heart and mind will cloud my thinking as before. I will do my best to give my trepidations and fears to God." The physician rose and gathered his belongings. At the royal coach, he warmly embraced his niece, in her full persona as Sister Sibyl, before he departed for Paris.

"Fare you well, Doctor. Rest assured knowing that I am still the stewardess of the gift you gave seven years ago. I will ensure that either newborn Isabelle or Jehanne will get it when the time is right."

"So be it, but only when the time is right," said Dr. Pizan as he once again made ready to part. "I will check upon the children in a month."

"As God wills it," said Sister Sibyl.

The horses whinnied and the coach stirred up the street dust of Domrémy once again. Father Minet waved from the door of the church.

"I will be here," muttered the sister to herself as she walked into the church.

26

Calling the Cavalry

Route to Saint-Quentin
Somme River Valley, France
Current day

Exiting the A-29 byway, which led from Péronne, and having passed every semblance of flashing, howling, emergency medical vehicle, Mickey screeched into west Saint-Quentin with a mostly unconscious Loni. *Please Lord, show me something, anything that is useful.* Frantically Mickey scanned for any sign that even closely resembled international medical aid. Finding none, his gut cramped. Mickey's eyes then riveted upon a pair of young men leisurely propped up against some fencing. They seemed to be waiting for a ride or maybe not—time held the same urgency for them as it did for the fence which supported them. Lowering the window, Mickey shouted out to them in French-accented English, "Pardonez me. Hospital?"

Mickey's tone, coupled with his exaggerated gesturing, fueled some energy into the young men and they began giving him directions in their regional dialect. Mickey spoke and confirmed the directions in English while the young men nodded and verified the same directions in French. Even though the language barrier remained undaunted, emergent communication was absolute, and the understanding was without error. Mickey looked at his wife slumped in the passenger's seat of the Beast. At least one thing was favorable: at present he could not feel the pain of his broken hand.

Minutes passed as the Beast climbed the hill to the rear entrance of the hospital. Mickey left the vehicle running in the patient delivery zone. In his arms, he carried Loni through a series of connecting breezeways, through some automatically opening glass doors, and into the sparkling hallways. He called for help and within seconds, a cloud of green and white scrubs surrounded him. Loni was mobilized on a gurney, and on her way to obstetrical medical care. Mickey looked at his hands and stared at the residual blood on his splint which must have trickled from the laceration in Loni's scalp. He wanted to cry but there was no time, not now anyway. He followed the medical personnel until they finally gave him the French version of the Heisman blocking pose. He went no further. The staff provided him a place to sit and wait. Instead, he about-faced to take care of the truck, and on the way, he punched a number into his cell phone.

"Mickey!" a jovial and friendly voice answered. "I really didn't expect to. . . ." From the pleasant sound of the voice, for a split second, Mickey had thought he had the wrong number and he glanced at his phone's display uncertainly. *Oh, yes, Suzanne is on vacation. Well, correction, she used to be on vacation.*

"Suzanne," Mickey interrupted, "I have Loni, and we are in the hospital. It's serious. She's in and out. It began—"

"Stow it, Mickey," Suzanne barked as she shifted immediately into her well-known Viking Witch mode. "Give me just the facts. Where are you and what is Loni's prognosis?" Now Mickey *knew* he had the right person.

"No matter how many times I practiced this call in my head—"

"Mickey, two eyes straight ahead, focus. Only the facts. Now."

"Saint-Quentin, the maternity hospital, the upper-west bank of the Somme River bordering the east side of town. Follow the hospital signs. I don't know about Loni. She really has been ill all day, and then came the attack. I am not sure if she passed out from illness or if her scalp laceration is indicative of neurologic trauma. I had just turned away for a moment when—"

"Mickey, I am in Poissy about an hour south of you. I'll call you back once I get on the road. Try to see yourself as the referring physician and get ready to present the patient in a way that would lend itself to the best help I can give."

"Suzanne, I *am* a physician."

"Not today, sweetie. Today, you are a family member. That's why you need me there."

"Roger." Mickey knew she was right. This whole being-a-family-member gig wasn't all it was cut out to be.

"Talk to you in a jiffy. Remember, present the patient to me as a doctor, then go do what you need to do best—be a supporting husband."

As she started to drop off the call, Suzanne could hear the hospital speaker in the background making announcements all in French. She began to wonder how much help she was really going to be in a French maternity hospital in the Vermandois. Murphy's Law always seemed to follow her, as it did her beloved Christine, like an unwelcome shadow.

27

Kindnesses and Kisses

Vouthon, Meuse River Valley
Lorraine region, France
15th century

As much as Christine wanted to see her cousin, Sibylle, she first had to take care of business back at home and at the Royal Palace of Paris—seemingly a litany of unending tasks. There had been two straight years of legal trouble as both the estates of her deceased father and her husband had been tied up in litigation. Furthermore, she was widowed, unmarried, and unsponsored. With no money coming in, Christine had become her own sole provider. So, it wasn't until 1402 that Christine de Pizan finally initiated the journey to Vouthon in the Lorraine to visit Sibylle.

Her heart was light, and her stomach was filled with butterflies as she entered the town of Vouthon. *Which house will it be, I wonder?* The royal coach trundled past a small graveyard, and she was forced to contemplate whether she had arrived too late.

The coach soon came to a stop at the town fountain, and Christine hastily tidied her hair. *Hennins just aren't conducive for long coach journeys*, she thought as she dismounted from the coach.

She looked around into all the faces of the curious townspeople who, these days, just weren't used to seeing royalty of any kind. She tugged her burgundy riding cloak straight and taut over her shoulders, settling its front hems over her chest. Then, Christine came to a sudden realization, and her brow furrowed. The only image she had of Sibylle was one of a fifteen-year-old girl some twenty-five years ago. *Well, Sibylle should be a woman in about her forty-second year of life. Start with that.* She made her way to the town fountain where she plucked up a conversation with a dirty-faced rotund townswoman. Christine wondered if, hidden under the facial grit, this was her beloved Sibylle.

"Is this indeed the town of Vouthon?" she asked the woman.

"It is, m'lady."

"You are a member of this community?"

"I am, m'lady."

"I am looking for a person by the name of Sibylle."

"We have none here by that name."

"Have you lived here long?"

"All of my life, m'lady."

"This would span twenty-two years?"

The townswoman blushed as she rendered an affirmative nod followed by gratitude for thinking her to be so young. "Yes, m'lady, that and twenty-two years more."

"It seems I have come a long way in vain." Christine cast her eyes down and turned away, one hand fiddling with the golden clasp of the cloak near her neck.

"Not entirely, m'lady," said the woman causing Christine to pause and turn back, her eyes hopeful. "I am but a humble baker's wife in this town. The parish church at nearby Domrémy has a nun who could help you find any person by name or description. If God wills you to find this Sibylle, then the sister might be your best help."

Christine brightened. "Thank you, dear woman," she said as she placed a coin in the hand of the woman.

The baker's wife smiled at the royal lady then motioned her to wait a moment. She whistled loudly, and a young lad arrived, equally grimy but with a shining smile. After receiving a few words in the local version of French, he shot around the corner and returned with a pair of a buttery brioche and a creamy cheese puff pastry.

"It's not much, m'lady. But it is from the heart," the baker's wife said as she passed the delights to Christine.

After packing away the food and securing directions regarding the southeastern route to Domrémy, Christine reviewed the woman's words and pondered the depth of truth in them. *If God wills it* circled round and round in her head until the coach again stopped, this time in front of the stone church at Domrémy. In the house next door, a girl in her mid-teens was hanging wash on a line. Christine motioned for her to come to the carriage. The girl hesitated, seemingly overwhelmed by the splendor of the ornamental coach—her keen eyes roved over its every detail. Again, Christine motioned to the young girl who, this time, wiped her hands on her apron and walked slowly over to the royal coach.

"Yes, m'lady? You summoned me?"

Before Christine could answer, a priest interrupted her as he came bustling through the church's front doors, shooing the girl away. The curious teen quickly moved to the tree line and perched on a stone bench located just off the edge of the road. She remained within earshot, taking quick glances at the beautiful woman in the burgundy cloak and her handsome carriage.

With the confident stride of a local church authority, the protective priest approached the carriage door, and with obvious intent, he placed himself between the young girl and the royal passenger. No doubt existed in Christine's mind that the priest would be the indisputable respondent for any further questionings.

"I realize you are a personage of great importance, my lady. I am Father Jean Minet. Please state your business with someone who might be able to best help you." The parish priest spoke gruffly, his eyes slightly narrowed.

"Forgive me, Father, I meant no harm to the child," began Christine in a politically trained voice with which she addressed kings and heads of state. "I am but a weary woman who has spent twenty-five years finding my way to this spot to ask but one question for an answer I fear greatly."

Somewhat mollified by her demeanor, the priest softened. "If that is the case, my lady, then the Lord wills it that you state your business within His house with nourishment placed before you."

In Christine's head the words *the Lord wills it* began again their circular journey.

"I have waited twenty-five years for this moment, I am sure that I am quite able to hold my query for a bit longer." Handing Father Minet the recently acquired brioche and puffed pastry, Christine spoke kindly as the accepting priest smiled.

From the doorway, with blue handkerchief in hand, a nun mopped her brow while taking in the scene along the roadside. She disappeared into the shadow of the door as she saw the royal lady dismount from the carriage with the help of the parish priest.

It wasn't long until the elegant lady sat in the small kitchen in the church. Clare, the cook, and her little daughter, Clarisse, whisked dishes, glasses, and flatware in and out of the room until nourishment had been completed and the traveler had been refreshed. The priest looked long into Christine's face before he felt that the time had come to re-engage. Christine never moved or spoke a word until the priest was ready. By yielding control and giving due respect to the clergy, she had successfully established command of this situation. Father Minet comfortably sat himself directly across the table from the royal lady.

"Now, my lady, how may I best help you?"

"Father Jean Minet, I am looking for my cousin from whom I was separated twenty-five years ago. I have traveled her path from Venice to Paris to Poissy to Vouthon and now to Domrémy. My dear cousin was more like an elder sister to me."

"So, my lady, you have lost a sister-like cousin and hope to find her here in the Lorraine. What if this relative does not want to be found?"

Before Christine could formulate a rebuttal, another voice entered the conversation. "What if she does?"

Christine looked at the intruder who stood fully in front of her. It was the nun Christine had seen from the road.

"God no longer wills my presence here," said the priest as he relinquished time and space to those who needed it most. "Sister Sibyl, I trust you will close the doors of the church as per usual. I must tend to the needs of the family next door. I shall be there if you have need of me." With that, the priest bowed, hid his hands in the folds of his sleeves, and quietly exited the small kitchen. Sibylle approached the table tentatively and then sat across from the noble lady.

Not allowing her eyes to leave Sibylle, Christine spoke as calmly as she could muster, even amidst the tears which streamed copiously down both cheeks.

"Never in my life has so much been taken from me." Christine searched frantically for something to wipe her eyes. "First my precious sister cousin Sibylle left without a word of goodbye." Christine spotted a blue handkerchief and reached across the table for it. Sibylle caught her hand.

"No, my lady. It needs a wash."

"Granted, as do I," Christine persisted. Sibylle yielded. "Then, my dear King Charles V died from a broken heart. My father died in the western marches along with my husband. My elder son died while I tended to the professional grooming of the younger." Christine blew her nose in the moist kerchief, then looked for another. Sibylle gently pulled one from Christine's own cuff. Christine looked at it and bawled. She dabbed her face and squeezed Sibylle's arm until her crying eased into sniffles.

"Marie, my only daughter, is separated from me," Christine said. "She lives enclaved at Poissy with a three-legged fox."

"Oh, how sad."

"I know. He probably had to chew his own leg off."

"I was talking about Marie, my lady."

"Oh? Yes, of course. And then there's the king who has lost his mind. His body moves unhindered through the palace like a foul pungency."

"My lady."

"I believe that God had willed it that I be left all alone in this world."

"My lady." Sibylle tapped Christine's arm.

"That is until now."

"My lady." Sibylle leaned across the table and held Christine's face in her hands. Christine cupped her hands over Sibylle's.

"Tell me, Cousin, am I destined to be all alone?" Christine asked.

"Maybe yesterday my lady, maybe tomorrow, but definitely not today." Rounding the table, Sibylle hugged the trembling noble lady tightly until they both lost feeling in their arms. Her tears dotted the shoulder of Christine's cloak with deep, dark circles. Sibylle drew away for a moment and kissed Christine on both eyelids and then lightly on her lips.

From the house next door, Father Jean Minet imagined the joy of the reunion. He had known that the time had come, and that the washing away of decades of loneliness could happen in a blink of an eye when the heart is involved. He mused that their reunion was like the celestial reunion all have waiting for them upon returning to the heavenly Father.

"Tell me of your daughter, Sibylle. I never knew her name."

"Her name was Isabella. She was a beautiful child. When she began her teens, her innocence had been advantaged by rogue Burgundians leaving her ravaged and with child. A child existing with a child—so history repeats itself."

"Did anyone come to love and care for this despoiled youth?"

"There was a man named Jean from Vouthon who had lost his wife in the same Burgundian raid. He gave Isabella stability, protection, and affection. He also gave her his two children, Aveline and Jean, to mother. She was so happy to love and be loved. You would have adored her, Christine. Even though she had lived a life filled with such great tragedy, her faith held her strong until the Great Pestilence took her."

"I'm sorry. I feel the pain of loss twice—first as mother who has lost a child, and second as her blood relative who never knew a soul so fair. How is it that we feel the pain from a heart we never knew?"

"It doesn't take earthly senses to have a memory imprinted deep within. I feel love for your children through you, Christine. Inasmuch I feel their loss as well. Before Isabella died, she had four children—twins from her womb and two adopted from Jean. Of the ones she birthed, one has since died. One now lives in the house next door. Her name is Isabelle. We call her Romée as she calls upon the names of the papacy in Rome more than names of the people in the house. God will bless her."

"I pray that He does." Then, with an almost imperceptible shift in tone Christine said, "The queen who lives in Paris will lose the kingdom."

The mission—which was started years before with an errant king, a naive maiden, a royal physician, a nun, a parish priest, a mother, and God's helper angels—was now on the verge of fruition, and both women could feel it in their souls. They could see it in each other's eyes.

"How bad is it in Paris?" Sibylle cringed. "There are rumors and there are *rumors*. Even if these ramblings are true, I'd rather hear your words. Tell me, Cousin, tell me everything."

28

Great Ball of Fire

Domrémy-la-Pucelle, Meuse River Valley
Lorraine region, France
15th century

"The king has had ten years of madness," began Christine, sighing deeply. "It began on a hunting trip when the accidental clinking of a sword on shield led the king to lose his wit. He slayed and maimed an abundance of his personal guard before he could be subdued."

"Your father feared exactly this," Sibylle said.

"Father had seen these signs for a while, yes." She paused. "But how did you know of it?"

"He told me," Sibylle said quite matter-of-factly.

"Where? Here?"

"Yes, here. He never told you he came here?"

"No." Christine's face fell a little, showing her puzzlement.

"Yes, dear Christine. It was his skill that saved Isabella from childhood death. It was his skill again that delivered Romée and Jehanne into this world. The heart, hands, and mind of Dr. Thomas de Pizan have repeatedly nurtured my family here in the Lorraine."

"Father did so much and said so little about it. He must have felt it important to keep your anonymity. I just wish he would have trusted me and my ability to maintain silence."

"Sometimes the need not to know outweighs the need to have information. The seed of Charles V still courses through veins in the Lorraine. That information could lead to dire consequences . . . for all of us."

"It may yet do so, Sibylle. Let's hope it is the English that receive the brunt of the consequences."

"The English and these local rogue Burgundians. I confess that I am still struggling with forgiveness for what they did to my Isabella."

"There are many such private wars within our people, and they will accompany the one war that will come to free all of France. However, France

125

must present to the world much more than was presented at the Ball of the Burning Men."

"I have heard tales of deliberate foolishness where the king nearly perished in a fire. Was he one of the burning men?"

"Yes, Sibylle, he was one of six men who dressed themselves as wild men and, I might add, he fully portrayed the part. It was in winter nine years ago. Her Majesty Queen Isabeau wished to honor the marriage of one of her chamber ladies. His Majesty, Charles, orchestrated a group of dancing wood-wose wild men as entertainment. Along with His Highness, five lords of France played in a charade which brought great merriment and laughter. The joviality ended when the costumes caught fire, igniting the lords one by one."

"How can that be?"

"The woodwose costumes were sealed to the lords by a substance which was susceptible to fire. More so fatal was the fact that the king, in his madness, had this cast of royal entertainers linked together with chain to enhance the comedic effect. Unable to escape, the fire jumped from one lord to another to the next until all were consumed with flames."

"How did our mad king survive?"

"By quick thinking and even quicker actions. The king was wrapped in the folds of the evening gown of the Duchess of Berry. At personal risk to her own life, she smothered the flames of the woodwose dancer closest to her. It was by the grace of God that the dancer closest to her was, indeed, His Majesty Charles VI."

"Did she know he was the king?"

"She says so. I don't see how anyone could really know. The costumes were an assemblage of tree trimmings and leaves plastered onto the green-painted bodies of the lords. One woodwose looked very much the same as the other."

"It made her look insightful. She might derive benefit from that."

"She might indeed." Christine smiled, remembering she had arrived at the same conclusion as well.

"The flames which burned the dancers—they came from malice?"

"No, it was the Duke of Orléans himself who playfully taunted the dancers with a torch taken from the wall. There was great horror when the fire leaped from the tip of the torch to the first dancer. It was then like a summer forest fire except the crackle of burning came from the bodies of the mindless lords of France. Even now, I can hear the screaming from the burning men."

"How many perished?"

"Four, initially. I am not sure of the fifth. He may have died later. I never heard. As for the king, his recollection of this madness is minimal. He continues to roam through the palace behaving, though not costumed, as a woodwose. His howling brings to my mind that night of the burning men so many years ago."

"Our queen has not compensated for this mental breach?"

"She has distanced herself from him completely. Unbeknownst to His Majesty, she has given him a substitute and surrogate wife—Odette de Champdivers of whom, in his state of mind, he knows not any difference."

Sibylle looked shocked and disgusted, but Christine simply shook her head and shrugged her shoulders.

"If the queen beds separately from the king, and the king, as a woodwose, desires no carnal knowledge . . . how can there be two more children in the House of Valois?" Even as the last word tripped off her tongue, Sibylle knew her answer, and in her most serious voice she intoned, "Apparently, there has been a miracle . . . of sorts. . . ."

The giggling at the table wiggled the candle so that the shadows on the wall danced giddily.

"In the absence of a miracle, Sibylle, reality suggests that the two children, Louis and John, are the offspring of the king's brother, Louis the Duke of Orléans."

"Wasn't he the person who torched the dancers?"

"Indeed. With so much intrigue afoot, can you see why my Marie should fare better in the Dominican abbey in Poissy?"

"Darling, are you convincing me or yourself?"

"A little of both, I suppose, Sibylle." Christine grew pensive and clinked the golden clasp of her cloak open and closed as she stared into the candle's flame.

Silence preceded a gentle touch to Christine's arm. Christine forced a small smile and continued. "Sibylle, these last five years without Marie have been so painful. To have her so close but only for brief moments over time, it drives stakes of agony into a mother's heart."

"It is good that at least when you saw your child and when she saw you, both could acknowledge the relationship. My plight was so very different." Sibylle folded her hands on the table and leaned in. "When Isabella saw me, she saw a loving, mother-like nun. Even until the day she lay dying in my arms," she swallowed hard, "she never knew that *through me* she came into this world."

Sibylle lowered her head onto her folded hands, sobbing. After a few moments of gradually accepting Christine's soothing compassion, Sibylle raised her head and pinched at her downward-cast eye ducts. "Some mothers are gifted," she said with resolving nasal intonation. "Others are aloof." She sniffled. "Either has a chance to receive their child's love." She looked up suddenly, anger in her eyes. "I never did. I never had the chance!" She pounded her fist on the table. "I was the mother that never was." She collapsed again in tears.

"Oh, Sibylle, please don't say that."

"Why not? It's true." Sibylle spoke nasally from the folds of her sleeves.

"Digging a knife into a wound doesn't heal it, *cherie*. It had to be so. You know this." Christine gently put her hands atop her cousin's head. "If there was any knowledge that the depressed King Charles V had another heir, both of you would be endangered. Father knew this and embraced silence in your best interest and in the best interest of France."

"I didn't even have a choice, Christine," she groused. "The justifications made it no less difficult for me." Sibylle snatched Christine's tear-stained handkerchief from the table and ground into her own eyes, her head hanging down.

"Nor for France. . . ."

"What of France, Christine?" Sibylle's head rose quickly. Eyes reddened, she clenched her teeth and sniffed. Her face hardened. "What about me?"

"Father always said, 'The kingdom of France will be lost by a queen and then saved by a maid from Lorraine.' We cannot change the past, dear Cousin, neither one of us. We *must* look forward. God is calling us forward. We are on the path of this prophecy. He has put us here and at least part of that prophecy is materializing, here, now. We cannot think of ourselves, only of His will."

"Yes," Sibylle conceded, putting aside her grief and anger, "at least here in the Lorraine we fan the flames of hope for a maid."

"Yes, but which maid?" Christine asked.

"You think the maid is Romée, don't you?"

"What I think doesn't matter. Only God knows."

"Christine, we must prepare Romée to be ready if it becomes her lonely lot in life to be the Maid of Lorraine."

"I wish no such loneliness on anyone," Christine replied as she stared down at her open, empty hands. "Imagine the painful processes needed to produce the stalwart leader who saves France."

"It would be difficult for any one man. I cannot fathom how it would weigh on the shoulders of a young maiden." Sibylle sighed deeply. "Separated from all others, she would have to be forged from iron and then tempered by the hands of our blessed saints."

"There may be many people who are willed by God to be alone in this world, but at least for tonight, Christine de Pizan will not be one of them." Sibylle placed her hands into her cousin's and squeezed tightly.

"By God's hand and with our diligence, we will continue the work that Father began."

At that moment the door creaked open.

"Sister Sibyl, will you study with me tonight?" said a rosy-cheeked maiden of fifteen years, pulling back her auburn bangs from a lightly freckled forehead with one hand as she widened the door with the other. Her piercing brown eyes slid over every facial feature of the elegant lady. Never straying her gaze, she repeated, "Will you, Sister?"

"Yes, my dear Romée, just like every night. I will come to your house." Sister Sibyl clapped. "Go now. Tell Aveline and Jean to prepare their lessons and prayers. I will tend to them as well." The teenager left after rendering the appropriate courtesies to both women and God.

It suddenly became clear to Christine that one additional degree of separation existed for Sibylle, a pain for which Christine could never have empathy. *Romée will never see Sibylle as anything more than Sister Sibyl, the church's recorder, and her godmother. The girl will never know that Sibylle is her birth grandmother and the living representative of her very bloodline—a royal one at that. Secrets and more secrets.*

Sibylle saw a profound realization creep into Christine's eyes. Christine hugged her cousin. No words needed to be spoken and none were for a long time.

After the evening study session with Romée and her siblings, the women returned to the church where they spoke together until deep in the night. The morning found Christine back in her royal coach, slouched in peaceful slumber, with a content smile on her face. Her trip back to Paris was accompanied by dreams filled with blissful satisfaction, a blessed gift from the hand of God.

29

Jilting Paradox

Maternity hospital
Saint-Quentin, Somme River Valley
Vermandois region, France
Current day

It was eight o'clock in the evening, and Loni didn't know she was Loni. The question on all minds was why?

With remarkable speed and efficiency, all medical, orthopedic, neurological, and obstetrical examinations indicated that she was fine. When all the imaging and labs had been completed and the results from the STAT blood testing had been reviewed, she was deemed physically stable. Everyone was in complete and total agreement that Loni and the babies were all sufficiently healthy.

The only remaining concern was that Loni, while currently awake, was not oriented to time, place, or person. The deficiencies within the parameters of time and place were acceptable and explainable since she had sustained a head injury and lost consciousness. The place where she was when she blacked out was not the same place she was when she woke up. Therefore, it was reasonable that she was confused as to the time of day and the place where she now sat. The fact that she didn't know *who* she was quite disconcerting. However, the amnesia was currently not an obstetrical issue for the French-trained medical staff. They felt that a tincture of time would heal it.

In such situations, time could never pass at an acceptable rate to appease Mickey. The only other person voicing more discontent than Mickey was the internal medicine physician scientist Suzanne Coletrane. Since her arrival at the hospital, Suzanne had been relegated to the friend-of-a-family-member position. This entitled her to even less importance and respect than Mickey, which went over as poorly as expected. Mickey and Suzanne were not experienced in the patient or family-member-of-patient role, and they certainly weren't good at it. They sat sulking outside the private patient room, listening intently as Loni was sequestered and tended to by the attentive fifth-floor maternity acute care staff.

130

"You know, Mickey, if you didn't look so much like a patient yourself maybe they would let us be more involved in Loni's care," unsheathed Suzanne.

"Wait a minute. Are you saying that because my arm is in a splint that I suddenly have a total absence of professional bearing?" Mickey flared.

"I don't have to. You already said it." Suzanne glared coldly. Mickey ran his hand over his splint while frowning at the less-than-happy medical internist. He tried to pose a retort but before he could, Suzanne went for the two-point conversion.

"So, how'd you jack up your hand? Slice it on the jagged edge of a broken fallopian tube?"

"You're an internist, Dr. Coletrane. You'd be the one eliciting the help of the third-shift night watchman to help you find a box of fallopian tubes from the laboratory supply room."

Suzanne stared back with pursed, frosted lips. Then, her lips twitched. Soon they both broke out in a laugh.

The moment of levity was short lived, and a moment later they both resumed their protracted silence.

Suzanne's thoughts were betrayed by her face. Finally, she turned to Mickey and said, "This is a maternity-gynecology hospital, Mickey. You know they are not prepared to address the nature of Loni's medical issues."

"I don't think they are about to credential you to be her primary medical attending, Suzanne," sneered Mickey.

"Of the two of us, at least my medical degree is recognized internationally. What is yours again, Mickey?"

"Bite me, Suzanne." Mickey huffed, sat back in his chair, and stared up at the ceiling.

"Now look at who is in Viking witch mode." Suzanne took a deep breath and ran her hands over her face in frustration. "Look, Mickey, I'm sorry." She winced. "Really, I am. It's just that I'm worried and I don't speak French and I don't like being illiterate to a culture that prides themselves in their Frenchiness."

"Ditto." Mickey rose to his feet. "I'm going to make a call."

"Excellent idea—*Art of War*. Place the strongest and bravest leader in the position to lead the fight! Begin by recommending staff changes to the CEO of the Centre Hospitalier de Saint-Quentin, *Monsieur Docteur Américain*."

"Nope, not even close."

Suzanne arched an eyebrow in response.

"I'm going to engage the help of a long-lost friend."

"Ooh. Anyone I know or love?" Suzanne asked coyly.

"Yes."

"Ahh. Well, tell him to bring those Romanian toothpick-meat delicacies he knows I love."

"Will do . . . but I'm not sure he will."

"Come on. You know Russell would do anything for his Suzanne, don't you?"

"I'm not calling Russell. I am calling the best person I know for the job."

"Then who are you—wait a minute, you aren't calling—"

"Still want me to ask about delicacies?"

The blood from Suzanne's face drained, then immediately went into a beet-red flush. Her shoulders locked and loaded, starting a shock wave that tensed every fiber of her body. From her eyes, daggers were replaced by spears.

Mickey averted his eyes to his phone and mumbled under his breath, "*Art of War: The Sequel*—venomous hate stares, an underrated weapon of destruction."

30

Prepping of the Maid

Domrémy-la-Pucelle, Meuse River Valley
Lorraine region, France
15th century

T he thunder echoed in the Meuse River Valley heralding the torrents of
rain which washed the dusty roads of the Lorraine. Lightning preceded
clap after clap of rolling thunder. Amidst the formation of a multitude
of tiny rivers, Romée, beginning her early thirties, took a break from her mundane housewife duties, scarfed her head so that it would stay dry, and went next
door to the church to talk to her spiritual mentor, Sister Sibyl. Romée's scan of
the homestead accounted for all the children save one. That one was last seen
heading for the church some time ago.

Even the deadly lightning wouldn't keep away the dukes of Burgundy and
their English allies who, regardless of the weather, managed to greatly trouble
the simple peace-loving inhabitants of the tranquil valley. Through the power
of prayer, Romée knew that God would one day give peace and prosperity
to France. Today was like the hundreds of days before except that there was
heightened talk about the Burgundians who, in league with French Queen
Consort Isabeau, had just given away Paris.

Romée moved swiftly through the torrential rain and into the refuge of
the church.

"Sister Sibyl, have you seen Jehanne?"

"She is here with us."

In her haste to find her child, Romée did not see that the room had many
occupants. In the rectory sat Sister Sibyl flanked by Father Jean Minet on her
left. Seven-year-old Jehanne sat at the end of the table with her lessons in front
of her. In the shadows, standing by the window, was a woman Romée had often
seen in greater frequency for the past four years. Looking out the rain-speckled
glass was Christine de Pizan.

Although it had been five years ago in 1415, the adults in the room were
discussing the Battle of Agincourt as if it was yesterday. Like the water pitcher

with big ears that sits in the corner of the room, Jehanne sat quietly turning the pages in her book.

"The defeat of our noblemen at the Battle of Agincourt spelled doom for the kingdom of France," spoke Father Minet. "And though they were in the very capable hands of Charles d'Albret, Count of Dreux, he could not bring the nobility under his leadership that day."

"Reports said the heavy rains resulted in lakes of mud. Our heavy-armored cavalry sank and drowned," recounted Sister Sibyl with great despair. "Those who were knocked off their horses fell to the sharpened pikes and the arrows of the English longbowmen. That fact alone sealed our fate."

Christine moved to the table's edge and plucked at her sleeves. "France lost hundreds of her noblemen, thousands of her warriors, and the greatest part of her army all because of me," she said morosely.

"You, my lady?" Sister Sibyl defied. "What responsibility could you have had in such a battlefield disaster?"

"It was a day not unlike this one when the Templar Peter Coimbra came to me."

"You have been deceived, my lady. Templars have been gone for over one hundred years. If anything, you spoke with a Templar ghost."

"I thought the same until I realized that the greatest power of presence is held when none seek to persecute you. Templars do exist, I assure you, but under a self-imposed cloak of invisibility."

"What did this no-longer-invisible ghost tell you?" Sister Sibyl asked, as she leaned in closer.

"Peter Coimbra said that the same fears that the French had with the English were being experienced in Iberia with the Moors. He asked if I could reveal to him the location of the Staff of Moses and the Rod of Aaron. He said that the time had arrived to wield these weapons in defense of the Christian nations of Portugal and France."

"Why would he ask *you* this?"

"There are secrets and there are *secrets* . . . and this Templar had his, believe me—"

"Are you saying you have this information?" interrupted Father Minet.

"Me? No. Of course not," Christine laughed. "I am saying that in the royal court of France, I know people who know people. Such information could come to me. However, because I knew not this strange Templar nor his secret purpose, I did nothing. Taking no action is also an action in and of itself. In so doing, or rather, not doing, our military died, and thus there was little left behind to defend France from further English incursions. Because of this, the enemy came into France as the Moors have into Portugal. The women of France have had to deal with the loss of many husbands, fathers, brothers, uncles, sons, and nephews. The true power in France has now shifted to the strength of its women."

"All but one woman," reminded Father Minet. "Queen Isabeau has claimed the Dauphin to be a bastard and has weakened the legitimacy of Mad Charles VI."

"In defense of our queen," spoke up Romée, "the king is mad and needs not to be seen as the leader of France."

"True enough, Romée," commented Sister Sibyl. "However, throwing her royal weight behind an English heir rather than her own son is a slap to the noble face of France. Isabeau has now poised an English competitor for the throne of France."

Though not one of them spoke it, they all looked at the quietly reading Jehanne with the same thoughts in their heads. The Maid of Lorraine was desperately needed, and the current hope sat in the small church in Domrémy amidst a humble church priest, a nun, the king's recorder, and a fretful mother.

Romée took Jehanne and sat the girl on her lap then began braiding the child's hair. The tension in the room broke, and the conversation topic moved to Paris and the rumors of the present day.

"The Burgundians took Paris a year ago and have been promising to return the city to Armagnac control," said Christine. "As of last week, the Burgundians, traitors to France and the crown, have handed over the city's keys to the English. I fear for any Frenchman who publicly speaks loyalty to the lineage of Charles."

"This would mean the Dauphin is now disgraced and must relocate to the Loire," Father Minet surmised. "There are many fortresses, like those at Orléans and Chinon, which can protect the remainder of France, but they cannot hold out forever. What can we do here in the Lorraine to help the Dauphin?"

"We must continue the work we have done from the beginning," stated Christine. "We must be God-fearing, loyal, and ever vigilant in the shaping of our maid. Mother Isabelle Romée has worked hard at being the best wife and mother she can be. She and Jacques d'Arc have reared a family of great character."

As they spoke, Romée took the tie out of her own hair to secure Jehanne's braid. She then looked at her hands—worn and aged. The years had been hard for her. Together, she and Jacques had raised a handsome family of children which included Jacquemin, Jean, Jehanne, Pierrelot, and little Catherine. The toll had been high on all of them and was reflected in their hands and faces. Now Christine, Father Minet, and Sister Sibyl were looking to place the recovery of France into the hands of one of her children. Besides book studies, her little Jehanne—a potential future savior of France—could spin, weave, and pray. *There is not much there worthy of leading great armies into battle. Yet, with God's divine leadership, this little maid from Lorraine is still a worthy hopeful.*

Jehanne was both the best and the worst candidate for the hope of France.

She was good and pious to the point of being mocked by the town's children. When the other children were at play in the fields, Jehanne would play in and around the church next door to her home. Wherever and whenever the children of the town heard the church bells ring, only she, Jehanne, would kneel in place and pray to God and her patron saints. She spoke to them often.

Because of Jehanne's extreme beliefs, her father worried about her. He mandated that if either of his girls showed any inclination toward the military—such as the following of troops, camps, and armies—he would personally drown them in the Meuse River. Such a disgraceful daughter would not embarrass the family name. To his mind, Jehanne could boast faithful spirituality to support France, but never would she be a warrior.

Life in Domrémy was particularly difficult in these times. Jacques ensured that his children were kept strong, focused, and skilled by keeping up the business of the farm. Romée had done well teaching them to be pious, reverent, and God-fearing.

Romée touched her daughter's head lightly. *Does it really come down to you, little Jehanne? If my sister, Jehanne, had lived and remained chaste, would she now be groomed as the Maid of Lorraine?*

Romée wrapped her arms around little Jehanne. Just as she knew every strand of hair on this head, she also knew, in her heart, of the work began by Dr. Pizan. He was gone. In his stead, his work had been continued these many years through his daughter Lady Christine, Sister Sibyl, and Father Minet.

Will it be enough to save France? Probably not.

Romée believed it would take the power of Saint Michael, Saint Catherine, and Saint Margaret—the saints who were dearly loved by Jehanne—to bring to life the Maid of Lorraine as the savior of France. These saints would have to lead her daughter to the fulfillment of such a prophecy. There was no doubt that they certainly gave Jehanne heavenly spiritual growth. Sister Sibyl, Father Minet, and Lady Christine would always be there to give Jehanne earthly guidance for spirituality. And her own mission to ensure that her daughter Jehanne was strong of body and strong of will seemed to be complete already at the age of seven.

Despite an overprotective father, maybe the debut for Jehanne as the Maid of Lorraine is truly in the offing.

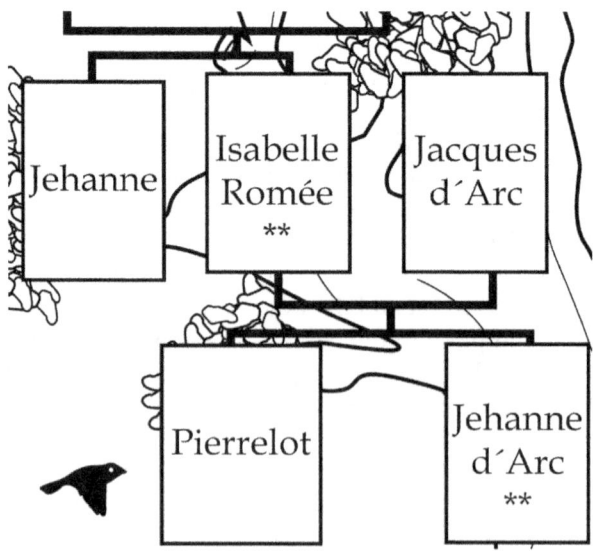

31

Lucky Rabbit

Douglas Odysseus Coletrane watched as streams of salt poured from every one of his skin pores still able to function. This attempt of his body to cool itself in the face of rising mercury was failing miserably. Already insufferable, it seemed as if the suffocating heat was literally broiling his body. He knew he needed fluids, lots of them. Douglas also knew that such mercy would not be forthcoming. He felt his tongue grow thick, dry, and swollen. He realized that if he had to speak to save his life, he couldn't. That moment had passed. He reached for a pebble from the dirt floor, but his hand groped aimlessly. Sucking on a small stone always managed to moisten his mouth. However, his fingers could locate no stone and consequently, in his immediate future, there would be no moisture for his blistered lips.

Douglas stretched his gaze to envision the world beyond. The noisy vegetation outside the window was plush, rich, and green. He was tirelessly taunted by the verdant hue which telegraphed the message that there was, indeed, water nearby. The proof lay in the giant plant leaves which drew moisture from their deep-searching roots. Regretfully, Douglas had no such adaptation. He wished his feet possessed water-seeking roots. As a further insult, he could hear the distant sound of a gurgling brook, but he could not appreciate a single drop from the spray of the swirling eddies.

Frustrated, he pushed himself away from the bamboo window and any hopes for water. With the earnest soul of a choir boy, he prayed for night to come quickly. Although he might not be able to control the water loss from his body during the heat of the day, at night there came the promise of condensation. He could lick the moisture off the bamboo surfaces in the morning. This was the only hope he could muster in his prisoner-of-war hotbox deep in the smoldering jungles of Indonesia.

At a sound of a telephone ring, Douglas's world lost focus. The clamoring of the Southeast Asian foliage began to fade into a distant rustling. Even the feel of the heat that pressed against his skin lessened, as cooler air bathed his face. His heart lifted as the flashes of the past began to relinquish their hold on his present.

137

As they had done so many times before, the jungle dreams which were part of his post-traumatic stress disorder were releasing him back to reality. The phone rang again but stopped in mid ring.

In the world of PTSD, Dr. Douglas Coletrane was unique. First, he did not look like a person in traumatic distress. Outside he was neat, trim, and competition for anyone caring to pose as a well-tanned fifty-two-year-old beach model. His black hair had only tiny flecks of grey which added the austere professionalism he needed when he spoke at conferences. His brown eyes, also verdantly flecked, were well distanced and bracketed a broad nose bridge. Douglas's lips were full and framed in a gracing jawline. As half Central American and half Caucasian, he sported the best in both genetic pools.

Second, he was in the rare position of having the first-hand experience of horrific stressors, reliving the trauma through dreams, and fighting the recurring disease. With his professional skills and training as a doctor of alternative medicine he could help others overcome the stigma. The demon of PTSD victimizes each person in its own manner. For Douglas, the demon found fuel in the several tours of Foreign Service with the Defense Intelligence Agency in Mongolia, Indonesia, and Thailand, which had led him—on more than one occasion—to live life behind bars at the hands of political extremists.

However, today in Ieper, Belgium, Douglas couldn't be farther away from bamboo, triple-canopy jungles, and POW hotboxes. Nevertheless, the sweat still poured rivers into his clothing. Douglas carried his PTSD demon with him everywhere.

Among metaphysicians, Douglas was a respected therapist. His integration of multiple therapeutic techniques often found resolution where traditional medicine failed. Douglas's mastery of hypnosis, and especially hypnotic regression, helped select patient populations. His colleagues called it the management of pediatric and preadolescent pathologies with latent manifestations. In other words, adults who were screwed up as kids, and never knew it, now had hope of dealing with their problems. Using hypnosis, Douglas took these adults back and resolved those childhood issues, paving the way for a potential normal adult life. There were many medical and metaphysician colleagues who worshipped the talents of Dr. Douglas Coletrane. Unfortunately, he was not one of them.

He had no ability to fix himself. Self-hypnosis and self-directed hypnotic regression were not skills he possessed. In his personal medical management, he had to resort to the lack of wisdom in others.

Douglas sat in his hotel room smiling because he finally had the definitive solution to his recurring problem of jungle flashbacks and PTSD. He sat with three friends who promised an instant resolution to this problem. Mr. Smith, Mr. Kline, and Mr. Beecham seemed to have what Douglas couldn't give himself. Indeed, the pharmaceutical company of SmithKline Beecham touted pharmacotherapy and pill-popping as a method to solve medical issues. Positive that the recommended dosing wouldn't work, Douglas multiplied by forty the milligram dose in order to put his misery to an end.

He held a half-empty glass of vodka and a fist full of pills.

Will I just go to sleep and then be found dead in the morning? What will Suzanne say? Wait, wait, I know that answer already. She will say that she had predicted this move of applied self-harm to the year, month, week, day, hour, and minute.

Douglas scoffed aloud to the empty room.

After my death today, it'll be hard for her to blame all her future shortfalls on me. He sniffed hard and wiped his nose with the back of his fist. *Ahh, but Mickey and Russell will help her find some way to attribute blame to me even after I'm gone.* He shrugged. *So be it.*

He swallowed hard and, now empty fisted, put down the dry glass.

No matter what successes he achieved, these physicians had never displayed any genuine respect for what he did or how he did it. The ultimate irony was that none of the accepted medical professional community understood his life in the Defense Intelligence Agency. Filled with self-importance, they were blissfully unaware that his so-called business trips were, in fact, top-directed intelligence-gathering missions into the world of terrorism. Unlike the arrogant physicians, not only did his medical skill sets provide answers in the world of medicine, but they also made him the tip of the intelligence spearhead in the world of clandestine remote viewing.

Douglas's head began to spin as the excess volumes of alcohol and drugs worked their way farther and farther into his system. In this vortex, Douglas remembered the one person who believed in him.

Maybe she believes in me because she also knows the world is gray—not stark black and white, not entirely linear, like so many others believe. We stand in that gray together, she and I. Her realms of special education and children's literature, my alternative, holistic medicine—all gray zones, all ways of looking around and through and in between. She'll grieve for me . . . I think.

He pulled his hands through his hair and blinked hard.

She'll have to manage the Missing Art Project all by herself now.

Regret creeped up on him as he thought of Loni. But the time to turn back was many pills and several glasses of vodka ago. He flopped back on the hotel bed.

Too bad that today, of all days, we're supposed to meet. It makes no difference. She'll just join the long line of Douglas-bashers who say I've never been a good gamble.

Douglas felt the blackness starting to overtake him. He felt the rising heat of the jungles returning him back to that Indonesian hotbox for one last stint. He welcomed the night which always followed this jungle trip behind the bamboo bars.

✠ ✠ ✠

For all the genius that Douglas possessed, he failed to remember one simple lesson. In the circle of military medicine, what he failed to recall was something titled the Napoleon Effect. Not being a historian, it was quite possible that it slipped his mind. Physician historians had learned an important lesson from prima donna Napoleon Bonaparte. Napoleon believed that a normal level of ingested poison would not be enough to kill him. Believing he was superhuman in every way, Napoleon knew only a massive dosing of poison could kill him. Thus, in his darkest hour of depression, Napoleon took an excess of poison. The result for him was that his stomach rejected the poison, and when he awakened from his attempted suicide, he was left with a residual headache and the stench of encrusted vomit.

Thanks to the Napoleon Effect, the non-historian Douglas Coletrane awoke next to an ice bucket filled with vomit, a headache and, again, the annoying ring of a hotel phone. Through the foggy hangover of drugs, alcohol, and a failed suicide, he could ascertain two pieces of important information from the phone call: Loni was in trouble, and he was the only who could help her. Douglas's time at the Rabbit Hotel had just run out albeit not in the manner he had planned.

Even with his pounding headache, it didn't take long for Douglas to pack his things. After all, most of his suitcase had remained unpacked since he arrived at the hotel five days previously. Sitting on the bed's edge, he stared at the three remaining items still needing to be secured for the journey. One by one he considered them.

Trancelike, he sat picking at the shards of glass still wedged under the broken picture frame. He remembered the day of that photo session with Suzanne. *Until now, I believed that love existed—at least it did once for that couple.* Reluctantly, he threw the now glassless broken frame with the picture into the open suitcase.

He reached for the next item under speculation. It was the vial of remaining pills. He looked at the sixty or so remaining tablets, judging their recent inability to get the job done. He set the vial down hard on the dresser. *There are other ways to skin that cat if I want to.*

The last consideration was on the fourth finger of his left hand. *Too easy.* He never wanted Suzanne to see the symbol of her broken promise to love him forever, and he knew she would be there. Douglas uncapped the vial of medication, shoved the gold wedding band into the gaping mouth, and recapped it. Then he bounced it off the wall and into the trash can overflowing with stale, aromatic pizza crusts and Chinese fast-food boxes. The vial perched precariously atop all the other discarded waste from his life.

With that done, Douglas gathered up his things and did a last-minute scan of the room before he departed. As he proceeded out the door, his suitcase skimmed the top of the trash, knocking the medicine vial out the doorway and into the hall. Not bound by superstition, Douglas remained unperturbed. He shuffled into the hallway and restacked his bag and coat into a manageable arrangement. Conscious of littering, he kneeled to pick up the errant medicine vial which managed to escape the fate of the fast-food debris.

A loud bang behind him startled him into a defensive stance. His DIA-trained hands gripped into fists. His pupils dilated and his heart raced. In seconds, he realized it was only his room door slamming shut behind him. Before his body could return to normality, he noticed a rising discomfort. His right hand surged with pain. As he released the crushing grip of his hand, he noticed a deep imprint in his skin highlighted by the yellow glimmer of the escaping medicine vial. Releasing a deep breath, he shook his head at the vial and shoved it into his blazer's front pocket. He gathered his dropped baggage and took a moment to center himself.

All superstition aside, a sign is a sign after all. There is no decision here that needs to be made now. As old pappy once said, "There are some times that are good times to decide not to decide."

With that, Douglas Coletrane left the building accompanied by the echoes of baggage clunking and pill shooping after every other footfall.

32

Mother's Pendant

L'Église Saint-Remy
Domrémy-la-Pucelle, France
15th century

The light that shone directly above the praying teen's face was the only source of natural illumination in the dark, dank church. Sister Sibyl silently watched the young Jehanne kneeling in prayer at the small chapel altar. The child who once knelt piously had evolved into maturity, La Pucelle. The eyes and facial expressions were the same but framed now within more mature features. The flow of her drab tunic cascaded over rises and dips consistent with that of a young woman. Her hair was long and straight with paired temple braids secured to the back of her head. Sister Sibyl looked at the peasant girl and knew that the blood of the ruling royalty of France, as well as the potential duties of the Maid of Lorraine, had been passed to her.

Sister Sibyl thought of her lineage and her mind flowed down through the women connecting herself to this young woman, this hope of France. She thought of her own daughter Isabella. Then, Isabella's daughters—one with God and the other, Romée, a mother herself. Finally, Romée's daughter, Jehanne, a budding woman.

A legacy of daughters. God has seen to it that Jehanne has guiding saints. There will be little more that Father Jean Minet, the Church, or I, myself, can do. The will of God is now playing out before our very eyes.

Sister Sibyl looked down at the heavy pendant which hung from her own neck. It was weighed down with the promise she made to Dr. Pizan when he gave it to her so many years ago in Vouthon. In the execution of that promise, she had thought to give the crucifix to her own daughter, then perhaps to one of her granddaughters, but time and again God's hand took and led her away from bestowing the sacred gift. Now this Jehanne, her great-granddaughter, seemed to be the current one destined to take the gift.

How can I be sure that Jehanne truly is the one? What if I give away the pendant to Jehanne and then fate alters her life—as it did to Isabella and her daughters Jehanne and

Romée—rendering her an unworthy candidate? Dr. Pizan said that I would know, but now—many, many years later—I am not so certain.

Sister Sibyl turned the pendant forward and backward in her palm as if the answer would be inscribed on the crucifix itself. Her eyes focused on the workmanship as they had countless times before, but no answers were forthcoming. In her periphery, the sister saw movement, and as her body startled involuntarily, she dropped the pendant back to her chest. She then relaxed slightly as Jehanne came into view.

"Sister Sibyl, have I ever told you I love you?" Jehanne began.

"Countless times, my dearest one, but never enough. Have I told you how much I love you?"

"Countless times, Sister, but I always need to hear so at least once more."

"And so you shall receive it, I promise. What is on your mind, child?"

"This year is my sixteenth. I need to tell you that the voices have spoken to me yet again."

"Are these the same voices that you first heard four years ago here in the church?"

"They are."

"They are Saint Michael and Saint Catherine, yes?"

"There is Saint Margaret as well, Sister."

Sister Sibyl nodded sagely. "What do the voices say to you, darling?"

Silently, Jehanne closed the distance between herself and the nun, lifted the pendant crucifix, and held it in her hand. The afternoon sun streamed in over her shoulder lighting up the front of the nun's habit. The metal front of the wooden crucifix shone brightly.

Again, Sister Sibyl asked Jehanne what the voices said. Jehanne cleared her throat and squared her gaze directly into the nun's eyes.

"The voices say that you are my mother."

Sister Sibyl's heart stopped, and she gasped. The word *mother* echoed in her head with a fading resonance. Her knees went weak. Jehanne never moved, and her sharpened gaze never faltered.

"Darling, that can't be." The nun reached out to the wall to steady herself. "I am a—you know your father and mother, they are—the church would never allow—I know that to you I am *like* a mother. In God's way, I have a love for you maternal in nature, sure but . . . I . . . I . . ." She searched for an answer that would be acceptable for Jehanne. The youth remained stalwart, holding both the crucifix and the nun's gaze with a gentle, but unyielding, strength.

"I don't understand how this can be, but I do not question what the voices say to me, Mother Sibyl. I just know that they have spoken the truth and I in turn only tell you what they have said."

Hearing the title *mother* attached to her name, Sibyl's tears flowed uncontrollably as they did the day Isabella, her daughter, was born in Poissy. Jehanne continued in the same quiet, respectful tone.

"The voices tell me that I am to go to the Dauphin at Chinon and tell him

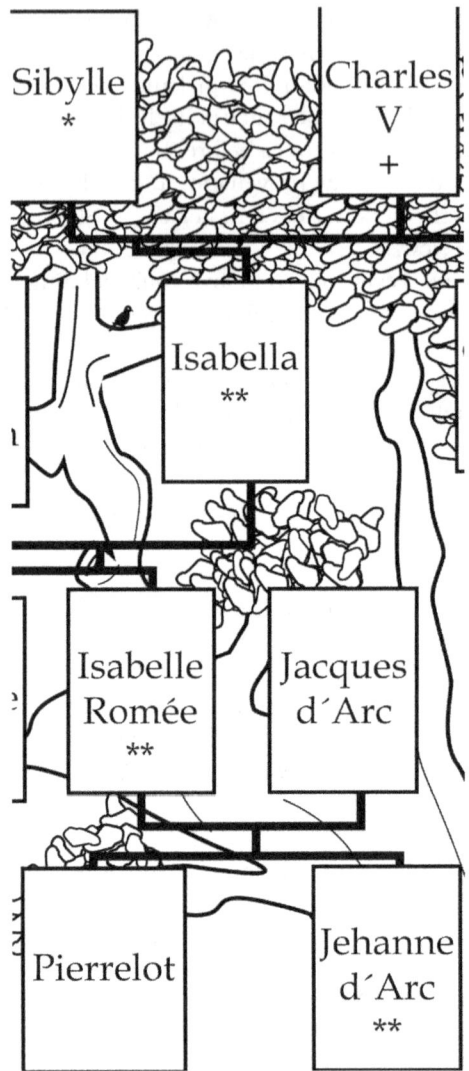

that I am the Maid of Lorraine. I am to lift the siege at Orléans. I am to see the Dauphin crowned at Reims."

Speaking through her tears, Sibyl responded, "Are you telling me . . . that you will present yourself to the Dauphin as the Maid of Lorraine . . . and the proof is that your mother is a nun? Why would this . . . insanity . . . ring any note of believability in the mind of the Dauphin?"

"Why indeed? It doesn't seem possible, does it? I know only this, Mother Sibyl: I am to go to Chinon to seek out the Dauphin. The voices tell me that my mother will go with me. The voices indicate that the mother is you. Therefore, you, my mother, will help me find what to say to convince the Dauphin."

Jehanne kissed the nun's two eyelids. With her two fingers, she touched the quivering lips of the blubbering nun and then leaned down and kissed the crucifix she still held in her hand. She placed the crucifix back against the habit of the nun.

Jehanne started to turn and move away when she paused and listened carefully to unseen sounds. In a moment, Jehanne turned back and lifted the pendant. With her thumb, she slid up the crucifix on the metal plate which formed the front of the cross. Behind it was a chamber. Jehanne alone looked in the chamber and then glanced back up at the wide-eyed Sister Sibyl. As quickly as she had opened the chamber, she closed it with a click. As if tacking it in place, Jehanne patted the pendant crucifix against the nun's chest, then turned away. Neither spoke a word.

33

Burying Hatchets

Route to the Vermandois

Ieper, Belgium

Current day

The headlights from oncoming cars hammered thorns into Douglas Coletrane's already aching temples. This made the one hundred miles of night driving which lay between Ieper, Belgium, and Saint-Quentin, France, a continuous grinding of his teeth. Douglas's jaws ached, and his eyes grew weary as the miles clicked by.

Why did God spare me when everything I did guaranteed me death? Why am I worth saving? Who am I really?

His mind carried him back through the waves of emotion that had brought him to this lonely stretch of highway. As there was no other form of diversion available, he allowed himself this parallel journey into his own psyche. *Am I just the sum of my experiences? More than that? Huh, less probably.*

Douglas O. Coletrane was considered quite memorable by all who knew him—regardless of whether he was liked or not. Even his nickname, Doc, was notable because it projected a bit of irony. In his circle of friends, physicians, and researchers, only Douglas lacked a universally accepted professional medical degree. Suzanne had always refused to call him Doc. Douglas would watch as her jaws tightened when anyone used this nickname for him in her presence. People referred to him as Doc but she, a genuine physician, was almost always addressed as Mrs. Coletrane or Colonel Coletrane. When this happened, Douglas could see the absolute loathing in her face. In later years, he thought that perhaps this was the seed that eventually led to the end of their marriage and began his marriage to his profession.

Douglas, in every way, was fully qualified to enter traditional medicine. He was academically accepted into every medical program to which he had applied. But he chose to shun allopathic M.D., osteopathic D.O., and chiropractic D.C. medicine. Instead, he studied and practiced energy weaving, ear coning, aroma therapy, massage therapy, acupuncture, homeopathy, hypnotherapy, among other holistic medical curricula. He felt this approach did more to facilitate the healing of a patient. Douglas knew that the services he provided his patients were deeply entrenched in a patient-centered approach, and it wouldn't be long before *traditional* medicine would have to catch up with Douglas's alternative medicine. Until then, Douglas professionally often had the fast lane. Relative to professional acceptance, he definitely had the slow lane. Socially, among medical professionals, he wasn't even in the race.

Douglas wasn't secretive about his hatred of what he loved to call fast-food medicine. Therefore, throughout the professional medical circles, he evolved to become a rebel without a clue. When his ex-wife or her professional medical colleagues were stymied or satisfactory progress of their treatment plan was lacking, they looked to Douglas for definitive care. Rather than be the professional, a bitter Douglas Coletrane often emphasized the shortfalls that brought others to his door. Normally, this was done within the confines of the US border. However, the telephone call this evening came on a relay from his home in Steinhatchee, Florida, currently to his international cell on an evening drive from Belgium toward Saint-Quentin in the Vermandois.

✠ ✠ ✠

"Douglas, did I wake you again?" Echoing on the cellphone speaker within Douglas's car, a voice from the past inquired with a sense of sincere concern.

"No, not really. I had to answer the phone anyway," Douglas retorted with his pat answer which could be taken humorously, or not.

"You really sounded out of it before, Douglas. I wasn't sure you were processing—"

"Who is this?" Douglas mocked.

"This is Mickey."

"I'm processing the image of a beggar with his hat in his hand, Mickey. How good is my processing now?"

"Spot on, Douglas. I'm kind of in a bind."

"So, why is your bind my problem?" Hearing the stammering attempt of a response, Douglas squeezed off another round. "How long has it been since we had a good heart to heart, Mickey?" *Not long enough*, he thought.

"It's been too long, Douglas, way too long . . . but with the divorce—"

"You're divorced?"

"No, I was talking about you and—"

"Stop right there, Mickey! There was no *divorce* between Suzanne and me. We loved each other, we still do. The opposite of love is not *hate*." Douglas paused trying to pull his hungover mind together. "No, the opposite of love is indifference. In the end, through indifference—not hate—the marriage dissolved. The legal beagles called it a dissolution of marriage. It wasn't a *divorce* . . . it was never a divorce."

"Yes, dissolution, I remember now. Nonetheless, there were obstacles produced that made talking to you . . . well . . . an uncomfortable situation."

"For whom, Mickey—me or you?"

"Yes."

"Some things never change, do they?"

"Maybe, maybe not."

"Give me a reason not to hang up." Douglas wiped the dregs of vomit off his lips with the back of his hand.

"Douglas, I. . . ."

"Out with it, Mickey. How can I best help you on this fine crisp evening?"

"Well, if you would stop pouncing on me," snapped Mickey, "maybe I could tell you." Douglas heard him take a breath. "Could we start again, possibly a bit friendlier?"

"Why would I want to do that, Mickey? Apparently, you need something from me or else you wouldn't have reached out to me. I would say that you seem to be wasting an inordinate amount of your own time. My advice to you, Doctor, is for you to get to your point—that is, if you even have one."

"Look, Douglas, Loni is in bad shape. I need your help, professionally."

There was a long, protracted silence while Douglas considered the situation. He rubbed his eyes with his free hand, ending with a pinch to apply pressure above the bridge of his nose and just below his eyebrows. *Must be bad if he's calling me. Okay, Douglas, get it together.*

"Douglas? Are you there? I said—"

"I heard you, Mickey. You know you have my Achilles' heel. Mind you, this changes nothing between you and me."

"Are you saying you won't help us?"

"I am saying I won't help *you* . . . but as you already know, there is nothing I wouldn't do for Loni. If that helps you, her husband, then I guess I will just have to live with that sad consequence."

"Then on Loni's behalf, let me say thank you."

"Don't, Mickey, don't say it. I haven't done anything for Loni yet. What's happened to her that *you*, as an allegedly competent physician, need to seek *my* help?"

"Do you have to be so ugly?"

"It's part of my charm, or haven't you heard."

"Well, I—"

"Come on Mickey, you're a doctor. Let's get to this. You know, doctor to doctor. Present the patient to me."

Mickey and Douglas simultaneously drew in deep breaths. Mickey spoke with utmost courteous professionalism while quietly, with an expert ear, Douglas carefully listened.

34

Oil and Water

Route to the Vermandois

Ieper, Belgium

Current day

"Loni, now a forty-nine-year-old white female, sustained an injury to her head a little over two hours ago in a manner which is still unclear. Initially, she lost consciousness. Later, she became intermittently conscious but with amnesia. Right now, this is how she presents." Mickey quickly catalogued, in depth and detail, personal and family medical history, surgical and social history, vital signs, laboratory values, radiographic images, and specialty consultant opinions.

Douglas grunted affirmations of understanding through the phone as Mickey spoke, trying hard not to interrupt. *I asked for a cup of information, and I get a fire hydrant's worth.*

"There is nothing we seem to be able to do, Douglas, but as a metaphysician, I know you can help her."

"That's more than I know, but I will try—for her."

"There's more."

"I know already. You probably called Suzanne before you called me." Douglas could almost hear Mickey's teeth gritting through the phone. "Well, Mickey, did you call Suzanne, the physician, before me?"

"Look, I'd like to tell you I didn't, but I can't. Yes, I called Suzanne before I called you."

"There's a surprise."

"It's not like that. Suzanne was already in Paris waiting to join us. It was as much a personal call as it was professional. Anyway, Suzanne is here as we speak."

"My God! Really?!"

"We *really* need you, Douglas," pleaded Mickey.

Douglas cleared his throat. "You said something about there being more. Besides Suzanne, what more is there?"

"When I said there is more, I meant it from a patient's perspective—that is, Loni's perspective."

"Please don't tell me it's some obscure cancer or a microtumor or something like that."

"Actually, it is a tumor. In fact, there are two highly efficient parasitic tumors."

Douglas gasped and his stomach lurched as if he'd missed a step while walking downstairs.

Mickey quickly resumed. "Don't worry, Douglas, all is okay. The tumors are twin babies."

"Was that some kind of attempt at humor?" Douglas jabbed.

"Look, forget it, okay? I want this resolved ASAP as Loni is due to deliver soon."

"Loni is pregnant again. Well, isn't that something?" Douglas remembered how much Loni wanted a sustainable pregnancy though it always seemed to evade her. *Maybe the fertility specialists finally did the trick.* "Tell me where to meet up so that I may see my patient."

"We are in the city hospital in Saint-Quentin forty minutes east of Péronne, France."

"I know Péronne. Nice place. Nice castle. Nice museum. Nice art exhibits. Antoine's is the best bistro in the Vermandois." *With our agenda being spy business, I know why Loni was there, but the fact that Mickey came as well makes for an interesting story. Loni will have to fill me in.*

Douglas tried to ignore the fact that it was his duty and responsibility to meet Loni and Asaad in Péronne, and by Douglas's truancy, he had failed her. He wasn't sure if Mickey knew this and said nothing, or if he just flat out didn't know. Mickey's voice terminated his stream of thought.

"As you wish, Douglas, I can tell you more specifics when you arrive. Do you need directions? I can turn you over to someone who can give you better directions than I."

"No need, I know the area of the Vermandois. It's just south of here."

"Where are you exactly, Douglas? I'm guessing not Florida."

"I'm in Ieper, but don't worry, I'm a dot on the horizon."

"You are here in Europe?"

"Yes, unless you know of a different Belgium than I know."

"What are you doing in Belgium?"

"Does it really matter? Just let Loni know I still keep a grass skirt, garlic beads, and a bison head in my suitcase just in case. I would say it will be nice to see you again, Mickey, but that would be a lie. As for Suzanne, tell her what you want. I am sure she is bracing herself for the worst."

"Maybe this wasn't such a good idea . . . you, Suzanne, both here occupying the same place with all the baggage you two carry."

"Yeah well, it's a little late for that concern, Mickey. I know you. You already decided that you need me there. Maybe I can help where the professionally medically trained couldn't succeed. Suzanne will have to deal with that. I guess she'll just have to move over and make room."

The sound of Mickey sucking in a tight breath whizzed through airwaves and into Douglas's ear. Some part of Douglas enjoyed having the upper hand on Mickey, but as soon as the thought crossed his mind it was swallowed in a surge of guilt. *The power scales are only tipped to my advantage because Loni is in danger. And maybe part of that danger was my fault. Had I been more available to Loni, she would have been able to update me on her most recent intelligence. With the sharing of that, the whole Péronne rendezvous would have played out differently. Now, Loni is not Loni and in danger of never being so again.*

"There's a lot at stake here," Mickey swallowed audibly.

Douglas thought hard about these words. He knew that Mickey was right because both Loni and the twins' well-being was on the table. What Mickey didn't know was that under the operational name Missing Art Project, DIA Agent Loni Peronne was the only person who seemed to have a bead on two of the components of the Rods of Power. The most current intel on both the Staff of Moses and the Rod of Aaron was likely what Loni needed to tell him but only—as the Germans say—*unter vier Augen*, that is, face-to-face. With Loni's amnesia locking down this information, Douglas alone fully understood the value of his skills as the key.

"More at stake than you know, Mickey."

"Well, I guess I'd better let you concentrate on your route planning."

"Give me two hours." Douglas glanced at the car's clock.

"Roger. Out." As the phone clicked off, Douglas's mind went back to DIA business and the scheduled meeting with Loni.

If I had been there, would she have passed me a picture, a document, a thumb drive? She never said. So, unless there's something that Mickey is not telling me, at least the Staff of Moses is still at the Péronne Castle Museum. Maybe when we resolve this, Loni and I can pick up with the project. Maybe there is still hope.

✠ ✠ ✠

Douglas focused on the road and tried to put the tension-filled phone conversation out of his mind. He could only guess at the turmoil brewing at his destination in France.

He knew Mickey would be wondering why a phone call to Florida found Douglas less than two hours away from Saint-Quentin in the European low countries at this particular time. *How much does Mickey know? Or worse, what will he suspect? Will he buy into the idea that my presence here was just a coincidence? Gosh, I hope so.*

In the hospital, Mickey was reaching the conclusion that Douglas's fortuitous presence in Europe probably had something to do with a convention.

He recalled that the last time he knew Douglas was in Europe was to attend the annual convention of the Circle of Friends. It was not at the usual alternating location between Cologne, Germany, and Vienna. That year, the convention had been at Rosenheim, near Munich.

Mickey remembered well that week as a very unhappy Suzanne Coletrane diverted her preferred plans to go to Poissy, France, and instead went to the freshwater lake at Chiemsee where the US military held a resort area. She, a person with a universally accepted professional M.D. medical degree, did not get the respect she sorely wanted from others at the convention. Treated as a non-professional spouse, Suzanne usually ended up sitting in the military hotel at Hitler's breakfast nook downing her trademark drink—seven and seven, double, shaken, tall glass, salted rim, slice of orange. Even back then, there were troubled waters brewing.

Mickey knew, in his gut, that having Douglas and Suzanne Coletrane both in the same place at the same time tonight was going to be a tidal wave of misery with the potential for a long night of conversational fireworks reminiscent of New Year's Eve. *There may indeed be a death in the Vermandois tonight. That dead body will most definitely be a victim of a brutal strangulation. And either way, it'll be wearing a toe-tag labeled Coletrane.*

35

Of Vans and Grands

Outer beltway
Paris, France
Current Day

The needle on the rental van's fuel gauge sat squarely on empty. Monique Meriwether knew what the dispatch clerk said about the gauge being broken. *What if the clerk was wrong?* She puckered her face into a scowl, making those usually subtle lines around her lips and eyes reveal her advanced age.

Monique Fabienne "Babe" Auger was a world-class French beauty and former actress. She was born in the French city of Oger in the Champagne region but raised in the Parisian suburb of Saint-Denis. She could easily steer herself and her husband from the airport to all points in France if there was enough fuel in the tank. *What if empty really meant that the van was on fumes?* Being out of fuel and in the inside lane during morning Paris traffic did not spawn happy thoughts. She tapped on the fuel gauge and, much to her surprise, the needle responded by sliding over toward the full side of the gauge. Monique let out a big breath of relief as she tabled all those mental scenarios that had her attempting to elicit help from indifferent French motorists trying to get to their downtown offices on time.

It wasn't long before the snarling sounds of the early morning airport traffic were far behind them, and as Monique's demeanor eased a bit in intensity, she could finally appreciate being back home in France, her place of birth some sixty-seven years ago.

This is vacation. Monty and I should be vacating all our worries and woes. She took a deep breath and settled in for the drive.

Negotiating the suburbs of Paris with ease and confidence, Monique checked her hair and makeup in the mirror. Her hair, streaked gray in black, looked intentional and added beauty instead of years to her appearance. Pleased with what she saw, her mind moved on to the greatest concern on her plate right now—whether her son-in-law Mickey was going to spill the beans on the surprise they had concocted months ago. She mulled on this as the street signs clipped by quickly. Her chauffer-like skills directed them westward to Saint-Denis. The evening would not end until they finally made it to the Auger family homestead in the little village of Oger. Monique broke the extended silence in the direction of her pensive husband's frown.

"Monty, I know you wanted to drive. It's just that this is my home sandbox and I know each curve in the road." Monique shot a glance at Monty scowling while mindlessly toying with his pocket watch.

As a retired military man, Monty, formally known as Harmon Fairmont, could still find his way through foreign terrain. Even without a wife of French descent, he still possessed enough of his army skills to find his way if dropped in any reasonably inhabited portion of greater France. In fact, a scrutiny of his left wrist showed that he still wore a compass clipped onto any watch he happened to be wearing and, quite comically, on the chain of his pocket watch.

"Look, Monty, if you insist on pouting, we'll switch drivers."

"I'm not pouting, Monique. I'm worried about Loni and how pregnancy has altered her moods."

"I know. Maybe to keep Loni's swinging mood changes on the positive side, Mickey will have to reveal the surprise and tell her that we are coming."

"Mickey is a military man," defended Monty. "There are things he knows that we couldn't pry out of him with a P-38."

"Darling, I hate to tell you, but P-38 can openers went out with C-rations."

"C-rations are obsolete?" Monty echoed with false horror which quickly eased into a soft chuckle as he reigned in Monique's laughter. Monty's greatest joy was to see his Monique laugh. In the presence of his wife, his flag officer–stern features were softened by her laughing eyes and a wide, beaming smile. The years had not been as kind to him as they had been to his wife. Nevertheless, they kept each other young with mirth at every possible moment.

Monty continued. "Anyway, I can't believe that anyone would do away with the C-rations John Wayne candy bar." Together they burst into a tension-releasing laughter. A few moments later, Monty again continued. "Even if Mickey does tell Loni we're here, we will still get to be with her as the twins are delivered. It's not every day that we get to experience grandparenthood with our youngest daughter."

"That's a fact, Monty," said Monique. "But, you know, I was really betting that Jillian and EZ would have already made us grandparents by now. Since she was a little girl, Jillian always said that she would be a mommy and fill her baby's room with every version of unicorn and flying horse."

"Getting pregnant is not the problem with our girls, honey. Staying pregnant is."

"Could it also be the quality of his little guys, *cheri?*"

"EZ is a teacher and researcher. It is a horrible work pace he keeps. I imagine the energy of his little guys is probably at an all-time low by the time he gets home from work."

"Teachers and researchers have been known to have children," Monique rebutted.

"I believe that God has deemed that it just wasn't right for them, honey. EZ and I have discussed this at length."

"Honestly, Monty, I think it's the fiddling with all those lasers down in his labs. No telling what that is doing to his . . . to his . . . his . . . *you know*." She waved a hand in the air to indicate the obvious omission.

"His pointer?" Monty fought hard to suppress a chuckle.

Seeing the absence of the faintest of smiles from his wife, Monty continued. "After all, he is head of the Chemistry Department at West Point. One would expect a man who will pin on a star as a general officer at retirement to have a significant pointer." Monty felt the laugh rising within and let it out this time.

"Laugh if you will. We don't know everything about the health drawbacks of lasers. His laser *pointer*, or whatever else it may be called, certainly hasn't brought us any grandchildren. Has it?"

"I've seen him in the Bartlett Hall laser lab. He wears protection."

"Laser glasses? You call that protection? He should be wearing a lead apron or something similar. Every time I go get an x-ray, they make me wear that stinky lead apron—which, I might add, is made without any remote sense of fashion—and I'm sure no one ever thinks about cleaning it. Tell me, if invisible rays are so harmless, why must I be stinky and tacky?"

"To protect you from the unseen, harmful x-rays. We're talking about laser rays, not x-rays. Lasers are safe."

"Yes indeed. So, where does the idea of a laser gun come from? Hello?"

"Honey, cool your jets. Have you thought that Jillian might be a factor? She may just be too old. Maybe she can't physically have children."

"I have two words for that, Monty: Im-possible." She drew out the *m* sound with great exaggeration and pronounced the word in French for additional emphasis.

"Actually, that's one word, Monique . . . even if you say it in French," he smirked.

"Monty, don't you taunt me. I know that since Jillian began her art studies at McGill University she spends beaucoup time with her tin-glazed pottery. I also know that working with those kinds of products can't be good for anyone."

"Monique. . . ."

"I know what you're going to say. They have visited fertility specialists, and they both have been checked out. They have a plan."

"Well then, I guess lasers and ceramics aren't the issues."

"Maybe not lasers and ceramics themselves, maybe it's just spending too much time in the science laboratories and art studios." Monique's tone drifted into a sense of impending defeat. Before Monty could shift into the perk-her-up mode, his cell phone rang, and he answered it.

"Honey, we're on vacation," whined Monique.

Holding his index finger up toward her to pause her speech, Monty continued speaking into the cell phone with a series of grunts of affirmation.

"Monty. . . ."

Monty spoke into the phone, "Wait a minute, wait a minute." Looking at his wife he said in a very grave general officer tone, "Pull over here, Monique, please. It's important."

Monique quickly pulled the van into a nearby highway emergency phone parking place. Once the idling engine had been turned off and the keys removed and placed on the center console, he switched the phone to speaker and handed it to his wife. His face remained drawn as he looked out the passenger window and then back at her.

"Hello?"

"Mother?"

Monique immediately recognized the voice. "Jillian, baby, what's going on? Is everything all right?" Monique looked at Monty and saw that his eyes were welling up with tears. Monique listened in horror as she felt her eyes well up also.

"Mother, are you there?"

"Yes, darling, I'm here." Monique spoke into the phone. She looked over to Monty and whispered, "She's crying. Monty, why is she crying?" Monty didn't answer, he only looked away.

"Mother, I know we haven't always had the best relationship. I never spent enough effort respecting what you have done for me in my life. I've always known your motives were honorable and good and the richest that there can be. I'm so sorry I was ever mean to you. I want you to know I love you."

"I love you too, Jillian. I—"

"We've had some horrible times, terrible times. You've said some hurtful things. I responded with a string of hateful things. Sometimes we think we have all the time in the world to correct these awful actions. Sometimes we put things off because it is too inconvenient to deal with them. Mother, you really need to know how so very sorry I am for the way I have treated you and Daddy. I really am. I can't tell you how much I regret—"

"Jillian, I—"

"Understand this, Mother. No matter how much I have grown to love you, respect you, and adore you, it won't be more than our children will."

"What?"

"I'm pregnant, Mom. I'm pregnant!"

Monique squealed, dropped the phone, and grabbed her husband's arm, shaking it vigorously. "Oh my God! Monty!"

"I know, Grandma. It looks like we have a doubleheader," said Monty as he wiped his eyes.

"Yes, three grandbabies!"

"Is that what you think?"

"Well, yes."

"Monique, we have two daughters each with *twins* on the way." This time the scream of joy was followed by hugs, kisses, and rivers of tears.

Meanwhile on the floorboard of the van, a cell phone lay totally ignored.

"Mother . . . Mother . . . Mother?" The voice faded away. "Honey, I didn't even get to tell her about the maiolica ceramics, the blue-horned unicorn, and the wallpaper with. . . ."

36

Speech and Hearing

Outer beltway
Paris, France
Current Day

With the exception that traffic sounds were fading in and out of Monty Meriwether's failing hearing, the trip from the airport to Saint-Denis continued to be uneventful, by comparison to the news they received, for the Meriwether doubleheader grandparents-to-be. Monty was mostly deaf to Monique's recurring angst as the van's fuel gauge needle bounced to and from the empty position. With one more gorilla double-tap on the fuel gauge, the problem was permanently solved. However, Monty thought that having a mangled gauge needle limply dangling from the dashboard might take some creative explaining upon the returning of the rented vehicle.

But it didn't matter. Monty was so very thrilled that his elder daughter was finally on the verge of motherhood. He wanted to tell everyone at Saint-Denis but unfortunately, Monique's side of the family there only spoke French. He held on to the feeble hope that perhaps, when he and Monique arrived at Oger later that night, someone there would have enough mastery of English for him to brag in his native tongue. However, he knew it was a foolish hope. Unless Mickey and Loni were there for the surprise rendezvous, French, German, and Flemish would be the languages spoken between family members.

Deeply lost in thought, it seemed to Monty that only a little over ten minutes had passed, and yet there they were, pulling into his in-laws' driveway. For Monique, because of the numerous fuel stops, the trip seemed to have taken over ten hours. After the oohs and ahhs of the initial hugging, beginning at the grapevine-framed front door, continuing room by room through the house, and finally into the kitchen where filled champagne flutes were placed in hand. Drifting out the back door onto the covered porch, Monty migrated to the rear garden. Meanwhile Monique engaged relative after relative, catching up with news and learning all about the mechanism of fuel gas gauges. Within the solitude of the back porch, like a cancer, Monty's pensiveness persisted and grew.

157

"People who speak three languages are trilingual," commented Monty aloud from the trailing edge of the garden behind the farmhouse. "Too bad one of the languages can't be English tonight." He took another sip of his champagne and continued to nurture the thought streaming through his brain cells and their sizzling synapses. In the distance, he could see more of the swaying grapevines with his eyes than any vine rustling could be heard with his ears.

Vaguely he could track his wife moving across the living room cheerfully chatting in French with her brothers, sisters-in-law, and Grande Madame Meeley, Monique's elderly mother. No doubt the conversation with the grande madame would lead, as it always did, to her namesake, Amelia Meeley Earhart. Back in the 1930s, Amelia Earhart, Elvy Kalep, Marie Marvingt, Bessie Coleman, and the grande madame's mother, Jasmine Hertz, were besties as well as historic female pioneer aviatrixes at a time when sky adventure belonged only to men. When Amelia disappeared in 1937, Grandmother Jasmine began calling her daughter, Monique's mother, Meeley after the lost pilot. Since the age of fifteen, the nickname stuck. Monty knew there were so many more interesting details of that story to uncover. However, his lack of understanding of the French tongue kept mountains of knowledge hidden from him.

As much as Monty's French was criminally absent, Monique's French remained impeccable. After all, having been born in Oger, she was a home-grown product here in the Champagne region of France, and she never let her time in America diminish her native tongue. However, in this family aptly blessed with linguistic prowess, Monique was the weak link—she only spoke two languages, French and English. Turning away from the view of his conversing wife, Monty looked back at the multiple garden statues bathed in the light of the nearly full moon.

"Bilingual. Monique Auger Meriwether is *only* bilingual because of me," Monty muttered aloud. Before he could take another sip of his champagne, he saw a distant, but familiar, shadow move closer into the margin of his periphery.

"Broadcasting my shortcoming to these moon-drunken stone animals, are we, Monty?" Monique questioned him in her British English as she pressed her ageless body against his. She believed that her hyperacute hearing was as much an impairment as Monty's not hearing well enough. Regardless of whether voices couldn't be heard, or conversely, were lost in a cacophony of too many sounds, for both Monty and Monique the distinguishing nature of speech was often lost.

"If anyone could be accused of having a shortcoming, my dear Monique, that person would be me. I have spent my seventy-five years mastering just one language. And you know what they call a person who can only speak one language, don't you Monique?"

His wife answered without hesitation, "Of course, Monty: monolingual."

Monty searched the face framed in absolute confidence; he smiled and drew his beautiful bride even closer to him. He planted a warm wet kiss on her painted red lips. *How can one man be so lucky? She is as ravishing as she was when she was in films. Doesn't look a day over fifty. However, be that as it may, she is not correct.*

"No, Monique, they call that person an American. How can you find it in your heart to still love a monolingual person like me?" His deep-pitched rumble of a chuckle was joined by her melodious laughter. But the smile on his face could not stay there long. There was trouble brewing inside him, and he had to ensure that she was on the inside track of what he was about to say.

37

Probing the Lost

Maternity hospital
Saint-Quentin, Somme River Valley
Vermandois region, France
Current day

Inside a couple of hours, Douglas had traversed the expanse which separated him from the Peronne family, proceeding quickly past all the checkpoints, until he stood outside Loni's hospital room door. It was ajar. Inside the room was dark but he could make out the outline of Mickey standing next to the head of the bed, shifting pillows from the bed and arranging them carefully in the bedside recliner where Loni sat. Shuffling into the room past a silently sitting Suzanne, Douglas freed the lowest button on his vest. Giving a slow solemn nod to Mickey, Douglas knelt in front of a very pleasant-faced Loni dressed now in a hospital gown. *This is not the woman who planned to meet with Asaad and me at Péronne Castle.* In her eyes was every courtesy and kindness which hallmarked her personality but missing was any hint of her recognition of those who looked upon her.

"Douglas, is there anything I can get you?" Mickey asked after waiting long enough for Douglas to make his initial assessment.

"Can't think of anything," replied Douglas, never breaking eye contact with Loni or releasing her hand. He concentrated hard as Loni spoke.

"I wish I could help you. You all seem like very nice people," Loni commented as she surveyed the room from her bedside recliner.

"Looks aren't everything, honey," knifed Suzanne as she drew first blood. Ignoring the jab, which was pretty much intended for him, Douglas groaned, stood up and squared off in front of Suzanne and Mickey.

"I want to hypnotize Loni and carry her back within herself until she has a comfortable memory." Douglas shot a wayward glance toward his ex-wife, adding, "I wish I could do this for other un-named people in this room, but I doubt I will have time."

Suzanne shifted her weight from one foot to the other and drew in a breath, but before she could speak, she felt Mickey's hand against her wrist giving it an almost fatherly pat.

160

Having returned fire, Douglas switched his method. He spoke directly to Mickey, but it was quickly clear that the message ranged wider. "I have had unbelievably great memories with everyone in this room. I hope you all can believe that. There have been times when my life was on the line and any, or all, of you were there to save me, even from death. Though I wouldn't have assembled this cast of characters, the very people in this room are the exact ones needed to bring back Loni." Douglas tried to read the faces of Mickey and Suzanne. He couldn't decipher if what he saw in the two physicians was confusion or disbelief.

"Rest assured," Douglas continued, "I didn't come here for a friendship reunion. I'm not sure what that reunion would bring. I do know this, though. There is enough tension and emotion in this room to fuel this hospital's energy needs for weeks to come. What I need right now is that energy, that skill, that expertise, that love, to be focused in one direction only. And that direction is toward Loni and in helping give me the best chance to bring her back."

It looked to Douglas that there was a slight softening in the brick wall. Mickey's focus had moved down to his shoes instead of doing the thousand-yard stare. Suzanne was harder to read. *Well, I've gone this far. I might as well bring the point home.*

"In one way or another I am indebted to each of you beyond words. If we can't rise above our internal issues within ourselves, we are lost before we start. I need no war here. I don't need you to respect me or what I do. I only need the lot of you helping to shoulder the burden of work that I must do while I'm on point. If I ask for something, I need you to see that I receive it. My promise to you is that I will not quit until I have tried every technique that I have in my repertoire. Can you do that for me? Will you do that for me?"

The shuffling of feet was not the answer for which Douglas had hoped.

"This is not rhetoric folks. I need an answer and I need it now. We all must be on board here."

Loni shifted in her seat causing all eyes to lock onto the movement. Suzanne pursed her lips.

"Not for me, guys. For her." Douglas nodded his head toward Loni.

Mickey cleared his throat to speak. "Douglas, in your area of expertise, I'm not sure I can be an asset to you. Tell me, what do you need me to do?"

"Thank you, Mickey. Suzanne?"

"I can offer you silence. Be grateful for it."

"Well, there you have it. Sit down, folks. Get comfortable because this night will begin when Loni connects with what she remembers last. I hope it is a pleasant memory."

Throughout all this dialogue Loni never lost her blank stare. In fact, it appeared she never blinked.

From his blazer pocket, Douglas produced Mad Max, his silver medallion on a chain. He tapped it on his forehead as if the engraved image of Robespierre would impart some obscure knowledge to him in this, his time of need. Then, swinging Mad Max and engaging a soothing tone, he began the psychic journey to go where no one had previously traveled with Loni.

"Loni, I want you to focus on this shiny object." Douglas's eyes searched for the desired response in Loni's face. Soon, her head tilted forward, and her chin rested on her chest as if she was intensely scrutinizing the pendant that hung around her neck.

"Loni, can you hear me?" Douglas nervously plucked at the whiskers on his unshaven chin. A low ebb of nausea began to rise within him. *She doesn't hear me.* Douglas thought he saw lip movement of impending speech. *No dice. No more than a sad attempt to moisten a dry pair of lips.*

"Loni, I really need you to concentrate on the sound of my voice. Can you hear me at all?"

"I hear a voice in my head very, very far away. Who are you?"

Douglas cringed at the aloof echo in the voice of his dear friend. Nonetheless, through his pulsating headache, he kept his voice true and steady.

"It's me, Douglas Coletrane. Remember me?" Douglas held his breath as he waited for an answer. After many instructions and many seconds, Loni's voice again filled Douglas's ears.

"Douglas Coletrane, I do hear you." Loni's head rocked from side to side, her eyes scanning a far horizon until she rested that rocking head upon her pillow. "Your voice echoes of a home I once knew but now can't find. Are we . . . were we . . . friends?" To Douglas, Loni's voice was a symphony flavored with sweetness, but it was completely devoid of any sense of recognition. Grateful that he had made psychic contact, Douglas pressed onward, cloaking the residual sting of a dear friendship lost.

"This is good, Loni. I'm so very glad you can hear me." He drew in a deep breath and then resumed his query. "I need to ask you some questions."

"Questions? What kind of questions?"

"They are questions about you."

"Me?"

"Yes, you, Loni, I need you to tell me—"

"Douglas Coletrane," Loni interrupted with marked dismay in her voice.

Douglas's voice remained liquid velvet. "Yes, honey, I'm listening."

"You need to know that I'm fine answering any questions you may have. However, Douglas Coletrane," ceasing her head rocking, Loni lifted then turned her head toward Douglas. Her eyes sharpened as did her voice, saying, "there are some things I need to know from you."

"Sure, Loni." Douglas softly chuckled. "Go ahead, but please just call me Douglas."

"Who am I and why can't I remember anything about anything?" said Loni, resting her head back on her pillow, her eyes opening and closing slowly.

"Your name is Loni, and you have had a terrible mishap."

"Loni . . . Loni . . . Loni. It is a gentle name, isn't it? Just speaking it is pleasurable. It's like a sigh and a smile in one. Loni . . . Loni. Just look how the word leaves the mouth parted in such a way that wet lips are instantly dried with the sweet savor of human warmth. Loni. I wish I knew why this beautiful name was given to me." After a moment of silent pondering, Loni queried, "What was the mishap?"

"You were brought here because of a—"

"Where's here, Douglas?"

"You are in the Vermandois in a hospital, a maternity—"

"Vermandois. That's in northern France. France? I'm in France? Why am I in France?"

"You were on vacation. You were on the way to—"

"Has northern France lost all electrical power?" said Loni sitting upright, her head surveying slowly. "Why is it that I can hear you but can't see you?"

"Well, Loni," said Douglas, gently easing Loni back into her pillow. "That is part of the problem. You were traveling on vacation in France on the way to the castle in the city of Péronne when you—"

"They have no electricity in the city of Péronne?"

"Yes, they have electricity in Péronne."

"Well then, why are you a voice that speaks to me from the darkness that surrounds me?"

"At the castle your head was struck and later you passed out, Loni." Before Loni could respond, another voice interrupted in a loud whisper.

"We don't know the sequence, Douglas," Mickey said. "It may be that she passed out and then hit her head. It was not a witnessed event. It becomes a chicken-or-the-egg scenario."

"I chose the chicken, Mickey. So what?"

"So, we should not make any assumptions. In the absence of the medical evidence, we—"

"I have an assumption for the both of you," groused Suzanne. "I assume you two are boorish and annoying. Period. How's that for an assumption?" Before Mickey and Douglas could further parry, Loni probed the darkness.

"Douglas, who else is there?"

They all watched as Loni pulled herself forward and, with her hand, tried reaching into her darkness.

Then, with a tremor in his voice, Mickey answered his wife. "It's me, Froggie. It's me—Mickey. Suzanne is here too."

"Mickey . . . Mickey. . . ." Loni was quiet for a moment and then she continued, "Why do you call me Froggie, Mickey?"

Mickey choked on his silence. He put his fist to his mouth.

"Suzanne, why does he call me Froggie?"

Suzanne looked hard at Mickey waiting for him to make a move.

"Mickey, is it Froggie that everyone calls me? Do I have an oddly shaped birthmark? Is that it? Oh God, don't tell me I have a frog tattoo."

Mickey's eyes welled up with each passing word from Loni. He turned and stumbled toward the door. Providing what little comfort that she could, Suzanne left with him.

"Mickey? Suzanne?"

"Mickey had to step out, Loni." Douglas's voice was strong and reassuring.

"Oh, sorry. I hope I didn't anger him. Is Suzanne still there?"

"Suzanne went with him. I guess they needed to talk."

"It's odd that Mickey can't explain calling me Froggie, don't you think, Douglas?"

"It may be more about your need to have it explained, Loni."

"Are you saying this is all about my head injury?"

"I would say the two things are connected."

"Why do you suppose Mickey needed to know exactly when my head was injured?"

"It's a physician thing, I guess. His review of the present illness leads him to his diagnosis."

"He's a doctor? I would think with his animal verbiage he might be a veterinarian. Is he my doctor?"

"Yes, he is a doctor."

"Is he my doctor?"

"Yes and no, Loni."

"More yes than no?"

"His name is Dr. Mickey Peronne. Do you have any recollection of that name?"

"Well, it sounds like he has the same name as the city where I was injured. Does he live there? Don't tell me, his family owns the town—"

"No, he doesn't live in Péronne. You may be right though, there may be a connection to his family and the town. In fact, that may be the reason you both were traveling there."

"We were there together? Maybe we are friends, close friends. Is that why he called me Froggie? Is it, Douglas? Is that the reason he called me Froggie? Tell me, please tell me, that I don't have a frog for a tattoo."

"I am not aware of any tattoos, Loni." Douglas smiled. "However, my knowledge in that area is limited. Since I have known you two, he has called you his little frog."

"Oh." She nodded mutely for a moment. "I wish I could remember more,

Douglas. I wish I knew how Mickey arrived at that nickname. I'm sure it was special. Maybe if I could see him, I would remember more."

Having failed to restore Loni to herself under hypnosis, Douglas began to wonder if this hypnotic approach was a very good idea.

Of course it is! What other recourse is there? Traditional medicine had its turn and has stabilized everything medical in Loni's pregnancy. But here she is, thirty-five weeks pregnant and she doesn't even know who she is, or where she is, or that she is even pregnant. Mickey is her husband, and she has no idea who he is.

Douglas began to think of a pain from deep within him. He remembered the friendship and collegiality that he and Loni had shared over many years. His mind then moved on to Mickey. Loni's unwitting stab to Mickey's heart was more than any war wound that the army colonel had ever experienced. Douglas's bruise of an unremembered friendship could in no way compare to the depth of pain in the failure of Mickey's beloved spouse to recognize him.

Douglas tried to regroup.

"Give me a moment, okay, Loni?"

"Of course, Douglas."

He turned away from Loni and began to reassess the situation. Strolling away from Loni's bedside, Douglas slid into the chair once inhabited by Suzanne. He began picking at the stubbles of whiskers on his chin, contemplating just how much spiritual healing he would have to engage in to support the hypnotherapy he was using in this approach. Without bridging the minute fractures in Loni's positivity, he knew that she would not acquire the courage to engage the memory gaps and thus, healing energy could not flow. Douglas understood that spiritual healing had a strong history here in the war-ravaged areas of the Vermandois. In fact, Douglas's metaphysical studies had specifically included the history of the people of northern France. Living during the devastation of two world wars, their spirits had endured so much trauma.

As a population, the people in the area had to learn to embrace the concept of healing energy streams of positivity just to get through the day-to-day desolation. It was the one greatest healing power they had, and it kept their bodies, as well as their minds, well and healthy despite everything they faced. Once he completed the healing of Loni, Douglas knew he would have to address the holistic needs of Mickey, the accidental patient. Mickey's heart was deeply traumatized in a way few could fully understand.

The teachings of his mentor, Bruno Groening, kept spinning in Douglas's head. *People lose their pain by releasing it in the stream of life that reverberates throughout their entire spiritual and physical being.* Bruno taught that first the patient needed to be one with God. *Once this happened, illness had no choice but to retreat and give way to life.*

Douglas looked again at the absence of recognition in the face of his patient. *How can Loni look at me so expressionless? It's like she is looking through me into a world beyond where spiritual healing coexists on a different plane.* He watched as Loni tapped rhythmically at the crucifix suspended from her neck.

She is already one with God. Her heart is basically so pure that all I need to do is to confront that one psychic source of illness within her inhibiting her positivity and then her own spirituality will lead the way to healing and ultimately remembering.

Having reviewed the teachings of his mentor, a hope-revived Douglas drew in another deep breath, stood, and squared his jaw. *It's time to make that connection.* With heightened confidence, he went back to Loni's bedside, and into the fray.

"Loni, I'm back now. Can I ask you some questions?"

"Yes, Douglas."

"I want to take you back to the castle where you became ill. Do you see it? Do you see Péronne Castle?"

"Yes, I see something that looks familiar, a castle, although I can't remember why it feels familiar. The place is very strange, Douglas. The towers—they're are all wrong."

From just outside the door, Mickey and Suzanne heard Loni's voice and returned to the edge of the room. They stood, motionless.

"Why is it very strange, Loni?" Douglas asked.

"It's like I was here before . . . maybe as a child? Yes, that's it. I was here as a child. I was here struggling with those oblong towers."

Douglas shot a glance at Mickey to get confirmation if Loni had been there as a child. Mickey shook his head from side to side and shrugged his shoulders. Nothing in his memory recalled a time when Loni or her family ever visited the city of Péronne or its castle towers.

Douglas's eyes now shifted and focused on Suzanne, whose face grew long and pale. Without a doubt, the blood was draining from her cheeks. Douglas peered at her intently.

What on earth does Suzanne know that is upsetting her?

38

A Hidden Vision

Maternity hospital
Saint-Quentin, Somme River Valley
Vermandois region, France
Current day

Douglas's breathing quickened as he watched Suzanne's arms drop limply by her sides. *She is remembering something significant, something that is taking her where she doesn't want to go.* Douglas nervously studied the stunned expression in Suzanne's face as he saw her thoughts turn inward.

What does Suzanne know that I don't? Did my hypnotherapy management go sour? Could it be that I have taken Loni to a place in time where I have no ability to control her psyche? Look at her unseeing eyes. Have I taken her to a threshold before her current age—somewhere beyond the twilight? He tried reining himself in. *Even a mild temporary loss of absolute control would be okay if I could be sure that when the final leg of hypnotherapy is completed, Loni's psyche would be back.*

However, Douglas had no good feelings about this. Instead, he was on the edge of panic. Right now, it appeared that with bugs in their teeth and their hair on fire, the four of them were in a downward spiral. Douglas tried again to take hold of himself and control the situation. He moved over to Suzanne and Mickey.

"Suzanne, I need to know what you know," Douglas groused. "Tell me something, anything . . . even if it sounds trivial." Douglas watched as Suzanne, now recomposed, cleared her throat. In a glance, Douglas also noted that a muted, but intently listening, Mickey Peronne morphed into a proverbial sponge.

Suzanne's reply began in a slow, emphatic coarse whisper. "Loni's sister, Jillian, has a home at West Point. There is a sketch that she keeps on the wall in the library. It is a castle with towers."

"Yes, I know the sketch," Mickey chimed in with confidence. "It is a striking castle with beautiful round battlements and towers. It was drawn and painted by Loni."

"Okay," Douglas stretched the word. "I did ask for trivial. I'm not sure why any of this matters . . . but, okay." *Why does she always begin at the fringes of understanding?* He opened his eyes wide and raised his eyebrows in anticipation of explanation.

Suzanne ignored him and spoke instead to Mickey. "That sketch wasn't drawn by Loni, Mickey; it was drawn by Jillian. She signed Loni's name to it."

"What? How do you know that? Why would Jillian credit Loni for a sketch drawn and painted by her hand, Suzanne?"

"Hold on, folks," Douglas interjected. "I'm not catching the overall significance here."

"It's hard to explain," Suzanne said, turning to Douglas. "Once at Jillian's house, I was poking fun at how Loni was the true artistic talent when it came to the Meriwether sisters. I used the sketch, the one currently framed, as an example. Evidently, that struck a nerve with Jillian. Anyway, Douglas, Jillian took out her diary and from it produced a sketch of that same castle drawn by Loni with oblong battlements. Odd-shaped towers, if you will."

"So, you are saying that Loni drew a castle with oblong towers which then Jillian chose to hide in her diary. Right?"

"Right. Jillian redrew a similar sketch to replace it but without oblong battlements and signed it with Loni's name. That's the one that resides on the wall in her library today."

"Okay. So what, Suzanne?" Douglas still looked puzzled.

"So, what I am saying is that Loni—as a child—drew a sketch with incredible detailed accuracy of Péronne Castle. A castle that she had never ever visited or seen."

"Maybe she saw it in a picture, photograph, home movie, or on television in a documentary."

"That was my first thought as well. But no. Even if, by chance, Loni did see a likeness of Péronne Castle, how would she have remembered it in such explicit detail to accurately reproduce it in a drawing? No other sketch that she has ever made could ever be mistaken for an outright photograph."

Douglas paused to absorb the depth of what he just heard.

If she's right, then this visit to Péronne *Castle was, in fact, also a psychic revisit for Loni. Somehow, someway, little Loni connected with this castle long before her human foot ever crossed its threshold in France. But, then again, if this wasn't the first time Loni has been to Péronne Castle, why this visit? Why this time?*

Shaking off his worst fears, Douglas looked at Loni, rolled his lips tightly inward, dug in his heels, and ratcheted up his game. Douglas returned to Loni and spoke in a voice neither Suzanne nor Mickey had ever heard.

"Loni, tell me about the castle."

Douglas's voice was strangely musical, but it was still endowed with a fatherly strength. It was rich and kind, yet firm and directing. It made one want to follow it in any manner that the voice so decided. Never had the shear vibration of vocal cords impacted Suzanne and Mickey more than at that moment. Each in their respective minds, they wondered if they too would become inadvertent subjects of hypnosis as well.

"Tell me everything you think important about the castle," Douglas repeated.

After a few moments, Loni slowly responded. "The castle towers are oblong, not round. It is not what I thought it would be."

"What expectations did you have?"

"Castle towers are always tall and round. They are battlements for defense. An oblong tower is strange . . . possibly appropriate, but nonetheless strange."

"Tell me what happened there."

Loni's face had a look of searching, but no spoken word left her.

"What else do you see, Loni?"

Douglas kneeled closer, propping himself on Loni's armrest.

"What else do you see, Loni?"

Loni's lips moved but there was no sound. Douglas looked back to Suzanne.

Suzanne's eyes were locked on Loni, but she spoke to Douglas in a strained whisper. "Jillian told me that Loni's sketch was emotionally distressful for both of them. For some reason, probably artistic pride, Jillian *had* to tell me about the hidden sketch—Loni's sketch."

"Why? Why would she tell you, Suzanne? And why not tell you why the hidden sketch was so distressful?"

"I already told you, Douglas." She broke eye contact with Loni and resumed her usual harsh tone. "I don't know why."

Douglas disengaged from Loni. "Guys, this stop-and-go isn't helpful in hypnosis. Suzanne, spill it. All of it. Now."

Suzanne scowled at his gruff tone. "Jillian and I have known each other since high school. When I commented on her library sketch, she mentioned the hidden drawing and then she abruptly shifted gears. She went from friendly and jovial to dark and gloomy. For some reason at that moment, she felt the need to purge her soul. She took me to her personal vault."

"She has a vault in her house?" both Mickey and Douglas asked simultaneously.

"Not a vault per se. Not in the manner of a bank or bullion reserve. We're not talking about Fort Knox here, guys. You really need to understand something important. Every woman alive has a place in her home where she keeps her personal treasures—yes, a place of secrets. In it every woman keeps her most personal things away from prying eyes and nosey people. In Jillian's special place there is a folded piece of paper—the sketch that her sister made."

"I got it, Suzanne. Get on with it," Douglas prodded. He glanced quickly to Loni who stared off into nothingness.

"There's more. Loni and Jillian once lived at the Presidio in San Francisco when their father was stationed there on military assignment. Jillian and Loni were enrolled at the Saint Joan of Arc School. According to the two sisters, it was a beautiful school. It was filled with art and music and was the absolute one single reason Jillian sought a life of art and creativity."

"I thought we were talking about Loni, Suzanne?"

"Ditto," Mickey parroted as he dropped into a chair at the small table in the room.

Suzanne spoke with marked emphasis, jabbing her finger on the table between her and Mickey. "Loni drew the sketch with oblong towers *at the school* when she was a *child* from her *memory*—a memory that never existed in her lifetime."

"A unique castle with oblong towers drawn from the memory of a child who had never physically been there. . . . That is strange," admitted Douglas. "Maybe that is why Jillian felt the need to hide that sketch. Maybe she was fearful and thought people would question the sanity of her little sister?"

"Possibly."

"What was the inspiration for a child living in California to sketch something she had never seen? And in perfect detail."

"Exactly!"

"You don't know these answers, Suzanne?"

"No, Douglas."

"Jillian never told you why she hid the drawing after Loni made the effort to make such a sketch?"

"I never asked."

"But you have the very source of all the answers—right here—right in front of you. All you have to do is ask the correct questions to the heart and mind of a child."

"You are kidding, right?"

"You can do this, Douglas," urged Mickey.

"Yes, I can do this. But the question is: *Should I?* Mickey, Suzanne, I am quite comfortable opening Loni's mind with hypnosis. I have little fear of taking Loni back in time a few hours, days, weeks, or even a month or so. However, taking Loni back several years—no, several decades—to when she was an elementary school child really gets into the realm of playing with matches . . . in a psychic sense." *If I psychically change a childhood memory, the Loni that we knew may not be the same Loni today.*

"But, Douglas," Mickey began, "Loni checks out physically. The problem is elsewhere, presumably in her psyche. If the root of it has to do with the castle and if the root of the castle is in her childhood, then that's where we must go."

"Agreed," Suzanne chimed in.

"I see your logic," replied Douglas. "I really do. But this can be tricky. We don't even know of Loni's child self has the answers."

"Well, adult Loni doesn't seem to," posed Suzanne.

"Why the trepidation? Why the fear, Douglas?" Mickey asked. "You have a proven record of success in this very area of retrograde hypnosis."

"I know. I know." Douglas held his hands up, then ran them through his hair. "People always remember the achievements made and the great strides forward," he said. Then he mumbled, "They tend to forget the stumbles, trips, and falls on that curvy path to ultimate success and glory."

39

The Battle Begins

Maternity hospital
Saint-Quentin, Somme River Valley
Vermandois region, France
Current day

Douglas shook his head to clear it and then stretched his neck. After a deep breath he spoke with absolute authority to everyone in the hospital room. "It's called *regression* hypnosis. Regressing people backward in time is something I do. If I'm going to do this, let's get something straight. Surgeons do surgery all the time. That doesn't eliminate the fact that what they do is very delicate. I am fortunate that it has almost always gone well. It is not something I ever do as a first choice. There are other options here. Can't we just ask Jillian why all the secrecy? Why she felt it necessary to hide the sketch that Loni made?"

"Yes, we could, Douglas," said Suzanne, thinly masking her annoyance. "However, Jillian is not here and might not be accessible. Anyway, we have the source right here, right now. Jillian, in her best rendition, could only provide an adult's recollection of her own childhood. Additionally, this would be skewed by her own slant of life *now* and how she remembered her life *then*. More important, maybe Jillian doesn't *want* to tell us why. She never offered the information to me in the past. Even under hypnosis, Jillian might remain blocked in her cover-up. It is absolutely, positively better for us to take the plunge now, Douglas. On top of that, we already know that Loni responds well to hypnotism."

"That is debatable," said Douglas. "As you have seen, I have had no success in bringing her out of her amnesia. She doesn't even recall the visit to the castle hours ago." Douglas glanced at Mickey who had clammed up and sat incessantly picking at the bandage on his hand. *There are no assurances I can give this tortured soul.*

"Delve now!" urged Suzanne. "Delve into the thoughts Loni had as a child—a child who drew a castle with oblong towers that was so incredible her sister needed to hide it for all time."

171

"Till now, Suzanne. Till now."

"Yes, Douglas."

Douglas pushed his two fists together until they audibly cracked. He looked back at Loni then down at his shoes.

"Douglas, I may have seen you in many ways," said Suzanne, "but never as a coward."

"So *now* you're calling me a coward?"

Suzanne put her hands on her hips. "No, let me clarify. I'm calling you a highly trained, skillfully proven, credentialed metaphysician coward."

Suzanne leaned into Douglas in a way that made Mickey understand the strain existing between the former couple. He leaned back in his chair to avoid the inevitable crossfire. He fixed his eyes on his dear Loni.

"I don't want to do this, Suzanne. We might lose today's version of Loni. It's dangerous territory."

"Yes, I see that. Cowards fear danger."

"I really don't want to do this. There are no guarantees."

"Noted."

"I'm going to end up doing this, aren't I?" Douglas looked to Mickey for a cue.

"Yes, Douglas," Suzanne snapped. "You must. You know you do. None of us can do what you do. You must be okay with that. Are you?"

"No."

"Thank you, Douglas. I'd just like to say that you humble me with your skill, your patience, your—"

"Shove it, Suzanne. I have been the mirrored reflection of your career all our previously married life. I've grown accustomed to being ignored in your presence. When you were heralded as the next Jesus Christ of medicine, I gladly learned to accept my role as the anti-Christ. Thank you for your slick words but I'll do this for Loni. It will never be about me or cowardice!"

"Whoa there, and they call *me* the Viking Witch." Suzanne rolled her eyes as her tone went from complimentary to icy. "Anyway, I always thought we had more good times than bad."

"You always did."

"What's that supposed to mean?"

"Why don't we just stay the course with Loni."

"You never could handle a compliment, Douglas."

"Maybe it's because they came so few and far between."

"The course—stay the course, remember?"

"Right . . . for Loni, I'll stay the course." He turned away from the table.

"Good. That'll be more than you ever did in any of the years we were married," hissed Suzanne.

40

Losing Sense

Auger residence
Oger, France
Current day

"*The future belongs to those who can hear it, one decibel at a time.*
Standing on the back porch of the Grande Madame's house, Monty Meriwether edged closer to his wife, Monique. *Monique needs to know about my hearing problem, and she needs to know it now.* Monty pulled Monique close, gently tickling her and reveling in what sounds he could still enjoy of her laughter. He remembered this to be one of her characteristics which was most endearing at their first meeting.

How am I going to break the news to Monique that I might never hear the voices of our grandchildren in the years of life I have remaining? I can hardly stand the thought.

Hearing loss was an occupational hazard for a retired general having spent most of his professional army life in and around guns, tanks, and cannons. Now, the medical experts all agreed that he was suffering from a progressive tinnitus that would eventually leave him without functional hearing.

Well, maybe the time isn't right, but at least the acoustics in this relatively quiet place are perfectly suited to give some bad news about hearing deficiencies.

He was glad he had Monique at the back of the house. The noise from the house was distant, at least for him. He had to take this opportunity to tell her what the doctors were saying about him. One thing he learned from all his years of army service was that bad news never gets better over time. After a deep inhalation, Monty tapped gently on his wife's forearm.

"You know, Monique, if we play our cards right, we two might be a part of the study that EZ is revving up."

"Are you talking about the study involving sensory-impaired people?"

"That's the one."

"I thought it just dealt with blind people."

"No, it studies both blind and deaf people. At least that was my understanding of it as it was explained to me."

"I don't think I'm quite following you, Monty. Why should we be a part of EZ's study?"

"I'm saying that it might be time for me to find a new job."

"Monty, don't be a fool. You're retired, for God's sake. What craziness have you been listening to lately?"

"That's my whole point; I have trouble listening to any craziness these days. Monique, I am losing the ability to hear . . . and to listen. . . ."

"Says who? Doctors?"

"Yes, hearing specialists and ear physicians."

"Remember what Voltaire said about physicians?"

"No, what did he say?"

"'Doctors are men who prescribe that of which they know little, to cure diseases of which they know less, in human beings of whom they know nothing.'"

"Okay. That still doesn't change the fact that the world is filled with sounds. Many of which I am losing the ability to hear." Monty blinked back the moisture starting to accumulate in his eyes. Tugging on his ear, he continued. "Anyway, Monique, if we—*if I* become part of the study—maybe I can pick up some tools which will let a deaf man communicate."

"The last time you had hearing concerns, Monty, an earwax flushing fixed it." Monique pursed her lips. "I guess that was in the last millennium. Time surely flies. Doesn't it?" Her voice softened. "What exactly is this study?"

"Well, dear, it appears that quite some time ago, EZ, Mickey, and Loni began working on a project design which could create a new field in osteopathic medicine. They called these folks osteopathic medical assistants. With the help of Loni's colleagues at Nova University, a new study format will be developed to train these hearing- and vision-impaired folks to perform in a technical capacity with manual aspects of therapeutic treatments."

"Isn't that what Loni studied when she was working on her special education doctorate there at Nova?"

"It started in that direction but her passion and interest in autism took her into developing children's books instead. So, as a result, she never followed up beyond the curriculum design, but a lot of groundwork was already done. It is interesting how the reboot came about.

"One night," Monty continued, "Loni mentioned to both Jillian and EZ how much she wished she could have fleshed out this project to completion. Mickey himself had once presented the concept as a major paper for his family practice residency. Thus, Mickey had already done the outline, Loni had designed the academic curriculum, and after this discussion with Jillian and EZ, Loni contacted the bigwigs at Nova University. EZ found the funding, but he needed a full-time academic researcher."

"Did he find one?"

"Yes, he did. He found Dr. Charlotte Benjamin, a volcanologist, who is a West Point visiting professor of chemistry. This volcano lady—she goes by Charlie—had worked for four years writing research requests in the late nineties for an internationally acclaimed geologist called Walker. Then, once EZ had a solid researcher as a ringer and a bag full of research money just waiting to be spent, the idea was ready to become a marriage of three, potentially four, great minds."

"So, what is the study?"

"A hearing- or vision-impaired individual can be taught how to do osteopathic manual medicine. Basically, it's based on the idea that people who are worse in one sense, like sight or hearing, will be able to perform better with the remaining senses they do have, such as touch. Makes sense?"

"I see."

"So, in other words, the abilities of bad seers and bad hearers are switched over to the fingertips of these blind and deaf people. I'm not blind—at least not yet. However, my bad hearing might be used to treat and maybe teach deaf people osteopathic medical techniques."

"But you know nothing about medicine or communicating with deaf people."

"Exactly, neither does this volcanologist, Charlotte—or Charlie, as she goes by. Like her, I'll bring something unique to the research experiment."

"But I don't understand how just because you have eyes and hands—presto chango—suddenly you can be a medical assistant. It sounds too easy."

"For me to be part of the study, they will have to teach me some basic techniques and some common skills so I can work with hearing and non-hearing people alike. I have a leg up from all the rest of the deaf people in that I have a lifetime of having lived in the hearing world. That means I can serve as the bridge between the deaf and the hearing population."

"How does any of this improve your hearing?"

"It doesn't. That is the downside."

"I don't understand. You want to learn ear medicine along with sign language so that you can be part of an experiment that won't even help your failing hearing. I don't get it, Monty."

"I was just thinking I could help the kids with their study and get a leg up on communicating as a deaf person—which I will be soon. Kill two birds with one stone. Anyway, it might work." Monty shrugged.

"Have any similar studies worked?"

"I don't know. Mickey did say that it had long been supposed that blind and deaf students had other abilities in areas not affected by their loss. This is where Loni comes in."

"How so?"

"Being an expert in communication disorders and autism, Loni has learned not only to think outside of the box, but also to work outside of it as well. Very early on she saw how savants and autistic people had lost abilities in one sense, and yet they could do marvelous things through other senses."

"You're not a savant, Monty."

"No, but there's always hope."

"Hope only gets the journey discussed, Monty. Money makes it so."

41

Honors and Horns

Auger residence
Oger, France
Current day

"You're right, Monique. You are spot-on," Monty nodded affirmatively. "The study needs to be much more than a funding kiss and a promise." Monty smiled with confidence and continued. "With barrels full of research money from EZ, the idea which started with Mickey and Loni can now lead to an experiment funded by EZ and performed by Charlie."

"I agree, Monty. For you, it is a way you can learn to continue to communicate with our future grandchildren once your hearing is completely gone. But no matter if it is you or others, I see that the project will be very good for the patient."

"Yes! People who come to doctors get a ten-minute patient visit and then can be turned over to a paraprofessional like the future me. Despite my hearing impairment, I too can become a trained healer. Here." He handed Monique a folded paper from his pocket. "Read EZ's funding proposal for yourself."

Monique looked at the paper and spoke with a sense of growing pride. "Monty, our kid's idea could provide careers for people who never could get a job because their eyes or ears didn't work. I don't know this Dr. Benjamin, but the title of the experiment alone sounds great: *Osteopathic Medical Assistants: A study of increased diagnostic capability of manual medicine practitioners by capturing profound touch sensitivity of sight- and hearing-challenged individuals by Dr. Charlotte Ives Benjamin, Army Physician Colonel Dr. Michael Philip Peronne, Civilian Educationist Dr. Loni Leigh Meriwether Peronne, and Army Chemist Colonel Dr. Emerson Doyle Zimmerman.*' It could get even better, you know."

"Better?"

"Yes. EZ will probably get a second doctoral degree out of it."

"And . . .?"

"Well, he would become Dr. Dr. Zimmerman."

Monty raised an eyebrow at his wife. "In the European system he would be called Dr. Dr. Zimmerman, but in the United States, he would just be called Dr. Zimmerman. Why would that be better?"

"Even if he wasn't addressed as Doctor Doctor, he would still be a doctor doctor."

"I think we've covered this already, haven't we?"

"You're not following me."

"Correct, I am *not* following you. Why is this better?"

"Because, my dear soon-to-be-stone-deaf husband, in both systems, Doctor Doctor Emerson Zimmerman would owe you for his success. That being the case, he could—and I know that he would—invest some of that newfound money into the repair and restoration of the hearing of one Monty Meriwether."

"That's quite a leap," Monty said.

"Yes, it is. Rather well done, don't you think?"

"Sure. But, Monique, even if they didn't divert a penny toward my worsening hearing, I still couldn't be prouder of them. They have accomplished so much already."

Monique folded the paper up, put it in her husband's chest pocket, and tapped it lovingly. "Which leads to yet another problem, Monty."

"Problem?"

"Yes, what does one give to children who have done so much in their lives?"

"I don't think they are doing any of this to get something in return, Monique."

"That's not what I meant. It's not about what the world can give them. It's about what we can give to them to show how much we love and appreciate them as people, professionals, and future parents. It took Jillian and EZ so long to get pregnant—and with Loni nearly due with her babies, I don't want Jillian to feel overshadowed."

"Can I tell you what I was thinking while I was standing here on your mother's back porch alone?"

"Staring at the stone statues against the vine canopy doesn't count." She paused and raised an eyebrow at Monty. "Do you think?"

"Yes, I do. These beautiful statues are spectacular. In the moonlight, I really thought they were alive at first."

"Well, you aren't the only one. That's what they're talking about in the house. My brothers said that they often tiptoed on the porch as children, not wanting to scare away the deer."

"Deer in the vineyards can't be a good thing."

"No, Monty, they are a nuisance. Even as children we knew this. The elders used to point out the neck chain and the uni-horned forehead on the statues. They chided us about our belief in mythical beasts. Our minds knew they weren't alive, but our hearts wanted them to be."

"That was my exact feeling, Monique. In a whirlwind of fascination, it sweeps me away. Today's world sorely lacks these gifted artists. Doesn't it?"

"I heard that specific question only moments ago, inside the house."

"What was the answer?"

"Florence."

"Italy?"

"Yes, Florence, Italy."

"No surprise. It was the home of so many artistic heavyweights—Botticelli, Michelangelo, da Vinci, Donatello, Ghiberti, Raphael." Monty recalled his Italian history from the three years he spent in duty assignments in Italy.

"Not to mention Cavalli, Coveri, Ferragamo, and Gucci." Monique had a better grasp on Italy's modern fashion industry.

"I suppose fashion is art that we wear."

"Yes, and I prefer art to be on me more than on my walls, Monty."

"Did your family say where in Florence the statues were sculpted?"

"Possibly. To be honest, Monty, I just caught gubbins."

"Well then, what bits and pieces did you catch?"

"Except for Master Gilberto Fermi, most of the artists were not Florentine, but instead were from nearby towns like Prato and Fiesole. But no matter . . . whether they were city talent or not, they used Carrara marble."

"Well sure. Why not? That is the finest marble in the world. In Florence, did they see mythical creatures sculpted as well?"

"By mythical, you are asking if they saw statues of winged horses like Pegasus?"

"Yes, and—"

"—classic shapes of sculpted unicorns?"

"Yes, that is what I wanted to know."

"They didn't say but I could ask."

"I would like that very much."

"I have an idea, Monty."

"I'll bet I have the same idea."

"It *has* been a long time since I was in Florence."

"I think that a road trip is well in order, then. We could leave at first light."

"Great! That's settled. Now, Monty, please say yes."

"Ask your question first."

"Not until you say yes."

"No, Monique, every time I say yes it convinces me I should have said no."

"So that is your answer?" she pouted.

"Yes, Monique. To the question I have not heard, the answer is already no. So, what is the question?"

"Monty, do we have to leave so early?" Monique smiled roguishly.

"I don't believe this. You've done it to me again. Okay, tell you what. We will leave later and break the trip up over a few days. But remember, our main mission was to be here for Mickey and Loni and to help at home after the birth of the twins."

"You are an incredibly wise man, Monty."

"Yes, I am a veritable owl."

"You are."

"So, Monique, we can stay here and listen to Flemish and French, or we can go where the language changes from French to Italian."

Monique smiled, but then her face shifted. Monty could see her maternal radar kick in. "What if Mickey calls, and we are needed here but we are so far away?"

Monty squeezed her forearm firmly but gently to let her know that such a thought never escaped him. He spoke reassuringly. "Then we stop where we are and return quickly. If it means we overnight train or fly back, so be it."

"Do we need to call Mickey to tell him we are not in Oger?"

"I say no, Monique. I say let them enjoy their vacation. They don't need to worry about what we are doing and where we are doing it."

"Sounds like they are the parents and we have become the kids."

Hearing this, Monty unsheathed an impish grin. "Why not? They will be parents soon enough. This will be good practice for them."

"And for us, Monty?"

"We'll consider it our duty to provide a parent-in-training mission for them."

"Spoken like a true general. What about EZ and Jillian? Should we be telling them that we are looking to buy them life-sized sculptures from Florence?"

"I am sure Jillian would have no problem with that. In fact, if I remember correctly, she has already created a pair of unicorns which she was planning to give to Loni as a baby gift. The *Blue Horned Unicorn* and the *Brown Horned Unicorn*?"

"I never really got that." Monique shook her head slightly.

Mesmerized by the shimmering moonlight on Monique's face, Monty's eyes drifted out of focus.

"Monty."

"What?"

"Are you listening?"

"Of course, dear."

"I said, I never got that."

"Got what?"

"The whole colored-horn thing, Monty." Monique put a hand on her hip and shifted her weight dramatically. "Is it a mythical thing or an art thing?"

"Come on, Monique." Monty pinched the bridge of his nose and refocused. "You know it's most likely a Jillian-being-an-artist thing. She has a million reasons for doing what she does when she does it. God forbid you should ask her the why and wherefore about it though."

"You never asked?"

"I just guessed."

"Is that father's intuition?"

"Maybe. Anyway, Jillian would well appreciate two full-sized mythological horse statues, if we could find them."

"What about EZ? He might not appreciate them. Anyway, he certainly has a right to know that the total baggage weight of his household goods just doubled, compliments of his in-laws and Carrara marble art."

"He's a colonel, Monique. He can afford it."

"True. I guess the worst-case scenario would be that they couldn't ship them and then we would have to keep them at our home."

"Honey, the next shipment for EZ is the same for every department head at West Point. He stays in place till retirement. Then when he announces it, he pins on brigadier general for one day and retires as a one-star general. His household goods get shipped to his home of record with general officer allowances."

"Monty, do you think EZ has intent to go back to Ohio?"

"I really doubt that since his parents are both dead."

"I guess that makes him our son, Monty. I guess he will have to claim home as Marlboro, New York."

"But we have two married daughters. Therefore, we have inherited two sons, albeit one son is shared."

"Shared?"

"Mickey still has Franklin and Elfie. It's a blessing that he works so hard at being our son as well."

"And soon we will have spread the nest to include two sets of twins."

"Yes, two sets of twins."

"Well, I guess we better get on with being big kids ourselves since in the very near future we are not going to have that opportunity anymore, Monty."

"That's right. We must go back to being parents again. Parents of parents. That's a whole new role."

"And for the first time in our lives—grandparents."

"I hear you, Monique. For now, I hear you."

42

Losing Michael

Maternity hospital
Saint-Quentin, Somme River Valley
Vermandois region, France
Current day

Douglas really didn't want to take this path with Loni, but what Suzanne said was absolutely correct: There was no one better postured than he to move this psychic therapy to the next phase of hypnotherapy, reaching deeply into Loni's childhood. Nonetheless, a rush of nausea was surging within Douglas as he crouched, almost nose to nose, with his hypnotized patient. It had been thirty full minutes and Loni remained in an unanticipated prolonged hypnotic silence. *Psychic break? Psychic shutdown. Neither bodes well for Loni. Have things gone belly-up already? God, I hope not.*

"Loni, can you still see the castle with oblong towers?"

With his fingernails, Douglas vigorously clawed at the hairs at his temples. He could feel the sweat trickling down his neck. He glanced over at Mickey who truly looked like death warmed over.

"Loni, can you see anything?"

Loni's face was unmoving.

"Loni, can you hear me?"

Silence bounced off all four walls. Douglas's gut heaved.

"Loni—"

Suddenly and quite unexpectedly, Douglas gagged and lurched from his kneeling position. He blew by a surprised Mickey and Suzanne and planted himself face first in a hallway trash bin. The rising wave of deep stomach contractions finally gave way to a profound vomiting. His brain reeled. His arms encircled the top of the bin. He rested his head on one arm and thought, *I've done it now. I pushed the envelope too far. I have become the worst version of myself. My arrogance and overconfidence have doomed her.* He spit into the bin once more then stood up and sucked in a deep breath. He tried to steady himself and organize his thoughts. *With her mind separated from her body, the chances of sustaining the pregnancy drop to zero. After all, if Loni can't acknowledge herself, then the childbirth that follows belongs to someone else entirely. Forget the possibility of taking Loni to her childhood. If her mind totally disconnects from her body, then her will to live might hit baseline as well.*

The stench of acidy, acrid globules of green bile mixed with trash wafted up to Douglas.

"Wait a minute, that's it!" he shouted, automatically leaning over the bin. Douglas accidentally caught another full-face whiff of his own vomit and dry heaved. His eyes watered.

"Gads, I hope not," said Suzanne handing him a dripping wet cloth.

"Loni can't see it, Suzanne."

"Thank God. It's not a very pleasant sight from here either."

"Not the trash bin, Suzanne. Loni cannot see the castle. That's the toad in the road." He leaned against the hallway wall and mopped his face.

"Actually, I think what's in the trash can looks more like what was *left* of the toad in the road." Suzanne dry heaved herself then glared at Douglas in disgust.

Unable to be distracted in the new revelation, Douglas eagerly embraced hope where a moment before there was none. "Honestly, I've got this figured." Douglas's bowl of newfound confidence was topped with Suzanne's icy disdain.

"Are you just now figuring this out? If that's true, Douglas, then we are truly in a bad way." Suzanne's sarcasm was thick, but Douglas ignored her and thrust the lumpy, chunk-covered cloth into Suzanne's hands. He strode confidently back into the room, wiping the residual moisture from his face using the back of his hand.

"We might not have to regress her, Mickey." Douglas sat down. "Loni, can you hear me?"

Loni remained unchanged. Douglas looked at Suzanne and Mickey, then gave a nodding wink.

"Loni, I know you can't see the castle, but I know you can smell it. It's strong. It fills the air. What is that smell?"

All watched with apprehension as Loni's nose dilated and contracted.

"Loni, what is it that you can smell?" Douglas's heart lifted as Loni's lips began to move slowly. Soon a rumble deep inside of her bubbled her thoughts up to the surface.

"I . . . I . . . can smell a combination of dank water . . . with a stale bouquet of something like dying flowers." Douglas pumped his fist hard, feeling glad that he had recalled that the memory of smell far exceeds the memory trace of what is seen. He vividly felt joy and relief at the same time—so much so that he also gave way to another dry heave. There was no time for back-patting. He now had Loni back, and he needed to move forward in her psyche.

"Can you see a castle in the direction of the fragrance?"

"Yes, I see a castle."

"Can you tell me what happened to you there?"

"I try and try to remember, Douglas, but my mind doesn't connect with any familiar memories. What is wrong with me?"

"The mind is a funny thing, Loni. When it feels pain or fear it goes into a protective mode. Unacceptable things that we see and easily recall are taken away in the name of self-preservation."

"Do you know what happened to me there?"

"I know what people who were there say. What I need though, is everything from your point of view."

"But I can't remember. Maybe it would be easier if you just tell me what transpired, and that will help me to remember."

"It doesn't work like that."

"I knew you were going to say that." Hopelessness was etched in Loni's voice. "Where do we go from here?"

"Loni, I'm going to let you rest for a moment. When I tap twice on your arm, you will fall into a restful sleep. When I tap you twice again, you and I will talk again." Douglas sighed deeply. "Rest now." Douglas tapped Loni twice. Loni eased into a relaxed mode as Douglas cupped his mouth and nose in his hands. He was crestfallen that the olfactory approach didn't work completely. *Still, it revived her. . . .* He shuddered to think that he was standing at the beginning of a road with no visible end point.

Douglas looked to Mickey. "Maybe we do have to take her back to her early childhood memories after all." Mickey gave a somber nod.

Douglas knew that in the business of managing the human psyche, this next step was like Russian roulette. Nevertheless, suppressing another rising dry heave, he placed a metaphorical bullet in one of the empty chambers of the revolving cylinder. Douglas reached over and tapped Loni twice.

"Loni, can you hear me?"

"Yes, Douglas."

"Loni, I'm going to snap my fingers, and you are going to wake up." Once Loni's eyes had cleared, Douglas squared off with her.

"Loni, I would like to take you back to your childhood. I'd like to take you back to when you were eight years old or less."

"Excuse me?" Loni gripped the bedsheets with her hands.

"Loni, please. We believe that the answers to your confusing memories might be tied in with some childhood experiences."

"I don't know. What if you can't bring me back, Douglas?"

As Loni spoke these words, Mickey's gut sheepshanked into a tight knot. Though he had encouraged this next step, he was still uneasy about it. He said nothing. *I must trust Douglas. Douglas is the answer. But then again, what exactly is the question to be answered now? And what if the answer isn't in the past?* His thoughts were halted by Douglas's slow and careful explanation to Loni.

"Well, Loni, it goes kind of like this. Time and memory lie in a continuum. They wrap around us like a coat sleeve around an arm. The arm is the present moment—right now, here in this place. Whereas normally an arm does touch the inside of a coat sleeve, in this case—with time and memory—it doesn't ... until we make it happen purposely by making contact here at the wrist." Douglas placed his finger on Loni's wrist. "Then, we reach to the sleeve and slide along its length, moving back in time and memory." He traced his finger up her arm. "So, in order to move ahead in understanding what happened to you, we must consider stepping backward in time."

"I don't like it." Loni frowned. "But I also don't like the situation now. If there is a possibility of change, we should do it. One more thing, Douglas."

"What's that?" Douglas closed the cylinder to the imaginary revolver in his mind and gave it a hard spin.

"If I don't make it back to this place and time, please have those who knew me remember me as I was."

"I promise to do my best."

Douglas adjusted his posture, cracked the knuckles in each hand, and with two taps on Loni's arm, initiated a hypnotic regression back to a time before Loni knew anyone in the French hospital room.

"Loni," said Douglas softly, "you are a child living at home with your parents. Your sister, Jillian, and you are going to an elementary school named—"

"—Saint Joan of Arc School. I remember. I remember." Shifting herself to the side of the bed, Loni began curling and uncurling her hair with her fingers and swinging her legs as she spoke.

Seeing this girlish change in Loni's outward behavior, Mickey and Suzanne inched forward.

Douglas remained focused from this distraction and continued the prodding. "Go on. Tell me what you are doing today."

"I'm in art class. We are studying the saints. We all got a saint to study. We are going to draw and paint different things about their lives. I was given Saint Michael."

"Excellent, Loni. Saint Michael, a warrior saint, is a very fine saint to have."

"Wait a minute. Something is happening."

For the first time since the hypnotism began, Mickey and Suzanne stood and crowded up against Douglas's shoulders. The center of the room became very tight, almost suffocating. Douglas watched as the smoothness in Loni's forehead became deeply furrowed.

"What, Loni? What's happening?"

"I am being told that I am getting a different saint." Loni picked at her eyebrows. "It is Jillian. Why is she doing it?" Loni's voice began echoing the tone and pitch of a whining eight-year-old child about to cry.

"What did Jillian do?"

"She just switched saints with me, Douglas. She says that Saint Michael is hers and that I must get another saint. I don't want another saint. I was given Michael. He's mine. I want Michael." Loni covered her face with her hands and became silent.

Burying his face tightly in his hands, Mickey's eyes streamed.

43

Before the Beginning

Maternity hospital

Saint-Quentin, Somme River Valley

Vermandois region, France

Current day

"Of course, Chaplain. Whether he's called Michael or Mickey, I take him forever." That's what she said on that cool October day twenty years ago, Mickey thought. He spun his wedding ring around on his finger nervously and swallowed the rising lump in his throat.

"What happened to Saint Michael, Loni?" Douglas asked as he gently brought Loni's hands away from her face and back down to her lap.

"He's gone. He's not mine anymore. I never got him back. Jillian never gave him back," she said.

Noting the shift in tense, Douglas matched it, "What did you do?"

"Nothing," Loni frowned. "I had to take her saint, Saint Joan of Arc."

"Is that so bad?"

"Yes, it is. I got an F on my sketch. That wouldn't have happened if I had Saint Michael." Loni's hands became fists.

"The teacher gave you an F for your artwork?"

"Yes, she did."

"Why, Loni? Why did you get an F for your artwork?"

"Teacher said I was angry and just being rude, and that I was drawing and painting the castle badly on purpose. She told me that nowhere in the world did such a funny-looking castle and towers exist and that unless I changed it, I would get the worst grade she could give me."

"Did you try and change it?"

"No, I had to draw it like Sibylle told me." Loni relaxed her fists, folding her hands on her lap.

"Sibylle? Who is Sibylle? Is she one of your classmates?"

"No, Douglas."

"Tell me about Sibylle, Loni."

"I don't think I can."

"Is she an imaginary friend?"

"No, she is real. She is like you—a voice inside me."

"Can I talk to her?"

"I don't know."

"Loni, I am going to tap your arm twice and let you sleep now. I'll be back. When I come back, I will have found a way to talk to Sibylle." With a double tap of Douglas's hand, Loni's body ceased all its girlish mannerisms of hair curling and leg swinging. Douglas eased her back in her previous posture with Loni sitting against the elevated head of the bed. Watching Douglas make final adjustments to Loni's pillows, Mickey and Suzanne remained speechless. Douglas turned and engaged Mickey first.

"I need to talk to this Sibylle. If she's connected with the sketch and the sketch plus the episode at the castle triggered this amnesia, then maybe she can tell us what we're looking for. I am not sure exactly how to do this except to regress further back in time until I connect with her."

Douglas peered at a dour-faced Mickey whose lip movements brought forth no intelligible word.

"Mickey, I need to know if it's okay to take Loni further back in time."

Mickey combed his good hand over his scalp and turned away. He pivoted back to Douglas, but words did not spring forth from his pursed lips. He stared at his hands and then clenched his unbroken left hand into a fist.

"Mickey, you were the one encouraging regression therapy—"

"I know. I know. But don't think any of this is *okay*, Douglas!" Mickey snapped. "I don't like traipsing around in Loni's psyche like it is a laboratory. At first, she's a woman. Then she's a little girl. Mix a little of this from this bench with a pinch of that from that bench. When it's all over, we may have created something that can never be Loni again!" Mickey stretched out the fingers of his left hand and sighed deeply.

"Understood, Mickey. We stop here."

"I didn't say that. Did I?" Mickey stared at the sleeping woman and proceeded with a voice of forced calm. "What we have now is not Loni—even before you regressed her. This is a whisper of the person I married. I don't *want* to go on, but I am smart enough to know that if we don't do it, Loni will be what she is now—an eight-year-old or an amnesiac—forever." He looked back at Douglas, "It's not *okay* to go back further in time but what choice is there? I caution you, Douglas, if things go awry, I will hold you personally responsible for it."

Douglas knew Mickey was being unfair. There was no way to be sure things wouldn't go sideways. *Even if they do and Loni becomes erased psychically, I have little control over it.* But as Douglas looked into the eyes of Mickey, a husband who was caught in a huge dilemma, Douglas understood. Nevertheless, in his mind's eye, he placed the revolver to his temple and put his finger firmly on the trigger.

"All right then, Mickey. Fingers in your ears. This is where the trigger squeezing begins."

"What?"

"Nothing, just triggering the next step." No sooner than those words left his mouth, Douglas turned to Loni and engaged the hypnosis that would take him to the time in Loni's life where reality and fantasy walked hand in hand.

"Loni," said Douglas, "I want to speak with Sibylle."

Loni shifted but remained silent.

"Loni, I'm taking you deeper into your past. Can you please let me speak to Sibylle?"

Loni's motionlessness began to drive daggers into the hearts of the three physicians.

"Loni, let's go back further and further until Sibylle is the only voice I hear."

Suzanne's hand grabbed Douglas's shoulder but was shrugged off immediately. Douglas pressed on.

"Loni, I want to—"

A husky feminine voice cut off Douglas before he could articulate another syllable. "Loni?" Loni's hands grasped the later sides of her pregnant belly. "Why do you call me by that name?"

"Who is this? Identify yourself."

"This is Sibylle. You called to me. Who are you?"

"I am Douglas Coletrane. I was speaking to Loni. She tells me about a voice named Sibylle. Are you Loni's voice?"

"I am my own voice. I am Sibylle." Loni gathered the sheets over her belly.

"What can you tell me about your friendship with Loni? Do you go to school at Joan of Arc?"

"I don't know that school or this person Joan. I schooled in Paris with my cousin."

"Would that be Paris, France?"

"Is there another one?"

Douglas arched backward at the poke in the face. *Is this wanton sauciness or an absence of world geography?*

Before he could regroup, the voice speaking through Loni continued. "My family and I came to Paris from Venice. Christine's father, the king's chief physician, helped us get there."

Hearing the name *Christine*, Suzanne sucked in an involuntary, and quite audible, gasp which cleared the room of all the settled dust. Having only experienced a one-sided discussion with a Christine hologram of sorts, she couldn't wrap her mind around the fact that they had arrived, conversationally, with one degree of separation from her life-long idol.

"My Jesus!" Suzanne said. "Christine de Pizan? Is her father the doctor named Thomas?"

"Yes, it is," said Sibylle as Loni scanned the room "Do you know Dr. Pizan and Christine?"

"I most certainly do!" Suzanne pushed ahead of the men and squared herself in front of the hypnotized Loni.

"Suzanne, I—" Receiving icy darts from Suzanne's eyes, Douglas's words froze in his throat.

"I must tell Christine and Dr. Pizan," said Loni as Sibylle locked her gaze. "What is your name?"

"Suzanne. Suzanne Coletrane. But Sibylle, they won't know me." Suzanne leaned forward. "Can you help me answer a question? Do you have time?" Suzanne demonstrated that females of all time periods had a social lubricant that allowed them, even as strangers, to converse as long-lost friends.

"Not really. I need to go." Sibylle made no movement to turn away.

"It won't delay you," said Suzanne as she touched Loni's arm. "It's a quick question. I promise."

Sibylle hesitated, but then said, "All right, if it is a quick question."

"What year is it, Sibylle?"

"I thought you had a serious question, Suzanne."

"I am serious, Sibylle. What year is it?" said Suzanne, as Loni fidgeted annoyingly.

"It is the year of our Lord 1375."

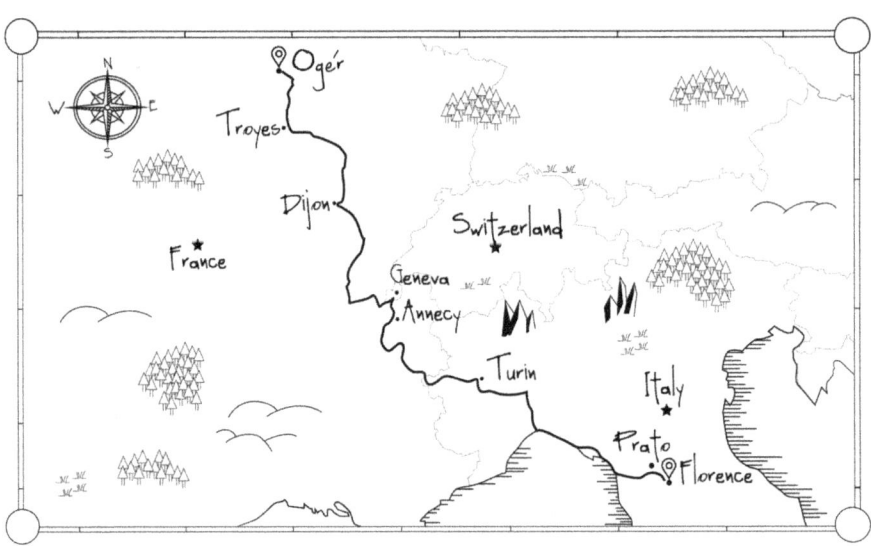

Oger, France to Florence, Italy

44

Path to Unicorns

Grand Est region
France
Current day

Monty and Monique were stimming off the strong, French-brewed coffee that Grande Madame had prepared them before their southward departure. Monty had taken the first driving shift, and over the sound of their humming engine, they recapped the events of the last twenty-four hours. The pair reveled in the good news regarding Jillian's pregnancy, the potentiality of participating in a meaningful research project, and the thrill of visiting Florence, albeit for purpose rather than leisure. At this point, life couldn't be better. However, as always, there were two sides to every proverbial coin. Despite the rising surge of joy, a steady dose of remorse was slowly settling in. Monique wondered about the timing in taking this unexpected shopping trip to Florence to buy a gift for the expected parents.

"Should we have waited a couple days before leaving the family in Oger?" Monique twisted her lips. "There were family members wanting to see us but unable to do so. They would have had to cease work at the vineyards to come visit."

"Probably so, but you said that your artisan sister's recommended artisan, Master Gilberto Fermi, could be inaccessible if we piddled around in the vineyards," said Monty, gripping the steering wheel firmly.

"Yes, that is what Louise said, and the family did toss his name about." Monique's eyes went up and left as she recalled. "If Master Fermi is alive and still in business, Louise said he would be the best choice, as he is a profoundly accomplished sculptor in fantasy sculpting."

"But darling, couldn't we have called Master Gilberto?"

"No, Monty, these things need to be done in person."

"Fine, but with these sudden change in our plans, it's quite possible that we offended some of your folks."

After a brief pause for consideration, Monique responded. "Mother was certainly expecting us to spend the better part of ten days with them in Oger. The family hasn't really seen us since we retired from Europe seven years ago."

"That's not entirely true. Since the kids got assigned to Heidelberg in 2007, we have been in and out of Europe on visitation."

"Honey, visiting the kids in Heidelberg, Germany, is different from visiting my family in and around Paris."

"Are you saying we didn't visit your family?"

"No, it's just that when we stay with the French side of the family, you tend to be a lot stricter with the three-day rule . . . or in this case, the three-hour rule. When we are with Loni and Mickey, you seem to have a sudden loss of time limit."

"The three-day rule is meant for the in-laws, not for the children."

"Honey," she put her hand on his leg, "when we stay with Mickey and Loni in their home, we *are* the in-laws. Although you see Mickey as your son, he isn't."

"Well, it's a good thing they don't have a three-day rule, isn't it?" Monty laughed thinking he would be joined. He wasn't. He cleared his throat and resumed his defense. "It wasn't that we weren't ever planning to stay for an extended period with your family. It was those garden statues that were to blame. Not a member of your family can argue that those garden beasts aren't spectacular. The workmanship on the Carrara marble is unbelievable. It is almost as if the animals are about to move at any second."

"Was it that or was it just that Monty Meriwether needed a solid excuse to leave his French in-laws early? *Very early.*" Monique removed her sunglasses to clean them.

"Objection! Counsel is hitting below the belt."

"Really, Monty, I know that you have never mastered the French tongue. Can you see how not being able to be a part of any conversation automatically excludes you? Even though you are there, you aren't."

"I guess you are right, Monique. The issue behind the issue is that I really should have learned French—a long time ago. It is not my fault that the world spoils Americans by speaking English every time we appear on foreign soil. Further, in my military position, I was always blessed with a competent translator." He paused and glanced to his wife. "I must say that in my own defense, I chose to marry the most beautiful French translator of all!"

"I seem to recall that Infantry Second Lieutenant Meriwether, whom I met at my dressing room after the theater play in Trier, did not need a translator to get his message across." Monique smiled as she rubbed her eyes.

"Your English was wonderful."

"My English was horrific. It's just that your French was worse."

"Must have been ample enough to win the heart of a fair maiden. . . ."

"How can one say no to an army officer?" She repositioned her sunglasses and put on her haughtiest voice. "After all, they are skilled in the art of seizing the high ground and taking victory."

"Ah, the art of making war and love." Monty looked over at her. "Sun Tzu meets Ovid. Sometimes there is a fine line between the two."

The truck zipped past a home with two great stone lions standing on either side of the driveway. Seeing the magnificent statues reminded Monique where the conversation began.

"Monty, I will have to say that my family understood our need to go to Florence to find the statues. After all, they shared the same intensity when they first laid eyes upon the figures. I believe they are hoping that we will have enough time after our travels to come back and be with them for a while." She paused and drew in a slow breath. "If I am honest, I have the need to spend time with them as well. True, America is beautiful, and I love my home and family there. We are blessed to have Jillian and EZ so close to us there at West Point. But, honey, there are places in my heart that cannot be filled by anything except by the people and places of my first home."

"Speaking of such, did you ask this morning if they had seen statues of mythical creatures—most specifically, unicorns?"

Monique rolled her eyes at her husband's attempt at diverting the conversation. "I did ask. They said that they remembered a Pegasus. They could not come to an agreement whether a one-horned creature was seen."

"Did they at least remember the shop that made creatures?"

"They gave me names of several shops. Our work will be cut out for us once we get to Florence."

"I look forward to the challenge: finding a unicorn, and—"

"—making a hasty return back to Oger where you and your beloved can spend time with her family and friends to refill the parts of us that only France and the Champagne region can aptly do."

"Champagne in Champagne. It just doesn't get better!"

The sign for the Troyes city limit passed. Monique, as navigator, drew her husband's attention to it.

"Actually, it does. We are now entering the only town in the region whose city planners laid out the city center in the shape of a Champagne cork."

"I can't recall much about the town."

"Aren't you glad you have me along?"

"I'm always glad I have you along, Monique. Troyes is another of the early Roman outposts in France, yes?"

"More like a serious crossroad. If you were Roman and you wanted to go anywhere that was important, then a journey through Troyes was a must."

"Well then I guess the town must be held in great esteem."

"For the English, yes. Around the time of Joan of Arc, there was a move to make Troyes the capital of all the French lands held by the English. The Treaty of Troyes signed by the Queen Isabeau of France tried to disinherit the Dauphin as the true ruler of France. The geographic map of France looked much different in her time than it does now."

"The French people agreed to this?"

"The French people did not, but the French leadership was divided. The people sided with the Dauphin, who harnessed the power of the Maid of Lorraine along with many other great military leaders. After a three-day siege in the summer of 1429, Troyes was recaptured for France. The letter written by the Maid of Lorraine was beautiful. I don't remember it precisely, but it went something like this: In the name of Jesus and Mary, Jehanne la Pucelle announces that in the name of the King of Heaven, her rightful and sovereign Lord, in whose service she remains every day, which the people of Troyes should render true allegiance to Charles VII, the noble king of France. I promise and guarantee upon your lives that we will enter, with the help of God, and there will be a peace despite whomever may come against us. I commend you to God, and may God have mercy on you, if it so pleases him."

"So, basically, it says that if you oppose God, you will lose," Monty summarized. "Was the city destroyed in the siege?"

"No, not in 1429. However, about 95 years later, a fire consumed the whole city. Much of what remains of the medieval city today is what survived afterward."

"I never knew my wife to be such a historian."

"I'm not. I'm a French actress turned educator. One cannot play the part of a historical character unless one truly understands the history. It's like a body without a skeleton. It doesn't work if there is no basic framework of understanding."

"I don't think I knew that my wife acted as Joan of Arc, either."

"Hold on to your hat! Your wife was also Duchess Anne of Brittany, Anna of Denmark, Duchess Anne Geneviève, Lady Claudine Guérin de Tencin, and Marie Antoinette."

"So, you lost your head, Miss Antoinette?"

"Not before the statue of my husband was destroyed here in this town."

"I had a statue here in Troyes?" Monty teased.

"No dear, before the Reign of Terror, my husband King Louis XIV had a statue at the Hôtel de Ville—which by the way, sells the world's best chocolate made by Pascal Caffet . . . and a must-stop."

"Is this candy man one of your ex-hubbies?"

"No dear. Pascal Caffet is a chocolatier par excellence, not a historical figure . . . at least not yet. I prefer to study roles associated with leading men who are long dead."

"Well, that doesn't say much for me, now does it?"

"That says a lot for you!"

"Where do I rank in this long line of ex-hubbies?"

"Don't worry, Monty, rest assured. You are in the top ten—fifteen—okay, twelve—more or less."

45

Losses and Gains

Maternity hospital

Saint-Quentin, Somme River Valley
Vermandois region, France
Current day

The numbers that made up the year 1375 seared like a flaming brand onto the brains of the American healers. After placing Loni back into a restful but still hypnotic state, Douglas, Suzanne, and Mickey plopped themselves into a small patient waiting area outside Loni's room. Each seemingly unaware of the other, they sat in a stunned, somber silence. Meanwhile, the French hospital maternity team bustled about in her room doing their routine checks and monitoring, completely unaware of the significance of what just happened. However, the Americans sat outside the room ruminating on the truth that the regression hypnosis, employed by Douglas, had transformed Loni from modern-day woman to a person who has been dead for six hundred years.

Mickey's face was chiseled into absolute amazement. He had just lost his wife to the distant past. Yet, there she sat in the room across the way, quite alive, resting. Mickey aimlessly stroked the bandaging on his hand splint, trying to work his way through his roiling emotions of pain, confusion, and denial.

With some cajoling, the three migrated to a table as Douglas attempted a productive round-robin discussion to try to make credibility of the incredible. *Before I can re-engage Loni's psyche,* Douglas thought, *I absolutely must have a plan . . . or at the very least a list of questions to ask Sibylle. Otherwise, 1375 might be the year where Loni, connected to Sibylle, will dwell forever.* Douglas began the dour powwow.

"Folks, it's time to proceed beyond the dark," Douglas said. "There are multiple pieces here which don't seem to fit. I know if we can put our collective minds together, we can make sense out of this. Mickey, Suzanne, you are the two greatest sources of history here. Who is this Sibylle?"

Upon hearing this, Suzanne scowled. "History for me is only a job. Always has been. I don't love it. I won't love it. If we need expertise on dead people and

193

their doings, then I fully defer to Mickey." Suzanne pointed across the table to Mickey in a tapping motion.

Douglas peered at Mickey. His gaze was locked on a fixed point somewhere in the distance.

Oh, great. He's shut down completely. With the Loni he knows and loves presenting as a character from the year 1375, this should be expected. It's too much information for him to process. I guess no historical support from Mickey for a while. Douglas folded his hands on the table, leaned toward his former wife, trying a different approach.

"Suzanne, in this forum, a *love* for history as a subject matter is immaterial. Your *knowledge* runs deep in forgotten areas where few care to tread. You and I both know that in certain, specific areas there is no one with greater expertise than you. Long before I was your ex-husband, I was a widower to your commitment to the study of women's history. There is no substitute for the depth of knowledge within Suzanne Coletrane—especially in women's studies. Am I right, or am I right?" Douglas spoke kindly but firmly, thereby eliminating debate as an option. Suzanne's rebuttal died in her throat.

She stared down at her hands. *I don't want to be the subject matter expert on history. What if I am amiss? What if I jumble historical facts?* Suzanne sucked in a deep breath. *Jesus, blaze me a history path and let me travel within your wake.* Then, her eyes were pulled up—drawn away as if of their own accord—tugged from the contemplation of her own personal misgivings. She looked beyond the table to a large glass window which kept out the waning night. In the reflection stood a silent Christine de Pizan dressed in full regalia—perfect in her floor-length blue dress and her bleached-white, twin-peaked veiled headdress. Her hands were clasped, with fingers entwined at her tiny bodice waist. Suzanne felt her breath catch in her throat and her heart lurch. The reflection's piercing gaze looked confidently and directly at Suzanne, then nodded. Suzanne thrust her chin up in affirmation and nodded her head minutely in return. Christine winked and smiled.

Suzanne closed her eyes. She brought her hands together, prayer-like, and rested them upon her chin as she had seen Christine do in the garden. After a moment, she opened her eyes. *Time to engage.*

46

Of Owls and Scowls

Notre-Dame de Dijon
Dijon, France
Current day

The four hours that separated the city center of Dijon and the city center in Troyes were akin to the inscription on the Troyes church spire clock: our time here on earth *passes steadily like the shade*. The Meriwether pair seemed to have just blinked and Dijon appeared.

In whispered conversation, they sat inside the Dijon's namesake religious structure which they had always affectionately called the Owl Church because of its iconic 300-year-old owl carving on one corner. Despite the popular owl of Dijon, the memory of beautiful Troyes was still the burning topic at hand between the Meriwether travelers.

Monique, a brilliant child-actor product of the Sorbonne School of Drama, had learned intricate French history through acting on stage and in films. Later, in her years as a Department of Defense Dependents School teacher, she taught the history that she had portrayed dramatically in her youth. Troyes was the city where so much of what she acted became her reservoir of knowledge.

"Mother used to bring Louise and me down to Troyes to the Église Saint-Remy, Monty. Louise loved to hear the story of Marguerite Bourgeoys, a daughter of Troyes. Marguerite left her family inheritance and sailed to the French frontier to start a church and nunnery in the fledgling city of Montreal. As a mother superior there in Canada, she was responsible for teaching students as well as educating teachers."

"I never knew that your sister wanted to be a nun."

"She didn't. Louise was rebellious. The adventure she most desired was that of any journey going to anywhere that would leave her misery behind."

"Oh, come on, Monique, everything I know of your family is like the French version of the *Brady Bunch*. It's a never-ending story of blissful happiness."

"That's because you know the story of my family as revealed through my eyes. Through Louise's eyes things were a whole lot different."

"How could that be? Your parents were the same."

"Yes, but like actors in a play, the scripts that we received were performed by the interpretation of us as individuals."

"How so?" Monty's mind kept drawing parallels to their two daughters, Loni and Jillian. *Loni was the pristine obedient child while Jillian was so argumentative.*

"I enjoyed the structure that Father provided me. Instead, Louise took it offensively. Louise felt that structure stifled her artistic creativity, and so her joy became suppressed. Honestly, Monty, I reveled in the hours and hours of formal study in the Parisian schools of arts and drama. It felt so good to feel the richness of the world's greatest talent surrounding me."

"Well, at least now I know now why Louise went to Canada. She was escaping from her life as it was rigidly handed to her."

"Perhaps. But her part in my family play has played its part in ours. When our Jillian was struggling—you know, going through life at her pace—Louise, as an elder sibling herself, could understand Jillian and be a confidant and trusted counselor in ways we couldn't."

"Monique, I don't know about you, but there were times when I really wondered if Jillian was a child of ours. Being heavily artistically inclined, she is everything neither you nor I ever chose to embrace."

"True, Monty. I will always be grateful that she and her Auntie Louise were a match made in heaven. I believe Jillian's success as a ceramicist arose due to Louise's tutelage. Weren't we blessed when Jillian's love for Italian Renaissance pottery made her passion blossom into a *mon seul desir?*"

"Agreed. Being a ceramicist is indeed her heart's only desire." Monty smiled cautiously, noting a hint of pain in Monique's eyes. "So, there is nothing of us in that child—only Auntie Louise?" Monty laughed.

"*Au contraire.* True, there is much Louise in her, but there is more. She has gained a devoted passion for God."

"Well, Monique, I guess we did something right with that child."

"We did indeed." She looped her arm around his waist. "We passed on what was poured into us by our parents. My sister found strength in her faith in Montreal at Notre-Dame-de-Bon-Secours—the very church that her idol, Mother Superior Marguerite Bourgeoys, worked to build."

"So, thank Jesus for Louise and Mother Superior Bourgeoys both. I am glad that they were there to provide Jillian with what she needed spiritually at the time she needed it."

"Aside from other people, churches have a funny habit of doing that too. I do so love visiting them for that very reason. They seem to give what you need—even if you didn't know you needed it. Because I am French, I seem to be drawn closer to the churches and cathedrals of Europe."

"I'm here to say that I am not French but, nevertheless, like you I also feel a closer presence with Christ in the European houses of worship—much more than those in the United States. Why is that?"

"Because the imprints of the footsteps of the Templars aren't in the churches in America."

"Okay, granted, not when America began being the United States. However, there is much that makes me believe there has been a Templar presence everywhere in the Americas. For me, the logic of it bolsters the existent subtle evidence of pre-Columbian America visits. Don't forget, the Vikings became Christianized in the 900s. That means the visits of the Norsemen to upper–North America and the Great Lakes were that of Christians. As Christians, they would be sensitive to the Templar predicament in the 1300s while also having a pool of nautical intelligence which would reasonably give a westward direction to Templar fleets. For Christ's sake, Monique, Pedro Teixeira, a Templar in the Order of Christ, was in South America in the seventeenth century as a—"

"Whoa there, general! Easy, Monty. I didn't say there weren't Templars in the Americas. I was just saying the footsteps of the Templars in the Americas did not echo within the church walls that exist there today."

"In my mind, Templars were in the Americas."

"Still are, Monty. Take a knee."

"Okay, but it just frustrates me to know that as a modern order today, we Templars are so few in a world that needs us in so many places. My prayer every day is the same. Give the world more Templar hands to protect the holy shrines, the holy relics, and most importantly the Christians at risk."

"If God indeed grants a wish for any prayer given in a newly visited church, you'll have your increased number of Templars tomorrow," said Monique. Her smile made Monty revel in the fact she had so much love for the cantankerous old curmudgeon he had become. He softened a bit.

"With you at my side, Monique," said Monty, stretching back in the pew, "I feel the need to visit and pray in every beautiful church in Europe." His arms waved circularly to encompass all numerous chapels in proximity to their seating, all lit with candles and adorned with art throughout.

"Well, if you do, you'll get more than just answered prayers." She nudged his shoulder playfully. "You will get a powerful history lesson."

"True enough."

"That brings immediately to my mind the greatest son of Troyes, Hugues de Payens."

"Hugues de Payens, the founder of the Knights Templar? I don't believe I knew that he was from Troyes. Few churches stateside are famous for having their sons crucified on a church door."

"Do we really know that this crucifixion ever happened, Monty?"

"There are those who not only believe that it happened, but that instead of Christ, he is the figure under the Shroud of Turin in Turin, Italy."

"I don't believe it." Monique's voice was appalled.

From one pew behind them, in a gravelly voice, another woman opined, "I don't either. That's nonsense. Sheer balderdash!"

Monty and Monique simultaneously turned rearward to gaze into a rather disfigured face sporting large disproportionate eyes which bracketed a beak-like nose and button-shaped mouth. Monique involuntarily gasped. The woman rested her walking stick against the pew as she lifted a black veil from its dangling position from her left ear fully into position as she hooked it over her right ear. When in place, the dark veil covered nose and mouth, leaving only her eyes exposed. With stick back in hand, she tapped it on the stone floor with a nod to add emphasis to her commentary.

Unmoved by the shock of the speaker's appearance, Monty spoke to the issue raised by the uninvited conversant conversationalist.

"Hugues de Payens was a knight of the First Crusade," Monty said. "He was not Christ. His success and leadership led the Christians to take Jerusalem and the Holy Land within three years. Alas, it was all lost when Mehmed II retook Constantinople, and with it, the last vestige of what our crusaders and Templars died achieving."

"I defer to the gentleman's knowledge of Templars," said the veiled lady.

"I defer to the kind lady's knowledge of Hugues de Payens," Monty continued. "However, the debate here revolves around who is the crucified person underneath the Shroud of Turin." Monty momentarily paused, placing a hand against his lips. "I am not sure I know you, madam. Have we met?"

"Only by the hand of God. By our effort alone, we have not, kind sir. Not officially." The Owl nodded her head in a slight bow causing her walking stick to tap the top of her head.

"I am Monty Meriwether. This is my wife, Monique. We welcome your thoughts on the topic if you wish to continue to share," said Monty.

The Owl raised her gaze and spoke through the fluttering of her face veil. "Indeed. Monty, Monique, I am sorry for interrupting your private conversation. I hope you can believe no malice was intended. The topic of your conversation stirred me into rudeness. For my interruption, I apologize . . . for my opinion, I do not harbor regret. I am Szkolna Gora."

"Why do I know that name?" Monty rifled through the rolling card file of names in his head.

"We have a common acquaintance. I work with Elior Yahel at the World Templar Order."

Recognition dawned on Monty's face. "Of course, you are the Owl."

"Yes, people find it easier calling me the Owl." She paused for a moment and then resumed the lead in the conversation. "Actually, I believe I recognized you both when I first noticed you at the stone carving of the owl outside—at the corner of the church wall, just to the left of the entrance. You were next to the lady tourist in the black quasi-military outfit. She was plotting the quickest way to stroke the owl statue."

"You stalked us from outside?" Monique's voice displayed her profound dissatisfaction. The Owl breezed onward, ignoring the obvious distaste.

"Many believe that the owl figure is a good luck charm," the Owl continued. "I have seen many people—like the tourist just a few pews ahead—touch it with their left hand, almost religiously, and make a solemn wish. I noticed that you looked but did not touch it for luck. Instead, you both appreciated it for art, then came into the church, kneeled reverently and said your prayers. Thank you for being respectful." She nodded again. "Since you looked familiar, I chose to follow you and—yes, Monique—listen to what you two spoke of as you sat here in the back pews of the Owl Church."

Upon hearing this, Monique's feathers became further ruffled. "You admit it? You eavesdropped on us and politely sit there admitting it?"

"Not for reasons of malice, Monique. You see, so many people come here to the church to find, in some undiscovered hidden crevice, the Holy Chalice of Christ or they sit discussing the multiple types of mustard for which Dijon is famous."

"Of course, I am of French origin, and you probably know that already, but that is beside the point. You boldly stalked us then eavesdropped on us. It's not okay." She looked to Monty for support. "Not even a little bit." She turned back to the Owl. "You need to know that."

Monty's voice, however, remained objective, almost soothing. "Honey, true, she was gathering intelligence on us. For the reasons she gave, I can live with that."

"But she violated our privacy, Monty. What kind of person does that?"

"Honey, she meant us no harm."

"No, Monty," said the Owl. "Monique is right. Although I meant no harm, what I did was wrong, and I am truly sorry. It was wrong for me to invade the private conversation of a famous French actress and her accomplished soldier husband, but I truly believe that God wanted us to meet. You can imagine that whether veiled or unveiled, meeting people is not my forte. I chose to sit behind you two, wait for an opportunity, and then take a liberty. Please, Monique, forgive me."

Monique paused, noting the sincerity in the woman's voice. She drew in a deep breath. "Nothing to forgive, Madam Owl." Monique punctuated her forgiveness by folding her arms forcefully in discontent.

"Thank you, Monique."

Monique nodded curtly while Monty took the conversation lead.

"Is this your church, Madam Owl? That is, does it belong to you?"

"Well, yes and no."

"Now there's indecision for you," Monique whispered. "That's an answer Mickey would give." Though she intended her comment only for Monty's ears, it unintentionally reverberated louder than she desired.

The Owl quickly parried with a wisp of annoyance. "Are you comparing me to a cartoon mouse?"

"Oh, no, Madam Owl." Monique's face flushed hot for a moment. "I meant no offense. Our daughter's husband prefers the nickname Mickey to his Christian name, Michael. Anyway, Miss Eavesdropper," Monique resumed her haughty tone, "my commentary was meant for my husband, not for you."

"I see."

"Pardon me, Madam Owl," Monty asked gently, "could you please slowly repeat your Christian name?" As he said this, Monty motioned a raised index finger from his lips outward.

"Yes, of course. But why, Monty?"

"No reason, I just wanted to hear it again as you pronounce it."

"Szkolna Gora. It is a Polish name and very hard for many to pronounce. Most just prefer to call me the Owl. You are still welcome to call me by that name."

Monty smiled. Monique grimaced with continued discontent.

The Owl continued. "To answer your previous question, the Owl Church—Notre-Dame de Dijon—belongs to no one and everyone at the same time. The owl on the façade of this church and the name that I bear gives me a natural relationship. That makes this church, metaphorically, mine over all the others."

"So, the church is the reason that you are called the Owl."

"No."

"Then why do they call you the Owl?" Monique furrowed her brow.

"What you seek is easy to ask but very difficult to explain. If you were going back to Poland with me today, we would have plenty of time to discuss it as we visited my home, the Owl Tower. But, alas, my guess is that you have left Oger with the intent to go on to Florence. So, for now, the best answer to this question will be that you will have to wait until you get back with your children."

"Monty," Monique whispered. "She knows—"

"I know." Monty whispered back. "Not now."

"It's been a pleasure," said the Owl as she steadied herself on the back of the pew as she rose. She began shuffling to the end of her bench. Without turning back, she spoke. "Monique, when you are safely in the folds of your home with your children seated comfortably around you, ask your daughter's husband, Mickey, 'Why is it that the Polish woman Szkolna Gora is known as the Owl?'"

"Madam Owl—" Monique bristled, paused with Monty's grip on her arm, then took a slow deep breath. "Aren't you forgetting your walking stick?"

"No, Monique, I didn't forget." She turned slightly toward the pair. "I left it for Monty."

"Thank you, but no. I just couldn't." Monty reached over the back of his pew and gently retrieved the stick for her.

"After all my transgressions, consider it a gift in apology."

"Again, we must decline." With great reverence, Monty made his way to the Owl and held the walking stick out to her.

"I see. There is pity for an old woman today." The Owl pursed her lips and nodded sadly, then she raised one hand to stop Monty. "No means no."

Confused, but not willing to argue with such a formidable force as the Owl, Monty brought the walking stick back toward his chest and set the end point at the ground near his feet.

"Don't you need this to help you exit the church?"

"As I get older, I find that I am often blessed with the unexpected kindness of others."

As the Owl rounded the end of her pew, the same tourist from the owl statue outside caught her eye. In a moment, the woman pushed a brochure into one of her many cargo pants' pockets, stepped forward, and extended a helping hand toward the frail old woman.

The Owl smiled toward Monty and said, "See what I mean?" She tapped her chest with her thumb.

The Owl patted the woman on the arm kindly. "Thank you, my dear. I won't keep you for long. I don't have far to go."

Then she turned briefly back toward the pew and, shaking a finger at Monty, she said, "Remember to ask about the mystery behind my name. I am quite sure that your son-in-law, Deputy Command Surgeon Colonel Sir Doctor Michael Philip Peronne, will be glad to tell you that and much, much more. Monique and Monty Meriwether, God bless you both and keep you safe in your travels and in the search for your unicorn statue." With a nod, she turned to leave, but then paused and spoke over her shoulder to the couple. "When you see him, give DCS a hug for me and extend my very best."

47

Deciphering Yesterday

Maternity hospital
Saint-Quentin, Somme River Valley
Vermandois region, France
Current day

Cocking an eyebrow at Suzanne's strange response to his pep talk, Douglas looked around the empty waiting room to see what, if anything, he was missing.

"Ummm, okay," he mumbled. "So, the current task is to decipher who this Sibylle is and why she has bridged to the child psyche of Loni all the way from the year 1375. Anybody?" Douglas asked, still watching Suzanne closely.

"That's difficult to answer, Douglas." Shaking out of his trance-like mode, Mickey joined the conversation abruptly causing Douglas to give a little start. "Sibylle may be as unknown in her past as she is in our present. We must remember, folks—just like many people today will never be of sufficient significance to be historically remembered, this is also quite true of the past." Mickey nodded toward the patient room where the nursing staff was leaving with carts, instruments, and a rolling clothes hamper. With the passing by of the last staff member, he then continued. "Whereas this person Sibylle is indisputably significant in the history of Loni, that in no way indicates that Sibylle herself contributed significantly enough to be placed into the historical record of France in the late 1300s."

Rebutting, Suzanne leaned over the table. "Are you saying that this woman is of no historical significance?"

"Well, maybe I am," Mickey said. "As cold as it might sound, I cannot remember any Sibylle in France in that time period being prominently recorded in any historical document that I know of."

"So then where do we go from here?" Suzanne asked the group. "Are we stymied from the git-go?"

"Maybe not," said Douglas. "Sibylle clearly links with Loni at the oblong towers. Can we deduce that the oblong towers are absolutely Péronne Castle and no other?" Douglas searched Suzanne's face.

"My vote is yes," she nodded.

"So is mine," concurred Mickey.

"Agreed. Okay, so what we need to know now is what happened at the Péronne Castle in 1375. Anyone?"

"Nothing comes to mind in that year for me." Mickey shrugged. "Suzanne?"

"I got nothing," Suzanne growled. "Wait a minute, Mickey. Maybe something didn't necessarily happen *at* Péronne Castle but instead happened *about* the castle in 1375."

Mickey's eyes moved up and to the left, concentration furrowing his brow. "All right, if you put that way, here's something . . . in fact, I was telling Loni about this earlier . . ." He paused and shook his head to clear it of emotion. "Péronne Castle was the site of a significant find in the mid-to-late 1100s—"

"But we're talking about the 1300s, Mickey," Douglas began, but Mickey held up a hand to stop him.

"A lost scroll was found when King Philip II of France decided to expand the castle fortifications there. Hidden for 200 years, the newly found scroll was discovered to discuss intimate details about the Sword of Charles Martel. As such, it was carried to Paris where it was placed in the castle at Vincennes. Sad to say, due to disorganization and neglect, the Péronne Castle scroll was again lost at Vincennes. Then, two hundred years later in the *mid-to-late 1300s*," he cast a significant look at Douglas, "a pair of apprentice scribes looking over court recording documents for King Charles V found the lost scroll. Say!" Mickey rapped the knuckles of his good hand against the table loudly. "That might be it!"

Suzanne picked up his trail. "Well, if either of the two apprentice scribes at the Vincennes castle has a connection to this lost scroll, then maybe we have an explanation of why Péronne Castle's oblong towers would be a bridge to the past for Loni."

The image of Christine reappeared in the window and again beckoned to Suzanne. Pushing her seat back from the table, Suzanne stood up and walked to the window, listening acutely as Douglas continued the conversation. Wanting so much to interact with the image, Suzanne pressed her fingers against the cool glass. Finger for finger, Christine pressed back. The darkness behind Christine yielded to the cresting sun, but her reflection remained vivid.

"How then does this fact link to Loni? In other words, why Loni? Why now?" Douglas pulled his hands through his hair.

"I see the foundation as threefold," said Mickey. He jabbed his finger at the table with each point he made. "First, Loni's whole day today was matrixed in an investigation of the northern arm of the Joan of Arc trail beginning at Joan's home in Domrémy and proceeding to the city of Péronne. Next, the castle of Péronne with oblong towers appears to have been part of Loni's life from her time spent at the Joan of Arc School in San Francisco. Last, via regression hypnosis, Loni seems to have a connection reaching back to fourteenth-century

France involving a personage who *could possibly* intersect with Joan of Arc in that it is the correct time span."

"Yes, I see the recurring pattern's central theme as Joan," said Douglas. "However, what is the connection between these three foundation stones and Sibylle?"

At that moment, Suzanne's eyes whipped away from Christine's face to their mirrored fingertips. The air smelled electric, and the same warm, tingling pressure that she had felt in the abbey garden began again, this time where their fingers met. Suzanne saw her own reflection's eyes grow wide with a mixture of fear, excitement, and anticipation.

"Well, I'm not sure," Mickey said. "The three stones are in some way associated with Joan of Arc, if only tangentially. The last is only associated because of the lineage of French royalty in the era of Charles V who later appreciated and honored Joan of Arc."

"Is Joan connected to King Charles V?" Douglas asked.

"Not that I am aware," Mickey stated, shaking his head. "There is no historical data known that supports that theory. However, his grandson was the Dauphin whom Joan returned to the throne of France thereby re-instating his ruling lineage. Hey, wait." Mickey spoke his revelation rapidly. "Medical history does record that the chief physician for Charles V was Thomas de Pizan, who practiced healing arts during the bubonic plague. But, when Sibylle spoke to us through Loni, she mentioned his name. She said he helped get her, or her family, to Paris. Is there a connection there that we are missing?" Mickey paused, looking at Suzanne who stared intently out the window into the dawn.

Like the sun's light beyond the window, the warmth was spreading to her palm, and Suzanne was reticent to break the connection.

"Well, geez, Mickey why didn't you start with that? It's a better lead," Douglas scowled.

Christine pulled her hand from the glass and nodded to Suzanne.

"Let's see, Douglas," Mickey snapped back, "maybe I'm a bit exhausted, and distraught about my wife, and my babies, and—"

Suzanne cleared her throat and turned to the group. "We also know that Dr. Thomas de Pizan was the father of my role model, the great Christine de Pizan, royal secretary to King Charles V." She crossed her arms over her chest and leaned her shoulder against the window. "History connects Christine to Joan of Arc, the Maid of Lorraine, in the form of Christine's published literary praise of Joan as a female warrior."

"A feminist author in the fourteenth century?" Douglas challenged skeptically.

"Yes, gentlemen, and she was the very first acknowledged feminist in history. Lord Jesus bless her. Although if you asked her," said Suzanne, bouncing her gaze off Christine, "I'd wager that she wouldn't agree. My guess would be that Christine would claim that Joan of Arc, and the many like Joan, were the true feminists." Suzanne glanced to the glass, receiving Christine's nodded affirmation.

"Those like Joan?" Douglas asked.

"Sure," Mickey said. "History accounts for some very significant female warriors in Asia and in the Greco-Persian era. The one probably known by Christine would be Queen Boudicca who fought against the Romans near King's Lynn, England."

"Ahh, yes, King's Lynn. Home of one of the two leaning towers in England." Suzanne winked at Mickey. The Leaning Tower affair, hallmarked by a race between good and evil from tower to tower over four European countries. In the wake of that race strode modern-day Templars girded as meek tower keepers holding on to secrets two-thousand years old. Clearly this experience was still fresh in the minds of these two newly knighted Templars.

Douglas, used to being on the outside of their personal interactions and agendas, shrugged and brought everyone back on track. "All this conjecture and history is great, but we still don't know who this Sibylle is who resides as the current voice of Loni."

Mickey rubbed his forehead vigorously. "I only recall a very few Sibylles in that era." *It's like dredging a river!* he thought. *If only I could get some rest, this would be so much easier.*

"Well, at this point, any Sibylle would give us a jumping off point."

"I think there was a scribe," Mickey said, thinking. "Yes, an apprentice scribe named Sibylle. And another near the same timeframe, I think, named Christine." Mickey stood and began pacing. "Incidentally, history notes that there were two apprentice scribes in the employment of King Charles V, but I can't recall any names specifically listed." Mickey shrugged, strode over to the table, and frowned as he slumped back in his seat. "It doesn't mean it was *this* Sibylle." Utterly dejected Mickey muttered, "Not much to go on, really."

Over her shoulder, Suzanne saw the silent reflection of Christine tap on the glass. Suzanne felt her fingers tingle and the warmth spread again to her palm. Suddenly, a thought came to her as clear, sharp, and real as a bolt of lightning and just as fast too. It was something she had never known before, yet she did not question its validity. She felt its truth in her very atoms.

She squeezed her hand into a fist and then rubbed her thumb over the tips of the other four fingers. She proceeded tentatively. "Christine de Pizan had a cousin named Sibylle. Maybe it's the same girl, I think. . . ."

"Where's that coming from?" Douglas cut in. "What is it with you both?" He bolted upward, knocking his chair over. "Why didn't you tell us before?" Douglas bounced his gaze from Suzanne to Mickey. "This is about Loni being Loni again. Folks, the decisions I make here aren't trite!" Neck veins began bulging above Douglas's collar. "Loni's life, or at least her consciousness, is on the line here—and in my hands—and you guys are holding out on me with essential information? Enough!"

"Whoa! Whoa! Douglas, take it easy," Mickey put his hands up in surrender. "None of us is firing on all our cylinders, we—"

"I didn't know it before, okay?" Suzanne shot back as she crossed her arms again. "It's just . . . just a feeling."

Douglas scoffed loudly, collected his chair from the ground, and slammed it back upright. "I didn't know you had any of those left."

"How would you know? You couldn't find my feelings with two hands and a flashlight." Suzanne scowled. She turned her attention to Mickey. "Well, I *know* Christine's cousin earned the right to be cloistered at the abbey in Poissy. And. . . ."

She paused as the warmth in her hand surged again. As the sensation became more familiar, she spoke with confidence and certainty of what she had not known before—of what no one knew before.

"Through Christine's daughter, Marie, Christine obtained knowledge of a past librarian's assistant by that same name at the abbey in Poissy." Suzanne cast her eyes over her shoulder at a smiling Christine.

"But *was* it the very same Sibylle?" Douglas winced.

"I thought you said *any* Sibylle was a good start?" Micky challenged.

Douglas rolled his eyes.

Suzanne pressed on. "Most likely it was the same, but it's hard to decipher and prove beyond coincidence. It may be a *feeling*, but it's more than we had to go on before." *It's coming more easily now.* "Also," she rubbed her fingertips, "before Marie's time at the abbey, Sibylle, the librarian's assistant, left to go to Vouthon."

"Well, Vouthon is right next to Domrémy," Mickey elaborated, "the home of Joan of Arc." Suddenly, Mickey sat up at attention and snapped his fingers. "There was a nun at the Domrémy church named Sister Sibyl—*S-i-b-y-l*— who mentored Joan of Arc. She appears in the records in Vouthon, Domrémy, Burey-en-Vaux, and later in Vaucouleurs—all in the Lorraine!"

"I understand that there was a Sister Sibyl there in the Lorraine, Mickey," Douglas nodded, trying to regain some professional composure. "However, does the historical evidence indicate that there was a *Sibylle* from Poissy there in the Lorraine?"

Mickey and Suzanne shook their heads and shrugged. The elation of the moment dissipated as quickly as it had arrived.

"No, Douglas, there isn't indisputable evidence. However, the names Sibyl and Sibylle are very close in appearance, although quite different in pronunciation," offered Mickey. "Relative to appearance, it could be a misspelling or typo." Mickey's voice clutched at the wisp of hope which seemed to constantly evade them.

"Oral and aboral are close in spelling too, Mickey. However, they are at opposite ends of the Good Idea Pig."

"Fine then, Doubting Douglas! Ya know," his voice broke, "we're all trying our best."

The two men locked eyes. The stress and strain reflected in both faces.

"I'm sorry, Mickey, I'm just—"

"I know. We all are."

They nodded curtly to each other. Suzanne sat down next to Mickey and pressed her hands together prayer-like.

"Where do we go from here?" she asked.

A collective deep breath circled around the table.

Mickey was the first to speak. "We follow this Sibylle—whoever she is—into the Lorraine."

"I agree." Douglas stood calmly and placed his palms on the table. "Are you all ready? Mickey? Suzanne? There's no turning back. Is there *anything* else I should know before I go back to Loni—feelings or otherwise?"

Suzanne flashed a scowl in his direction but softened when she saw the sincerity in his eyes. She shook her head slightly. Mickey copied.

"No? Okay, folks, it's show time." Douglas led the team down the bright, sunlit hallway and back into the unknown.

48

The Captain and the Maid

Lassois residence
Burey-en-Vaux, France
15th century

W hen is a captain not the captain?" Sister Sibyl asked as she darned a
sock. She and the girl sat by the fire in a house just south of Vaucouleurs, on the road leading from Domrémy leading toward Chinon.
The flickering firelight played against the girl's features lending her a new
fierceness. Although Sister Sibyl periodically looked placidly upon that angelic
face, her thoughts were far aloft. *This path to Chinon to visit the Dauphin is far and
filled with peril. It seems odd that the way to Chinon leads through Vaucouleurs and its captain. Yet, it does. Because of her faith in her three guiding saints, I know Jehanne is ready to
meet the captain and all that lies beyond, but am I? Will I be strong enough for Jehanne when
she faces off with the captain?*

"When is a captain not a captain, Sister Sibyl?" Jehanne eyed the sister.
"When he is confronted by the indomitable Maid of Lorraine."

The time had come to begin her journey to meet with the Dauphin. Captain or no captain, Jehanne would not be deterred from this journey.

✠ ✠ ✠

Captain Robert de Baudricourt was the proverbial big fish in a little pond. Being
the captain of the Royal Garrison and master of the castle gave him great power
in the town of Vaucouleurs in the Lorraine. Comfortably settled on one end of
the power spectrum, he always had the advantage.

This day was no different than the countless others before it. He was certainly in no mood to listen to the babblings of yet another Maid of Lorraine
candidate, who would be the savior of all France by leading French armies to

208

victory over the English. It was February 12 in the year 1429, and the castle walls retained winter frigidness as proficiently as his frazzled frock. Prior to her presentation, he had thought to himself, *Perhaps bringing in a few advisors to hear what this precocious adolescent has to say might be somewhat entertaining, or at least less monotonous. Even if it doesn't help, having more warm bodies near could help shake the chill out of my bones.*

As he reflected now, several days later, he had to admit that she certainly was the best Maid of Lorraine he had seen thus far. He sat huddled near the fire, deep in solitary contemplation, trying to ward off the creeping cold.

But the whole concept of a farm girl leading the armies of France into victory after victory is complete foolishness.

Still . . . her words kept echoing in his ears, just as they did off the walls of the hall a few days before.

How does a sixteen-year-old maid from Domrémy have the gumption to bellow at me—the captain of the Royal Garrison—in my castle, in my hall? "The kingdom of France is not the Dauphin's but my Lord's," she had said. "However, God wills it that the Dauphin shall be made king and be given rule over France. The Dauphin shall be king despite the best efforts of his enemies, and I shall lead him to his anointing at Reims." *The audacity!*

He rubbed his hands together and reached toward the fire, his palms tinted orange by the light.

Then again, what if she is right? Can I afford to be so wrong in not backing the one true Maid of Lorraine, savior of France? There is more than one way to spread light. The source. . . . He watched the fire crackle. *And the projection. . . .* He turned his hands to and fro directing the orange flickering light over his hands. *Even if this maid's whole presentation is a façade, a faux Maid of Lorraine could still do much to inspire the armies of France against the English. Maybe she is worth my investment in time and effort—it could have benefits.*

"Guards!" Robert de Baudricourt shouted in his most commanding tone. He paused as the scurrying of feet brought armored soldiers kneeling to his feet. "Bring me Father Jean-René Fournier. Tell him I have a mission for him. He is to find this Maid of Lorraine from Domrémy. He is to tell Jehanne d'Arc to ready herself to meet the Dauphin."

He clapped his hands together, smiling to himself.

This is a gamble I cannot lose. If she is truly the legendary maid, then the Dauphin will be eternally grateful. If she is not, the Dauphin can create any ruse he so wishes to use her as a convincing actress. However, if I do not send Jehanne, and she finds the ear of another supporter, there will always remain the question of why I knew of her claims and yet failed to send her. Now, having the priest confirm her intent and validate her claims, if worse comes to worst, the Church can take the fall for the misinformation. Either way, he nodded at the fire, *I will arise from this without my good reputation and solid credibility being questioned at Chinon.*

The main room in Jehanne's aunt and uncle's home was small, but it was warmly lit and full of family. A sudden knocking sound disturbed the conversation of the evening.

"Open the door. I have been sent by Captain Robert de Baudricourt," said the stern voice.

In a voice loud enough for the person outside the door to hear, Durand Lassois said to his wife, "Jehanne-Marie, pass me my sword and shield!"

Durand Lassois, husband of Jehanne's cousin—having married the daughter of Aveline, Isabelle Romée's sister—made him a family cousin by law. However, the title of uncle served him better. To Jehanne it was a natural part of his name.

In response to Durand's command, the voice on the other side of the door softened. "I have no intent of harm. I am but a poor, humble priest sent in behest of the captain to speak to the Maid of Lorraine."

The door opened slowly, and the priest's timid eyes fell upon a poor wheelwright prepared to defend his house and all hands within, with his wife's butter churn paddle as a sword and the butter churn lid as a shield.

"May God bless this house and all the butter produced here," delivered the relieved priest with a sigh. With two fingers up and two down, his thumb extended outward, he motioned the sign of the cross toward all the occupants. After which, he saw Jehanne, eyeing his religious garb, immediately kneel before him. He watched as she reverently kissed the front hem of his robes. Father Jean-René gently tapped the girl's head, helping her to her feet. *Her face is angelic and her demeanor sublime.*

"The captain wishes to send you to Chinon with an armed escort," Father Jean-René announced. The entire room erupted with cheer. A crying Sister Sibyl rushed over to Jehanne and hugged the child dearly.

After several moments, the room quieted, and the priest continued. "The vanguard that brings me here will leave tonight with a message that says you are who you say you are—the Maid of Lorraine. It is my charge to ensure the message is sent with the captain's seal."

"What was it that changed his mind?" Durand asked.

"There were two things which softened his heart, kind sir. First, the news of the defeat of the French at the Battle of the Herrings was confirmed." The entire room looked at a stone-faced Jehanne. She did not flinch at this announcement nor at the attention suddenly placed upon her. The priest looked directly at the young girl.

"Tell me child, how is it that you knew of something which happened so far away? And with such detailed accuracy?"

"I will tell you what I have been saying since I first arrived at Vaucouleurs, Father. I have no knowledge of anything save what the voices of the saints tell me. They told me that a wagon of herring and arms were being transported to support the siege at Orléans. They said that in this battle, the French would be defeated and their allies, the Scotsmen, would be almost destroyed. I, myself, have never seen a Scotsman, or an English war wagon. Can everyone not see that there are divine forces leading me to the Dauphin and, ultimately, the Dauphin to Reims?"

"None doubt that there are forces leading you, child. But until I arrived here tonight and gazed upon your face and touched your head, I knew not that the force was divine."

"Have you doubt now that I am sent from God as the Maid of Lorraine?"

"Do you think you are the Maid?" the priest posed while gazing deeply into Jehanne's eyes.

"I know that I have been born and raised to fulfill this purpose. Whether I believe I am the Maid is not so important. I think it is important that the Dauphin believes that he is in the presence of the Maid of Lorraine and that all of France believes me to be so."

"You are truly wise beyond your years. As for me, a humble priest in the service of our Lord, I most certainly have no doubt you are who you say you are. I will release the vanguard with the message legitimizing you, and I will return now to tell Captain Baudricourt that you accept his support and will be ready to depart in a fortnight."

"A fortnight?" Jehanne raised her eyebrows at the priest. "Fifteen days? I think not, Father. I hope to leave much sooner than that. You must go tell the captain that we must leave tomorrow or the next."

"Easy, child," consoled the priest. "There are many preparations that must be made for the two-week trip to Chinon. Two weeks are marginally enough time for the bare minimum of preparations. I really believe more time will be needed."

"Father, I must insist. We cannot keep waiting. There has been too much time lost already. We must leave inside of a fortnight—the siege on Orléans must be lifted, and the Dauphin must be crowned king at Reims. Please remind the captain that he will have his favorite breakfast only when the escorted party leaves for Chinon." Father Jean-René smiled, nodded, and prepared to exit the house.

"What of the second issue softened the captain's heart?" Sister Sibyl asked.

Pausing as he crossed the frame of the doorway, Father Jean-René turned and responded. "As the Maid says, it is the gold that sits in a field of white." Raising his thumb and first two fingers in holy configuration, the priest again gave the sign of the cross, blessing the occupants in the house in the name of the Father, the Son, and the Holy Ghost. Then he left as abruptly as he had arrived.

As the door latch clicked down, Uncle Durand engaged Jehanne with a look of confusion sitting on his brow. Jehanne walked across the room and sat next to her uncle, placing an arm around his shoulders with steadfast reassurance.

"The gold that sits on a field of white describes an egg, Uncle. Captain Robert de Baudricourt loves his eggs as the sun rises." Durand searched the confident face of Jehanne, but his confusion persisted.

"So, does he like eggs served golden-side upward, or does he like eggs for breakfast as the sun rises in the morning sky?"

"Yes," smiled Jehanne.

49

Jacques and the Thief

Lassois residence
Burey-en-Vaux, France
15th century

To leave or not to leave?
The thought of a fortnight of preparations weighed heavily on the inexperienced shoulders of young Jehanne. She was weary of waiting despite the promise of support and protection offered by Captain de Baudricourt.

Leave. I will start to Chinon without them. The Dauphin needs me to crown him king. Despite the possibility of being attacked by English, Burgundians, or just everyday rogues, I can wait no longer. What supplies might Uncle Durand have available for an eleven-day trip?

"Jehanne, I've found you a horse. It cost sixteen francs . . ." Pulling a horse by its reins, stable hand Jacques Alain rounded the corner of Uncle Durand's home expecting to find Jehanne, but instead he found one of the village boys rummaging through some of the storage trunks out under the eaves of the stable.

"Stop your pilfering, lad, immediately!" Jacques told the young boy, then glanced around anxiously; there was no sign of Jehanne. Caught red-handed, the mischievous boy could do no more than grin.

"Jehanne! Durand!"

The furtive boy, sporting a badly bobbed-off bowl haircut, maintained his hand in the trunk without moving. Errantly, Jacques expected him to run off at any moment.

"You there, boy, can you not hear? Those things don't belong to you!"

The lad looked down at the dress he had pulled from the trunk. His dirty hands attempted to wrap it around what seemed to be a pair of women's shoes. Opening his mouth to speak, he instead clamped it quickly shut in the presence of a shaking fist.

"I'm serious," said Jacques. "Put down whatever is in your hand, else you will find yourself the subject of a sound thrashing—if not from me, definitely from the girl who owns that red dress."

Jacques cocked his ear. He hoped his scolding would bring a response from Jehanne or, even better, Uncle Durand. Hearing none, he rang the alarm.

"Thief! Durand, come at once!" The impending threat of bodily harm did not even make the boy flinch. Shoving the dress-wrapped shoes into his shirt, the boy's eyes darted left and right as if to look for a quick escape route. Noticing this, Jacques, still holding the reins of the horse, squared off in front of the lad with a posture that said, *There is no possibility of escape.* There was no doubt in Jacques Alain's mind that his words would soon be backed with strength, if not by his hand alone, then most certainly by Jehanne or Durand who were running to his aid this moment. Trapped without a venue for escape, the boy's grin nonetheless widened into a beaming smile.

As the moments crawled by and no help arrived, Jacques began to feel quite nervous. *Why does he just smile? Is it an ambush or trap? Are other thieves lurking nearby?* He subtly scanned his periphery but saw and heard nothing.

"Jehanne! Durand!"

He narrowed his eyes at the boy, imagining the worst. *Why hasn't he made a move? At least there are no weapons in his open hands.* Jacques swallowed dryly. *Where can Jehanne be? What if she is somewhere nearby injured, maybe even dying. Uncle Durand too.* These thoughts distressed him greatly. He needed to find her, and he also knew he must not show this ruffian any sign of fear, or the hunted would soon become the hunter.

"You have tested my patience beyond words . . ." His voice broke with nervous tension. It was too late—as the fish dies by his mouth, Jacques had tipped his hand.

The boy smelled fear and sensed a shift in the advantage of the situation. He leaped upon Jacques with great speed and agility, knocking him back into the horse and to the ground with a thud. Whinnying, the horse scampered off to a far corner of the stable. Jacques saw stars as he struggled to get his wind back.

Jacques was hopelessly pinned. Straddling Jacques's chest, the boy let loose a war whoop. Jacques struggled against the boy. He cast his eyes around wildly for Jehanne or anyone who could help him, but he saw no one. Jacques closed his eyes and covered his face, preparing for the pummeling that would soon begin.

Shaking him by the shoulders, the boy said, "Jacques, Jacques, open your eyes! It's me! It's me."

Jacques tightened his protective grip around his face.

"Don't you recognize me?" The boy laughed. "I am preparing to leave today for the trip. I am not a thief. These are my clothes and shoes. Open your eyes, Jacques. It's me—Jehanne. I am wearing Uncle Durand's riding clothes."

Jacques peeked through his hands.

"I am off to Chinon. I will need the horse." She got up off his chest, but Jacques didn't move. "Are you coming or you just going to lie there?" Pretending to be disgusted, Jehanne picked up two fists of straw and threw them at Jacques's face.

Stupefied by her masculine appearance, Jacques wriggled his elbows up under himself, spat out the residual hay, and gawked directly into the laughing face of the Maid of Lorraine.

"Jehanne? What did you do to your hair?"

Standing above him with one hand on her hip and the other hand imitating shears, Jehanne replied, "The same thing I will do to your nose if I have to wait another moment longer for my horse." Jehanne smiled as she helped the now completely befuddled Jacques to his feet.

"Uncle Durand, come, we have passed the test! I do believe that dressed as a lad I should be much safer for traveling."

"Jehanne," said Uncle Durand as he walked around the corner of the house leading the horse that Jacques released when he was tackled, "we have had our fun at poor Jacques's expense." Rolling his lips inwardly and slowly shaking his head, Durand shot Jacques a look of mock pity, then leveled his gaze on Jehanne. "I am glad that your new disguise is validated. However, I cannot, in my heart, take a step from this house without first offering you this sage advice: Wait for the morrow's preparations. I think it unwise to leave without the help that you have sought out and obtained from the captain. I believe God has given you key people to help you in this mission. I think it is wrong to decide not to include them." At the steely look on Jehanne's face, he continued. "This is not to say I won't go with you. For better or for worse I have promised my services to the Maid of Lorraine, and I will not strike my colors because my opinion differs from hers."

"I appreciate your advice, Uncle, but I feel it in my soul that we must not wait. I sense the forces against the Dauphin are amassing. He must know that I am—"

"Jehanne . . ."

"Yes?"

"Will anything I say change your thinking?"

"No."

"Fine!" Uncle Durand motioned Jacques to ready his steed, then eased his own horse toward the riding gear table. "Then let the three of us go now."

☖ ☖ ☖

Mounted on their horses, Jehanne and Jacques watched as Uncle Durand kissed his tearful wife before climbing on his horse. Once Uncle Durand was on his horse, Jehanne eased hers forward away from Jacques and him, steadying it broadside next to her snuffling aunt. Once her horse settled, Jeanne leaned forward in her saddle to hand her aunt a hanky to dry her crying eyes. Jehanne spoke in a coarse whisper.

"Please, Auntie, tell no one that we departed toward Chinon." Jehanne bit at her lower lip. "Also, send a message to Sister Sibyl over at the church in Domrémy that, regretfully, I could take her into danger that has been preordained for me. Please ask her to ease the mind of my parents with the thought that this was not an act of disobedience to them—it was an act of obedience to God."

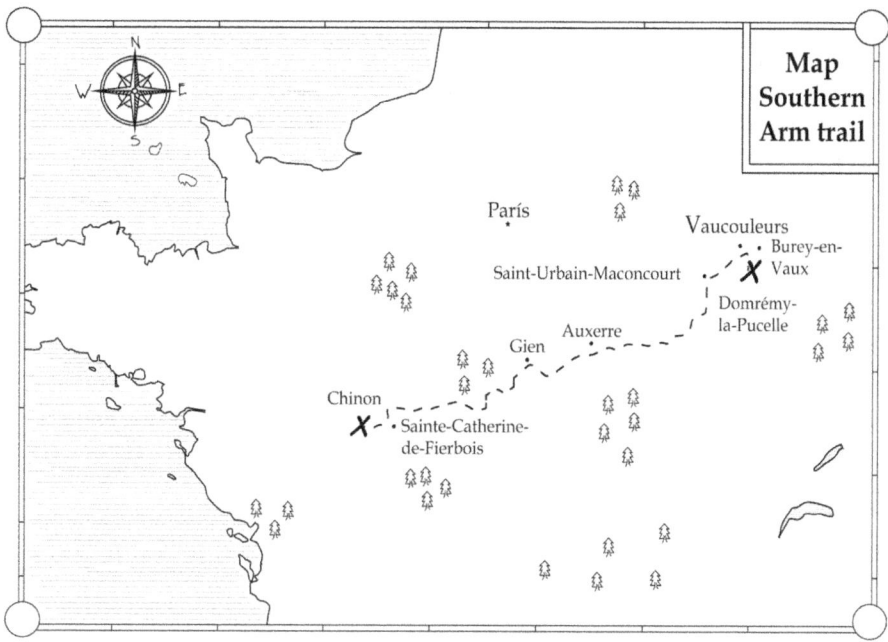

With this said, the three-person travel party slipped away in virtual secret, galloping along the roadway until the path turned into the high grass. Their silhouettes could be seen against the trunks of the tall trees until they were swallowed by the forest. Soon they were gone.

Having gone only a very short way, Jehanne stopped at a forest chapel— Chapelle de Saint-Nicolas. Ruminating on Uncle Durand's advice, Jehanne sought this opportunity to pray for guidance. She knelt humbly at the altar supporting a life-sized carving of Jesus Christ and crossed herself devoutly.

"Dear Lord, I come before you with deep misgivings," she whispered in the stillness of the chapel. "You know I have internalized the charge you have given to me through your three most venerated saints. I wish now only to move forward in great haste to ensure your will is done. Have I miscalculated your intent? Have I sought that my will be done over yours?

"As you have asked of me, I have gone forth, sought out, and received help from Captain Robert de Baudricourt. If his help was timelier, Lord, I most certainly would be willing to accept his support. What good is help when those who wield it cannot deliver, and those who can deliver can only do so when the need for it has passed? Also, most willingly, I have left my parents who have guided me thus far in my life. I have also left behind Sister Sibyl, whose purpose you said was to guide me along the journey and and—oh, Lord, what have I done? Uncle Durand is right. I have forsaken all those who can greatly strengthen my mission. What have I done? What have I done?" Jehanne hurriedly made the sign of the cross and rose without another breath.

Jehanne gathered her devoted companions and returned to Burey-en-Vaux. Uncle Durand smiled his silent *I told you so.*

Jacques still wrestled with the reality that he had been bested by a short-haired maid. *But not just any maid,* he consoled himself, *the Maid of Lorraine.* The whole ride home he continued to spit out tidbits of stable hay which remained stuck between his teeth.

50

A Sooner Departure

Château de Baudricourt
Vaucouleurs, France
15th century

In the late afternoon shadows of the wall at Vaucouleurs, the escort party saddled up in final preparations. A pair of sunsets had passed since the joyful besting of Jacques at Uncle Durand's stables, but Jehanne's face portrayed a hint of sadness despite all the happiness that the moment could provide. Although she had thought that this moment would never be realized, the day of days finally arrived. In fact, it came three days earlier than had been originally predicted.

The waning sun began to set on Wednesday, the twenty-third of February 1429. The late afternoon shadows against the city walls made the departure seem disproportionately larger than life. To Jehanne, it seemed an endless process, getting everything tightened down, supplies secured, horses and the supply wagon marshaled, and the whole array lined up for departure.

Mounted on horseback, Jean de Metz was at the lead, followed by Bertrand de Poulengy, then came Julian and Jean de Honnecourt, Richard the Archer, and Colet de Vienne. Julian and Jean were the designated domestic help for the trip since Father Minet would not release Clare and little Clarisse from their responsibilities at the church in Domrémy. Colet was the royal messenger. Notably missing were Uncle Durand and Jacques Alain who were scheduled to be part of the original itinerary. However, a current illness at the Durand home took them out of the manifest. Saddened and almost angered with their absence, Jehanne jerked hard on the canvas over the wagon of supplies. *How could God do this to me? I need them.* She was interrupted in her self-pity by an intentional cough.

Jehanne looked up from this business of tightening wagon straps to survey the dauntingly handsome figure of Jean de Metz. His brown shoulder-length locks swayed as sat on his mount. He had ridden over to where she wrestled with the uncooperative canvas strap.

217

"Pull harder on that strap and supplies will be popping out the back of the wagon," he told Jehanne with his clean-shaven half grin.

Jehanne glared up at Jean then tugged even harder on the straps before tying them off with a snap, pop, and loud crack.

"Fear not, dear Maid, we will soon be ready." Jean de Metz exuded confidence despite a general tone of group apprehension accented by the Maid's disappointment.

Jehanne had met Jean de Metz and Bertrand de Poulengy on some of the previous interactions with Robert de Baudricourt here at Vaucouleurs. With her confidence in presenting herself as the Maid of Lorraine, she had impressed them far earlier than she did the captain. Within their hearts, she *was* the Maid of Lorraine, whether the world chose to believe her. Jean de Metz knew that one day all the armies of France would arise with her charismatic leadership.

As the late-day shadows stretched longer, the town's children raced along the city egress and cheered as Jehanne mounted her stallion and rode through the castle arch and gate known by all as the Port de France à Vaucouleurs.

She held her head high. *It has begun. France will be saved.*

Although this day saw a Jehanne with cropped hair, dressed masculinely in her uncle's riding clothes, nothing in the hearts of the city folk could hold more promise of hope for France's redemption. To further accentuate the importance of the event, Jehanne rode with her sword drawn and waving high. This sword was the weapon given to her by Captain Robert de Baudricourt. Jehanne appeared confident, but the stark reality was that her mission to see the Dauphin was now officially at its beginning, and for her, that was frightening.

The screeching of wooden wheels broke Jehanne's fearful musings. Pulling up to her was a squeaking wagon laden with additional supplies for the perilous trip to the first stop at Saint-Urbain. The horses which pulled the wagon seemed to be a bit skittish at the late afternoon start. Fortunately for all, they were skillfully steadied by a strong hand accompanying a very familiar face. Jehanne smiled and pulled her horse along the side of wagon master Sister Sibyl. Jehanne's horse kept pace with the slowly moving wagon.

"Who's your friend?" inquired Jehanne, pointing to the wagon bench.

"Actually, *he* came with the wagon," said Sister Sibyl as she looked down next to herself.

"Indeed, that rascal is a *he*?" Jehanne shifted in her saddle. "Does *he* have a name?"

"*He* doesn't say much at all."

"Excuse me, sir," Sister Sibyl elbowed the furry creature sitting beside her. "By what name may the Maid of Lorraine call you?" Sister Sibyl shrugged her shoulders as the occupant wagged his tail. "Anyway, Jehanne, I call him Papillon. He seems to like it."

"Does he? That's nice. How is it that he comes by that name?"

"It comes about for two reasons. First, on his white short-haired fur, he has a distinctive tan-colored, butterfly-shaped spot on his left flank. Second, he seems to enjoy chasing and jumping after the butterflies foolish enough to cross his path."

"What has become of his left eye? It looks injured."

"He seems to have damaged it in a scuffle."

"Overall, he seems none the worse for it."

"Does he have sight in it?"

"Not that I can tell. It doesn't seem to slow him down, although he tends to circle more than I have noticed in other dogs."

"Nonetheless, Sister, he is a pretty dog. What breed is he?" Papillon's tail began to steadily wag as he seemed to understand that he was the focused object of the present discussion. With his good eye, he intently surveyed the cropped-haired girl on the horse leaning toward him with kind scrutiny.

"A Sooner," Sister Sibyl smiled.

"Sooner? I don't believe I have ever heard of that breed of dog."

"Yes, well, he'd sooner be one breed of dog as another."

Jehanne laughed. "Well, Monsieur Papillon, Sooner extraordinaire, I am quite pleased to meet you and look forward to your contributions on this journey—sooner rather than later. With his functioning good eye and his keen, sharp nose, it's good to know that he is on watch so that our rest may come more easily." Upon hearing his name spoken by the rider, Papillon stood adeptly on the slowly moving wagon bench and wagged his tail briskly.

Scratching behind the ears of the happy dog, Sister Sibyl leaned in toward the Maid. "Since I have your attention, Jehanne, I would like to ask you a question which has been plaguing me since Father Jean-René's visit." Sister Sibyl stroked Papillon thoughtfully as she formulated the way to ask her question. "The eggs, dear, I just don't understand how eggs softened the captain's heart."

Jehanne nodded with a small smile. "Sister Sibyl, the hens of Vaucouleurs have been made barren by God until the time this trip begins. The voices of the saints allowed me to pass along this warning to further spur our dear captain into action. The fact that he is a lover of this fruit of the hen gave leverage enough to provide us a three-day earlier start to Chinon." Jehanne pointed to the tower which overlooked the arch. The captain could be seen waving his fork with one hand, while a plate domed high with eggs was held in the other.

The pair burst out in cheerful laughter at the spectacle while children ran in the streets mustering up unbridled vocal support for the Maid of Lorraine. Papillon barked along with them.

In the distance, voices could be heard calling, "The hens are laying! The hens are laying!"

51

Wag the Dog

Route to Saint-Urbain

French-held territories, France

15th century

The furrow in Sister Sibyl's forehead ran long and deep. Sitting restlessly on the wagon bench next to the sister, Papillon was not doing well. More so, he had not fared well over the night-long journey from Vaucouleurs. Only hours before, he had spewed up a bloody clump of worms. She kept one hand upon his panting chest and murmured softly to him as the caravan continued its long journey.

It was a cool, overcast Thursday morning as the eight-person and one-dog entourage finally arrived at the Abbey of Saint-Urbain at dawn. This was the first stop on the route to the Dauphin at Chinon. The messenger who had been sent ahead to the Dauphin by Captain Robert de Baudricourt had already passed through the abbey and had left a message to the abbot that Jehanne and seven riders would be soon arriving. Then, the messenger continued rapidly onward to Chinon.

Abbot Arnould d'Aulnoy stood at the front archway instructing the guard that visitors would be arriving within the day. With mild consternation, the abbot and the guard turned to find their immediate horizon silhouetted by several horses and some wagons. With a degree of caution, the guard hailed these earlier-than-expected travelers.

"Halt, who goes there?" The guard stood fast with his hand raised but no weapon visible. The abbot stood with his hands hidden within the folds of his sleeves.

"Have no fear. We come in peace," greeted Jean de Metz, holding his weapon-hand high and away from his side, his fingers widely splayed.

"I believe that we have an escort for the Maid of Lorraine," whispered the wary guard to the abbot.

"Have you sanctuary and safe haven for weary travelers who have left the security of the castle at Vaucouleurs?" Jean de Metz hailed.

The abbot responded, "Yes, we do—as we have done so for the past three hundred fifty years. Welcome, I am curious what news you have of my family from Vaucouleurs." The riding party approached the abbey and halted.

"Of that I cannot say except that Captain Robert de Baudricourt sends wishes for your good health and good fortune."

"Is the captain well?"

"He appeared so as we set forth from his castle yesterday at sundown. That is more than we can say about the smallest of our traveling companions."

"Then you have sufficiently satisfied my concerns regarding the well-being of my family," boasted the abbot with a beaming smile. "Come and rest within God's arms today. I will tend to the little sick one once you have settled in." The abbot was warm and friendly and made sure that the travelers knew that they would be able to rest without fear or molestation. "Whom may I ask the doctor to tend?"

"Send the good doctor to see Papillon," Jean de Metz said.

"As you wish. Tell Monsieur Papillon that help will be here within the hour."

Very quickly the troop settled into the modest accommodations that the abbey had to provide. All the horses were washed, brushed, and given fresh hay. Special care and attention were given to Jehanne's horse which was a last-minute substitution to the trip. The original horse, a gift from the Duke of Lorraine, was suspect and was therefore replaced for reasons unknown to Jehanne. It was very important to the people of Vaucouleurs that the Maid of Lorraine be carried safely onward in the completion of her mission. Thus, because of the confidence they had in their own stock, the originally slated horse of unknown breeding and rearing had to be replaced even if it was the gift of a nobleman.

Jehanne didn't balk at the last-minute horse substitution. She never liked Charles I, the Duke of Lorraine, because he was a man of dubious morals. She had learned that his persona was rich with infidelity and debauchery. Additionally, his loyalty to her blessed Dauphin was in question. During his youth, the Duke of Lorraine had been very close to Philip II, Duke of Burgundy. They had served together several times on various military campaigns. Further, Charles I was openly defiant against Louis I, Duke of Orléans, a friend and supporter of the Dauphin. The Duke of Lorraine's inconsistent pattern of genuine loyalty was well established and well known.

Jehanne had the misfortune to have met Duke Charles I recently in the city of Nancy. She had accepted his invitation, which turned out to be no more than a ruse to bring the Maid into juxtaposition and hopefully her healing powers as well. Charles was afflicted with a social disease in a form of the harlot Alison du May, whom he would not forego despite the sanctity of his wedding vows.

Instead of getting healed from disease by the Maid, Duke Charles I got a reprimand regarding his cavalier approach to marriage. As for Jehanne, instead of getting a robust armed escort from the duke, she got a black horse and a meager bit of change to defer her travel expenses. Neither received what they had hoped to gain.

The duke's splendid black horse, however superior it could be to any other horse, was a constant reminder of the ill reputation of Charles I, Duke of Lorraine. It was probably all for the best that his gift horse stayed in Vaucouleurs while the locally reared white-stocking horse bore the precious Maid to Chinon.

Having refreshed in the abbey enclave quickly, Jehanne announced to the group that she wanted to rest only briefly and then continue to press on. Hearing this, Metz advised against it.

"I think if we can minimize our rest here," postulated Jehanne, "we can cover more ground later today."

"We must be fresh of mind and vigilant," reminded Metz. "It is better to arrive a bit later rather than not at all."

"God will protect us in this travel. The angels have promised this."

"God protects the person who engages measures to first protect himself. My job is clear. I am to see you arrive safely to Chinon. You can assist me by allowing me to do my job unencumbered, my dear Maid."

"I have no wish for you to poorly execute your task, my pushy Jean de Metz. I just want it to be done more quickly." Jehanne turned abruptly and left the group.

"Most honorable Jean de Metz," Sister Sibyl spoke, "your leadership is greatly appreciated. However, please remember that your tasking by your captain is to ensure the safety of a party of eight. Jehanne's task comes from Lord God Almighty and it is to ensure the safety and deliverance of all of France. Keep your priorities straight."

All the men nodded solemnly in response.

"Tomorrow's travels must take us toward Clairvaux and Pothières," Metz pondered aloud. "There *may* be some ways to safely accelerate our pace both to please the captain and our heavenly Father. But Sister, I fear no pace we set will ever be fast enough for our Maid."

Sister Sibyl nodded, smiled, and appreciated the efforts made to ease tension in the ranks. As she followed after Jehanne, Sibyl reflected upon how much Jehanne trusted Metz and the routes that he recommended. Jehanne had to do so—God had selected him from all the rest.

The selection of Jean de Metz may have been clear in the sight of God, but it took some warming up on the part of the Maid. Although she had won his heart quickly, she did not remember him with great fondness regarding their very first encounter outside the captain's keep, right before the first meeting with the captain at Vaucouleurs.

☩ ☩ ☩

"What are you doing here?" Jean de Metz had asked. "Shouldn't the Dauphin be thrown out? Why not just allow us all to become English?"

Jehanne bristled at these words. "Kind sir, I came here to Vaucouleurs to speak to Captain Robert de Baudricourt. I need him to see to it that I am taken to the Dauphin. To date, he fails to see the importance of my request.

Nevertheless, it is important that I be at the Dauphin's side even if it means I should walk until my feet are worn down to my knees. Besides me, there is no one else who can recover the kingdom of France. Can *you* save France, sir? I think not. The blessed Dauphin will have no help, save through me. Though I might prefer to stay home and spin wool with my mother, and though I may be adept at the craft, God has determined that such is not my proper station. *Your* proper station is that you must either direct me, assist me, or just stand out of my way. I must go and I must do it. My Lord wills it."

"I know of no lord in Domrémy. Who is your lord?"

"The same as yours—our Lord God."

"Indeed." Metz looked at her in keen interest. "Sheath your tongue and give me your hand, lass. With God's aid, I will lead you to Captain Robert de Baudricourt. If God so permits, I will also take you to the Dauphin. Are you ready to go?"

"Better yesterday than today. Better today than tomorrow. Better tomorrow than afterward."

✠ ✠ ✠

At the dining table, centrally located in the abbey's transient quarters, Jean de Metz called the traveling group together at the abbey to discuss the particulars of the morrow's quick and safe journey. Still covered in road dust the weary crew sat in varied stages of attentiveness. Some picked at the fruit and vegetable basket on the table while others stared up aimlessly into the rafters. Despite her fatigue, Jehanne listened with a special intensity. Amidst the discussion, a knocking on the meeting room door rudely interrupted. The opened door revealed an austere presence.

"Greetings all. I have been asked to tend to the health of the smallest traveler of this entourage. Please direct me to where I might find Monsieur Papillon."

"Are you a capable healer?" Jehanne asked glumly.

"I am and have been the finest tender of health these parts have seen for well over thirty years."

"That is well and fine, but are you capable?"

"Sir, I assure you. I am a physician of the finest order. I have trained in Paris with the best and have even spent extensive time working with His Highness's staff of court physicians."

"Actually, I am not a *sir*. My name is Jehanne. You know me as the Maid of Lorraine. I am not convinced that you are capable to tend to my friend Papillon."

"Why do you disgrace me so in front of everyone, dear Maid?"

"Sir, my intent is not to demean you in any way. It is just that the health problem of vomiting blood might be something that your Parisian training may have missed."

"Again, dear Maid, I assure you that I was not absent when the art of medicine was taught to me many years ago by Dr. Pizan himself. Rest assured that a malady such as this is well known to me. I have treated many during the several epidemics of pestilence we have endured. Take me to my patient, and I will prove myself to you."

"You need not prove yourself to me, Doctor. You are a healer. Please heal Papillon. He is with the nun in the room beyond that door. I will accept only your best work and your solemn promise of a recovering health for Papillon else you will not leave this building in the same health as you now enter. Do we have an accord?"

"We have it, blessed Maid. I promise. Is it this door?"

"Yes. Tread quietly, as Papillon needs not to be startled."

"As you wish, dear Maid."

The local doctor crossed the room in a stunned silence. If ever his confidence had been shaken, it was today. He gave himself internal reassurance that a patient presenting with bloody vomit had the wherewithal to heal under his trained hand. He only hoped that Monsieur Papillon had no other comorbidities or secrets which might confound any progress toward healing.

The door opened and the voice of Sister Sibyl was heard giving due respect and greeting to the doctor as he closed the door behind him.

"Good day, Doctor. It is a great pleasure to meet you. If you need anything, please do not hesitate to ask. I am here for you."

"Where is my patient, kind Sister?"

"He lies there under the covers. He moans frequently but moves little. It worries me so."

"My goodness he is a small one. Is he a midget?"

"I have no reason to believe so, Doctor," said Sister Sibyl as she pulled back the blanket uncovering the head of the canine patient.

"Sister, where is the patient? There's nothing here to treat but a mangy dog."

"Mangy dog? A mangy dog? I think not. He is one of God's creatures and a chosen one for this most perilous mission. That's more than I can say about you. Your patient's name is Papillon, and he is quite ill."

"Sister, I have no knowledge of your mission, what it entails, or what will result from its completion. But whatever it is, surely the health of this hound cannot not weigh greatly in the outcome."

"Whether the dog wags its tail, or the tail wags the dog, please be advised, Doctor, Papillon has the esteemed favor of the Maid of Loraine. You would do well to remember that. Further, you are bound by your solemn promise to her. I heard you say so."

"But Sister—he's a dog."

"Shhh . . . in the ears, straight to the heart. Papillon may have only one good eye, but he has two good ears. He does not know he is a dog. He does not need you to herald it to the world."

"Sister, I'm a physician. I heal—"

"—God's creatures . . . and so you shall. Papillon is one of God's finest creatures. If you are a quality healer from Dr. Thomas de Pizan's court of physicians—"

"You know Dr. Pizan? How can you know of such things, Sister?"

"Don't trouble yourself deciphering how I know what I know. If I have correctly heard you boast your skills, then it shouldn't matter whether your patient has two legs or four."

"But Sister, you don't understand. This is a dog."

"If you insist, Doctor. Then know this—your patient, Papillon, is a sick dog. May God himself strike you down if you fail to practice your sworn oath to the blessed Maid and her faithful canine. You are a healer. So take this *dog* and heal!"

52

Amassing the Maid

Route to Auxerre

French-held territories, France

15th century

A blanket-covered Papillon gingerly rode on a firm pillow on the wagon seat next to Sister Sibyl on the morning of the twenty-seventh of February. On this, the second day of travel from Saint-Urbain, Papillon's gums were still a little pale, but his vomiting of blood had stopped. The medicine that the good doctor gave seemed to be working. At least he was not getting worse. The same could not be said for the rattled Saint-Urbain physician.

The formation of eight passed numerous vineyards filled with fruit-laden vines of white Chablis grapes. They occasionally stopped to taste a sample of the commercially grown product now being raised in quantities to support the economy of the beautiful city of Auxerre. This normal Sunday had its usual millings which totally ignored the austere presence of a most distinguished group of travelers.

Unbeknownst to the weary personages, Auxerre had its own level of accomplishments. It had been a flourishing town across the Yonne River since Roman times and even served as provincial capital in Gaul. As Jehanne passed beneath the center city archway, she noted the time on the old tower. She came to the realization that she arrived just in time for Mass. Since the trip began, Jehanne had great trepidation in the fact she would not be able to sufficiently attend Mass and give due praise to Lord Jesus.

Jehanne took this moment to again advise her companions to place God first in their lives. "If only we could hear Mass, all would be well. We must all give our thanks and due respect to God." Papillon weakly wagged his tail in agreement.

Auxerre boasted both the ancient Roman-built Église Saint-Eusèbe-en-Champsaur as well as the grand gothic Cathédrale de Sainte-Étienne. The stained-glass windows of the grand cathedral were renowned to be the most elegant glasswork in all France. Here, between the multicolored artistic religious

226

images, Jehanne accepted Holy Communion and lifted the burden of guilt from her heavy heart—at least for a while.

Upon gathering after Mass, Metz spoke to the travelers. "We must be increasingly stealthy as the next few days of travel will go into the English-held territorial towns of Mézilles, Viglain, La Ferté, and finally Gien. Once past Gien, we will be back in friendly territory. But until then, danger will lurk around every corner. Because we are at war, within every shadow will hide the enemies of France—the English, the Burgundians, and even some French who all wish ill upon the Maid of Lorraine. Folks, our lives are all in danger. We all must be at our sharpest watch—especially our smallest one who, thankfully, seems to be improving by the hour, Monsieur Papillon."

53

Epistles of Jehanne

L'Eglise de Sainte-Catherine-de-Fierbois

Sainte-Catherine-de-Fierbois, France

15th century

After five days of having to pass through English-controlled territory, the loud barking of a mixed-breed Sooner dog announced that Jehanne's party had finally arrived at a small namesake church in a demure village. The church honored one of her three saintly voices. The arrival spawned great emotion from within Jehanne, for Saint Catherine had guided Jehanne's fluid metamorphosis into the Maid of Lorraine.

It was now the fourth day in the new month. March was as blustery as February was cold. It felt good for the band to warmly bivouac in the safety of church grounds once again. Jehanne knew that she must now announce their presence to the town of Chinon, located twenty miles away as the deer runs but seven hours by wagon ride or just two hours by lone horse rider.

"The Dauphin must know that we have arrived here in safety," Jehanne requested of Jean de Metz.

Bertrand de Poulengy shook his head in stark agreement. "Maybe now we should dispatch Colet de Vienne as he is the king's messenger."

"Agreed," said Jehanne.

"With a caveat," interrupted Sister Sibyl. "I believe that the Dauphin must know that this is not a ruse—the message which accompanies Colet must come from you, Jehanne." Sister Sibyl's voice portended insistence.

"But, Sister, you know that I struggle with writing. You tell me the letters are reversed or upside down. Even with all your years of help, I can write little more than just my name."

Sister Sibyl's cheeks grew red as she came to the realization of the depths of Jehanne's humbleness. God had certainly selected the most unseasoned pick of the litter. Of all the d'Arc children, Jehanne never could master the art of hand-writing. Sister Sibyl regrouped her emotions in stalwart fashion.

228

"The scripting of your name by your own hand will be enough. If it pleases God and his Maid of Lorraine, I will humbly write the message as you best dictate it to me."

"Sister Sibyl, please write in a manner that will convince the Dauphin that I am truly the one whom he seeks to aid France in this, her hour of greatest need."

The nun nodded her accord. Having then secured writing instruments and paper from the clergy of the church, Sister Sibyl annotated the date and place of the letter.

"I am ready to scribe. Speak, child."

Placing her hands at her chin, Jehanne interlaced her fingers, looked up at the church ceiling, and then began a discourse. Her voice rang melodically.

"My precious Dauphin, I have come to you upon the guidance of three blessed saints. In each of three masses I have attended on this journey, they have revealed to me that I must come to your aid in the saving of France from the English and Burgundians. Although I have traveled unrestricted for nearly one hundred fifty leagues to come to your aid, the last few steps must be granted by you. You must allow me to see you as I have much good news in what I have to say and in what I have to show you. Be of good cheer—I need no help in finding you as I am sure that the angels will help me to recognize you amongst all others."

Jehanne affixed her signature to the letter, and Colet rode hard the twenty miles which separated the travelers from the castle at Chinon. For the remainder of this Friday, with moistened cheeks, Jehanne worshipped God before the statue of Saint Catherine. After she had completed this spiritual cleansing, she once again approached the devoted nun.

"Sister Sibyl, if it pleases you to assist me once again, I need you to draft a letter to my parents. I fear that they thought my departure from Domrémy was one where I sought to leave them. I want them to understand that I needed to start upon the execution of the mission God."

As before, Sister Sibyl took up quill and parchment and wrote the words that Jehanne's heart purged.

"My blessed parents, I implore you to reach deep in your hearts to forgive your daughter who has left you without word. Had I had a hundred parents or been the king's daughter, I would have had to go. I know that I have left you with an empty seat at the table and without an extra pair of strong hands to help in the home. Please know that I am guided by God and His holy saints. Along with me I have taken from the church Sister Sibyl as she has consented to be my spiritual guide while we journey. When the opportunity arises, please extend my deepest gratitude to our dear friends and family in Burey-en-Vaux. Uncle Durand was noble in his support of this cause. I assure you, Father, that our family honor will never be questioned. I am proud to be your daughter. Please explain to the family that the love in my heart for all of you will never fail. God bless you all."

As before, Sister Sibyl watched Jehanne write her name upon the letter. Sibyl placed the rolled-up letter in a special tube she had brought from the church at Domrémy. She had used the tube to carry paper for notes she wrote at the Château de Beauté many years ago. It also served to carry select pages from her book of prayers. The book itself was left back at her work area in the church at Domrémy. To ease matters presently at hand, the notes and the prayer book's loose leaves could easily be moved to another secure container. This, now vacant, tube could justifiably be raised in its level of important service to protect the in-transit message Jehanne wished her parents to be given. Sister Sibyl gave the newly refilled tube to the clergy at the church who would see to it that it would be delivered to the church at Domrémy. From there, Father Jean Minet would open the tube marked "Domrémy" and read the feelings and thoughts of Jehanne to her devoted family.

Jehanne returned to the chapel within the church and immersed her soul in the voices of the three guiding saints. Papillon pitter-pattered after her, demonstrating great energy that he had not had for many days. Jehanne's exhaustion eventually carried her into a dreamless sleep. Papillon watched over her silently as she slumbered. When she finally awoke, information had been received from Colet who had just returned from his morning sojourn. It now appeared that Jehanne would be expected at Château de Chinon in five days hence.

The ninth of March could not and would not arrive soon enough. Knowing that the city of Orléans was still under siege, and that every day of delay meant that it could fall, left little to stop the English from marching down to Chinon. Jehanne quickly surmised that they certainly could not wait there at Fierbois. *When the Dauphin summons me, I must be close. We must leave at the earliest opportunity— the morning of the sixth. I will wait for the Dauphin in the town of Chinon itself. Today and tomorrow will be very taxing for all, but especially for me.*

Angst again consumed her. Jehanne knelt and prayed to God and her three patron saints for that which her vestment of character sorely lacked—a blessed shroud of patience.

Afterward, Jehanne's mind continued the forward planning.

Once we arrive at Chinon, three more days of waiting will proceed at a snail's pace. Worse yet, no person in the city can hospitably keep us. Curiosity seekers and meddlers will come. What if I unwittingly lead this troop to ill will and harm? What if God and the blessed saints lose confidence in me—in the manner I present God's mission? France could fail and it will be I alone at the core of the defeat.

She closed her eyes. The scarlet syrup in her veins morphed into the molasses of winter.

54

Voices in Chinon

Chinon, Loire River Valley
Loire region, France
15th century

It was high noon on the sixth of March when the bedraggled group arrived without pomp or circumstance into the ingress streets and migrated toward a local traveler's inn. Immediately, Jean de Metz dispatched Colet to announce to the royal staff in the Chinon fortress that the party had safely arrived in the city. Meanwhile, the troop busily shifted travel gear to support a multiday stay in the local hostel. The security of the items that they could not stow indoors was ever present in their minds.

Papillon, the one-eyed guardian, growled at all of the city's curious inhabitants that passed too closely to his wagon. Even though it was a reasonable distance from the busy street traffic, all pedestrians gave him a wide berth.

The flow of the first day in Chinon was periodically interrupted with royal probes in the form of visits from the king's advisors and counselors. These men had been sent out to give the Dauphin advanced knowledge of the Maid of Lorraine. Jehanne was honestly as glad to see them as they were glad to see her. *What makes you so special among all the maidens there in the Lorraine?* they asked. *Are you sure it is our Lord God that speaks to you?* She was happy to acquiesce to the image of their fluttering coattails as they headed back to the castle. After they had departed, she always felt violated—like a rigorously handled vegetable on the stand of a local greengrocer. Emotionally, she felt poked and prodded—constantly having to defend herself and her God-given mission. If it was only this, she could live with the rude annoyance. However, there was something else bothering her. In solitude, the meaning evaded her.

"I need your help, Sister Sibyl." Jehanne hurriedly pulled the nun to a place where their conversation would be out of earshot. They sat on the bench of the wagon, knee to knee, only separated by the presence of a blanket-

231

covered Papillon who was, already, a master of keeping whispers, securing secrets, and encasing surreptitiousness.

"What is it, child?" Sister Sibyl's voice had a ring of alarm.

"I have heard voices."

"Yes, dear, I know."

"You don't understand—these aren't the same voices," Jehanne whispered.

"Whose voices are these?"

"I am not sure. And I cannot hear them distinctly, at least not yet. It is like a murmur that surrounds me. It is growing stronger. They speak in a language I have never heard. It sounds like the language of the Godon."

"The Godon?" Sister Sibyl asked, cocking her head to the side.

"Yes Sister—the English. In my experience with these invaders, it seems that every other word they speak is 'Godon.'" Jehanne shifted Papillon's head onto her lap. "I collectively call the Englishmen who use the Lord's name in vain Godons." Jehanne leaned in. "These new voices do not curse our Lord, but they do speak in English. Sister Sibyl, when I focus on the murmuring, I can almost understand it. It is an unsettling sensation. But even so, I believe the saints want me to communicate with them. Yet I am afraid."

"Are you *sure* these voices aren't those of Saint Catherine, Saint Margaret, and Saint Michael?"

"Yes."

"Could they be other saints? English Godon saints?"

"It is possible. My fear. . ." Jehanne paused and drew in a breath, "is that they are from evil sources."

"Nonsense, child. God would not permit it. Get that thought out of your mind immediately." She placed her hands firmly on the girl's shoulders. "I do not know who has been allowed to speak to your mind and heart, but I will guarantee you, as God is my witness, it will not be evil."

"How can you be so sure?"

"In my life, I have heard voices as well." A sudden rustle overshot their whispers. They turned toward the street to find the source. "I need say no more now," the nun whispered. Papillon emanated a deep growl.

Richard the Archer slowly passed by on his way into the city. From his initial downward gaze, he glanced left at the closely huddled feminine pair but rendered no more than a smile. His footsteps disappeared into the usual noises of the city. A brief hush followed. Papillon ceased his low growl and placed his head back in Jehanne's lap.

Jehanne scrutinized the nun's face closely. After a moment, she paused then spoke softly. "They are returning to me now, and the whispers are getting louder. Sister Sibyl, if they speak to me should I answer?"

"As God wills it, Jehanne. As God wills it." Sister Sibyl held Jehanne's hand as the girl's eyes fluttered closed, and she drifted into a quieter state.

Papillon edged his way fully into Jehanne's lap. Counterclockwise he circled and circled methodically then settled himself peacefully.

The nun sat anxiously waiting, worrying. She prayed that her counsel had been good and true—that she had not led Jehanne off the righteous path. She closed her eyes to calm her unease, but they snapped open instantly as Jehanne began to speak aloud in a language that the girl had never known, and the nun could vaguely remember.

55

Unexpected Parade

Maternity hospital

Saint-Quentin, Somme River Valley

Vermandois region, France

Current day

Step right up, folks. . . . Douglas scratched his forehead as the last of the hospital's nursing staff departed, leaving Loni in a bedside patient recliner. Douglas pulled up Suzanne's chair and settled in to re-engage Loni. *Pay your money and take your chance.* He knew that Mickey and Suzanne agreed on this talking to historical voices—and he did too, for that matter—but it didn't make it any less dangerous or nerve wracking. *If through this course of action, we find the key to make Loni herself again . . .* Douglas cleared his throat. *It's showtime.*

"Hello again," he said to Loni, whom the hospital staff had moved to a patient recliner, her feet were slightly elevated in the patient recliner, and on her pregnant belly she rested her pair of folded hands.

"Hello."

Douglas's finely tuned ears caught an increased coarseness in Loni's voice. "With whom am I speaking?"

"Jehanne."

Douglas looked to Mickey and Suzanne, his face wide-eyed and questioning. "What happened to Sibylle?"

"Am I supposed to know that?"

"Where is Sibylle?" he asked.

"I don't know. I am Jehanne. Who—"

"Why are you using this name?"

"Because that *is* my name."

"Where is Loni?" Mickey surged forward, uninvited, into the dialogue.

"Who is Loni?" Loni's face turned toward Mickey. Her vocal cords reflected a slight hint of consternation at the second voice which spoke to her. "And who are—"

236

"Jehanne, what do you see?" Douglas cut across the new voice, simultaneously holding up a hand to halt Mickey from further interruption.

"I see Richard the Archer walking up to the castle. There is a river that flows down below the bastion."

"Why do you suppose you are at a castle?"

"I am here because I traveled eleven days and many leagues to get here," she responded, with a tone of proud defiance.

"Why did you travel so long to get to the castle?"

"God willed it."

"Loni!" Mickey again knifed in.

"Who?" she responded.

Douglas sternly pulled Mickey's shoulder down and hissed into his ear, "Mickey, there is no Loni right now. Let me guide this interview the best way I know how. I am the lead doctor here, so *stand down*. You asked me to help. So let me help."

Mickey felt his face flush hot. Pushing Douglas's hand off his shoulder, Mickey threw himself into a chair.

"Why does that voice call me Loni?" she again asked.

"Jehanne, I am going to ask you to focus on my voice and no others. I mean you no harm, I wish only to ask you some questions. Can you do that? Do you understand?"

"Yes."

Within moments Loni was comfortably more upright in her recliner, her feet less elevated. Loni's hands were at her neck scraping her pendant on its chain.

"Give me one moment, Jehanne." Gently, Douglas placed his hand atop Loni's, stopping the pendant crucifix from scraping on its chain. *It's amazing that such a uniquely beautiful crucifix, affixed there on its Jerusalem cross, could pique the hairs of my neck just by its grating on its serpentine neck chain.*

"As God wills," said Jehanne slowly, relaxing her grip on the crucifix slightly. Douglas and the others had no way of knowing that across a time continuum, Jehanne now sat statuesquely on the wagon bench outside her lodging there in Chinon. Quietly she sat with Papillon, who had comfortably relocated in her lap. Her hands were folded over the butterfly mark which graced the flank of the sleeping dog. She, so very gently, stroked his soft fur.

Turning away from Loni, Douglas stood up and again squared off his shoulders. He corralled the others away from Loni and began talking in the direction somewhere between Mickey and Suzanne. Wanting to address each simultaneously, his eyes focused on neither.

"Can either of you tell me about the castle that this Jehanne is talking about?" Douglas asked.

"I am guessing it's the castle in Péronne where she was when she passed out and struck her head," offered Mickey. He flexed the fingers of his unbroken hand.

"Are you saying that Jehanne went to Péronne?"

"I don't think so. I was talking about Loni," Mickey replied.

"Guys, Jehanne said *nothing* about paired oblong towers. She just said a castle," Suzanne affirmed.

"Good point. I agree that it isn't Péronne."

"Well, without further information, I have no other guesses at this time," Mickey's voice trailed off with disappointment.

"Anyone want to pose a guess why the voice of Sibylle has gone?" Douglas scratched at his forehead again.

"My guess is that both Sibylle and this Jehanne are linked in Loni's psyche in a manner that is unclear to us at the moment," Suzanne responded.

"I'm not sure I understand what you are saying, Suzanne," Douglas raised an eyebrow at her.

She held up a finger to say *Wait a minute*. Suzanne leaned her back against the wall and placed her middle and ring fingers on her temples with her palms just hovering over her cheeks. She closed her eyes.

Mickey took a step forward and began to speak, but Douglas held out his hand to stop him. With a look from Douglas, Mickey understood. The men waited.

Suzanne tried to align her thoughts. She swiftly amassed all the seemingly surreal events of the last several hours: the shimmering edges of the holographic Christine in the abbey, the sensation of her touch, the wisdom of her words, these other voices within Loni, Christine's reflection in the waiting room window of the hospital.

Suzanne spoke slowly, with her eyes still closed. "Maybe the point where we engage Loni links to a specific person, and *who* it is depends upon the nature of what is happening in the past." Having arrived at a satisfactory theory based on her experiences, she lowered her hands and opened her eyes.

The looks on the faces of the men made it clear that they were not tracking. They cast each other sideways glances.

"How can I put this . . . ummm . . . Okay, eyes on me—good. Now, imagine Loni is no longer a single entity we know as Loni Peronne, but instead, in her psyche, she is a parade of characters lined up in a definite order relative to each other—but that order is unknown to us."

"Okay," said Douglas, stretching the word.

"We are the sidelined spectators of this parade. Inasmuch, we can have visibility to all the parade of characters—Sibylle, Jehanne, and who knows who else—but only little by little as they pass our scope of vision."

"Okay," Mickey echoed.

"The problem is that we don't have a program, right? So, we don't always know who is in the procession, in what sequence, or what purpose they have in Loni's psyche. Further, I think maybe the characters themselves may not know each other—or if they do, they don't know that they are part of a cavalcade."

Suzanne's analysis metaphor was interrupted by the shooping of the pendant necklace, its metal flashing brilliantly in the sunlight. All eyes turned to Loni.

"Loni—as Jehanne—keeps fiddling with the pendant around her neck. Could it have something to do with this persona?" queried Suzanne. "Did it once belong to a Jehanne?"

"No, not to my knowledge," said Mickey. "It belonged to Loni's grandmother, Grande Madame Fabienne Auger. She inherited it from another parade of characters who willfully entered a tontine." He followed up with, "I know, right?" and a small smile.

"A tontine?" Douglas queried. "Why would Loni's grandmother enter a group legal agreement leading to an inheritance? Who was part of this tontine?"

"Oh, how I wish Loni was here. She could tell you exactly." Mickey rubbed the back of his neck and cast a glance at his wife. "Here is how the story goes according to Loni's great grandmother—as best as I can relate it. Four dear friends came to accord that whoever of the three of them lived longest would inherit a gift, the pendant that was as rich as it was precious."

"Who were the four friends?" Suzanne asked.

Mickey smiled broadly, "These women were only the three most famous aviatrixes of the time—Elvy Kalep, Amelia Earhart, Marie Marvingt, and Jasmine Emma Hertz."

"My Jesus," exhaled Suzanne. "That is one heck of a parade."

"In 1936, these three agreed to place the pendent with a New York law firm as a tontine with the stipulation that the last of them would receive the gift. That last person would then wear the gift, remembering and honoring the dear friendship that they all possessed." Mickey paused.

Douglas rubbed his stubbled face then commented very sadly, "Well, we know that Amelia Earhart disappeared in the Pacific."

"Yes, the very next year in 1937. GiGi died in 1978."

"GiGi? Who is GiGi?" Suzanne asked.

"Oh, sorry. GiGi is short for great grandmother. I guess Loni preferred this nickname rather than Great Grandmother Jasmine Emma Hertz. Anyway, GiGi died in Loni's very first year as an undergraduate at the University of Pennsylvania."

"Well, that would mean that Elvy received the pendant from the New York law firm," mused Douglas.

"And she did," Mickey confirmed. "Elvy possessed the pendant until her death in 1989. That same year, Fabienne Auger, GiGi's daughter, received a summons to appear in a Palm Beach courthouse. She had to attend the reading of the will regarding the estate of Elvy Kalep. Because neither Amelia Earhart nor Elvy Kalep had any surviving family, Elvy willed the pendant to Jasmine's child, Fabienne. The very next year, Fabienne presented the pendant to Loni in a beautiful, and explicitly private, ceremony on our wedding day."

"That's nice for Loni, but I wonder why Grande Madame didn't give the pendant to her daughter, Monique, or even to the elder granddaughter, Jillian," Suzanne mused.

"Whatever the issue was, even with the privacy of the gifting, I know Loni did not wear it for years. She kept it in her mother's jewelry box."

"Sounds like somebody gifted an heirloom while having a burr in their saddle."

"For that answer, you would have to go to Oger, France, and ask Grande Madame herself. She loves to tell the story but only in French, German, or Flemish."

"Actually," said Douglas, "I was more curious about how the pendant found its way to the three pilots in the first place."

"I'm guessing Loni or Monique knows. Grande Madame surely knows. However, I could only lie to you from this point on. I can tell you with candor that—at least to Loni—that pendant has an inexplicably deep association with Joan of Arc." Mickey's face suddenly brightened, and he opened his mouth to speak again.

"But . . ." Douglas cut across, "this voice calls herself Jehanne."

"Yes!" Mickey tapped his splint into his open palm. "Jehanne was the name Joan of Arc *called herself*. It was the one word she knew to spell!"

"But that still doesn't explain anything!" Douglas whispered back harshly. He combed ten fingers through his hair and stared at the ceiling. "How are Sibylle and Jehanne connected? What is this castle? Why doesn't Jehanne know Loni?"

Douglas groaned and leaned against the room's sink. *This whole thing is spiraling aimlessly, and the answers I need to bring back Loni aren't getting any clearer! If I fail, Loni ceases being Loni. She devolves into whichever character that we intersect in this bizarre parade across time.*

Mickey hesitantly took a step toward Douglas and put his good hand on the man's shoulder. "Maybe she doesn't know Loni because the guiding angels and voices in her head only revealed the part of the future that Joan—or Jehanne— needed to know to accomplish her earthly mission."

Suzanne stood squinting at the glass window in the room. "Oh, Jehanne knows Loni." The two men stared at her, but she kept her eyes on her own reflection. "Jehanne knows Loni," she repeated, "just not by name. Jehanne was an embodiment of female strength long before her time—and a main inspiration of it afterward. Jehanne *is* Loni and Loni *is* Jehanne. Names are irrelevant."

The room went quiet for a very long time. The light from the window crept its way across the tile floor, casting leaning shadows.

Douglas finally broke the silence. "What of this Richard the Archer? Jehanne spoke of him in our conversation. What association does Richard have with Jehanne and the castle that sits on their horizon?"

"I can't remember a Richard the Archer in any historical annotations," replied Mickey. "But as we have all witnessed, I'm not exactly sharp as a tack right now."

"Richard was obviously a warrior. Russell might know," posed Suzanne. "Shall I call him?"

Douglas displayed a tight-lipped grimace. Responding only to Mickey, Douglas summarized, "Okay, that is helpful. Using Suzanne's paradigm of a parade, I am going to work with Jehanne for now. I can tell you both that I honestly don't know where this will lead."

"Hopefully in the direction of recovery, right?" Suzanne asked, inadequately obscuring the desperation in her thoughts.

Douglas was not going to reinforce any doubt. He picked up the pace without missing a beat. "Recovery . . . maybe. Discovery . . . most likely. Mickey, do you want me to continue what we're doing?"

"Is this, in any way, hurting her?"

"No, not to my knowledge, Mickey. However, there may be sides of her that we may uncover that none of us ever knew existed."

"Like the multiple personalities cases in the twentieth century; like Sybil or Eve?"

"Maybe. We can always pull the plug. But the further down we go on this road—even if we back out—we may have forever lost Loni as we know her. Think about this before we take the next step." Douglas looked squarely at Mickey who gazed toward his precious Loni.

Mickey heard Suzanne's critique in his ear. "If we don't do anything, we have lost her forever anyway."

"True enough," answered Douglas. "Mickey, it is your call. Where do we go from here?"

"Don't ask me, Douglas. Ask Joan of Arc." Mickey clenched his jaw at the decision just made and prayed silently to God that he had done what was best for Loni and the twins. Then, the prayer of the fourteen angels came to him, and clearly, without error, he recited it in his mind.

56

Spies and Secrets

Chinon, Loire River Valley
Loire region, France
15th century

From time to time a person with a spyglass could be seen on the tower of Château de Chinon looking out over the town and often in the direction of the most recently arrived town guests.

Jean de Metz looked out beyond the rooftops of the town to the solitary, tall oblong tower of the castle. The feedback from the morning visits of the king's counselors began trickling back to the travelers.

"Apparently, some have reported that the Maid is a fake. Others say she is a lunatic. Still others say that she is divinely possessed of God." He stroked his chin thoughtfully. "At this rate of advisement, we will never be permitted to visit the Dauphin," Metz concluded, his heart heavy with the mixed bundle of news received.

"Do not worry," said Sister Sibyl. "God would not have let us travel this far just to have us be defeated by the snake-tongued advisors of the Dauphin."

"They have the ability to obstruct our meeting," reminded Jean.

"Yes, they do."

"This does not bother you?"

"I have said my piece, Jean. The Dauphin's heart will be swayed by the merits and virtue of our blessed Maid. Don't you feel her power?" Sister Sibyl boasted.

"It matters not what I feel. It matters only what the Dauphin feels. It is he—not me—who must grant her an audience."

"Honorable Jean de Metz," began Sister Sibyl in a more encouraging tone, "tell me what you saw in the distance this morning."

"I saw a man with a spyglass looking in this direction."

"How many people would have the authority and freedom to be on the castle bastion at Chinon?"

"Not many."

"Would it be safe to say that the man who holds the spyglass is of relative importance?"

"I would say that."

"He could even be the Dauphin himself?"

"Yes, he could."

"After hearing the words from all the advisors which have categorized our Maid in every way, from demonic to depraved to insane to divine, he still has mustered enough energy to look and seek answers for himself."

"Yes."

"He is a man who thinks for himself."

"I concede that the man with the spyglass is a man who thinks for himself. However, dear Sister, I cannot be sure the man with the spyglass is the Dauphin."

"Even if he isn't, I believe the spyglass belongs to the Dauphin. The fact that he owns it makes him a man who wishes to better understand things which are far."

"Yes."

"So, whether the man on the bastion with the spyglass is the Dauphin or one just directed by the Dauphin is of no matter. The Dauphin will seek to query our blessed Maid because he desires to know. Even if it is out of mere curiosity, he burns to know. I believe that God has placed the burning in his heart."

"I believe *you* should be on the king's royal staff."

"How do you know I wasn't?"

"Were you?"

"I was."

"I mean really."

"So do I."

Jean studied the face of the nun carefully. "Nuns are not permitted to speak falsehoods."

"No, they aren't."

"Have you always been a nun?" Jean de Metz displayed a wry smile.

"That, monsieur, was the correct question. There are secrets and there are *secrets*." Sister Sibyl smiled back at the beaming Jean.

Sister Sibyl knew that what Jehanne needed was much more than a man with a spyglass, be he the Dauphin or not. Jehanne needed the fulfillment of the promise from the angels. And how these new voices played into this process still needed to be fathomed. But most of all, Jehanne needed to have the ear of the Dauphin, and it needed to be soon.

As the moments passed in Chinon for the anxious travelers awaiting audience with the Dauphin, Orléans—the last city to hold out against the English—continued to weaken. The people of Orléans could not withstand the siege much longer. They were running out of tomorrows. It seemed that every failed attempt of gallantry had put the city on the same path as that of the Battle of the Herrings. Morale was slowly weakening and some feared that soon, even the discovery of the fated Maid of Lorraine would have no bearing. The king's ears were being filled with the fears of less virtuous men while sand continued to fill the bottom of the hourglass. Every moment without salvation was a lash against the hope the people of Orléans tried to muster in their hearts.

Sister Sibyl went to Jehanne to update her on the conversation that transpired between herself and Jean de Metz. Out in the carriage house, Jehanne sat in her usual spot on the wagon bench with Papillon well in place. The sounds of chickens clucking could be heard from the pens on the far side. Sister Sibyl kicked at stones under the wagon until Jehanne opened her eyes. The sister smiled motherly.

"The new voices are with you, aren't they, dear?"

"Yes, Sister. They need me to be here, now, alone."

"Without me?"

"For now, yes. Please don't go far. I sense I will need your company sooner rather than later."

"I will be just inside the doorway of the house. Use your solitude to its best advantage. I will be close. Do you need me to take Papillon?"

"Papillon stays. You don't. Thank you, dear Sister Sibyl. That will be all."

57

Reaching Sorrow

Maternity hospital

Saint-Quentin, Somme River Valley

Vermandois region, France

Current day

Douglas re-engaged Loni's hypnosis, and after the appropriate set of commands he brought back Jehanne. What he was about to do next was unfathomable—he was about to use regression hypnosis on a person six hundred years in the past. Through a hypnotized Loni, he was going to hypnotize Jehanne to find what he assumed might be the source of the psychic problem dwelling in both their pasts.

"Jehanne, are you alone somewhere quiet?"

"Yes. Voice, please, tell me who—"

"Jehanne, I need you to concentrate on my voice and nothing else. Just my voice. My voice is enough to guide you."

"Very well."

"I need you to go back and recall the first thing in your mind that you clearly remember."

Loni's body relaxed more deeply, eyes closed, her face like still water.

"I see a bearded man in a mirror." Loni tilted her head to the side as if with curious observation. "He looks very old and very tired. He is a reflection of me." Her eyes popped open. "No, he is me. I am that man in the mirror."

"Who you are, Jehanne?" Douglas's voice strained. "Can you tell me?"

"I am very, very important." Loni's eyebrows rose. "I am a king. I see my coat of arms. It is on many things that I wear and around my house."

"Tell me about your house."

"It is a castle."

"The same castle as before?"

"Before what?"

Douglas changed gears seamlessly. "Tell me about this castle."

"No. I can't. There is much sadness here." Loni's forehead furrowed. "I don't want to stay."

"Tell me why there is sadness and then we will go."

"There is a woman sitting near me. I think she is the queen. She wears the same coat of arms. In her lap is a blanket with the same symbol. I think the bundle is the focus of her despair."

"Tell me about the coat of arms."

"It is a blue shield and on it are three golden fleur-de-lys."

"Is the woman there crying?"

"She is beyond tears. She is at the silence which follows when no further tears can be shed and only the sadness remains."

"Why is she sad?"

"Joanna is sad for the same reason I am weary. It is because the royal line faces tragedy after tragedy. My house, the House of Valois, is in distress."

"How do you know this?"

"I am the king." Loni held her shoulders back, her posture strong despite her pregnant belly. "I am King Charles the Wise. I am King Charles V."

"Why is there so much grief?"

"Of the nine children born into my household, six have thus far died."

"I am so sorry to hear of your losses, Your Highness. If you will, can you please tell me what year this is?"

"Yes."

Douglas shifted forward in his chair. "If it pleases Your Highness, what year is it?"

"It is the year of our Lord 1375. The tragedy began so many years ago. My first two children died two weeks apart. Now arrives the final insult. Queen Joanna gave birth to Princess Catherine. I see Catherine moving in the lap of her mother. But not even this life can return joy into the face of my queen. Nothing can."

"Nothing?"

"No. The dead can't feel anything."

"Your queen is dead?"

"Dr. Pizan tells me so."

"Your Highness, I will take away your sadness, for now." Double tapping Loni's arm, Douglas returned the king to a state of quiet. Loni eased back into the chair; her hands drifted up to the pendant around her neck.

58

Secrets Unfolding

Chinon, Loire River Valley

Loire region, France

15th century

A steady rain announced the morning of the seventh of March. It had been twelve days since Jehanne left the city gate at Vaucouleurs. Today, she prepared to face the continued annoyances of the king's counselors. She wondered which of them would appear and what foolish questions would they pose. In the distance, the top of the castle tower was shrouded with a haze. Since the tower's head loomed far above the level of the street, she wondered if maybe the man with the spyglass had a clearer view of the world. Here, below the level of the clouds, the world was dark and dreary. Jehanne felt further from the Dauphin and her goal than she did back in the Lorraine.

Sister Sibyl, with Papillon afoot, scooped up a distraught Jehanne and took her to their private corner of the world under the thatched roof of the carriage house.

"Did the voices come back, child?" said Sister Sibyl as she situated herself on the wagon seat.

"Yes."

"What did they say?" Sister Sibyl chewed on the inside of her cheek.

"It is not what they said, Sister Sibyl. It is what I have said."

"I don't understand." The nun stroked Papillon's fur.

"Nor do I."

"Speak not in riddles, dear Jehanne."

"The voices took me deep inside myself to another place, another life. I saw the world through the eyes of another person," said Jehanne, shuddering.

"How can that be?"

"I'm not sure. It was like I went to sleep and woke up as a different person. Almost like a dream. The voice carried me to a castle."

"This castle?" Sister Sibyl pointed toward Chinon.

"No, the castle of King Charles."

Sister Sibyl trembled slightly as she inhaled. "Darling, did the voice say Paris? Was the castle in Paris?"

"I don't recall the name of the castle. I remember the face in the mirror. It reflected the eyes from which I viewed my world."

"In whose face did those eyes reside?"

"His name was King Charles. His bearded face was old and very sad."

"Maybe it was Charles VI."

"He said . . . I said . . . the year was 1375."

"Then Charles VI would have been a boy," said Sister Sibyl nodding. "The face you saw was King Charles V. We called him Charles the Wise."

"Yes, he called himself this name. He said his wife was Queen Joanna. She had given birth to Princess Catherine. Then I said that my queen was dead."

"Then it was certainly Charles V. He so despaired over the loss of his queen."

"He was so very sad, Sister."

"Yes, I know. I remember."

"You remember?" Jehanne peered at the nun, puzzled.

"Yes, I remember that his heart was so heavy with the loss of so many of his children and then with the loss of his queen. I always wished that his pain would go away. No one deserves such sadness. It consumes the soul and sucks the light from the eyes."

"*You yourself* remember?" Arching an eyebrow, Jehanne picked up Papillon and moved him to her lap.

"Child, I thought if the king could see the world as it once was, maybe his happiness would return." Sister Sibyl audibly inhaled. "So, I would show him small kindnesses—a smile, a nod—just to let him know the world was not all darkness and dismay."

"You spoke to him . . . knew him?"

"Yes, darling." Sister Sibyl winced a half smile. "I was once your age—young and frightened. My intention was to comfort the king in his sadness by being kind and then before I knew it . . . he . . . he. . . ." Sister Sibyl's words died in her throat, and her face contorted. Her hands flew up, palms outward, and she twisted her face away in a painful grimace.

"He what? He what?" Jehanne looked upon her mentor with a mixture of wonder, terror, and great concern.

"I can't say it," she bawled. "I can't say it to you." Sister Sibyl rested her face in her hands and cried rivers of pent-up guilt flowing from her tortured soul. "I don't deserve to be here with you, Jehanne. You deserve so much better than a . . . a. . . ."

"Sister Sibyl, it is not determined by you or me but by God alone who should be here with me. He has found you most worthy. It may be that I am not worthy of your love and devotion."

The nun lifted her tear-stained face and sobbed, "Don't you say that! Never say that, Jehanne!" She continued to scold the child with unconvincing authority, sniffling as she spoke. "You are worthy, child! It is me who is the chink in your protective armor."

"Sister Sibyl, why am I seeing King Charles V in my vision?"

Sister Sibyl took a deep, shuddering breath. "Time will tell you when you need to know. Until then, comfort an old nun who loves you more than her own life, and do not ask me again."

Suddenly, Sister Sibyl felt Jehanne clench down forcefully on her arm. In Jehanne's lap, Papillon tensed at the motion.

"The voices are returning. Hold me, Mother Sibyl." Jehanne's body swayed slightly.

"I am here, child. If God finds me worthy and allows it, I will always be here." She lightly kissed her great-granddaughter's eyelids and then her lips, steadying her for what was coming.

59

The Angel and the King

Maternity hospital
Saint-Quentin, Somme River Valley
Vermandois region, France
Current day

Having just seen Loni's mind open into the world of a person named Jehanne and then that person's mind opening into that of a fourteenth-century king, Mickey and Suzanne sat dumbfounded. Loni's body rested in a state of suspended hypnosis.

Douglas kneeled in front of them and again, using a tandem retrograde hypnosis through Loni and Jehanne, he tried to engage past characters in discourse. The late afternoon shadows lengthened around them. After a moment of verbal prodding, a conversation ensued.

"Douglas, what are we witnessing?" Suzanne inquired through a veil of disbelief.

"I am thinking Bridey Murphy," said Douglas.

"Is this another character we have yet to meet?" Suzanne asked, almost despondent in her inability to wrap her head around the present reality.

"Let me answer that, Suzanne." Receiving a nod of affirmation from a weary Douglas, Mickey rose and went to Loni's purse. He began explaining, his voice monotone due to unrelenting consternation. "In the early 1950s, a man named Morey Bernstein hypnotized a housewife named Virginia Tighe from Pueblo, Colorado."

Mickey took the balm out of Loni's purse then held it up toward Douglas questioningly. Upon received an approving nod, Mickey went over to Loni, speaking as he went. "He took her back before her date of birth into the soul of a nineteenth-century Irish lady, Bridey Murphy. Bernstein used a technique called hypnotic regression."

Using his unbroken hand, Mickey gently massaged the healing balm, used for headache relief, onto Loni's neck. Feeling her body respond to his touch, even in this suspended consciousness, gave him a hope he could not explain. *At least I can still do something to help you, my dear Loni.*

"I know about this," commented Suzanne. "What we're talking about is past life regression, right?"

"Very good, doctors," commended Douglas. "Past life hypnotic regression is the basis for a therapeutic approach called past life therapy—PLT."

"Like the sandwich or the Middle East organization?" Suzanne mocked.

"Funny." Douglas shot his former wife a cold stare. "That would be BLT or PLO, Doctor." Douglas resumed his most professional tone. "As I was saying, PLT allows unconscious experiences from past life traumas or emotionally charged events to become fully conscious. Past life therapy aims to resolve any unconscious emotional pathology affecting a person's present health, behaviors, or quality of daily living. Some folks propose that it can allow for better healing since it gives the mind permission to locate past-life sources affecting present-day challenging obstacles."

"Is that what happened with the housewife Virginia?" Suzanne asked, regaining a smidgen of her professional bearing.

"Actually, no. Bernstein was trying to engage the precepts of past regression *within* the lifetime of Virginia when he stumbled upon the experiences coming from the voice of Bridey. Can you imagine the shock of talking to a woman from Cork, Ireland, who existed in the early 1800s while hypnotizing a woman in the 1950s from Colorado?"

"No, really?" Suzanne again mocked.

"Sorry, brain cramp." Douglas realized that he was speaking to two people who had just heard a fourteenth-century monarch from a fifteenth-century farm girl via a twenty-first century woman sitting in the same room with them.

"At any rate, there are others who state that PLT can uncover or discover dialogue from many lifetimes of trauma associated with an event."

"Hold on!" Mickey exhaled. He slowly retracted his hand from Loni's neck. "It was right here in the Vermandois that a regretful Joan of Arc jumped from a seventy-foot tower to unconsciousness . . . at Beaurevoir Tower, I think. Do you think it has been incumbent upon Loni to re-create this similar experience as an attempt to heal an unresolved part of Joan's past life experiences?"

"Listen to your own babble, Mickey," interjected Suzanne. "You are saying that Loni is a residual, transmigrating soul embodying the tortured souls of both Charles V of France and Jehanne who potentially could be Joan of Arc."

"Don't forget Sibylle," reminded Douglas. "As I said before, I don't know which way this will lead, but along the way we are going to find some answers to questions asked and some answers to questions never asked. We can always stop. The problem is, right now Loni is a fourteenth-century monarch."

In a low voice, halting poetic verse could be heard filling the room. Suzanne and Douglas gave yield to Mickey who stood stock still with the uncapped balm container in his hand and a distant stare in his eyes. Colorlessly, and with small pauses as he searched his mind for another line, another stanza, Mickey spoke as if both everyone and no one were listening.

Perhaps I stabbed our Savior
In His sacred helpless side,
Yet I've called His name in blessing
When in after times I died.

Through the travail of the ages,
Midst the pomp and toil of war;
Have I fought and strove and perished,
Countless times upon this star.

I have sinned and I have suffered,
Played the hero and the knave;
Fought for belly, shame, or country,
And for each have found a grave.

So as through a glass and darkly
The age long strife I see
Where I fought in many guises,
Many names—but always me.

So forever in the future
Shall I battle as of yore,
Dying to be born a fighter
But to die again once more.

"I know that poem," said Suzanne. "It was written by General Patton. He believed that he had traveled through many lives to lead the US armies in a critical and desperate battle. It is Russell's favorite poem. The name?" She snapped her fingers repeatedly. "The name? What is the name?"

"'Through a Glass Darkly' was written by General George S. Patton in 1922," Mickey answered. "Even on his deathbed, as his eyes panned the walls of the hospital room on the first floor of Heidelberg Hospital, he felt that he would again appear in the life of another."

"Maybe Schwartzkopf?" Douglas posed.

"Maybe," mused Suzanne. "I mean, c'mon, we all know Patton's history, his poem, how he saw himself as a warrior of the ages—it's US military common knowledge, right? But I must be honest, as I have read Patton's work over the years, I keep thinking about all those lifetimes. . . ." Suzanne rubbed her eyes. "I keep wondering how he dealt with losing his Beatrice in the twentieth century and if he went from life to life losing love after love. He had to have loved someone in each lifetime. Everybody loves *someone*. You know, every soldier has someone worth fighting for? And, if he remembered all those past lives and, presumably, all those lost loves . . . how lonely would that be? Living every day, knowing all that had been lost and found and then lost again?"

Douglas caught Suzanne's eye and, knowing that he framed her comments in the context of their failed marriage, she looked hastily back at Loni and pulled the conversation into the present.

"Guys, is Loni really a French king in a parade of characters, or is this some demonstration of a long-lost memory of a character she studied to obtain her degrees?"

"I can't say," replied Douglas. "Besides, the construct of a parade of historic characters was your idea, Suzanne."

"Yeah, but I didn't expect. . . ."

"Well, what do we do?" Mickey's voice had a twinge of hopelessness. He threw the balm back into the purse.

"What indeed?" Suzanne echoed.

Douglas looked to Mickey for the go-ahead.

Mickey turned away and moved to the window. He gazed at the sunset, thinking about the rider in the clouds from the day before. "For better or for worse, we plod on." Mickey spoke the words confidently, but they possessed a hint of thinly veiled trepidation.

Only a few minutes had passed when again Douglas re-engaged Charles.

"Where are we now, Your Highness?" Douglas queried.

"I am in my castle. Dr. Thomas de Pizan tells me that I have already survived a fortnight which is all that medicine guaranteed."

"What year is it now?"

"The year of our Lord 1380. It is September sixteenth, a Sunday."

"Which castle, Your Majesty?"

"I am in my queen's palace—Château de Beauté-sur-Marne. To think, my queen never lived to enjoy it."

"Is anyone with you?"

"No, not right now. I sent them all away—the archbishop of Paris, the abbot of Saint-Denis, and Lord de la Rivière. They have been loyal, tried and true to the king of France. I wish I could have been such to them."

"I am sure you have."

"There is one among my subjects I have wronged. It was an act of the flesh and not the soul. I have asked forgiveness from my chief physician Dr. Pizan."

"Why ask forgiveness from your chief physician?"

"It was his beloved niece with whom I experienced the pleasures of the flesh. She was hardly more than a child . . . perhaps fifteen . . . beautiful . . . with the mark of a red flower on the lower right corner of her mouth." Loni's hand rose and hovered near her mouth.

"What became of her?"

"An angel came to tell me that she has forgiven me. I guess that God has dealt with her as he has dealt with me. We each have our crosses to bear. I only hope repentance and my gift to Dr. Pizan will, in some way, pave my way back into heaven."

"What is the gift?"

"For the flower, it is but a mere thorn. Even so, it is a gift that is the richest that there can be."

Mickey whispered into Suzanne's ear, "That's how Joan described her gift to Charles VII at Chinon to convince him she was the Maid of Lorraine."

"I hear steps. The doctor returns. Alas, it isn't him. It is the archbishop and the abbot. My heart saddens. My dear friends, I am afraid my time is at its end. The clergy must now step in when the healer has gone before and dares not tread again. Rarely in life does such a truth exist as it does at the end of a person's time. The healer becomes the failed symbol of hope whilst the clergy is the one who brings solace in despair."

"Goodbye, dear King of Hearts," a voice whispered. Loni lowered her eyes and nodded in the direction of the speaker.

The whisper came not from Douglas, but from Suzanne who knew the feeling of hopelessness all too well. It was always at certain death when she relinquished control to the chaplain to allow his work to continue when her work as a military physician could go no further. Seven centuries of medicine had not changed that interaction.

60

Of Flowers and Thorns

Chinon, Loire River Valley
Loire region, France
15th century

The day of the eighth of March was almost a nonevent. It had been thirteen days since the initial marshalling outside the walls of Vaucouleurs. Today the original escort party, minus Colet de Vienne, went to the smithy to have the animals tended. Jehanne had pulled the king's messenger, Colet, aside earlier in the morning. Only whispering could be heard between them. The interaction ended with a nod of understanding from Colet.

"Do not leave until you have cleared your absence with Jean de Metz," the Maid warned. "Although this mission belongs to me, your duty remains with him." Again, he nodded understanding and went in search of Metz.

Jehanne and Sister Sibyl sat quietly in the ladies' quarters, as the men had now begun to call the wagon seat in the carriage house. True to form, Papillon—although not a lady—was there as he had been from the trip's onset at Vaucouleurs. Jehanne was anxious. She had had another of the strange encounters.

But wanting to present her question before the Maid began speaking, Sister Sibyl struck first. "Where did you send Colet?"

"That, Sister, is between Colet and me."

Sister Sibyl recoiled at the sharpness of the tone. "Are there secrets between us now?"

"You tell me. Are there?"

"There are secrets and there are *secrets*," informed the nun.

"This one must stay within me for the time being even if the sword of heaven was placed across my throat."

"Your secret is safe within me," Sister Sibyl prodded hopefully.

"Right now, Sister Sibyl, it is safest within me. Please pursue this no further."

"As you wish, child," responded the nun, jarred by the tone Jehanne had taken. "Please, tell me what else weighs upon your heart. Does it involve your visions?"

"Yes, Sister Sibyl, I keep seeing the world through the eyes of the Dauphin's grandfather, Charles the Wise." Sister Sibyl's fleeting cringe did not go unnoticed by the Maid.

"What have you seen now, child?" The nun's voice had no conviction of intent.

"What do you know of Château de Beauté-sur-Marne?"

"I know it as the palace built for a dying queen who never got to enjoy the structure. What was the year in this vision?"

"The year was 1380." Jehanne watched the nun's reaction carefully.

The sister yielded a sigh of relief, the tension in her body lessened, and she responded a bit more easily. "I have only one memory of the Château de Beauté in that year. It is a memory that saddens me greatly. Tell me what you saw."

"The king spoke of his chief physician. . . . That is, I spoke of him."

"That would be Dr. Tommaso da Pizzano."

"I heard no name other than Pizan."

"That would be correct, dear. It is the French form of the Italian name. His name was Dr. Thomas de Pizan. He was an Italian physician from Venice."

"Did you know him?"

"Of course, dear. He was my father's brother and the reason my family moved to Paris. I was just a young girl. My cousin Christine was so happy to have me come along so she could have an island of comfort in a sea of French aristocracy. What did the king say regarding Dr. Pizan?"

"I said . . . I mean he said . . ." Jehanne heaved a sigh and shook her head. "He, I will say he—it is easier. He said he had a gift for Dr. Pizan. It was for a wrong he wished to right. He hoped the gift would help pave his way back into heaven."

"Did he say who was wronged?" Sister Sibyl licked her dry lips.

Jehanne reached out and caressed the strained features of the face of the nun. She traced her right thumb over the nun's red, flower-shaped birthmark near her lip. Sister Sibyl's lower lip quivered.

"He did not give a name."

The nun nodded. "What was the gift?"

"He didn't say. He did describe it in terms of a flower."

"How did he describe it?"

"He said for a flower it would be a mere thorn. Even so it is a gift that is the richest that there can be."

"I don't understand. How does a flower interpret its own thorn? Is it painful? Is it protective?"

"It is both, I believe."

Sister Sibyl looked at the sixteen-year-old girl's face—her maturity seemed to increase with every vision she experienced.

"What gift is the richest that there can be?" Sibyl asked the question to which she already knew the answer. Jehanne wrapped her arms around Sister Sibyl and embraced her as if her existence depended upon it.

"The gift? You know the gift?" the nun asked.

"Yes, Sister Sibyl, I know the gift."

"Will you tell me?"

"When the time is right."

"I knew you would say that."

"Then you are true to your name, prophetess."

"How is it that you know the meaning of my name?"

"God leads me, providing me what I need to know when I need to know it." Jehanne's tone sharpened again. "Why is it that you cannot fathom that which I already know?"

The nun slowly studied the face of the Maid of Lorraine, wondering. *How much does she know that she is not willing to share? It seems that the longer I spend with her, the less I know about her and the more she knows about me.*

61

Four of a Kind

Maternity hospital
Saint-Quentin, Somme River Valley
Vermandois region, France
Current day

Through the waiting room windows of the hospital there was a residual glow in the sky from the fading sun as Suzanne, Mickey, and Douglas discussed the bizarre events they had just witnessed.

"Suzanne, I'm impressed. You remembered the King of Hearts," nudged Douglas hoping to have a nonhostile conversation with his ex-wife.

"I will always remember the King of Hearts—it was the card you always sandbagged, holding it last in your hand," responded Suzanne.

"Old habits die hard."

"I'm sorry to interrupt but I'm not," chimed in Mickey. "I heard the King of Hearts comment too but wasn't tracking."

"The royalty in a playing deck of cards are actually representations of true monarchs," began Suzanne.

"No kidding. A place where gaming meets history," said Mickey. "I think I need to study more gaming to improve my knowledge of history. Wait a minute, you're kidding me. . . ."

"If she was kidding, she would have said, 'Horse walks into a bar . . .'" Douglas prompted, doing the famous Groucho Marx impression while mimicking the wiggling of a cigar in front of his face.

"Bartender says, 'So, why the long face?'" Suzanne finished the line.

An unbridled laugh erupted as Suzanne and Douglas collapsed into facing waiting room chairs. Mickey, more captivated by the sudden change in the interaction than the humor exhibited by the one-liner, returned the conversation to its original intent to inform.

"Ahem. . . ."

After shaking her finger at Douglas, Suzanne, with the trace of a residual giggle, continued. "Seriously, Mickey, the four kings in a deck represent

258

historical kings." Crossing her legs at the knee, she continued. "The English deck and the French deck have a slight variation on which monarch is highlighted." Suzanne nodded at Douglas and pointed to a table on the far side of the waiting room.

Meandering back from across the room, Douglas sorted through a French deck of cards in his hand. He handed Suzanne four kings, four queens, and four jacks. Mickey was amazed at the sudden synchronous flow of communication between the two without a word having been spoken. Then he mentally checked himself. *Well, after all, they were once husband and wife.*

Holding up the French king of spades, Mickey noticed on its margin symbols indicating its title, David.

Suzanne continued to narrate. "This king of spades represents David, king of Israel, significant in the lineage of Jesus. Diamonds indicates Caesar, most likely after Julius Caesar. Then the king of clubs—Alexander, Greece's Alexander the Great. And finally," she held the king of hearts card almost tenderly, and it was with a voice softened with emotion that she said, "Charles. There is a myriad of opinions and several schools of thought that support one great Charles over the other. Some say it was Charles Martel, the king who wielded the sword of heaven and saved France from the invading Arabs."

Mickey's eyes moved up and to the left as he engaged his logic centers. He remembered the dialogue with Loni in the truck as they negotiated the drive from the Lorraine.

Douglas stepped in. "Others believe it is Karl der Grosse, better known to you as Charlemagne or Charles the Magnificent."

Suzanne, smiling at the interplay between Douglas and herself, resumed her spiel. "There are then many minor camps that are divided among Charles V, VI, and VII. Mind you, the camp of Charles VI, the mad king, is very small, although formidable. There are many scholars that pose that Charles VI has the priority for selection. Apparently, playing cards were introduced into the French royal house by the Burgundian, Odette de Champdivers, who was the queen look-alike mistress to the mad king. Be that as it may, I have always chosen to believe it was Charles V, the favorite king of my hero, Christine de Pizan. She spent great literary efforts to announce to the world he was a good and honorable king."

"So, the king of hearts is speaking through my Loni?"

"Yes, through Loni, but also through Jehanne." As she handed the royal cards back to Douglas, one card slipped from the deck and fell faceup on the waiting room floor—the jack of hearts.

Awestruck, Suzanne looked at the card and then at Douglas who had the same expression of shock upon his face. Together they looked at a puzzled Mickey.

"What? What's wrong?"

Douglas picked up the card and handed it to Mickey. Front and back, Mickey inspected the card in his hand.

"Mickey, there is one more thing you need to know," iterated Suzanne.

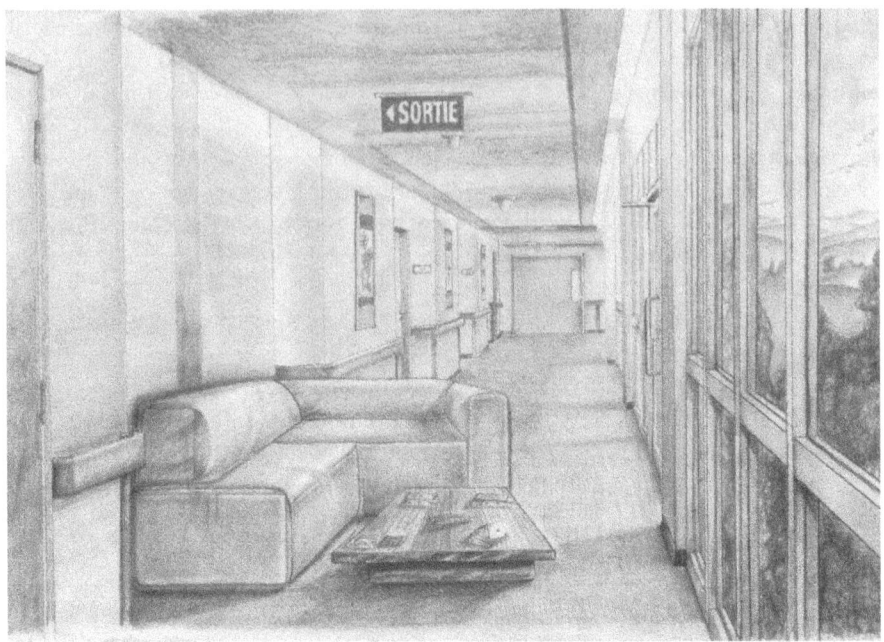

"The jack of hearts is also important in the scenario now being played out. He worked for the House of Valois under Charles VII as La Hire. Most specifically, he was the tried-and-true battle companion of—"

"—Joan of Arc." Mickey whispered the words, the name barely escaping over his teeth.

Mulling over this evening of incredible events, the three doctors topped off their coffee cups from the dispensing machine in the waiting area, still not very far from Loni's suite. Douglas stacked and restacked the cards in his hands.

Suddenly they heard an all too familiar sound which heralded the nursing staff to rush into Loni's room before the three could broach the frame of the doorway.

With her face in full strain, Loni breathlessly heaved and strained until she eventually held the baby within her arms.

The shock in the face of the maternity hospital's staff was only surpassed by the consternation in the faces of the three American doctors.

In front of them sat Loni—still fully pregnant with her fetal monitor tracking the stable evolution of her physical pregnancy—but in her arms she cradled empty air, and in her mind, she rocked a newly birthed neonate. Douglas dropped the cards on the table and quickly engaged hypnotics while Suzanne corralled the hospital staff out of the room. Mickey backed up against a wall, trying to slow his heart rate and steady his shaking hands.

62

Chinon Waits

Chinon, Loire River Valley
Loire region, France
15th century

The long-awaited day of royal invitation had finally arrived. Breakfast was served early and the group, minus one person, sat in chairs propped outside the inn which had become their transient home over the past week. The missing person, Colet, walked up from around the corner and whispered something into Jehanne's ear then walked over and handed Jean de Metz a rolled-up parchment which Jean read aloud to the group.

"'The ninth day of March in the year of our Lord 1429. Dear Maid of Lorraine, Please present this parchment at the front gate of Château de Chinon so as to permit passage to engage an audience with His Highness, Charles, Dauphin of France. His Royal Highness expects your presence in the Grande Salle no earlier than five o'clock. Please ensure all the party is present as His Highness may want to query members of the escort party as well. Please be prompt as you will be denied entrance to the castle after the clock has struck for the fifth time. Signed, Charles.'"

"Well, we have the whole day to wait," remarked Richard the Archer.

"Is there somewhere else you have to be?" Jean de Metz asked stiltedly.

"No disrespect intended to you, the Maid, or our sovereign Dauphin," Richard said, "but we have traveled from afar and have waited here like hungry dogs for the scraps he chooses to throw. Frankly, I have grown weary of the delays."

"Richard, I picked you because of your quick hand on the bow string, not your quick mouth," said Jean de Metz. "Your heart has great strength. Why do you choose now to become restless when we have endured so much already?"

"I just want that we be taken seriously."

"As do I. Don't you think the Dauphin has given us every chance to retreat? He must be sure that the Maid is who she says she is. If he falsely raises the hopes of our nation to a faux maid, then the people will see him as a weak and irresponsible ruler."

261

"Do you believe we are being treated fairly?" Richard asked.

"I believe what the Maid believes. Unless she stands up and renounces her claim to her identity, I will stand here and wait until Chinon's castle tower leans and then falls."

"As will I," piped in Sister Sibyl.

This was followed by a rousing cheer of support from every member of the armed escort party, including the vigorously barking Papillon. Jehanne, distanced from the tempo of the present conversation, went to the seclusion of her usual place of refuge on the wagon seat in the carriage house. Before long the voices of the men were cheerful and loud as in the days prior. Jean de Metz was a good leader and knew how to keep his men in line. Jehanne knew from the onset that she was in good hands. She wished that she had as much control of her visions as Jean de Metz had of the escort party.

The revelations of the recent visions had now become quite disturbing. Jehanne had hoped that Sister Sibyl would leave her alone this day—she sought seclusion. But there was a four-footed indication that this was not to be. Papillon whisked up on the wagon and into her lap. His face had a look of curiosity, as if wondering why she should be away from the very source where the fun was happening. He gave her a big, one-eyed wink before he curled up in her lap. He was soon followed by Sister Sibyl.

How will she come to terms with the latest of my visions?

Beneath them, under the seat of the wagon, lay a meter-and-a-half long package wrapped in cloth which had been placed there earlier by Colet, following Jehanne's instructions to the last detail, prior to presenting the rolled parchment to Metz.

Jehanne sighed wearily, so great was her burden. *How much longer must this secret be kept? The voices know. The voices will tell me when the time is right.*

63

Mother and Sister

Maternity hospital
Saint-Quentin, Somme River Valley
Vermandois region, France
Current day

Lathered and matted in the sweat of childbirth, Loni gave an exhausted smile to those around her, as though after a successful delivery. "Jehanne, what's happening?" Douglas asked, most bewildered.

"Jehanne?" The voice within Loni echoed with a distinct ring of unfamiliarity.

His gut lurched as though he missed a step, but recovering quickly, Douglas redirected his line of questioning, "With whom am I speaking?"

"Sibylle. Who is this? Come out where I can see you."

Suzanne cut in quickly, nearly slurring her speech, "Sibylle, this is Suzanne Coletrane—"

"Sister Catherine?"

Suzanne looked slowly, guiltily at Douglas. The words had flown from her mouth, almost as if of their own accord. *Why on earth did I do that?* she thought.

Douglas gave her an incredulous, wide-eyed stare.

Suzanne paused for a moment, then feeling her fingers tingle again as whenever with Christine, she offered an apologetic grimace as she sidled in between Douglas and Loni, squeezing him out. She knew she needed to pick her next words very carefully. No matter which way she went, there would be consequences to her integrity in this life or the next. "Yes," Suzanne stiffened, "this is Sister Catherine. Um . . . don't be afraid."

"Sister Catherine, blessed Saint Catherine, I have prayed long and hard for you to come to my aid. Praise heaven! Is Saint Michael with you there as well?"

Suzanne looked at a dumbfounded Mickey who was synthesizing the fact that Coletrane, now Catherine, and he by his given name, now Saint Michael, could possibly be standing in as two of the three voices that were said to have

263

guided the historic Joan of Arc. Not liking the implications of this, he held up his hands toward Suzanne indicating he wanted no part of this deception.

Suzanne continued, this time with more confidence. "Yes, Sibylle, Michael is here. He searches for you at my side. Time is fluid here, and it is hard for us to find you. Can you tell us in which year of our Lord you now reside?"

"It is the year 1375."

"And where are you, child?"

"I am here with the sisterhood at—"

"—the abbey at Poissy?" asked Suzanne.

"Yes," Sibylle answered.

Suzanne turned to Mickey and Douglas and smiled. They stood stock still and nodded back, anxiety etched in their every feature.

"Yes, Sister Catherine. You have found me, but I cannot see you. Where are you?"

"We are here, and it is all right that you can't see us. Just talk to us and help us to help you."

Suzanne caught movement at her periphery and turned momentarily to the room's window. Christine stood there, bold against the dusky night sky beyond her. Suzanne squinted at the figure and its metamorphosis. The reflection wore no pointed headdress as it had before, and it donned a burgundy riding cloak, but it was Christine, nonetheless. The golden clasp at her neck glimmered in the florescent light of the room for only Suzanne to see. Christine pointed back to Loni.

"Sister Catherine, in this, a time of blissful joy, there is an unhappiness which consumes me." Loni rocked an invisible child, holding it close to her breast. "I want that my soul be spared though I have committed a grave sin."

"This child you have birthed today, Sibylle, was it by choice?"

"Borne by choice, yes. Impregnated by choice," the young voice trembled, "no."

"I understand," Suzanne answered kindly.

Suzanne sat back for a moment, placing her middle and ring fingers at her temples, she relaxed her mind and let everything she knew, everything she had been shown, fill her mind. And then, all at once, it fell into place. *Just a few more questions to be sure.*

"Sibylle, you were brought here by your uncle, Dr. Pizan, after that unfortunate event, correct?"

"Yes. He said I would be safe here."

Suzanne looked to the others in the room, and they indicated that they were tracking with her method and results, so she continued.

"Sibylle, to my next question, please only answer yes or no."

"I understand, Sister Catherine."

"Is your child's father King Charles V?"

Loni remained silent, opening and closing her mouth like a fish, gasping for lack of water. Her chin quivered, and tears gathered in her eyes.

Suzanne hastily turned to Douglas and mouthed, *What happened? Have I lost her? No, keep going,* he replied silently.

"You will find no judgement from us, dear child. Is the king the father?"

"Yes," sobbed Loni.

"We understand. It is that act which brings us here today."

Loni sat up in her chair suddenly, posed as though she was protecting the imaginary newborn in her lap. "Just because I am young, unmarried, and now finished with this pregnancy," she choked out, "you aren't planning to take away my baby Isabella!?"

"No, darling, we will not take her. But you are not safe there. When it is proposed, you must accept the nuns' invitation to leave the abbey enclave." Suzanne paused and looked to Mickey for confirmation, mouthing, *Lorraine?* He nodded back emphatically. She continued. "Travel to the Lorraine. Isabella can go with you." She looked to Christine, who gave an affirmative sign. "But you must not give any indication that you are her natural mother."

"Why can't I be her mother?" the young voice was tremulous.

"I never said you couldn't provide for her as a mother would care for her child. But it would be safest for Isabella to be perceived as a product of a family in the Lorraine, rather than a contender for the throne of France."

"But if Isabella was placed with a family in the Lorraine, how would I gain access to spend time with her?"

Suzanne again looked to the window and the wiser, burgundy-clad Christine. Christine crossed herself, placed her hands in prayer, and then let her fingers interlace with slow and deliberate intention. With the warm fingertips of her hand, Suzanne repeated the first two actions, and she felt the tingling sensation spread as she spoke to Sibylle.

"As a sister of the Church, you would have the mission to teach the baby, the child, and then, one day, the woman to do God's will. This could be a calling for you in the name of the Church." As Suzanne interlaced her fingers, she understood Christine's final message. "Your darling Isabella will know you as Sister Sibyl."

Loni, as Sibylle, smiled through her tears.

"Will she one day become a queen or princess of France?"

"I don't believe it is God's plan to have Isabella enjoy a presence in the house of French royalty. Her regal bloodline is controversial. For now, her lot in life must be to stay shrouded in humbled anonymity amidst the cloistered walls of this obscure nunnery. Later, she will embrace the fruits that the region of the Lorraine has to offer."

"It hardly seems fair, Saint Catherine. To bear this fruit only to give it away."

"Pray to our Lord's mother, Mary, that she may guide you, Sibylle." Again, Suzanne turned to the reflection in the window who, with sad eyes, placed her hands upon her heart. "We do not always see the path God places before us. But rest reassured that through you and Isabella, France can be saved, and a prophecy will be fulfilled. You or your lineage will eventually present yourselves back to the royal ear of a French king in another place and time. France will reverently genuflect in acceptance of the greatness you brought to life this day."

"Bless you, Catherine. You have given me strength of heart when I thought I would have none."

"Bless you, dear, dear Sister Sibyl."

Suzanne looked to the window. Christine turned her open palms toward Suzanne and, giving a smile tinged with sorrow, she began to fade away into the night. Suzanne leaned on the hospital bed, burying her face and silent tears away from all who had eyes to see them.

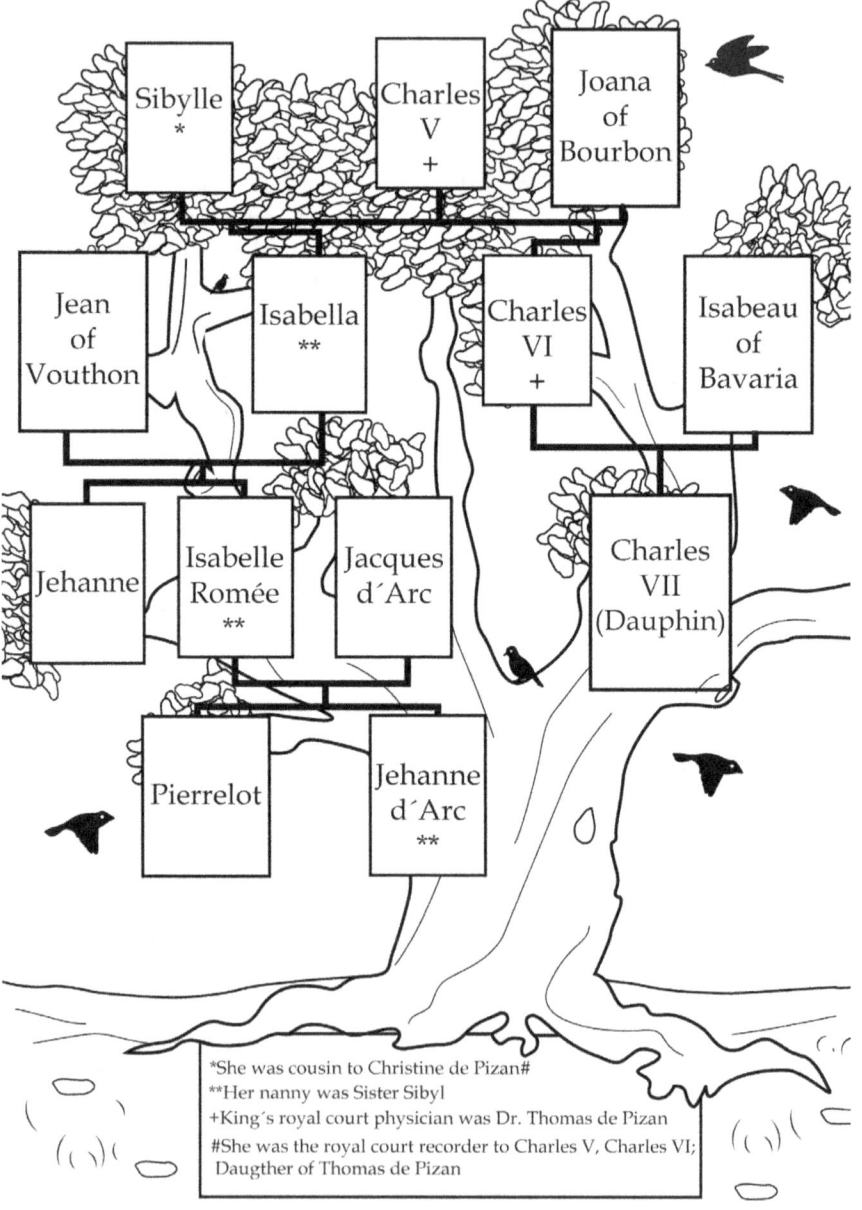

*She was cousin to Christine de Pizan#
**Her nanny was Sister Sibyl
+King's royal court physician was Dr. Thomas de Pizan
#She was the royal court recorder to Charles V, Charles VI;
  Daugther of Thomas de Pizan

64

A Lineage Revealed

Château de Chinon
Chinon, France
15th century

At half past four, except for horse-mounted Jean of Metz and Richard the Archer, Jehanne's escort traveled by wagon from the inn, up the steep hill to the main drawbridge of Château de Milieu and toward their long-awaited goal of an audience in the Grande Salle with the Dauphin. As Jehanne, now dismounted from the wagon, was about to access the entrance portal, a handsomely garbed man on horseback abruptly halted to engage the Maid of Lorraine. She smiled at him kindly. Exhibiting flawless courtesy in a remarkably grandiose bow he swept low his velvet cap, which was richly plumed with feathers of an exotic bird.

"Is this not the elusive *pucelle* from the Lorraine?" he asked and then paused, taking stock of the group. A haughty smile broke across his face as he continued. "Be advised, dear friends, if I could have had her for just one night, I am quite sure I would not have returned you a maiden." He laughed lustily as he replaced his cap.

Jehanne heard the creaking of Richard's bow from behind her. She motioned for Richard to stay his hand, and only after the passing of many seconds did she hear his breathing normalize and sense the tension release from the weapon. At the same time, the Maid heard the sheathing of swords from every one of the party who also had drawn full weapons to the ready upon the man's insult. From the wagon's seat, being restrained by Sister Sibyl's grip, Papillon continued his unrelenting low-pitched growling.

"Papi, stay!" Jehanne commanded the bristling dog. "As does a fish, he will die by his mouth." She turned her sharpened gaze to the rider. "Along with me you are attacking the Lord God with such vile words. I have only this statement of warning that can be said to you. Behold you right yourself with God. Before long, you will soon be in his presence. Forewarned is forearmed. I trust you will do right by God."

The rider spat at them. He spurred his horse on around the castle, nearly trampling a dirty street urchin, marred with green and brown slime, begging for her meal. The gray dust settled after a few moments.

In the courtyard, finely dressed squires took the horses and wagon. Such elegant reception was usually reserved for the most distinguished of visitors. The group was relieved of their arms and goods except for Jehanne who refused to release the wrapped package she held in her hands. It was agreed that the nun could hold the package since, of all in the party, she was perceived as the least threat to the life of the Dauphin.

The party was escorted over to an antechamber where the men were separated against one wall and, on a facing wall, Jehanne and Sister Sibyl were given chairs to sit upon.

Sister Sibyl leaned toward Jehanne and whispered, "Is this part of the secret I am not yet to know? What is it I am carrying?"

"This question is not easy to answer, Sister Sibyl. From the voices and our past conversations, I have learned that your ability to carry is great—it is, perhaps, your greatest gift. To best answer your question, Sister Sibyl, that which you carry is a gift to the Dauphin which is the richest that there can be."

"Well, I certainly can believe it because it is heavy."

"You have carried it thus far with little complaint. Why is it now such a burden?"

"You misunderstand me. It is not the weight of the gift that concerns me. It is the weight of my curiosity, no more," said the sister apologetically.

"Your curiosity is something with which you must manage. I laud you for having the discipline not to have revealed that which I know has . . ." Jehanne cleared her throat, "plagued your heart and mind."

The nun's brow lines crinkled at the strange intensity of the response with regards to the package in her hands. "You will let me know the right time?" she queried.

"I will let you know the right time when it is revealed to me."

After a brief pause, Sister Sibyl broke the silence with what she thought would be a redirection of Jehanne's focus. "What have you seen in your latest revelation?"

Jehanne looked upon the face of the nun debating whether to answer. She then began slowly. "I saw a time of blissful joy through the eyes of a woman who was involved in the active birthing of a baby."

"What woman? What baby?"

"She was young, unmarried, cloistered within abbey walls. She brought into this world a life that would never see her as its mother."

"What woman?" Sister Sibyl repeated as tears, unbidden, began to trickle down her face. Across the room, the men were caught up in conversation and unaware of the emotional moment passing by right in front of them.

"Do you truly wish me to continue, Sister Sibyl?"

The nun collapsed into the lap of the seated Jehanne, sobbing.

"You must hate me and think I am the lowest of the low."

"I could never hate you, Sister Sibyl. I have always felt that you were connected to me. I now know how. You are, and always have been, the link between me and the Dauphin. This is why God chose you above all others to journey with me."

"I only wanted to console a saddened king." The woman spoke into the folds of Jehanne's tunic, never raising her face. "I didn't want . . . what was done to me. And afterward, after it all, I had to give away my motherhood. I lost possession of my dear, dear, Isabella."

"I know."

"But at least before she died, she gave me your mother, Isabelle Romée."

Sister Sibyl felt Jehanne's body tense. Sister Sibyl raised her head. "The voices didn't tell you? They didn't say that Romée was the child of Isabella? That you were named for your aunt who was lost?"

"I think they left that for you to say."

After an audible gasp, Sister Sibyl buried her face in her hands and wailed outright. Jehanne lifted the blubbering face, gently pulling away the nun's hands, and looking her in the eye.

"Sister, I am so glad they did. Through your words, your truth, I can see how in every step of my life, your earthly charge has been to bring me to the Dauphin at this time."

"And do you still love me?" Sister Sibyl sobbed uncontrollably.

"More than any one human being has loved any other human being on this earth since the beginning of time. You are my blood. You have given me the love of a mother, a grandmother, and a great-grandmother all at once. On top of that you have been my church mother, always nurturing my faith and leading me in my devotion to God."

"I . . . I . . ."

"Please, Sister Sibyl, sit here next to me. The time has come. I need you to pass to me the gift that is the richest that there can be."

The nun wiped her eyes with the sleeve of her habit and recomposed herself in the best manner she could.

Across the way there were occasional glances but nothing which would lend acknowledgement to what just transpired. In fact, the men across the way saw only the deeply expressed devotion of a nun to the Maid of Lorraine, nothing more.

Sister Sibyl began unwrapping the package in her lap when Jehanne's hand stayed her motion.

"I thought you wanted me to pass the gift to you now."

"I do." The nun's hands again began the business of unwrapping when once again the Maid stayed her hands. Jehanne looked deeply into the eyes of Sister Sibyl and held her face in her hands.

"The gift that is the richest that there can be is with you and has been for a very long time." The nun's hands slowly moved from her lap to her neck where another precious gift had rested for many, many years. Sister Sibyl now understood the true depth of the Maid's words from earlier. Nothing in her life was clearer. She knew what to do. Sister Sibyl's hand clasped the crucifix which hung as a pendant around her neck. She looked to Jehanne.

"Now is the time?"

"Now is the time," said Jehanne.

Sister Sibyl, with a swift continuous motion, removed the chain from her neck. She then lovingly placed the pendant crucifix necklace around the neck of the Maid of Lorraine.

Pointing to the meter-and-a-half long heavy package in her lap, Sister Sibyl asked, "Will you need this as well?"

"Yes, but not now. Keep it covered for a bit longer. It is better that way."

"What is inside the hidden chamber of the crucifix? You opened it long ago at home . . . can you now tell me?"

"Yes, I can. It is—"

"Attention, those who seek the company of His Highness Charles, the Dauphin of France." A man of particularly fine apparel walked in and asked that the Maid and the nun be advanced to the Grande Salle. Jehanne could feel the eyes of the men upon her back and hear Papillon's bark guarding the wagon outside as she took her final steps toward the Dauphin.

65

Death and Departure

Maternity hospital
Saint-Quentin, Somme River Valley
Vermandois region, France
Current day

Sibylle, are you there?" Suzanne's voice carried great emphasis even though the sleepless night weighed heavily on her. She couldn't remember a time she felt so much fatigue. Shoulder to shoulder, the three doctors stood. None showed any indication that they were ready to rest though they all needed it sorely.

"Yes, but no. It's me, Sister Sibyl. Saint Catherine, Sister Catherine, is it you once again?"

"Yes, Sister. Tell me what you see."

"I see death in the eyes of my baby." Loni's hands fell limp and hopeless into her lap.

Suzanne's gut tightened. Even though it had only been minutes in the Vermandois, the time of the joyful birth at Poissy had long passed. *How can a blissful birth so quickly turn tragic?* Douglas nudged her gently, and Suzanne cringed as she squeezed out the next question.

"How old is Isabella now?"

"She is twenty-six, Sister Catherine. Even now as she lies before me, she still is my sweet little piglet, and she doesn't know I am her mother."

"What is the cause of her illness?"

"It's the great sickness. Some call it the Black Death. Others call it the Great Plague. It will take her as it did her adopted parents."

"You are not worried you will become sick too?"

"I don't care. Parents should never outlive their children, especially when they are so sweet and loving like . . . Isabella . . . my little . . . my . . . my piglet." Loni as Sister Sibyl began to weep with the grief that only a mother can fully understand.

"Sister Sibyl, there is much more to life than just your Isabella though it may not feel like it now. There are the lives that she has brought into this world. I believe you need to take responsibility for her family." Suzanne glanced at Mickey, and he nodded. "They will need you."

"Why? Neither family is mine. Remember, I am a sister of the Church. The lives that are mine become the children of others even though they belong to me. Can any penance be so harsh?"

"Do not worry. Do not fear. It will work out. God will see to it."

"I believe you are right. It's just that my heart grows so heavy, and my soul cannot bear the weight."

"You do not bear it alone," Suzanne told her. "I am always with you."

"Sister Catherine, did you say something?"

"Sister Sibyl . . .?"

"Saint Catherine, please . . ."

"Sister Sibyl, can you hear me?"

"Your voice is fading. Please don't leave me now. Please."

"Sister Sibyl?"

Suzanne turned away from Loni. "Douglas! Take me back! Get her back right now! Sibyl needs me—I can't have her thinking I abandoned her. Please, Douglas . . . please—"

"Saint Catherine? Saint Catherine? Don't leave me, please!"

66

Richest That There Can Be

Château de Chinon
Chinon, France
15th century

Jehanne and Sister Sibyl walked through the castle on the way to the Grande Salle. Jehanne was filled with wonderment for she had never seen so many people and such elegant things. For Sister Sibyl, it took her back to many other castles, far more elegant in and around the city of Paris. She said nothing except to echo the amazement of the Maid. When they passed by a small chapel, Jehanne asked to be able to delay the journey through the palace. "The Dauphin waits." The guide spoke with abrupt tonelessness.

"Indeed," responded Jehanne. "His Lord God has waited longer. I have not been able to give thanks for the safe journey today. I need the time to pray. You may wait or go tell the Dauphin he is second to God. The choice is yours to make." Having spoken, Jehanne took the elbow of Sister Sibyl and guided her into the chapel.

As he was unwilling to confront the Dauphin, the guide bit blood from his lower lip while lingering outside the chapel. Meanwhile, Jehanne knelt at the altar with her devoted Sister Sibyl.

Jehanne prayed aloud. "Precious God, one hundred fifty leagues you have brought me in fourteen days. Through your visions, I have seen the souls of my lineage and the greatness they have provided me. You have blessed me more than others. Instead of one mother, you have given me two. Instead of one set of voices, you have given me two. Instead of one angel, you have given me three. With so much assistance from all, I know I cannot fail.

"In a few moments, Father God, I stand before the Dauphin. Even now as I kneel before you, I don't know what I will say to him. I know that I have the two gifts to show him. What is it that I am to say to him so that he may see me as the Maid of Lorraine?"

She paused and went silent. After a few moments, the thoughts in Jehanne's head became distracted by the whispering nun who prayed beside her.

"Reverent Holy Father, please hear the prayer of this child who kneels before you and provide her the answers that she seeks. Lord, she is a good and holy child and has done all you ask and more. Although she is mine, I would not think otherwise if she belonged to a stranger. You have bestowed upon me a great blessing by allowing me the ability just to kneel beside her, let alone guide her. Lord, there are many other blessings in my life. I want to now thank you for them.

"You brought me from Venice to Paris with my blessed cousin Christine. You gave me the love for a king which went awry. Nevertheless, life brought me the maid who kneels before you. Guide her in your light as you did the spirit of the dying king in Château de Beauté so many years ago.

"Lord Father, please give Jehanne the wisdom of King Charles V the Wise. Impart upon on her heart and mind the words he spoke to the people who came to him to pay their last respects. From the abbot of Saint-Denis, he took the royal crown which had been brought from the royal reliquary. He placed that crown of man at his feet. From the archbishop of Paris, he took our Savior's crown of thorns and had it held high above his head to signify the true power of royalty. Such wisdom in man can only come from you. Please impart this wisdom upon my dear Jehanne who has blessed my life just by her existence."

Jehanne crossed herself, stood up, and helped the nun to her feet.

"I love you, Mother Sibyl. I love you now more than ever. Thank you for bringing me into this world. Glory be to God!" The two women again embraced. Jehanne kissed the nun on both of her eyes and then lightly on her lips. She turned and headed for the door. Before she left the chapel, she paused and faced the nun.

"Do you know now what is in the chamber of the crucifix?"

"Yes, I do, child."

"How?"

"You told me, child."

"No, I was interrupted—"

"You said if the gift—the pendant crucifix—was a flower it would be a mere thorn. Even so, it is a gift that is the richest that there can be."

"Yes, I said that." Jehanne reached over and brushed the flower birthmark on the corner of the nun's lower lip. "You are the flower."

"And in my heart resides a thorn. However, Jehanne, you are the gift that is the richest that there can be."

"Thank you, but no, Sister Sibyl, I don't believe so. I am glad we both know what the chamber behind the crucifix contains. Why didn't you ever look yourself?"

"It was not my station in life. It was placed with me for the Maid of Lorraine and no other."

"Thanks again to you, I now know what the Dauphin needs to hear from me. It will be good and honorable and the richest that there can be."

"I will see you when you return, child."

"As God wills it, Sister Sibyl, always as God wills it."

67

A Wish Realized

Maternity hospital
Saint-Quentin, Somme River Valley
Vermandois region, France
Current day

The night seemed to have gone for an eternity. Today already seemed an endless toil. Seven in the morning found Douglas, finally succumbing to an oppressive fatigue, curled up on the couch in the waiting area. Suzanne, amazingly energized with a second wind, continued to engage Loni in the hypnosis Douglas established. Although swiftly waning, Mickey stood nearby.

"Sibylle? Are you there?"

Loni's eyes snapped shut and a new voice from the past spoke as Loni's vocal folds vibrated creating sound waves in the present.

"There is no Sibylle here. Who is asking?" The new voice seemed more guarded than the others.

"You do not know Sibylle?" Suzanne cringed, feeling suddenly out of her league. She wondered if it was time to roust Douglas.

"No, should I? If so, why? Who speaks to me in my head?"

"May I ask you your name?" Suzanne held her breath in anticipation.

"Yes, of course, if you give yours first."

Suzanne looked to Mickey, wide-eyed and questioning. He passed her his travel notebook, open to a page upon which he had just finished sketching out everything he could recall from the family tree lineage chart they had seen on display in Joan's home in Domrémy. He pointed to a name and shrugged his shoulders. Suzanne nodded. As Mickey tucked the pen back into his travel vest he smiled briefly and thought, *See, Loni, you always laugh at my vest's pockets, but they save the day again, my dear.* His smile drifted away. *If only there were something I had that could save you.*

"You are Isabella's child, Isabelle Romée. Yes?"

275

"How could you know this?" the voice gasped. "Only God or his helper angels would know this."

"Romée, you are a devoted mother, and you protect a very, very special child—"

"You are Saint Catherine, as my daughter has said you are. You must be. Forgive me my rudeness. There is much evil afoot. There are so many who would destroy the Maid of Lorraine and France."

"God has laid a special path for Jehanne," said Suzanne as Saint Catherine.

"Yes, you angels have told her so."

"Yes."

"Why do you reach out to me?" Loni as Isabelle Romée asked. "Have I done something wrong?"

"No, gentle Romée, I just need you to tell me what you see. What year is it?"

"It is the year of our Lord 1419."

Suzanne did some quick math. "Jehanne is seven years old?"

"She is."

"Is she there?"

"She was here with Sister Sibyl when I fell asleep."

"Awaken, Romée. I hear your thoughts but describe for me the world you see through your eyes."

Romée opened her eyes, as did Loni, and scanned the living room of her home. "Jehanne is spinning yarn near the fire with Sister Sibyl. They are singing church verses together."

"Is there anyone else in the room there?"

"No, just us three. The others have gone to take food to the family in Burey near Vaucouleurs. Burgundians have pillaged the land again."

"Not just Burgundians. English too. They have taken our beloved Paris," echoed a new female voice through Loni, with austere undertones.

Chills shot down Suzanne's spine. *I know that voice. The abbey.* She drew in a deep breath and held it longer than she ever thought she could. Before her, through the mind, voice, and ears of Romée, Suzanne knew who had spoken those words even before the name was said aloud. *It must be. It must be. Good Lord, it is.* Suzanne took in another deep breath and tried to speak.

"Romée, can Christine de Pizan hear my voice as I hear hers?"

Suzanne's throat tightened. Her mouth went dry. She unconsciously wrung her suddenly freezing cold hands. She looked to Mickey and touched her ear, asking without words, *You heard the other voice too, right?*

He nodded his head in the affirmative and bit his lip. He then propped his elbows on his knees, interlaced his fingers in a double fist, and rested his forehead upon his hands. He listened with all his might, searching for an answer on how to bring back his wife.

"It would appear not, Saint Catherine," said Romée.

"Uh, okay," said Suzanne as Saint Catherine. *It appears as if Romée has become a distant speakerphone where through Loni's connection to her, I can hear the room, but the room cannot hear me. Wow!* Suzanne cleared her throat. "Would you please let Christine de Pizan know that I wish to speak to her—that is, if she isn't busy . . . of course she isn't busy . . . wait a minute, Romée, let me gather my . . . okay. Tell Christine to fret not because—Mother Mary, give me grace 'cause I really need it, now!" She tugged her hair back behind her ears. "Okay, okay, Romée . . . Paris will be okay, really it will. Honest. Oh boy, this just isn't coming out right . . . Romée . . . please, help!" Suzanne's voice ended on a high-pitched squeak.

In a slow steady voice, Romée began to speak. At this point, Suzanne could only hold her breath and listen.

"Lady Christine, there is a voice in my head, and she wishes to pass to you a message."

Suzanne cringed at the confusing and poor message she bumbled to Romée. *Oh, God, this is going to be awful!*

"The voice in my head wishes you not to be encumbered by your concerns for Paris," said Loni as Romée. "She says you should fret not. Even though things may not look to be coming out right for Paris, Mother Mary will grant her grace and, honestly, the help Paris needs . . . now."

I said that? I did? Yes, I did say that!

"Thank you, Romée," Suzanne exhaled.

"This voice, Romée," Christine asked, "it hears my speech?"

"Yes, tell her yes," whispered Suzanne. *Jeez, why am I whispering! Christine's on speakerphone, but I am not. Get it together, Suzanne. You were too scared to talk in the abbey . . . now's your chance!*

"Yes, m'lady," said Romée. "She hears through my ears. Speak to me and you will speak to her."

"Very well," said Christine with a note of skepticism that was picked up by Suzanne. "Paris has never seen such tribulations, Romée, how can we be sure of salvation?"

Romée parroted the more structured thoughts that Suzanne next offered. "M'lady Christine, the voice says that Paris has the blessing of God. He will not allow the guardian of his faith to fail. Since the Battle of Agincourt, the women of France who lost their men in battle have been made stronger with your help. Even as you and Sister Sibyl bring strength to young Jehanne, rest assured that—specifically because of your efforts—all of France will be saved."

"Can we truly prepare this child to be the Maid of Lorraine?" Christine implored dejectedly.

"Yes, we can prepare," said Suzanne as Saint Catherine. "But only God can make her the blessed Maid. It has been said that the one whose face and eyes look ever downward can never see the sun. Our job is to make her a child whose eyes seek far to the horizon."

"Romée, how can anyone know of such things?" Christine asked.

"I don't. I know only what the voice in my head is saying to you."

"Of course," Christine swallowed dryly. "I forgot, the voice . . . in your head . . . it speaks to me. I knew that. Dear me. I must appear the village idiot. With this, um, display of mental disarray, does the voice care to say anything else to me—that is, if it's not too much to ask? Of course it is . . . oh dear. . . ."

Suzanne stifled a chuckle. She smiled at the human frailty of her idol, recognizing in it her own frailty. Never had she felt so endeared to a person with whom she had never directly exchanged a spoken word. Suzanne pressed her fingertips together and warmth began to spread through them, overtaking the chill of anxiety she felt before. Tears began to brim in her eyes when she heard Romée begin to speak again.

"The voice says that women of all time are grateful for your strength and piousness, m'lady. Your strength is seen in women who are great warriors. Your lust for learning has been felt in women scientists and doctors. Your piousness has taught humility and servitude to the one true God. When strength through preparation is combined with belief in God, the force is undefeatable."

"Does this voice have a name?" Suzanne could hear the constriction in Christine's throat, and in Suzanne's mind's eye she could almost see her idol's tears matching her own.

"Yes, m'lady. I called her Saint Catherine. The angel calls herself Suzanne, Dame Dr. Suzanne Niles Coletrane, m'lady." Romée silently passed the message to Suzanne, that she had been adding the m'lady part because it seemed appropriate to her own personal station.

"Suzanne is a woman who is both a doctor and a great warrior?" said Christine, pressing her palm to her chest to quash the gasp.

"She says yes, Christine." Romée's voice inflected. "Suzanne is a physician, a scientist, a warrior, and a Lady Knight of Christ. All of this she has accomplished in her life, but she states that she is but a whisper in the shadow of your greatness."

Christine fell to her knees on the dirt floor. She buried her face in her hands. The tears streaming through her fingers darkened the earth below her.

Suzanne heard the crying through Romée and began to do so herself in earnest, trying desperately to stifle her noise so as not to miss a moment of this brief window into 1419.

Sister Sibyl and Jehanne rushed over to comfort Christine.

"Are you well, m'lady?" Jehanne asked with seven-year-old innocence.

"No dear, I am not well," said Christine. "I am better than well. I am the happiest I have ever been in my life."

Suzanne, in her own time, nodded vigorously in agreement.

"These are rivers of joy," said Christine. "These tears wash away all the years of doubt. I am cleansed of all the times I had ever wondered if my existence really mattered." Christine stayed upon her knees in supplication. She wiped her eyes with the backs of her hands, swallowed hard, and then directed her words to the woman beyond Romée.

"Dr. Suzanne, m'lady, I believe that God has seen to it that you speak to me through Romée. I thank you for your words and ask you to help me solve one thing in my life."

Romée spoke for Suzanne. "She would be honored. What do you wish?"

"How can one make a change in the spirit that will last beyond several lifetimes? How can one make such an impact that it will make the very foundations of towers crack and fall?"

"Give me a moment, Romée."

Suzanne scanned her own recent experiences from the Leaning Tower affair. She looked to Mickey for backup, and although he was listening, he seemed lost somehow. *Guess I'm flying solo now.*

Suzanne put her hands together, rested her chin upon them and, feeling the tingling sensation spread, she spoke again to Christine through Romée.

"Christine, m'lady, the answer is simple, yet difficult," Suzanne said. "The answer is that we live our lives such that God himself can use us to model for others. We embrace his Son as our Savior. We engage his Holy Spirit as our daily teacher. The difficult part in this is that we are human. We have within us the shortcomings of Adam and Eve. But we do the best with what we have. We can make every setback a challenge for success. We give our flaws, like anger, greed, and hate to God. He will ensure our legacy long after the towers have fallen."

"How do you know this?" asked Christine.

"He has led me to where towers lean. He has infused me with divine guidance to which, I must confess, at the time I was oblivious. Christine, m'lady, I know this through having faith in Jesus the Christ who gives us a chance at heaven. I know this because I have spent a lifetime internalizing the words and works of the great and incomparable Christine de Pizan, m'lady."

"You spoke of my greatness, but now you say you know of my words and my work. How can this be?" She edged closer to Romée. Christine raised her palms upward, and with a look of frank disbelief upon her face she turned her eyes first to Romée and then to the heavens, searching for answers.

"All the women of the world know your work, directly or indirectly," said Suzanne. "It is hallmarked in the great learned women."

"What of the men throughout all ages?"

"I cannot speak for all of them, Christine."

"Please, speak of the ones which you know. Have they read my words and ceased their misogynistic ways?"

"Those who can see beyond their own vices have learned the power of God through the love of strong, spiritual women." Suzanne's eyes caressed the pendant crucifix hanging on Loni's neck. "Just as Jesus embraced the strength of women like Mary Magdalene and Martha of Bethany, many have learned. M'lady, you remain a candle which lights the way from darkness."

"Bless you, Suzanne. Thank you for witnessing and validating my life." Christine's tears fell swift upon Romée's lap.

"Thank you, Christine. Without you I would not be closer to our God. He has blessed me in so many ways. I owe my successes to your words which have become my words. They have bolstered my faith. I love you very much."

Upon hearing these words, Christine rose to sit beside Romée. The noble woman caressed the face of Romée, kissed both her eyelids and then her lips lightly in the way of their family. Seeing the reaction in Loni's face, Suzanne placed her own fingertips upon her own closed eyes and then her mouth. Then she leaned forward and hugged Loni.

Without touching—and separated by time, space, and circumstance—Christine and Suzanne embraced each other, sharing a common flame stoked deep within their hearts.

Through God, all things are indeed possible.

68

Change of Station

Château de Chinon
Chinon, France
15th century

The Grande Salle, measuring almost ninety-two meters long, could hold several hundred people. But because it was disproportionately narrow, it appeared to all as a great hallway rather than a room of its own. At the far end stood an enormous fireplace. Tall windows let the most casual of visitors enjoy an aggregated view of the trimmed hedges and beautiful waterworks of the royal garden. For the scheduled event today, there were at least three hundred people assembled. Two men, the Count of Vendôme Louis I of Bourbon-La Marche and the Dauphin, stood at center stage discussing the nature of the meeting which was about to take place.

"Is Your Majesty convinced that this peasant girl is truly the Maid of Lorraine?" the Count of Vendôme asked.

"I am not convinced of anything save that there is no one charlatan thus far seen that can hold a torch to the quality of this maid. My advisors, counselors, and spies all say the same. Possibly yes, possibly no; but indeed possible."

"What do you suppose this meeting will provide His Majesty?"

"Insight? Amusement? Entertainment? All the above? None of the above? Who knows?"

"If Your Highness knows not, then who does?" The count feared that the Dauphin was beyond pessimism.

"I know this, my dear Louis. I know that it does not matter what I believe. It does not matter what my advisors, counselors, and spies believe. It only matters what France believes. The captain at Vaucouleurs, Robert de Baudricourt, sent ahead support for her position. Why would he do this? Why would he choose her over any other maid?"

"She has had support from within these walls as well?"

"You are talking about Jean de Castel, my court recorder?"

"Yes, Majesty. Jean and his mother, Christine, have supported the idea that the Maid of Lorraine is now a reality. It was predicted long ago by the Venable Bead, Sibyl the Prophetess, and Merlin himself."

"Ah, yes. I know of this prediction," said the Dauphin. "Jean's grandfather, Dr. Pizan, used to say to my grandfather, Charles the Wise, that France would be destroyed by a queen and saved by a maid."

"Begging His Majesty's pardon . . . your mother, Queen Isabeau, has done more to destroy France than all our enemies put together. It appears that the time is right for the Maid of Lorraine to appear and save France. If not this maid, then who?"

"I tell you what, my dear count. Let's put her to a test."

"A test, Majesty?"

"In this maid's letter written to me from Fierbois, she made the claim that she could pick me out from all others. Would you agree that is a bold statement in that she has never seen me or my lineage in her life?"

"Your Majesty, she might have a drawing of you or seen an artist's representation of you somewhere."

"A peasant girl has not those resources."

"Maybe she is not truly a peasant girl."

"No—she is a peasant. That has been verified both by Charles I the Duke of Lorraine and Captain Robert de Baudricourt. Thus, out of three hundred people, I think she would have difficulty choosing me from the imposter we will posture on the throne."

"Where will you be?"

"I will be milling around in the crowd."

"If she cannot find you, does this prove she is a fake?"

"If she cannot find me, I will still listen to what she says, but in my heart I will have trouble seeing her as the genuine Maid."

"If—by the grace of God—she finds you in the crowd, is that, in itself, a validation, Majesty?"

"If she finds me out of the three hundred, I certainly will give a greater ear to what she says." The Dauphin's voice resonated with authority.

Jean de Castel, who had been waiting for the private conversation to culminate, now approached the Dauphin. "Your Highness, the Maid of Lorraine is at your door."

"Count Louis, please announce her to the congregation. Jean, please exchange your smock and headgear with me."

Jean de Castel, although quite puzzled at the Dauphin's request, nonetheless immediately complied, "As you wish, my liege."

The Count of Vendôme moved to the doors at the end of the Grande Salle. Jean de Castel took the king's place, knowing in his own heart the true significance of the Maid. His mother, Christine de Pizan, had taught him well. Orléans needed to be saved. The armies of France needed inspiration. All this could be achieved with the guidance of the young woman now hovering at the threshold of the double doors of the Grande Salle. He knew all this without doubt, without question, and yet, the only thought burning in the mind of Jean de Castel was how uncomfortably he sat in the king's chair. *Why must I be the preselected charlatan in the room?* He looked over at the Dauphin. *Why me? Why me? That's what I get for being at the wrong place at the wrong time.* Jean watched as the king moved to the middle of the crowd. Here he could watch and not be obviously seen. Jean knew the moment was near. He diverted his gaze so as not to give away the location of the Dauphin. *This maiden must find him on her own.*

69

From All Others

Château de Chinon
Chinon, France
15th century

Jehanne arrived outside the closed doors—she knew the Dauphin was awaiting her. She wondered if he was feeling the same nervousness that she felt in the pit of her stomach. She was about to approach the door, but then she turned to the side and brought the nun with her.

"Sister Sibyl, the time is now. Please unwrap the gift that you hold in your hands." With that being said, the wraps were pulled away and a sword in a scabbard was brought into full view. Jehanne approached the guards and held the sheathed sword before her. They looked at it, then immediately barricaded her pathway.

"Relinquish the weapon or else you travel no farther," one guard said commandingly.

"I will do so if Sister Sibyl is allowed to stay here at the entrance with the sword until the Dauphin calls for it."

"That is acceptable," the guard said. "However, neither the nun nor the sword will be allowed in the room with the Dauphin until he says it can be so."

Jehanne nodded, turned from the guards, handed the sword to Sister Sibyl, and knelt one last time before the nun. In that moment, Jehanne heard the voices which had shown her much over the past few days.

"Jehanne, if you are there, please tell me where you are," said Mickey. Jehanne had no way of knowing but Mickey, in the twenty-first century, had been forced into action by Suzanne. Mickey prayed that the voice he would hear, if not his own Loni's, would at least it be someone he knew something about.

"I am just outside the door of the Grande Salle, Saint Michael." Jehanne spoke aloud in whispered reverence, though she alone could hear the other voices of Suzanne and Douglas.

"Is it really you, Jehanne?" With the myriad of characters presenting themselves through Loni's hypnotherapy, Mickey couldn't be sure anymore.

"Yes, Saint Michael. I have seen the lives of many in my heart and mind of late, but rest assured, the person who will soon walk into the Grande Salle is me, Jehanne d'Arc—a much more learned version but, yes, still me."

"In your mind, Jehanne, have you achieved the status of the Maid of Lorraine?"

"Many have prepared me to be so. God himself will let me know if His will has been done and if I am divinely sanctioned as the blessed Maid."

"Are you prepared, Jehanne?"

"I think so. I have the gifts of two Charleses. Unfortunately, I am barred from entering the room with the sword of Charles Martel." Upon hearing this, Sister Sibyl felt her knees grow weak.

The guards exchanged looks of shock with one another in knowing that the sword which saved Christianity was being held out of the presence of the Dauphin by their action alone.

"I also have the crucifix of Charles V the Wise around my neck."

In a moment, the guards reversed their position and stepped to the sides of the closed doors. Jehanne looked up at the sound and then stood solemnly. With a nod from the guard, a very relieved Sister Sibyl helped Jehanne strap on the sword of heaven.

Jehanne closed her eyes and spoke. "Saint Michael, I now have the sword and the crucifix upon me."

"Then, Jehanne, it is time to meet the Dauphin."

"Do not leave me, Saint Michael, please," Jehanne whispered.

"I am here always," Mickey answered. He reached out and held Loni's hands. Then he stayed his tongue in anticipation of what they might hear next.

Suzanne huddled close to Mickey, sitting at the edge of her seat. Silently they perched, listening to history unfurl before them through the ears, voice, and mind of Jehanne.

Jehanne steadied herself and drew in a deep breath. *The moment of moments has finally arrived.*

Simultaneously, the guards pulled apart the massive doors. Jehanne crossed the threshold at the centermost point of their union. The room opened in front of her with the bay windows overlooking the courtyard and gardens to her right and a small window off to her left which showed little more than the river below. There was a wall of people who filled the spaces on both sides of a long, narrow pathway leading directly to the Dauphin who was sitting in a chair.

In her ears, she heard her name announced to the French aristocracy.

"Behold, Your Highness, before you advances Jehanne d'Arc, La Pucelle, the Maid of Lorraine." The voice of Louis I, Count of Vendôme, echoed off the rafters.

Jehanne entered the Grande Salle and walked down the long aisle. She made confident eye contact with the elegantly dressed courtiers and tried to smile respectfully to everyone who filled the great hall. There was no sound except the swishing from the scabbard on her side and the pounding of her heartbeat in her ears.

Is it my imagination or has the aisle stretched yet another hundred and fifty leagues?

Jehanne advanced to the regal chair and began to kneel but then paused. The look of discomfort on the face of the seated man made her stop. Immediately she sensed that something was amiss.

The face of this man is familiar and kind, but this is not the Dauphin. There is some mischievousness afoot.

She stood erect, nodded her head respectfully to the seated figure just as she had done to all the other courtiers, but then she turned away. She began to scan the crowd for a face which most resembled Charles the Wise, her great-grandfather, whose tortured face she saw in the mirror of her visions and was forever imprinted in her mind. After perusing the room, she found the one face which must be in the lineage of Charles. She approached him, making her way through the surprised crowd, and knelt before him.

"Gentle Dauphin, I am Jehanne d'Arc, La Pucelle, the Maid of Lorraine."

The room erupted with applause. Jehanne ignored them, speaking only to the Dauphin.

"The King of Heaven sends me to you with a message." Jehanne remained piously positioned, waiting for the Dauphin to speak.

He thundered at the crowd, "Silence! Silence, everyone! This maid has a message for the Dauphin. Quiet now! Go ahead, my dear. What message have you for the Dauphin?"

"You shall be anointed and crowned in the royal city of Reims and become, among men, the undisputed king of France. Mind you, you shall be the earthly lieutenant of the King of Heaven, who is the true king of France."

"You have been misled, dear maid. You speak not to the Dauphin of France, earthly or otherwise. There, sitting in his chair, is the Dauphin of France."

Never raising her eyes or changing her voice or the temperament of her discourse, Jehanne continued. "As I have written to you in a message, I know you from all others. I believe, in God's name, that you are my Dauphin. It is only to you and none other that I will give the entire message that I have to bear."

"How are you so sure that I am the Dauphin?"

"I know it in my heart just as you know in your heart that I am the Maid of Lorraine that France sorely needs. Shall we continue to amuse this crowd while Orléans teeters on destruction? My Dauphin would not let this happen. Majesty, I bring you five signs which God himself has willed for only you to see. If you wish me to show it to the man over there dressed in kingly garb, I will now leave and stay gone until God—not you or your imposter—commands me to return."

The crowd applauded at the presentation displayed before them.

Charles VII, the Dauphin, doffed Jean's hat and removed the recorder's cloak, letting it drop to the ground. He ordered that the room be cleared immediately.

As the courtiers filtered through the doorway, the Dauphin thought, *There may be a few who depart today thinking that Jehanne is a charlatan. These few have blackened hearts that shun God—they know nothing of loyalty to France.*

As the doors of the Grande Salle shut, the Dauphin squared his shoulders and tried to look as if he had control of the situation.

The Maid began boldly, "First, you should know that I have three things to say and two things to present to you. If you give me your palm, I will reveal the first."

The Dauphin extended his right hand to the Maid.

"Wait, gentle Dauphin. There is something I must do first." She brought up the hilt of her sword, never removing it from its scabbard. With a flick of a protective cap, a small blade appeared from the hilt. She raised it and ran her palm across the blade leaving an incision across the inner creases of her hand. While he watched the blood ooze into the crevice, he glanced at the repeat motion which produced the very same slice in his palm.

"The blood in my veins comes from Charles the Wise just like yours."

"Making my hand bleed does not prove we have the same lineage, my dear Maid." Charles stared at the young woman expectantly.

Jehanne never moved or offered a response but kept her hand held toward him, palm up. He could see her lips counting. In a moment, her silent counting stopped. She looked at him with the greatest of confidence.

"In ten counts my bleeding will stop; yours will not."

He looked at her in frank disbelief, but he extended his hand in the same fashion as hers and listened as she counted down to zero. At the time predicted, all active signs of fresh bleeding in her hand had stopped. He looked to his hand—it still was bleeding.

"How did you know? What is this trick?"

She did not answer. He could see her quietly counting again.

"In ten counts, yours will stop." Together, they counted down. The bleeding stopped just at the time she predicted. She ran her fingertip over each incision and then held it to his eye.

"See? Both have stopped bleeding."

"How do you know such things?"

"I told you, gentle Dauphin. Your blood and mine are the same. You are my cousin three generations removed. Nonetheless, we are one and the same."

"How can that be? You are a peasant."

"The story is long and has just been divinely revealed to me as of late." She returned the small blade to the hilt of the sword. "I prefer spending this precious time showing you the second of the five signs instead. May I proceed?"

70

Signs

Château de Chinon

Chinon, France

15th century

Though presented with remarkable evidence thus far, the Dauphin remained skeptical, and if he were honest with himself, a bit shaken. *There have been too many faux maids in the past—and some weren't even maids! At least that one credential is easily checked. Still, the blood was strange. What else does this girl have to show me, I wonder.*

Straightening up his royal garb and adjusting his position upon the king's chair, the Dauphin tried to bolster his authority, but even here within the Grande Salle, he failed. Jehanne's words were weighted in iron, and they pulled at him.

"The sword of Charles Martel came from heaven and saved France from being overrun by the Arab hordes. As Dauphin and heir to the throne of France, you know your connection to Charles and the significance of this story."

"You aren't going to tell me that the sword in that scabbard is the lost sword of my bloodline?"

"No, I am not. I am going to tell you *and* show you that the sword in this scabbard is indeed the sword of heaven. It was hidden by Charles Martel, grandfather of Charlemagne, who is from *our* bloodline."

Jehanne held the sheathed sword out to the Dauphin.

"The sword of Charles Martel has been lost for many centuries," he replied as he took the sword from her hands. "In fact," he continued, "few know the distinction which makes the sword unique among all pretenders." He paused, looking to the girl for any sign of weakness, any tell of deception.

He began to slowly slide the sword from its sheath, watching Jehanne's face, not the blade. He expected an expression of despair, but instead he saw her confident smile.

He shifted his stance, looked to the sword, and deftly unsheathed it in one swift motion. Together they scrutinized the sword as it rested on the back of the forearm of the Dauphin. The quintuplet fleur-de-lys–shaped stars shone more brilliantly than any of the fifty torches which lit up the hall. The Dauphin was aghast.

"I . . . I can't . . . How?"

"May I continue?" Jehanne asked respectfully. The Dauphin nodded his head with weak affirmation.

"The third sign is the parting words from Charles the Wise witnessed by few prior to his death. He prioritized his kingdom in two manners. With his golden crown at his feet, he properly placed the crown of man. And with the Crown of God above his head, but not upon it, he signified that this is where the king of France should prioritize his nation. God is—"

"—the priority," finished the Dauphin.

"Yes."

"How can you know this, Maid?"

"Are you not listening, Your Highness? God has sent me here to you as the Maid of Lorraine."

"I am listening. I am just having trouble believing that all this could be true. There have been so many pretenders before you. How can I be so sure? How can *you* be so sure?"

"The 'how,' my gentle Dauphin, is not the important factor. Only the true God-inspired Maid of Lorraine would know such things."

"What of the fourth sign?"

"You are looking at the fourth sign. I am the answer to the legend that states that France will be lost by a queen and saved by a Maid from Lorraine. Do you doubt that I am a maid or that I am from Lorraine?"

"I will believe that you are who you say you are for now. Be advised, dear cousin, these things can be confirmed, and your claim to being a maid will be thoroughly checked in good time."

"With God on my side, I have no fear. I trust that your findings will be in line with all that you will have searched."

"There remains one last sign. I must warn you, Jehanne, that there is no way that any charlatan, however skilled, could ever fake or trick this into being. I know this because on All Saints' Day I prayed for three things to be revealed. I have told no one of these things. They are known only to God and me."

"Have I, at least, answered in part some of your prayer's requests?"

"I will concede to you now that two of these things have been part of what you presented to me. The third request in my prayer will have to be revealed in what you have yet to say or show me."

"I must confess I have no inkling of what your prayers requested. God has not revealed that to me. I can only tell you this: The final proof I offer is what God wanted me to show you. If what I show and what you prayed for are the same, then it is not because I arranged for it to be. It was God who willed it to be."

"I understand. Show me the fifth and final sign."

71

God's Will Fulfilled

Château de Chinon
Chinon, France
15th century

The room echoed the words of the Dauphin as he braced himself for what this sixteen-year-old girl had to show him. His fists drew tight in anticipation. As much as he wanted the Maid to reveal the fifth sign, he also wanted her to leave. She was formidable. *What if she turns her power against me?* He drew in a deep breath. The Maid reached toward her neck.

"As you command, my Dauphin."

Jehanne took the crucifix which hung from her neck. With her thumb, she slid the face of the crucifix upward to open the secret compartment. She tapped the contents of the chamber into the palm of her hand and then passed the sacred item to him.

His face grew pale as he stared at what he knew to be the answer to his third prayer request. He saw it, he felt it, but he did not believe it, not yet. The thought of it being held by him at this moment was beyond incredible. It was mind-boggling.

He had wanted to know the location of the missing thorns from the crown of thorns which was kept in the reliquary at La Sainte-Chapelle. He had prayed to God to reveal their location.

God has answered my prayers. He has enough faith in me and my ability to win back France.

His eyes scanned the tiny splinters of wood that once pierced the Savior's scalp. Brought now by Jehanne, a flower of France, there they lay in simple innocence—the blessed thorns in the palm of his no-longer-bleeding hand.

"Behold, Dauphin, like a thorn to a flower, in your hand lays a gift so honest and good. It is the richest that there can be. King Charles V gave this crucifix and its hidden thorns to his chief physician who, in turn, gave it to my mother three generations removed."

"Does this woman still live?"

"She stands outside your door."

"Then let her in. Jehanne, you two will no longer live the lives of the humble. Jehanne d'Arc, you are truly La Pucelle and the Maid of Lorraine. Everyone you deem worthy will bask in the splendor that this reign can possibly endow."

"Precious Dauphin, I can speak for Sister Sibyl, and I tell you now: 'Not unto us, but unto God give glory.'"

"Psalm one hundred fifteen."

"Yes, Dauphin. We want no riches. We want no glory. We want only to serve you and save France by rescuing Orléans. In this matter, we have already lost much time. After beautiful Orléans has been saved; we want to ensure that you make it to Reims where you will be crowned king of France. After that, let God's will be done."

"And so it shall." The Dauphin threw open the doors of the Grande Salle. By his command the restless crowd, containing a very pensive nun, regrouped and returned to the Grande Salle.

Motioning toward the quiet figure of Jehanne, the Dauphin stood by his chair and spoke. "Be it known this day that Jehanne d'Arc is the undisputable Maid of Lorraine."

The thunder which followed shook the dust from the rafters. It took many minutes before the Dauphin was able to continue.

"With God at our side and the Maid at our point, the time has come to recover our fighting spirit. We will wrest occupied France from the grip of the vile Burgundians and their ally, the Godon-English. I confess publicly, as you all are my witness, that the Dauphin Charles who occupied this room before the Maid arrived and the one that you see now before you are not the same person. I am changed. I now have the faith and strength I need to be the leader France needs. Let us save our country!"

Corralling from the room talents from the most critical people, including generals, engineers, strategists, cartographers, theologians, and a certain nun, the Dauphin went straight to work. Through the miracle of God, he had fulfilled the hopes of all Frenchmen. Working through the hands of very many people, the Dauphin was energetically inspired to begin the reconsolidation of France beginning with the rescue of Orléans.

Pulling Jehanne by both hands, Sister Sibyl guided her into a quieter recess of the Grande Salle. In a louder-than-normal voice, the nun cheered, "It is a great day for all of France, Jehanne! We have answered the will of God and have completed our mission!" Sister Sibyl's joy fell on a dour Maid of Lorraine.

"Sister, I fear we have completed only one of many missions yet to come. Right now, Orléans hangs on by tenterhooks, yet we waste time in celebration. The army must be mustered. Reims must begin preparing for the blessed coronation of our Dauphin. I will be more joyful once the work begins, and the voices return to tell me what lays ahead for the weary eight from the Lorraine."

72

Theft or Terror

Maternity hospital
Saint-Quentin, Somme River Valley
Vermandois region, France
Current day

After the Maid of Lorraine left the Grande Salle with Sister Sibyl, Loni became very quiet. Her eyelids stopped fluttering and her breathing deepened—becoming more regular.

Mickey and Suzanne were also spiraling into a post-adrenaline energy crash after the emotional marathon. Witnessing an event that no one in recorded history had ever seen had pushed everybody in the room beyond the limits of exhaustion, not to mention sensory overload—including Loni.

Thank God that the obstetrical equipment monitoring Loni is reading within normal limits—one less thing to worry about, Mickey thought.

Mickey and Suzanne staggered out of the patient room into the hallway and toward the waiting area where Douglas, having just awakened, sat on a couch stretching out his arms.

He began talking in mid yawn. "I take it you didn't get much sleep. Either that or you two were run over by a spiked steam roller," said Douglas playfully.

"So that was the splat I heard a few minutes ago. Silly me, Mickey, I just thought we were hallucinating from sleep deprivation. Don't you just hate cheerful morning people?" Suzanne turned away from the men and went back into the room.

The Viking Witch is on her broom, Douglas thought, and he attempted to duck as the broom did a fly over. "What can I say? Beauty sleep makes me charming." Douglas tried on a smile as he followed Suzanne into Loni's room.

"Get *more* sleep, Douglas," grumbled Suzanne.

"Right. Well then," he tousled his hair, "what did I miss?"

Mickey entered the room last and answered as Suzanne went over to the sink to wash her face.

"We were able to get back into Loni's psyche—"

"Say what?!"

"We re-engaged Loni through hypnosis."

"No, uh-uh, we're not doing this! This is *my lane.*" Douglas leaned uncomfortably into Mickey's space. "I am the metaphysician with the skill set to support the tools I use."

Before Mickey could answer, Suzanne rallied. "Douglas, you're brilliant and yes, talented as a metaphysician way beyond the two of us. There—I've said it without choking on the words. Nevertheless, as great as you are, your skill sets are useless when *you are asleep.* I've watched you hypnotize many patients in the past. I may not be as good as you, but we had to move ahead at a critical time. And besides, you yielded the controls to me back there with Sibylle—"

"Yielded? You hijacked the hypnosis!"

"Well, why didn't you stop me?" Suzanne challenged.

"I . . . I don't know, okay?" Douglas covered his face with his hands, his manner mellowed a bit. "I . . . God, this'll sound dumb, but I . . . I had a *feeling,* okay?" He watched Suzanne roll her eyes and continued with real sincerity in his voice. "Honestly, I had the feeling that I should back off. I can't explain it."

"Humph," Suzanne looked at him appraisingly, then shot from the hip, "first smart thing you've said all morning." She glanced at her watch. "It is morning, right?"

Douglas's face tightened and he started to interject but Suzanne's Heisman maneuver kept him muted.

"Look, I'm sorry," she said, without a trace of apology in her voice. "We probably should not have done what we did. Douglas, I know this is your lane, but I know Christine more than anyone, you included. I haven't just idolized her; I have internalized her in a way that I can't even verbalize." Suzanne leaned closer. "Look, in that moment I really felt I could be helpful. And guess what? I was. Look at the outcome. Mickey and I connected beyond Charles V. Come on, Douglas, you know me. When do I cherish the thought of sitting on the sidelines of anything—especially a parade involving the psyche of a woman very dear to all of us. If anyone can attest to this flaw, it is you, my dear ex-husband. If you want to me to sit idly by then go ahead and kill me now." Suzanne squared off with Douglas allowing Mickey to go to the sink.

Douglas tightened his jaw and wondered, *Prison or progress?*

"Well, Douglas?"

"I'm thinking. I'm thinking. How long will it take to get parole in the French penal system?"

"Look, let's make this easy for everybody. I'll just leave now." Suzanne patted her face with a paper towel and spun away toward the hallway.

Mickey reached out to her, but Douglas responded first. "Wait, Suzanne, let me reboot. You know, control-alt-delete."

Suzanne paused in her egress.

"I'm thinking that we are all in uncharted waters," Douglas said. "Deep waters, at that. We're talking like—chasms, okay? There is no way to know what a good risk is or what a pitfall looks like. *You're right.* With Loni's pregnancy progressing, coupled with Jehanne's fiery fate approaching, time *is* of the essence. Let's not invest further time in conflict. I'm just asking you two to let me navigate from the helm of this ship. It is closest to my expertise, and I want to guide it the best I can for Loni's sake." Then he added, "Or at the very least let me be on deck when we enter the storm, okay? Is that reasonable?"

"I dunno," Suzanne yawned. "Yeah, I guess. Tell you what. Let me sleep on that. In fact, let me sleep on anything. I am too beat to continue this." Suzanne then suppressed another rising yawn causing her eyes to water copiously.

"Fine," replied Douglas, "but someone is going to have to catch me up on what happened."

The other two doctors heaved a collective sigh and then tag teamed an abridged version of the last several hours. Douglas listened with his mouth agape.

"What do you mean *you heard* what this Romée woman heard?"

"We heard what we heard—" Suzanne began.

"And Jehanne too?"

"Yeah. We can't explain it, it just happened," Suzanne shrugged. *It's not the weirdest thing I've experienced in the last couple days*, she thought.

"Look," Mickey sighed, "even if we had your background, and we don't, we still couldn't explain it."

"But you can't expect me to believe—"

"Believe what you want," said Suzanne shortly. "*I believe* I am due for some shut-eye."

Not waiting for any more follow-up questions, Mickey announced, "Let's decide now who will sleep and who will have first watch."

"It looks like Loni is resting quietly." Douglas rubbed his red-rimmed eyes. "Why do we have to have any watch at all?"

"Hello? Captain of the ship? There is danger here that exceeds patient care." Mickey wanted to be wary without sounding paranoid.

"What kind of danger could exist in the Vermandois?" Douglas asked.

"Let's not forget that Péronne Castle is currently cleaning up from yesterday's bloodbath. *And* my friend, Asaad Baghbah al Bethany, was killed right in front of me." He glanced at the other doctors; his brow furrowed. "I believe the strike was to steal the Staff of Moses from the castle museum. Considering the weaponry used, I think it was a terrorist strike—not a simple act of theft," said Mickey.

The tension shift in the room was palpable.

Douglas's mind went into hyperdrive. *God! Why didn't he say this before?* He took a breath and surveyed the facts.

"The Staff of Moses has been taken in a terrorist strike? Are you *sure* the staff was lost?"

Recalling the moment that the thief, in full sprint, passed over him,

Mickey nodded in sad affirmation. Douglas sank into the nearest chair and drifted into a mind sink while Suzanne recovered and commented.

"The keeper and exhibitor of the Staff of Moses is the same Asaad that we saved in Bavaria during the Leaning Tower affair, right Mickey?"

"Yes, the same. After he left Bavaria, he went back to Istanbul as curator of the Topkapı Sarayı museum that exhibits the Staff of Moses—or should I say *used to* exhibit that component of the Rods of Power. . . ."

"I had not realized that the danger had already arrived. Does Asaad's son, Nabil, know?" Suzanne recalled the terror upstairs at Tegernsee Castle. *Yogi Wunschmann had crucified Asaad, leaving Nabil to initiate the rescue sequence ending with Yogi's death and our mad dash to escape from the demolition detonation countdown. Nabil was so instrumental in how Asaad, and the rest of us, was rescued.*

"I dunno. Since the melee, my focus has only been on getting Loni definitive care. I just can't say what Nabil knows, Suzanne," said Mickey. "I do know that Asaad would have tried to stop the theft of any component of the Rods of Power at the expense of his life. What chance did Asaad have against Haman, the modern version of Amalek, or his Amalekites?" Mickey drifted into a quiet sadness. He mused on how Amalek, first in the lineage of Jacob's son Essau, was cursed by God as he mistreated the Israelites when the Hebrews left Egyptian bondage. Amalek did not give sufficient respect to the power of the Staff of Moses and the Rod of Aaron even though, through God, these weapons had just induced the plagues of Egypt and defeated the pharaoh's army in the crossing of the Red Sea. In the eventual battle between the biblical Amalekites and Israelites, the Staff of Moses was instrumental in the destruction of the Amalekite army. God had ordained that no Amalekite should be left alive. Unfortunately for Israel, King Saul did not obey God's will. The result was that now modern-day Amalekites had again achieved power under the competent leader, Haman, who made it no secret that any terror was justified in righting the wrong that Moses had perpetrated on his people. The one symbol heralding the destruction of the Amalekites at the hand of Moses was the staff itself. "Today's Haman won't make that mistake," whispered Mickey half aloud.

Suddenly shaken out of a reverie by a full-body chill, Douglas shivered and rejoined the conversation. "It's true! Worldwide acknowledged terrorist, Haman, the Amalekite, has made it no secret that he is in a terrorist pursuit of both major components of the Rods of Power: the Staff of Moses and the Rod of Aaron. If he indeed has the Staff of Moses, then I hope that the Rod of Aaron remains sequestered from him."

"Is there a synergism—a force multiplier effect—that arises when the components are combined?" Suzanne's nerves tightened in anticipation of the answer.

"More than you know," Douglas replied somberly. "With the combining of these two components, as was done by the biblical Moses and Aaron, the world can be leveraged by a re-introduction of the Egyptian plagues of biblical times. Remember the force that was unleashed when the Rods of Power were held in the hands of Moses and Aaron?"

"Come now, Douglas, if Assad knew that the Staff of Moses was that deadly—even without being combined with the Rod of Aaron—he would never have brought it into an unsecured situation like an art exhibit. Why would he risk giving Haman or any terrorist the ability to kick off another plague?"

"Remember the fish in the leaning towers?" Mickey nudged. "Most were right out in the open for all to see."

"Granted, Mickey. But there's a big difference here." Suzanne picked up the deck of cards from the bedside table and threw it faceup on the floor. Cards scattered everywhere. "The ace of spades can still hide among fifty-one other cards. The fish were paper. Papers are everywhere. However, a staff wielded by Moses might not fit that 'in plain sight' MO. There aren't a bunch of staffs just lying around, ya know?"

Douglas kneeled to scoop up the cards. "Good point, Suzanne. We can hope that the Staff of Moses at the exhibit was a substituted replica and not the true relic."

"How would we know?" Mickey said as he kneeled to help.

"Since Asaad isn't a source for answers," said Douglas, "we would only know if or when Haman tries to use it. Once assembled with the Rod of Aaron, the duo that make up the Rods of Power would be armed. A replica would not."

Motioning to Douglas, Suzanne pointed to a card under the edge of the bed. Douglas retrieved the ace of hearts and handed it to Suzanne.

She tapped the card on the table, her brow contracted. "Hold on a minute, Douglas." She pressed the card between her hands, glanced at it, and then put it facedown on the table, keeping her hand over it. "Exactly what components would have to be assembled?"

"It's hard to say. The important fact is that there exists massive weaponry and an itchy trigger finger ready to engage revenge."

"That makes for a very dicey waiting game," said Mickey, combining Douglas's cards with his and stacking them all facedown on the table.

"To say the least," confirmed Douglas. "What we have today is the potential of a terrorist weapon that has no equivalent. Haman, as an Amalekite familiar with history, knows all this. The magnitude of his vengeful evil has potential for worldwide devastation. Remember, it was Moses and Aaron who used this weapon, under the guidance of God, against the Amalekites when they warred against the Israelites in Sinai. I am sure that Haman tastes that bitter defeat every waking day."

"Douglas, do you really, honestly believe that this was a genuine terrorist strike by Haman and not just a theft of precious art?" Suzanne's voice trembled. She pulled the ace from under her hand and raised it to her eyes. She bit her bottom lip.

"You have the luxury to hope that it is just an art theft. I can't, Suzanne. Sad to say but, probably Loni is the only one who knows for sure. She was the lead subject-matter expert in an intelligence arena which primarily included Assad and me. Because the world could potentially be thrust into a plague of biblical proportions, I must assume the worst, the absolute worst, and prepare for that."

Douglas's deepest fear was that Haman was already beginning a search to find where the Rod of Aaron was secured.

Suzanne gave a harrumph as she flipped the card in her hand onto the table.

Everyone looked down at the ace of spades, and Suzanne asked aloud what everyone was thinking.

73

Well-Earned Rest

Maternity hospital
Saint-Quentin, Somme River Valley
Vermandois region, France
Current day

"Where is the Rod of Aaron?"

Picking up the death card, Douglas looked deeply into the eyes of Suzanne and evaluated the simplicity of both her query and her card trick. Unfortunately, unlike the clear connotation of the ace of spades, the answer was very complicated.

"We know that the Rod of Aaron is the second major component of the Rods of Power. There are only two people who know for sure where it is sequestered. One is the person who holds it today . . . or whom *I hope* still holds it. The other was the person I was supposed to meet with after my conference ended in Iper. Unfortunately, I missed that meeting at the museum in Péronne."

"The late Asaad, it was he who . . ." Mickey surmised.

"Well, yes, Mickey. Asaad may have known at one time, but I'm not certain he presently knew. No, there was someone else, but she can't tell me until we find her."

"Szkolna Gora? The Owl?" Mickey guessed. "She and Asaad were World Templar Organization colleagues. Certainly she knows where the Rod of Aaron is secured."

"Yes, Mickey, she does know. However, I was not scheduled to meet the Owl. The person we need to find is right here." He motioned to Loni.

"Douglas, you're making no sense," said Suzanne. "Be direct for once, hubby."

"With her ability to remote view, Loni had recently located the Rod of Aaron. But I need *our Loni*, not Loni-Sibylle-Joan or whoever else I missed in the parade—"

"Loni?" Mickey interrupted in disbelief. "Loni is the one who knows the location of the Rod of Aaron?"

"Yes, Mickey, she tracked it from your journeys in the Leaning Tower affair. You saw the Owl wielding it on many occasions."

"What I saw was an impaired, disfigured old lady calling herself the Owl and using a walking stick to steady her gait."

"It's funny you should call the Owl impaired," Douglas said. "Loni seemed to think she was gifted. Anyway, Loni's review of that same data led her to believe that the walking stick was most likely the Rod of Aaron."

Mickey frowned. "How do *you* know this, Douglas? Loni is *my wife* and she said nothing to *me*."

"She may be your wife. But she is also DIA. You yourself are familiar with the tenet of a need-to-know basis of information sharing. Under the auspices of the Missing Art Project, you did not have a need to know."

"And you had the gall to complain about us not sharing all the information we had?" Suzanne sniped.

Douglas continued, unperturbed. "That was different. That was historical facts, research you had done . . . this is Defense Intelligence Agency business. When she contacted me, Loni said that she needed my help."

"What are you saying, Douglas? You're DIA?"

"I am saying what I am saying. Given the research Loni has done on the Missing Art Project, she knew where the Rod of Aaron was, and she was going to tell me. And yes, Mickey, *I am DIA.*"

"This is why you two had to meet face to face."

"Yes, Mickey."

"There was no other reason?"

"Nothing that you have a need to know of right now. I know that Loni hated not being able to pick your brain or share Defense Intelligence Agency data with you, Mickey. It comes with the territory. As a physician, you know this better than anyone. It's tough when professional secrets must be guarded between spouses."

Knowing the depth of her involvement in DIA secrets, Mickey's worry for Loni had now grown exponentially, and it showed on his face. *If Loni is the single greatest reservoir currently harboring DIA information and intelligence on the Rod of Aaron, there is a veritable target painted on her, and our unborn twins.* Mickey nodded with a grunt and left the room to clear his thoughts.

Douglas and Suzanne stood silently face to face. Suzanne shifted her hips and spoke first.

"I saw you looking at me when you said 'spouses,' Douglas. Be advised, I am not your wife anymore."

"I know that. But since you previously referred to me as your husband, I just reciprocated."

"I did no such thing. You are delusional."

"You said 'hubby.' I heard it."

"No, I didn't. I probably said chubby. It's a word I like to use . . . and . . . uh . . . even if I did say it—and I'm not saying I did, because I know I didn't—it would have been inadvertent, an accident."

"Yes, you did. You know it, and I know it." Douglas smirked as he basked in the fact that Suzanne tripped up. "Anyway, Dr. Sigmund Freud says there are no accidents."

"Be that as it may, this," she moved her arm in a circular motion as if lassoing the entire room, "is not about you and me having been husband and wife," Suzanne remarked most emphatically. "The subject at hand is the real-world danger that currently surrounds us. We need to focus on it. Mickey made that point well."

"Okay then, do you think there are people here in this hospital who think we are all involved in some kind of cloak-and-dagger intrigue?" He gave her a look that said, *Yes, you did.*

She responded with a cold, emphatic stare.

Mickey's return broke the silence, and he engaged Douglas's question.

"Picture this scenario through the eyes of the locals. Here sit three American physicians in Saint-Quentin, a place very close to a probable terror event. They each arrive separately to address a non-obstetrical medical issue in a maternity hospital. Two of the four are high-ranking active-duty soldiers. Two of the four are DIA. Three of four have recently been in the publicized Leaning Tower affair. How strange is that?"

"Coincidence, nothing more," Douglas commented.

"That's because you are looking at it through the eyes of a *civilian*." Suzanne's tone served to remind Douglas that he had never served a day of active service in his life.

"Maybe, but serving as your *husband* in the European theater taught me much about keeping a low American profile. Today's friends are tomorrow's enemies, right?"

"Having been my husband in the past should remind you that appearance far exceeds the reality of the truth. I am sure there are people here who think we are doing things that are not above board."

"Are we, Suzanne?" Douglas locked his gaze. "Are we doing things that are not above board?"

"I have no hidden agenda." Suzanne scowled. "Do you, Douglas?"

"Well, maybe just one little one," Douglas conceded, eyeing his wedding ring finger.

"Well, I for sure do not. I just want my wife to be like she was before." Mickey looked longingly at his exhausted wife.

"That makes two of us." Douglas pursed his lips and tilted his chin at Suzanne, again shooting her that *You did too* kind of look.

"The reality is," Mickey again interjected, "that we three are all fatigued, and there needs to be a first watch volunteer or there will be a volun-told."

"I vote for Douglas," said Suzanne. "He needs time to think and to clear his head of bizarre notions."

"What?" Douglas attempted a rebuttal. Mickey raised his splinted hand in a parlay gesture.

"Ditto, Douglas. You have my vote too. You are the only one of who has gotten any bit of rest recently. The good news is that I will probably only need a couple of hours," said Mickey.

"It looks like no matter how I vote," said Douglas as he inspected and then added the ace of spades back to the deck of cards, "the count, like this deck, is already stacked against me."

"If you need a shotgun sitting beside you to help man the watch, I guess I can muster a bit more energy," Mickey offered with little conviction.

"No, Suzanne's right. I need to think through the issues we have at hand here. Thank you, Mickey. You two secure a waiting room couch the best you can. I'll take point and keep first watch. Let the two military physicians get some very badly needed beauty rest." Despite the hint of cynicism, Suzanne and Mickey needed no extra convincing.

Suzanne glanced back to find Douglas looking at her mouthing the words *You did too*, adding to it a firm nod for emphasis. She rolled her eyes, yielding that she conceded the round.

Mickey and Suzanne settled into their respective corners of an L-shaped couch just around the corner from Loni's room. Both were out the moment their heads hit the cushions.

74

A Failed Release

Château de Chinon
Chinon, France
15th century

Mentally, physically, and emotionally drained, Jehanne gathered up the escort party from Vaucouleurs and proceeded from the holding area at the castle back to the inn. The band's number had increased by one—the Dauphin had assigned a page to personally assist the Maid of Lorraine. As they left, their wagon passed workmen who had just fished a body out of the moat.

"What happened here?" One of Jehanne's original escorts from Vaucouleurs, Jean de Honnecourt, inquired of one of the workmen.

"Accidental death," replied the workman, wiping the sludge off his hands. "Apparently, this gentleman's horse was startled by a barking dog. As the horse reared, the unfortunate noble slipped backward, falling on his shoulders and neck."

"Would that be enough to cause death?" Jean de Honnecourt's brother Julian pursued the inquisition.

"Probably not," answered another of the workmen. "However, landing on this arrow, which looks to have been wedged in the rocks lining the moat, might have hastened things a bit. He was impaled on the arrow and then rolled into the moat. At that point, that which was left still living in him drowned." The entire group of filthy workmen collectively let loose a grizzly laugh.

"Well at least he has left us this fine feathered hat. The selling of it will more than cover the time we have had to smell his stench."

From his horse, the mounted Jean de Metz looked over at Julian in the wagon. "Death evens the playing field. The haughtiness of this morning's rider has been mitigated by a dog's bark, a wayward arrow, and lastly, by vile, stale waters. We never stop to think how fragile life really is. We should always act as if we are standing before He who judges us in the next moment."

"We should indeed," replied Julian back to Jean.

Metz redirected the next comment directly at the bowman. "At least you know where your missing arrow went now, right Richard?" Richard the Archer sheepishly looked back at Jean de Metz. "I thought you went back into town to find your lost arrow," Metz scolded his archer.

"I did. The Maid and the sister can vouch for the fact that I went back into town. I never found it. Look at it this way, Jean, we have found an arrow and rid Chinon of a richly plumed pestilence, all at once."

"God works in mysterious ways," commented Sister Sibyl, seated on the wagon bench. Keeping the reins in one hand, with the other hand configured with her little finger and ring finger bent toward her palm, she made the sign of the cross over the dead body. Afterward, she stroked the fur of Papillon who was leaning forward to better sniff the scene. "Sit, Papi. Don't concern yourself with such matters." As Papillon lay back down on the wagon seat, the nun covered him up in his blanket.

"God's will be done." Jehanne also motioned the sign of the cross over the body while she urged her horse and the party forward toward the inn for their last night there.

That night the group enjoyed dinner and some time to unwind together in one last gathering. Tomorrow, the escort party would return to Vaucouleurs at first light. Louis de Contes, the page, was formally but briefly introduced to the group. A carefully rehearsed departure speech by Jean de Metz followed it.

"Maid," said Metz, holding his stein of cider high, "I have fulfilled my charge to you and to Captain Baudricourt." Cheers arose around the dinner table as all the escort party held their steins upward with a hoot and a holler. Metz waited until the revelry subsided and each sat back down in their seats. Metz remained standing.

"With your permission," said Metz, directing his comments to Jehanne who stood in the doorway of the kitchen next to Sister Sibyl, "I will take my armed escort back to the Lorraine. But before I depart, what more do you need from me?"

"I need nothing more than has already been given." Jehanne motioned Metz to sit. Leaving Sister Sibyl at the door to the kitchen, she strolled around the dinner table until she arrived in front of the seated Jean of Metz. "If you must depart, I need for all of you to have a safe journey back and to promise to support the Dauphin's efforts as he reconsolidates France—unless, of course, you all wish to tarry a bit longer and fight at Orléans."

"Will he begin at Orléans?" Jean de Metz asked.

"No, *we* will begin at Orléans." Jehanne patted Metz's shoulder.

"'We?' That would be us included?"

"Yes, dear Jean of Metz, but only if you are volunteering your services to the Maid of Lorraine."

"Oh, but I would," said Metz dolefully. "However, I have not the power to grant release of myself or my party from the service of Captain Baudricourt."

"No, but the Dauphin does. He did send forth the message today." The room exploded in a roar.

"Quiet, everyone," said Metz, now standing and waving his hand for the escort party to return to their seats.

"Sorry," said Jehanne, "I would have told you earlier, but I wanted to have a feel of your true wishes." Upon hearing these words leave the lips of the blessed Maid, Jean looked to his faithful traveling band.

"How many here wish to be relieved of any service to the Maid?" Jean de Metz asked sternly. He scanned around the table and not a single hand rose. Metz drew his sword, sticking the blade down into the floor. He kneeled. Within seconds, all who had swords followed suit.

"I regret I have no sword to give you, dear Maid," said Richard the Archer, kneeling behind his bow.

"Your arrow has already shown its worthiness, Richard." Jehanne returned to her place next to Sister Sibyl. "I accept all of you as I did that day at Vaucouleurs. I wish I could tell you the way ahead will be easier. I can only promise you that whatever happens, we will be serving the Dauphin as God wills it."

Their stay at the inn was brief. With the help of Louis de Contes, the new page, the transition to new quarters at the castle in the Tour du Coudray was seamless. Jehanne was exquisitely happy since the castle contained a chapel directly attached to the tower. She went there frequently to pray.

And yet, as content as she was to be near a chapel and to have forward action toward the salvation of Orléans, she still hadn't come to terms with what the voices in her head told her.

75

Housekeeper and the Angel

Maternity hospital
Saint-Quentin, Somme River Valley
Vermandois region, France
Current day

D ouglas sat heavy lidded for over two hours. From time to time, he stepped out from Loni's room into the hallway and looked toward the waiting area to see if Mickey was beginning to stir. Despite the daylight streaming through the windows, Mickey was a somnolent corpse. Even through his historical dislike of Mickey, Douglas felt that Mickey deserved the much-needed rest. *Afterall, he has been involved with Loni's medical management from the onset. That, and he looks like a pathetic lobster with that oversized splinted right hand.*

Douglas pivoted his sights and looked over at Suzanne. She was angelic in her appearance. Every now and again she would heave a sigh and shift a bit. These stirrings never awakened her—which was a good thing because he didn't want her to wake and see him watching her. He could gaze upon that face forever. So many times, in so many places, he had awakened early just so he could prop on his elbow and watch her sleep. Occasionally she had awakened and seen him staring at her. But he would always lie and say he had just woken seconds before.

"You love this one, no?" A soft, unrecognizable voice whispered behind him. Douglas whipped his head around to check on Loni, but there was no one in the room. Then he saw a cleaning lady who was vigorously dusting the hand panels along the hallway. She never acknowledged Douglas's presence or varied from her work.

"Did you say something to me?" Douglas asked earnestly, but the woman did not pause in her intense cleaning of the rails.

305

Douglas looked back at the sleeping Suzanne. The same voice again interrupted his gaze. Douglas turned quickly and found the housekeeping woman propped against the rail she had been dusting. This fair, lightly freckled woman wiped her forehead with the back of her half-gloved hand. From the corner of her mouth, she blew at an errant auburn curl that escaped from beneath her flower-printed headband.

The housekeeping lady looked him in the eye. "I only asked, Monsieur, because the look on your face tells more than any spoken word."

"Who are you and what business do you have with me?" Douglas wasn't sure if he was alarmed or annoyed or intrigued. His voice transmitted a combination thereof. Douglas scanned over the habitus of the slim, five-foot tall French woman.

There is a hidden strength in this one. Maybe it's the uniform.

Matching her hazel eyes, she wore a green smock over a white tunic. Douglas scrutinized her movements as she deliberated on her response.

"Me, Monsieur?" She put a hand upon her chest. "I am nobody. I live in the world that everyone tosses away and rejects. I live in all that is discarded in our world. I am nothing but housekeeping staff." She paused and made eye contact with Douglas. "But you, sir. You are a *somebody*. You contribute much to the world above me. However, you look, and you do not see."

Nope, not intrigued, thought Douglas, *just annoyed.*

"Don't you have some work to do?" Douglas said as he started to turn away from the woman.

"Don't you?"

Douglas turned back to face the woman, shocked at her response. "Why are you troubling me?"

"You are already troubled, Monsieur. I believe that you are in love and that pains your heart greatly. I believe that the woman who sleeps there doesn't carry you in her dreams. I believe—"

"Enough." Douglas swiped his hand in front of himself like a scythe. He was bewildered by the audacity of this woman. "I have heard enough. I am not going to stand here and entertain theories with a . . . with a . . . with no more than a—"

"—a bit of dirt beneath your feet?" The woman raised her eyebrows challengingly but with a serene demeanor.

Douglas turned beet red. *Was it rage or embarrassment?* He shook his head. He couldn't be sure. *What is it with this lady?*

"No. No, I was going to say . . . to say—"

"—to say what, Monsieur?"

"I don't know anymore. I just know that I am not going to have this conversation with you." He held his hands up in concession.

"But you already are."

"So it seems." Douglas pursed his lips and ran his hands through his hair. Round one went to housekeeping. Clearing his throat and adjusting his rolled-up cuffs, Douglas softened his gaze. "Okay, let's start again. I am Douglas Coletrane. I am—"

"—a doctor and you are in love with the angel that sleeps so sweetly."

"Well, I . . . yes, I am a doctor. As for being in love, *that* is certainly no concern of yours."

"What happened between you and the angel, Dr. Coletrane?"

Douglas looked at the woman and the earnestness in her eyes. He leaned back against the doorframe to Loni's suite. "It began so long ago I don't even know where to begin." He scanned over at the sleeping Suzanne and then down to his shoes.

"Begin at the beginning. We have time."

"I told you," Douglas gave a nervous chuckle, "I am not going to have this discussion with you."

"But your eyes are already telling the story. Please, Dr. Coletrane. This conversation began long before you and I met. Let's sit," she indicated the chairs in Loni's room, "while a *someone* tells a *no one* what has caused a *someone's* heart to become so heavy."

Douglas turned a little to face the woman, blocking the room's entrance with his body. "Why do you keep referring to yourself as 'nobody' and 'no one'?"

"It is not an insult to be a *nobody* if one chooses to be."

"I don't understand."

"Monsieur Doctor, the world of a *somebody* pivots every day around how the world views you. It is true for all you *somebodies* the world over. For me as a *nobody*, the world doesn't look at me. The world cares nothing about me. I have no concerns of how the world sees me, and so, instead, my energy is spent viewing the world from my perspective. I have the unique privilege of viewing the world outwardly. I choose to be an observer of the world—not the observed. Tell me, Monsieur Doctor, who has more freedom to see and understand?"

"You aren't a *nobody* even if you say you are."

"Really? Then, why then won't you sit with me?"

"I . . . I—"

"If I am a *somebody*, what is my name? You are a *somebody*, Dr. Coletrane. I know your title and your name. What is my name?"

"You never gave it to me," said Douglas defensively.

"Did you ask?" the woman raised one eyebrow at him.

Douglas pursed his lips and grunted. In Douglas's mind the bell rang and round two went to housekeeping.

"Monsieur, did you really want to know the name of the person who cleans the grit and grime that the world leaves behind?"

"Well, I—"

"No, I didn't think so. You have still not asked. However, I will tell you, nonetheless. My name is Clarisse."

"Does Clarisse, the *nobody*, have a surname?" He watched as she tucked a few auburn strands of hair back behind her headband, and he found himself wondering how soft her hair must be to escape its confines so easily.

"My family is Penez, but my name is now Saint Vincent."

"So, you are French."

Clarisse looked at him in horror, simulated spitting on the floor, and then grinding it in. "No, I am not French. I have never been, nor will I ever be French. I am French Canadian."

Douglas's lips curled into a poorly suppressed and quivering smile. "Do you not like the French?"

"Yes."

Douglas cocked his head, wondering if she meant that yes, she did not like the French, or yes, she liked the French. Before he could get clarification, she interrupted him.

"My home is in Guelph, Ontario."

"Ontario isn't part of French Canada."

"But I am Franco-Ontarian," Clarisse spoke with growing pride.

"But you live in France. That makes you blessed French." Douglas hoped his bait would clear up the previous confusion.

Clarisse continued without missing a beat. "My family sent me in the summers to live with my uncle here in France at Wimereux on the channel."

"Not here in the Vermandois?"

"No, I lived in France tending to the Canadians there at Wimereux."

"A Canadian colony exists in France on the English Channel? I have never heard of such."

"The Canadians at Wimereux are the ones who no longer laugh, sing, or play merrily."

"Why so? Are they averse to having fun, or are they ill?"

"No, they are not either anymore. They all dwell in the cemetery at Wimereux."

"How many of them are dead?"

"All of them."

"What I meant was—"

"You are American military, no? There is one there well known to you."

"I am not American military. However, I do feel that I am truly American military at times because my whole life has been in and around it."

"Then you may not know Sir John McCrae."

"Of course I know of Lieutenant Colonel John McCrae—an army physician, pathologist, and artilleryman. He wrote 'In Flanders Fields' from his forward battalion aid station during the Great War. He was a great Canadian military physician, soldier, and poet."

Clarisse smiled for the first time and, unbidden, a smile came to Douglas as well.

"He was from my home in Guelph. He is also from my home on the channel at Wimereux."

"I think I knew that from the Veterans of Foreign Wars banquets I attended with my wife. She would recite the poem with a patriotic video playing in the background."

"Your wife is the sleeping angel, no?" Clarisse pointed down the hallway but kept her eyes fastened on Douglas.

"No."

"Then who is the woman there sleeping peacefully in the shadow of your watchfulness? You must love the angel very much."

Douglas cleared his throat then asked kindly, "What does a cemetery groundskeeper turned hospital housekeeping staff know of love and marriage?"

She looked away. "Maybe nothing." She glanced at him from the corner of her eye. "Maybe something."

"Nice answer—short and ambivalent."

"I know that while keeping a cemetery, the people you observe freely display who they really are."

"How so?"

"Private cemetery visits are a time when emotions cannot be falsified. What you see is real love, grief, respect, and disdain in their most genuine forms."

"How do you know they are real?"

"Because, Doctor, there is no audience requiring the person to fake an award-winning performance."

"So—I ask again, with respect—what do you know of love and marriage?"

"I know that a woman's heart is made of the same substance as clouds. From a distance, the love can be seen and appreciated, but it is difficult to hold and analyze."

"Clouds, eh?" Douglas massaged his back against the doorframe.

"In a manner of speaking, yes, clouds. It is the winds of relationships that gust against and shape the emotions into thin airy wisps or dark troubled thunderheads."

"Sounds about right."

"The man's heart is different. It is more like the sand on the earth. It has clearly defined margins and obeys the rules and logic within relationships."

"Okay," Douglas stretched the sound, "I guess I can see that." Douglas scratched his stubbled chin.

"The wind, rain, temperature, and pressure—all elements of a relationship—affect each substance, cloud or sand, in a different way."

"I'm tracking."

"The man's heart is harder to move and be moved."

"Yes, I see that."

"But . . . a woman's heart can encompass much and yet not be defined by its borders which really don't even exist. Her heart moves on the tiniest of whispers."

Douglas nodded silently. Then he asked, "What do you know of marriage?"

"I know that I love Luc Saint Vincent even though he has left my life."

"Why did he go?"

"Death spares no one's marriage."

"Is that why you came to work here?"

"When Luc went away, I gave up my flower shop and the graveside business. I really wanted to keep working with my flowers. So I came to a place where flowers are brought to the living instead of the dead. What place boasts greater life than a maternity hospital?"

Douglas cocked his head at the cleaning woman and smiled warmly. "Clarisse, you are quite amazing."

"I know."

"I mean that."

"I know."

"I'm complimenting you. Can't you just say thank you?"

"Can't you?"

The bell in Douglas's head rang and the final round went to the small French Canadian. He chuckled.

"Thank you, Clarisse." Douglas reached over and hugged the insightful housekeeper. As in the way of the French, he kissed her on both cheeks before relinquishing her to return to her responsibilities. Her hair brushing against his cheeks was as soft as he had imagined it would be. After he released her, she combed out her ruffled shirt sleeves and smiled her acceptance of his gratitude.

"It is amazing what can be seen when nobody is around." Clarisse gave a knowing nod and proceeded down the hall, around the corner, and toward the hospital flower shop where the remainder of her work lay.

"*Unter vier Augen*, 'under four eyes,' face to face, *nobody* . . . does it better," Douglas murmured to himself.

Giving a final glance down the hall to the sleeping pair, Douglas turned from the hallway and disappeared into the darkness of Loni's patient room.

76

Struggles in the Dark

Maternity hospital
Saint-Quentin, Somme River Valley
Vermandois region, France
Current day

Douglas settled quietly in the chair facing Loni. *It is good that the others are asleep. I need to reach Loni on a whole different level. There are secrets and then there are secrets.*

Douglas knew something that Mickey and Suzanne didn't fully understand. *It has always been hidden in plain sight just like they said about the fish, or the papers, or whatever.*

Everyone knew that Loni worked as an agent for the Defense Intelligence Agency's Department of Remote Viewing. But, until today, no one knew that Loni's work in special education and Douglas's own metaphysical work overlapped when it came to this remote viewing.

Douglas surveyed the sleeping face of his work partner. *Many know about a special educator's insights into the impaired. Few understand your keen insights into the atypical, the gifted . . . and sometimes, the criminally gifted.*

He prepared himself mentally for his next task. *Okay, Loni, we've been working on this for a long time. You know the location of the Rod of Aaron, or at least you have a clue to its location. We know that if it is kept away from the Staff of Moses it is safe. Asaad knew that too—that's why he displayed the staff. That intel, that clue you have, is buried in your psyche. It could save us all. Why couldn't you tell me before on any the numerous past phone chats? Why?*

Douglas rubbed his face vigorously and leaned back. His coat fell off the back of the chair, and the medicine vial from the pocket clattered to the ground. He retrieved it and stared into the dull orange plastic.

She knew . . . she sensed my instability and wouldn't divulge anything until we met under vier Augen.

He tucked the vial back into the jacket pocket. *Thank God they don't know of my failed suicide attempt. But then again, if I hadn't missed our meeting, I could have been a*

311

casualty too . . . then where would they be without me? I can handle this. I CAN handle this. I must. Douglas set his jaw. *I have to know what you know, Loni.*

"How is she?" a voice from the hall sounded.

"What?" Douglas's body tensed.

"The pregnant lady, how is she?" Clarisse's concern rang genuine. She hovered at the doorway, cleaning supplies in hand.

"She's battling," he sighed. "We are having some progress."

"Good to hear. I will keep her in my prayers." With that said, Clarisse disappeared again.

There is just no privacy, no secure location—at least not here. For now, the Missing Art Project and its current focus on the Staff of Moses and Rod of Aaron will have to be tabled.

Douglas shifted gears in his mind. *As far as everyone on the French maternity staff here is concerned, I am her managing metaphysician. For now, that has to be acceptable. Mickey and Suzanne said Loni was stuck in the year 1429—that's an improvement of about fifty-five years but it's still only 8.7 percent of the way home. The secret of everyone's future is tangled with Loni and Jehanne's past and the intentional grooming process for a Maid of Lorraine. I wonder, though, how much of Loni's DIA life is tied into Jehanne?*

Douglas squatted in front of Loni who was asleep in her chair. Her hands were folded over her domed belly.

Well, that answer will soon be forthcoming. The historic Joan of Arc only has a few more years to live in her timeline, after all.

Loni shifted in her recliner causing the metal of her pendant crucifix to flash. Douglas rose to stand over her and slowly, he reached toward the necklace. *Suzanne pointed this out at the beginning of this mess. Maybe this pendant is the beginning and end of some mysterious race and Loni—as Joan—is in a countdown to a checkered flag. Mickey said that Joan of Arc died by burning at the stake in the city of Rouen in. . . .* Douglas screwed up his eyes trying to recall the date. *In May of the year 1431. Maybe Mickey is right, and Loni is trying to find the meaning behind psychically connecting with Joan here in the Vermandois.*

Douglas shrugged, jerking on the lower front edges of his vest. *Remember, you're in uncharted waters here, Douglas. When Joan of Arc dies, will Loni, as we know her, die as well? What happens to this necklace when Loni—as we know her—is gone and the pendant no longer has the intended neck from which to hang?*

Douglas retracted his hand and sat back down in the facing chair, shaking his head. *No going back now—time will tell.* He settled himself to clear his mind before engaging Loni again. He visualized a calm, soothing place and breathed deeply, willing his conscious mind to be still. However, the beeping of the monitor was hypnotic, and unbidden, sleep overtook him.

Douglas suddenly woke up to the sound of a struggle. As he scanned his surroundings through his uncoordinated gaze, he saw the nurses pushing Loni out of the hospital window.

What in the world are they doing? Mickey and Suzanne were right! There are dark forces employed here in the Vermandois. Et tu, Clarisse?!

"Hey there!" he shouted. His voice was shrouded in unfurling layers of sleep. "Hold on! Stop it! Unhand that woman!

Where are Mickey and Suzanne?

After a few seconds of wakening, Douglas arrived at a revelation. *They're not pushing Loni—they are pulling at her.* Quickly, Douglas joined the fray.

"Loni, what are you doing? Where do you think you're going?" From behind, Douglas grabbed Loni's shoulders. Twisting her upper torso, he corralled her shoulders within the crook of his arm. Initially her head did not follow. Douglas watched as Loni's head slowly turned toward him. "Loni?" *This is not a face I have ever seen. It reeks of defiance and desperation.* "Loni, what are you doing?" Douglas watched as Loni's eyes rolled up into her head. He felt her body go limp.

Together, Douglas and the staff gripped Loni to keep her from falling out onto the fire escape. In a few moments, Loni was returned to her bedside recliner. The hospital staff was all quite distressed. However, using sufficient sign language and the English-to-French language skills of a certain French Canadian, Douglas reassured all personnel that this issue could best be handled by him. As the hospital staff slowly migrated out of Loni's room, Douglas dropped into the patient visitor's chair. He combed his fingers through his hair. *I don't know who that was trying to jump out the window but that was not a Loni I have ever seen.* Douglas straighten himself up in the chair, pulling it closer to an open-eyed, non-seeing Loni sitting in the recliner. Leaning toward her, he eased back into the doc mode.

"Loni, I need you to turn and look at me," said Douglas. "Good." *At least she's back in the moment.* "I'm going to have you watch the shiny object just like we did before, okay? Help me to figure out what is going on here." Loni took in a deep breath, resituated herself in the recliner. Soon, she was again reclined peacefully in her chair, back in a deep hypnotic trance.

"Loni, are you there? Is everything okay?" His voice cracked. "Are you okay?"

This word sequence sent Douglas reeling back through time. He remembered Loni's face over him saying, *Douglas, honey, are you there? Is everything okay? Are you okay?* The memory string overrode his current situation and cast him back twelve years.

✠ ✠ ✠

It was the European Medical Command's 1998 Spring Medical-Surgical Conference at the Holiday Inn of Passau, Germany, and he was far more inebriated than he had ever intended to be. It was an evening he desperately wished to forget, but even then, deep inside, he knew he never would.

Douglas came to join his wife at her medical conference. Mickey and Loni came over from Wuerzburg, Germany. Suzanne was finishing out her stint at Keller Army Hospital at West Point and decided she would catch the conference en route to their new assignment in Korea. Douglas departed ahead of her to do some research in Augsburg, Germany, with some of his professional compatriots called the Circle of Friends.

The evening was snake bitten from the start. Douglas's late arrival to the hotel caused Suzanne some inconveniences to get him settled. She was quite underwhelmed in her happiness to see him. She was enjoying the lockstep tempo of the conference curriculum—chumming around with all her physician friends. She really didn't want him there. He didn't want to be there either. He had no love for her colleagues who said, with their looks, the words they wouldn't say to his face. To Douglas, they all were egocentric overachievers and the level of arrogance that simmered up when the number of physicians in a conference reached critical mass was too much for him.

Watching them verbally fencing with one another was absolute drudgery. Seeing them land their well-placed conversational thrusts and parries made Douglas, Loni, and many of the other professional spouses grow weary. Loni always found some way to extract harmless entertainment from the superfluous interplay. Douglas just preferred to be apart.

As the evening wore on, Suzanne, exhausted from the day's activities, turned in early. Douglas succeeded in finding alternative company to the spectator sport of immature bantering among the medical specialists. From his experience, a specialist was a person who had studied more and more to learn less and less until they knew everything about nothing. But he didn't have to tell his friends Iordanov and Tonic about that—they already knew.

77

Slam-fest

ERMC Spring Medical-Surgical Conference
Passau, Germany
1998

On a hotel balcony abutting a hotel salon on one side while standing over the Danube River on the other, Douglas listened to the water as it slammed and cursed the jagged river rocks. The black night on the unlit balcony made him an evening specter, quite typical of his DIA personality. He further accentuated his ghostliness by closing tight the red velvet curtain at his back. As a perk, this drape kept the hotel conversation din at bay. Unfortunately, he had enough remaining auditory acuity to overhear the salon conversation not meant for his ears coming from just beyond the drapes. He swirled the remains of a vodka tonic in his glass. The ice slid around and around, trapped in a vortex.

"So, Mickey, how's life at the mother ship?" said the Bamberg clinic commander. Mickey, seated on a couch with his back to the drapes, was ringed by no less than five of the ten clinic commanders. All sat in their respective chairs with cocktail in hand or resting on their notebook on side or center table. Each commander cascading into varied positions of uninhibited semi-drunken ease.

The alien reference to the mothership confirmed the fact that Wuerzburg Medical Hospital was the center support for ten outlying medical clinics throughout Bavaria including the cities of Bamberg, Ansbach, Grafenwoehr, Hohenfels, and Kitzingen, to name a few. This year, that mother ship provided support for the spring conference. The hospital commander at Wuerzburg was determined to top all previous conferences, so he staged the professional shindig for all his clinic commanders in the gorgeous German city of Passau.

"Mickey," Ansbach's clinic commander jeered, "aren't you going to divulge the doings of the great Wuerzburg Hospital?"

This jab simultaneously brought Mickey out of his memories about the beautiful host city and made him realize how boorish most of his colleagues

315

had become. Even though he had struggled with his peers through classroom didactics, clinical rotations, an internship, and then residency, he remembered most of his comrades being quite enjoyable company. True, they had all joined medicine for a variety of reasons, but he couldn't recall boorishness being one of them. *Is this the point to where we all have evolved? Or perhaps devolved?* Mickey shuddered as he began to respond to yet the third verbal probe of transparently cloaked sarcasm.

"Besides being at the point of excellence, what is it that you clowns need to know about Wuerzburg? Of course," Mickey propped his feet on his battle book for emphasis, "anything I tell you will mean that later I will have to kill you."

This brought a round of jeering calls followed by coarse laughter. Mickey continued playing at arrogance and answered the immediate question on the floor. He then expanded on the topic by talking about the hospital politics at Wuerzburg. His peers looked to him for his unique perspective, having been both commander of a clinic and a chief of a hospital clinic. This gave him insights from both sides of the proverbial coin. They all listened carefully—his opinions were widely respected.

Strolling into the hotel salon abutting Douglas's hidden balcony and listening to Mickey's slant was the deputy commander of clinical services from Landstuhl Hospital and two clinic physicians from outlying medical clinics in the Heidelberg footprint, Friedberg and Mannheim. Landstuhl's DCCS, Friedberg's, and Mannheim's commanders pulled up in three chairs, widening the ring around Mickey. After bushhogging through most of the mundane medical talk, the subject moved—as it always did—into the realm of gossip.

As the conference attendees delved immediately into the meat of tonight's topic, Douglas heard a familiar name surface. Even if he had been able to block out most of the conversation previously, now it was impossible. The ice in his glass swiveled to a standstill.

"I saw your buddy Douglas Coletrane arrive today," spoke the DCCS to Mickey. "What is he doing here? It's kind of odd to see Suzanne here also. What is a stateside-assigned physician doing at our European conference?"

"Didn't you hear, Sir?" said Mickey, returning his feet to the floor. "She landed the chief of primary care position at the army hospital at Yongsan, Korea." Mickey shifted his gaze to the drink he held in his hand. "Douglas will probably interface with the local host nation hospital and present an interchange between American and Asian alternative medicine techniques." Mickey stuck to the facts and said nothing of the tumultuous marriage which seemed to be in the final throes of death. He couldn't figure out why they weren't happy. He always thought they really loved each other.

"Really?" The DCCS sipped at his cocktail. "What happened to the golden girl from West Point? When Suzanne left Hudson High, our premier school for future army generals, I was sure she would be nailing all the killer assignments."

"The hospital at Yongsan isn't a bad assignment, Sir," defended Mickey. "She has done very well since graduating from West Point Academy."

"True, Mickey, but she was initially headed for much more . . . at least . . . before—"

"Just say it. We all know it," said the Kitzingen commander as she motioned for a refill from a passing waiter.

The Friedberg physician drew first blood. "Is she going to dump the albatross here in Germany or wait till she gets to Korea?"

"Does it matter?" asked the DCCS. "Why is a respected and accomplished internist like Suzanne playing patty-cake with an academic weak link like Douglas?"

"Who knows what makes Suzanne tick?" retorted the female commander from Kitzingen. "I mean, in 1976 she was selected to be in the first class of females ever allowed to attend West Point."

"And she was at the top of her class at the Medical College of Georgia," said her medical school classmate, the commander from Hohenfels. "That set her up for the next major career launch, right?"

"Truly . . . how many people get selected for a tropical medicine fellowship sponsored by Louisiana State University, University of Costa Rica, and Gorgos Laboratories in Panama?" The Kitzingen commander received and set down her new drink, passing the empty glass to the waiter. "Holy mackerel, when I think of experiencing tropical medicine full time in the tropics, I get a hormone rush."

"Being stationed in Panama is a gift," said the Mannheim commander as he struck a thoughtful pose. Listening quietly, Mickey nodded in agreement. *Suzanne is a rock star. Everyone sees it. But Douglas has skills too. Just ask Loni. Why won't he put his skillset on the world stage with Suzanne?* Mickey stirred his drink with his finger. His ears tuned back into the conversation. Mickey heard the Mannheim commander speak again.

"Wasn't it in Jurassic Park Land, just across the northern frontier border of Panama, where she first met that clown Dougie?"

Douglas listened quietly, hearing his name being volleyed back and forth like the ball on a ping-pong table. With each return, the slams came harder and faster. *Why isn't Mickey defending me? Is he still there?* Douglas gripped the glass tightly. The rising heat from his body had nearly melted his ice completely.

"I believe it was," chimed in Mickey, through the slanderous din. "I don't remember hearing the reason Suzanne was in Costa Rica at that time. I imagine visiting the fantastic volcano parks in the jungles would be a draw."

To Douglas, Mickey's voice was pale and anemic, not at all like a usual command tone. As he expected, Mickey's attempt to redirect the conversation failed miserably.

"What is the skinny on the male Coletrane?" said the DCCS.

"I got this one, Sir," said the Mannheim commander. "Here's what I know from several different sources—all of them disreputable, of course."

A generalized chortle ensued.

If I try and defend Douglas, these piranhas will just turn on me, Mickey groaned as he surveyed faces hungry for anything that could degrade and defame Douglas.

He knew there was no way he was going to subtly detour this slam-fest which was rapidly morphing into a train without brakes.

The Mannheim commander continued. "Douglas's father is the research geneticist and molecular biochemist, Dr. Remington Ellison Coletrane. Remember him from the scientific literature?" The commander waved his dripping cocktail straw at his colleagues.

"Remember him?" said the commander from Grafenwoehr. "Who wouldn't? He was an expert in protein chemistry and did some expansion work on increased thiol oxidation in sickle erythrocytes. Although the protein he selected for study was not the protein which caused sickle cell anemia, it added to the pool of scientific research knowledge." Grafenwoehr paused to slurp his drink, the ice clinking loudly against the glass.

Standing with his back against the cold stone balcony, Douglas stared at the drapes which separated him from the vile conversationalists beyond. Douglas imagined the condensation on Grafenwoehr's glass and the large, rotund ice cubes lolling about leisurely in their pool of alcohol.

"Was Douglas involved in the study?" The DCCS stoked onward.

"No, Sir," said the Mannheim commander, "but apparently, his father's love for science was embraced by little Dougie as he spent lots of time in his daddy's office at the Gorgos Laboratory." Mannheim's eye twinkled. "Wait, wait, here is where the story turns bizarre." The glass smacked against the table. "Dougie's mother was a mail-order bride, of sorts."

"Really?" The DCCS arched an eyebrow. "How's that?"

"Yes, how can one be a 'mail-order bride, of sorts'?" The Kitzingen commander patted her belly flanks. "Isn't that like being a little bit pregnant? Either you are or you aren't."

"Wait for it!" The Mannheim commander stood up. "Dougie's mother was the subject of an advertisement scheme for marriage."

"What?" said one commander. "No!?" remarked another. Murmurs rumbled through the group briefly.

"That's right, folks," said Mannheim. "His father, Dr. Ellison Coletrane, the quite wealthy and renowned scientist, put an ad in two Costa Rican papers for the Spanish and English clientele. There he advertised that he wanted to marry the prettiest Tica in Costa Rica. He promised to pay handsomely, but she had to be between fifteen and seventeen years old and be the richest flower in the land."

"What happened?" said the DCCS, as he preened his eyebrows.

"What do you think, Sir?" Mannheim gestured horse galloping. "Hordes of Costa Rican mothers and fathers brought their Tica princesses to his doorstep. From the multitudes interviewed, Dr. Coletrane selected a sixteen-year-old girl from the banana plantation of the United Fruit conglomerate. She became his wife."

"So," said Friedberg, "Douglas is a genuine fruitcake from one of the banana republics, eh?" This engendered another round of coarse guffaws.

Mickey stared at his battle book and said nothing. *No one deserves this berating.*

He cupped his drink. *Not Douglas. Not anyone.* Mickey's eyes began following the wavy pattern in the camouflaged cover of his battle book. *If a uniformed version of Douglas and I shared a foxhole and either of us received incoming fire from the enemy, both of us would return fire. The problem with me here is that in this situation, both the enemy and me wear the same uniform. How do I fight against that?* Mickey shifted his stare to the watered-down remains of his drink.

"When I heard that Dougie trained hard in biology at the University of Miami, then did grad work at Florida State University in medicinal chemistry," said the Mannheim commander, "I realized that if he continued on this track, he could almost be respectable . . . maybe." There were more chuckles from the group. "Instead, he decided to beach bum at every opportunity, spending time among the Hispanic communities in southeast Florida."

"Well, that's a no brainer," said Friedberg. "Douglas had to stay where the Hispanic population was the thickest—birds of a feather, you know. . . ."

"A drum roll, please." Mannheim seated himself, using the chair's arms for musical instrumentation. "Freaking out on sun and sand, he diverted from the hard sciences to—and this is where it gets weird—to the world of *occult* medicine."

"For real?" The DCCS flared his nostrils.

"Yes, Sir!" Mannheim slapped the table, punctuating the disbelief. "This quasi-capable science academician shifted his focus into metaphysical studies and herb biology—then on to the School of Homeopathic Medicine."

Douglas heard another round of drinks being ordered. He swallowed the tepid dregs of his cup in one gulp. *Useless. Mickey is useless.* He carefully placed the glass on the balcony floor.

"I heard a rumor." Friedberg scanned the faces in the group. "Is it true that Douglas worked some experimental therapy at Tripler with alternative medicine techniques—acupuncture and aromatherapy? Ha! Can you imagine! What's next? Ear coning?"

"Actually, all that's true," said Kitzingen. "Suzanne was an internist at Tripler Medical Center's Internal Medicine Department. Here is where the rift began. Suzanne *the good* probably decided that Dougie was a combo of *the bad* and *the ugly.*"

The drinks arrived and the piranhas took long draughts from their glasses.

"Bottom line," Mannheim smacked his lips together, "Dougie fell on his own sword and committed career hari-kari."

The chatter continued. Behind the curtain, Douglas stared at his feet, shaking his head from side to side, and squeezing his fists open and closed.

At that moment, Loni stepped a single foot into the salon. Pausing at the doorway to catch the drift of the conversation, she recognized quickly that she was amidst Doug-Slam '98 Festival. She looked to her mannequin husband and narrowed her eyes at him. Mickey was stone quiet; he would not meet her gaze. It only took two rounds of searing verbal degradation for her to interrupt.

"Excuse me, Doctors, and I do mean this title in the *least* level of professionalism it might allow. I happen to be a friend of Douglas Coletrane. I think what I see here is a bit of group envy among yammering eunuchs."

"Envy?" blurted a somewhat drunken Mannheim. "Envious of what? Medicinal needlepoint?"

Chuckles and snickers abounded. Even a few glasses clinked together in toast-like agreement.

"Yes, envy." Loni licked her lips. "Did you magpies know that Douglas Coletrane placed first in his class at University of Miami, at FSU, *and* at Hahnemann School of Homeopathy? Although he crushed the MCATs, he consciously chose metaphysical medicine. I don't imagine any of you managed to hit that out-of-the-park homer? He has been published in over twenty-two professional journals and magazines. *Count them, twenty-two.* I guess that's tough for most of you to understand—since most of you can't count higher than twenty-one unless you take off your gloves, shoes, socks, and unzip your trousers.

"Douglas's work in homeopathy has done more for alternative medicine than all of you so-called traditionalists have done in your field of *accepted medicine.* Personally, I feel fortunate to even be able to be in the same room with Douglas Odysseus Coletrane. Furthermore, I think Suzanne Coletrane is darned lucky to have someone like Douglas as a husband and a professional colleague. I am so glad to have him as *our friend.*" She put her hand on Mickey's shoulder and gave an obviously firm squeeze. "That is more than I can say for the rest of you who have never been to my home and most likely never will. So, if you don't mind, gentlemen and you too, my good lady officer, even if you do mind, good evening." Loni slapped Mickey on the back and walked off in a storm.

Standing quickly, Mickey attempted to vocalize an explanation to his colleagues but just stood there slack jawed. Finally, after a ten-count of silence, he closed his mouth, set down his empty glass, and departed with his tail tucked, leaving the conversation to broil on without him.

Beyond the drapes, Douglas slowly sank to the ground, slouching against the balcony rail long after the last of the salon's occupants drifted away.

What does Suzanne even see in me? Maybe I should step out of her life and not impede her success. Maybe I should have done it a long time ago. She's hooked her wagon to a flailing star. Maybe I just needed a drink—or twenty-two, count 'em, twenty-two.

Grunting, Douglas dragged himself up and yanked open the drapes which revealed an unoccupied couch, a coffee table covered with empty glasses jumbled between discarded cocktail serviettes, and a ring of empty chairs. He strode with determination to a smooth barstool which was to be his sheltered harbor of self-destruction. "Double vodka tonic!" he barked at the bartender. He drummed his fingers on the glossy counter. "Wait!" He reached out toward the bartender, "Double vodka tonic—hold the tonic."

"Double Iordanov, coming up."

Hours later it was Loni who eventually stumbled up on him at the bar. He was sloshed beyond all inhibition. He had hoped to forget the names and voices that trashed him that night; but even then, in his drunken haze, he knew he would always remember the one person who stood up for him—and the one who just sat silently.

✠ ✠ ✠

Douglas rubbed his eyes vigorously and sighed deeply.

I should have peeked beyond the curtains that night to see Loni's face as she thundered away at those pompous cronies. If only I had possessed more courage.

Through welled-up eyes, he saw his heroine placidly sitting before him. He gently shook her shoulder.

"Loni, are you there? Please be there."

"Loni isn't here," said an out-of-breath voice. "This is Jehanne."

78

Battle at the Gate

Maternity hospital
Saint-Quentin, Somme River Valley
Vermandois region, France
Current day

At Jehanne's unexpected response, Douglas quickly released Loni's shoulder. Wiping at the tears that had streamed down his cheeks, Douglas blurrily looked at Loni. As he surveyed her features, all he could see was only a whisper of what had been his most deeply respected friend, ally, and defender.

"I'll make it okay, Loni. I promise. Okay?" Douglas whispered to himself and the still air that clung about them.

Douglas regrouped and in a louder, more confident tone, he redirected.

"Jehanne, can you tell me what you are seeing now?"

"Yes, guiding voice, I see light from the far window. I had a chance to jump to safety, but the guards stopped me." Loni, as Jehanne, panted as if after a struggle.

"Why do you believe there is safety in jumping through the window?"

"Do you believe that there is not?" the Maid challenged.

Suzanne entered the room, rubbing the sleep from her eyes.

"What is the year and where are you, Jehanne?" Douglas asked.

Hearing Jehanne's name, Suzanne positioned herself just off Douglas's shoulder as he remained seated in front of Loni. With her eyes on Loni, Suzanne whispered in Douglas's direction, "Please don't let it be 1431."

Out in the waiting area, and still in blissful slumber, remained the snoring lobster. Mickey was far from ready to re-engage. His rapid eye movements indicated his energies were being utilized in a battlefield elsewhere.

"Is that you, Saint Catherine? Is Saint Michael there with you?" Loni's brow contracted and her head tilted to the side. "Please, blessed saint, who is this other voice? I have heard it before, and I have done its bidding, but I do not have a name with which to address it. I do not wish to be irreverent or disrespectful."

322

Without missing a beat, Suzanne, as the voice of Saint Catherine, responded. "I am always here for you, Jehanne. The other voice is a helper. He helps to bring us together. Know that you can trust in him as you trust in me."

Douglas gave Suzanne a small smile which she did not acknowledge or return.

"Michael," Suzanne continued, "with his arm draped for mortal combat, is wrestling with the dragons in another time and another place. In his heart, I know he supports everything you are. Be not sad that, for the moment, he is otherwise engaged."

Out in the hall sleeping on a couch, possibly through his subconscious, Mickey heard his name being discussed. He gave a particularly loud snort, followed by a snore and a growl.

"If my ears do not deceive me," said Jehanne, "I believe I hear the dragon's roar even from here."

"I am not surprised," iterated Suzanne.

Douglas rolled his lips in and bit down at Suzanne's art of skirting humor.

Loni sighed. "The tower that holds me is lonely. I need to go. My troops *must* find me." Loni looked to the ceiling. "La Hire and Arthur III de Richemont from Patay, if you could see me, you would be here now. From Orléans, Jean de Brosse, Lord of Boussac, come, free me now!"

Douglas thought hard before he spoke again. *Mickey mentioned a time when Joan of Arc was a prisoner in the Beaurevoir Tower in the Vermandois. He thought Loni was re-creating Joan's experiences. He said Joan jumped—that might match up with what just happened a few minutes ago. Maybe if we can find why Loni linked in with this moment of Jehanne's history, maybe we could get Loni back home and this amnesia would resolve itself. That is, if this current tower is the one in the Vermandois. There is another tower in the city of Rouen. . . .* He dared not think about that now.

"How is it you became held in this tower against your will, Jehanne?" Douglas resumed the quest at hand.

"It was in May, when the campaign to drive out the English began to mire down—"

"What year is it?" he interrupted.

He prayed she would not say 1431. The tower which imprisoned her in that year led to only one place—the streets of Rouen and a bonfire built to burn her as a heretic. Douglas held his breath and felt Suzanne's grip painfully tighten into his left shoulder.

"The year is 1430, one important in the year of our Lord."

Douglas and Suzanne together cringed at the ambiguity of the answer.

"Are you saying 1430 or 1431?"

The suspense dragged on, eons in every instant.

Haltingly, Jehanne enunciated her reply, "One . . . four . . . three . . . zero."

In unison, they audibly exhaled. There still was time to save Loni.

"Tell us about where you are and how you got there."

"I am at Beaurevoir, guiding voice. The English brought me here after they pulled me down from my horse in Compiègne. My misfortune began early. The

Duke of Burgundy came to battle me outside the city walls. I had to move my men to battle in a position that would favor our victory. We rode all night on the twenty-second from the deep ridges of Crépy-en-Valois to get to Compiègne. My troops were so tired. We were well received by Guillaume de Flay, the captain of the city."

"What happened next?" Suzanne asked.

"In the morning, we rested briefly, accepted Mass with the captain, and then by noon we girded ourselves for battle. With my armor covered in a golden cloth, I rode my gray stallion at the head of the army. He was so very handsome and proud—I knew the troops would be inspired to victory. Flapping sharply with every gust of a midday wind, my standard was raised high. The charge out of the city gate and over the bridge against the Burgundians was thunderous. The Godon ran back in fear of the Maid once . . . twice . . . thrice." Loni beat her fist on the arm of her chair with each count. "On the third charge, the English divided our troops, leaving those of us at the front encircled in a sea of enemy. They blocked our way back to the bridge so we could not get back into the town. We couldn't retreat."

"There is no disgrace in retreat if you live to fight another day," replied Suzanne. She wished she could change history—especially this history which she knew would lead to the demise of a precious maid.

"If it had been presented to me in that manner, I might have retreated. However, the words which reached my ears were that of fear and running to safety. I have no time for fear, and I will have no cowards in my army."

"So said General Patton! He then slapped the soldier who was suffering from battle fatigue." A new voice entered the room—the now widely awake Mickey, speaking as Saint Michael.

"Saint Michael!" Loni's face turned toward the sound of Mickey's voice. "I am strengthened by the sound of your voice. I don't know this General Patton, but I silenced our quaking hearted soldiers by using strong words and the flat of my sword on their backsides. 'Be quiet,' said I. 'The defeat of the Burgundians solely depends on what you do or do not do. Think only of striking at them. Make their wives widows.' Even though I said this, I saw in their eyes an inconsolable timidity. I decided to begin an organized movement back to the town. We needed to get back over the bridge."

"The English denied you, didn't they?"

"Yes, when the Burgundians and English saw that my men had lost heart, they came to capture the bridge. Here is where the true battle began. The fight was no longer about the city of Compiègne. The taking of me, the Maid, was a far greater prize. The captain of the city did not understand this and made the move to protect the city. Captain Guillaume raised the bridge and shut the gate. I knew then, the Maid was lost."

"Did you feel forsaken?"

"There comes a time when you have given away hope; it is then that the battle mind clears. You no longer worry of self-preservation, so you execute militarily as you have been trained to do. I reached deep within myself and knew that if the Maid was to be taken, it must be a moment which would be remembered long afterward."

"There will be a great poem written about you," interrupted Suzanne. In her heart, she remembered "The Song of Joan of Arc" written in sixty-one octosyllabic lines by Christine de Pizan. She recited her favorite stanzas aloud for Jehanne:

I, Christine, for eleven years
Shut in an abbey all the time,
Unceasingly have shed my tears,
Enclosed there by that dreadful crime,
Since Charles—what happened is bizarre—,
The King's son—if one can dare to say—
Fled from Paris, gone afar.
Now I can laugh again today!

XXVI
But people, I have never heard
A story of equal mystery,
For all the champions who lived,
As one goes back through history,
Could not compare in prowess to Joan,
Who strives our enemies to ban;
For God who counsels her gave her
A greater heart than any man.

XXXII
But by my faith, her holy life,
Shows well that she is in God's grace,
So that I more believe in her.
Whatever enemy she may face,
She always keeps God in her mind,
She calls upon Him, Him she serves
With all her heart in word and deed,
Her love for Him never ebbs or swerves.

XXXIV
Aha!! What honor for the female sex!
God shows how He loves it,

When the nobles—great, but wretched—
Who earlier the realm had quit,
By one woman were fortified,
No men could do this deed, but more:
The traitors were repaid in kind!
No one would credit this before.

XXXV

A girl of only sixteen years
(Does this not outdo Nature's skill?)
Who lightly heavy weapons bears,
Of strong and hard food takes her fill,
And thus is like it. And God's foes
Before her swiftly fleeing run,
She did this in the public eye.
There tarried not a single one.

XXXVI

She frees France from its enemies,
Recovering citadels and castles.
No army ever did so much,
Not even a hundred thousand vassals!
And of our brave and able folk,
She is the chief and first commander.
God makes it so; not even Hector
Nor Achilles could withstand her.

XLII

The Christian faith and Holy Church,
Will both be set to rights through her,
She will destroy the evil-doers,
To whom one sometimes does refer,
The heretics of filthy life.
For prophecy, which her foresaw,
Said that she would not mercy show
To those who soil the Holy Law.

XLVII

Do you not see, you purblind people,
That in this God shows His hand?
Only the witless do not know this,
For it is by his command,
That the Maid has come to France;
To the death fights La Pucelle—
You have no force to stand against her—
Against God would you rebel?

LXI

This poem was written by Christine,
Complete the last day of July,
In fourteen hundred twenty-nine.
About it I will prophesy,
That some will find themselves put out
About its contents, for the one
Whose face and eyes look ever downward
Cannot ever see the sun.
Thus ends a beautiful poem by Christine

"Jehanne, your actions and your devotion to God will be well documented in verse and rhyme," Suzanne, as Saint Catherine, said. "I know of what I speak."

"I understand, Saint Catherine," Loni nodded solemnly. "I am humbled by the words of Christine m'lady, for I am but a maid from Lorraine. The glory goes to God, and God alone." Loni crossed herself.

After a moment's pause, Douglas continued. "What happened next, Jehanne?"

"Kind voice, as the charge ensued, it seemed like everything was fluid around me. The sounds of metal on metal, screams of men and horses all swirled around me. I conjured up from within me everything that was taught to me by Sister Sibyl, Christine m'lady, and you, my helper angels. I waded into the fight, knocking men to and fro. They clawed at me, and my men hacked at them. Eventually, their many arms overcame us, and I was pulled from my gray horse. I was forced to surrender the Maid of Lorraine. They left the city untouched for they had what they believed to be the true victory. In such delusion, the city of Compiègne survived and I was brought to this tower."

"Are you alone? Were there not others taken with you?"

"Some of my men from Vaucouleurs were killed on the spot. Pierrelot, my

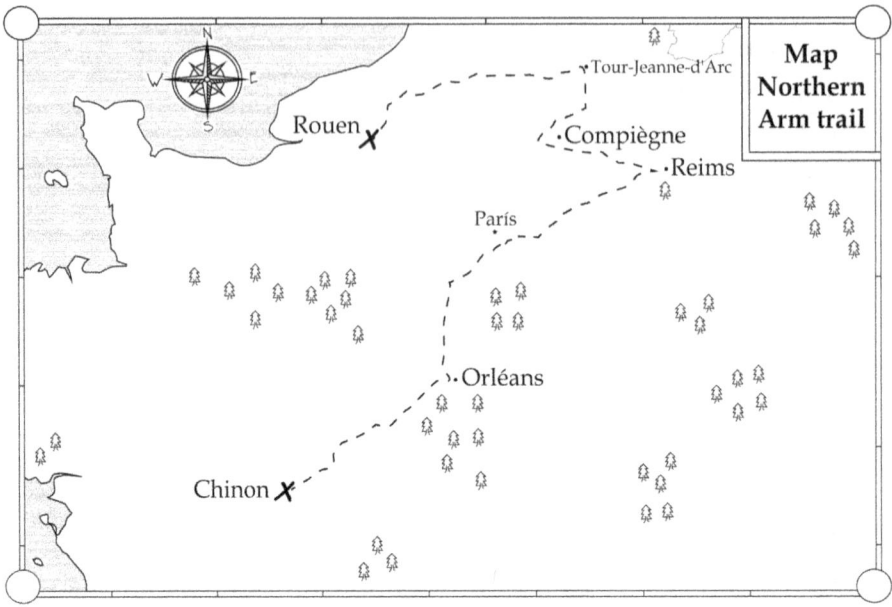

brother, and Jean d'Aulon, my bodyguard and squire, were spared and permitted to tend to me. I know not where they are now, but I fear they will be executed or ransomed for English profit."

"Are you being treated well?"

"Yes, for the most part. The ladies here are not English. They are from Luxembourg. I believe they want my heart to be at ease, so they treat me with great kindness. However, they tell me strange things to mislead me."

"What kind of things?"

"They tell me that across great waters there exists the power of God in a weapon so mighty that it could humble the Godon to the feet of the Dauphin. They said that such a weapon in the hand of the Maid could . . . could. . . ." Jehanne let out an exasperated growl. "Why would they tell me such things— tempt me so— when I am locked up in a comfortable prison while France struggles every day against the Godon? I must leave here!" Loni's hands gripped the arms of the chair, her knuckles whitened.

"Rest, Loni—I mean, Jehanne," Suzanne implored, putting a hand on Loni's. "Please do not try to jump again. God will ensure the victory of France. You must let His divine will supersede your desires. Do not meddle in His plan. Have faith." Loni's body relaxed some, and Jehanne's voice calmed.

"Why did you call me Loni, Saint Catherine? I have heard this name before. Why do you search for her? Is she here somewhere close? I will have the guards bring her to me. Perhaps I can offer her some protection."

"She is closer than you know, child. Keep in mind, Jehanne. If you jump— then most assuredly—she will also."

79

Towering Decision

Maternity hospital
Saint-Quentin, Somme River Valley
Vermandois region, France
Current day

After placing Loni back into a hypnotic rest, the three doctors stepped away and regrouped. All Loni's monitors related a stable evolution of pregnancy.

"So," Douglas began, "Jehanne is now here in the Vermandois at Beaurevoir's tower, and Loni tried to jump when Jehanne did." Douglas bounced his gaze between Suzanne and Mickey. "Though disturbing as it may be, the attempted jumping by Loni physically aligns with the previous encounters. We have seen Loni mimic other physical actions linking up with whomever the current character in the parade seems to be."

"Yes, Douglas, it is unsettling in many ways, but it tracks historically," Mickey replied. "Here is where I believe Loni has interfaced with Jehanne to close up a long-unresolved issue." He looked at the peacefully resting face of his wife.

"Yes, but what exactly is the issue?" Suzanne probed.

"Historically, here is the scenario," began Mickey. His mind felt sharp and clear after resting. All his faculties seemed to have rebooted, and he was thankful for it. "Jehanne is imprisoned at Beaurevoir in late spring-early summer 1430. It is a humane incarceration as she receives rather kindly treatment from three prison matrons serving as her guards. They are ladies in the royal family and members of the House of Luxembourg who fight alongside the English and Burgundians at Compiègne. It is the intent of the Duke of Luxembourg to sell Jehanne to the English. Jeanne, one of the matrons and the aunt of the duke, knows this will lead to the girl's death. This matron does everything to convince the duke not to sell the Maid. There is one point in time where the duke acquiesces, but then Jehanne's impulsivity reverses his mind to its original intent.

"Interestingly, these female guards are all named Jeanne, being the aunt, the wife, and stepdaughter of the Duke of Luxembourg. Jeanne of Béthune was first married to Louis of Luxembourg. They had seven children, one of them was none other than—"

"The issue Mickey; stick with the issue!" Suzanne curtailed Mickey's painful elaborations.

"Right. Sorry. After three months of imprisonment, Jehanne is fraught with angst."

"Angst?"

"Anxiety . . . ergo angst."

"I know 'angst,'" retorted Douglas. "I was wondering about the specific source of her anxiety."

"She knows that as long as she's imprisoned, she cannot help lift the siege of Compiègne. This upsets Jehanne. She desires to help her friend Captain Guillaume de Flay. She becomes stir crazy. She paces certain areas within the castle. Outside, she is only allowed to walk around the tower turret since its platform is over sixty feet from the ground. There is no threat of an escape from that height."

"She jumps," Suzanne raced ahead. "You told us before that she jumps."

"Not so fast. We're getting to that."

"Hurry up. I only have thirty days leave here in Europe."

"As I was saying, then came a day in late September or early October; historians never really can agree—"

"Mickey, I am going to strangle you!"

"Right. That autumn day, Jehanne received word that Compiègne was on the brink of capitulation. She knows that they needed the inspiration from the Maid of Lorraine."

"So, she jumps—"

"No, not yet. She recedes to an alcove for seclusion to pray to her voices to guide her in a course of action."

"Do they tell her to jump?"

"Stop it, Suzanne. Do you want to tell this story, or will you let me?"

"If I was telling this story, it would be told, published, and archived in the Library of Congress by now. I would guess the movie rights would have been sold into syndication as well."

Douglas wanted to grab Mickey and Suzanne both by the napes of their necks and shake them vigorously.

"Will you two quit the bantering? I am about ready to leap myself just having to watch you two."

"That may not necessarily be a bad thing," posed Suzanne, never missing an opportunity to dig in the talons.

Douglas shot her a *cease-and-desist* look, and Suzanne obliged.

Mickey continued. "The voices tell her that all will be resolved by the eleventh of November."

"Veterans Day?" Douglas mused.

"No, not in 1430. Well, you are partially correct, Douglas. Veterans Day did occur in France but not until the eleventh hour of the eleventh day of the eleventh month in the year 1918. World War One had just—"

"Mickey!!!" Douglas and Suzanne unanimously interrupted the meandering before Mickey really got off track.

"Maybe he was more help when he was exhausted." Suzanne groaned. "At least then he stayed on point!"

"Okay!" Mickey finally agreed. "In 1430, the eleventh of November was Saint Martin's Day. All Jehanne had to do was to bide her time and wait for the siege to be lifted the next day. However, being an impulsive young woman, Jehanne rejects the advice from her voices. She doesn't wait another minute. She climbs up to the top of the tower. Then she climbs up on the parapet within the turret. She commends her soul to God, takes a deep breath, and—"

A scream filled the room. Loni rolled from the chair onto the floor, doubled over, her screams echoing off the walls.

80

Consequences Accepted

Maternity hospital
Saint-Quentin, Somme River Valley
Vermandois region, France
Current day

Douglas barred the door with his body and waved off the hospital nursing staff who responded to the cries of pain. Mickey and Suzanne immediately knelt next to the writhing Loni. She clutched at her right leg and ankle.

Suzanne inspected the leg joints medically, while Mickey, hindered by his hand, interrupted her examination constantly with his own assessment. After she glared him into submission and silence and finished the brief exam, both doctors arrived at the same conclusion.

"The pain Loni is feeling did not come from the tumble from the chair," Suzanne announced.

Mickey, checking the monitors, reported to the group, "Everything looks within limits here."

"Get her back into the chair," commanded Douglas. Then, using his trained voice, Douglas eased Loni back into the world of hypnosis where he ascertained the etiology of the expressed pain faster than the two board-certified medical physicians could.

"Jehanne, are you okay? Tell me what you see."

"Hello, kind herald," Loni groaned, holding her ankle. "I am hurt and trapped."

"I understand. Please, tell me what you see. We will help you as best we can."

"I see a tower rising many feet straight above me. I feel stuck into the earth."

"Jehanne what day is this?"

"I know not anymore. I do know that September has come and gone and,"

Jehanne sobbed, "I have rejected the advice of my spiritual guides." Tears squeezed themselves from Loni's eyes. "God forgive my weakness. I just want to help, and I can't help if I am sold to the English."

"It is still 1430?"

"Yes. I am not a prisoner now—but soon I will be again. I can't get away. The guards are clamoring this way and they will take me back into custody. What will become of me?"

"Can you move?"

"No. I am like a stick stuck in the soft grass and mud at the tower base."

"Are you hurt very badly?"

"My right leg and ankle hurts. They don't feel broken. My head hurts."

Suzanne's eyes widened. She halted Douglas with her hand and cut in.

"Can you smell the mud?" asked Suzanne. She internally recited the mnemonic device used by medical students to remember the names of the twelve pairs of cranial nerves. *On Old Olympus's Towering Top, A Fin And German Viewed Some Hops. Okay, go, Suzanne.* She immediately began testing Jehanne despite the separation of space and time.

"Yes, Saint Catherine."

"Can you stick out your tongue?"

"Yes."

"Can you rotate your hands around each other?"

"Yes."

"Squeeze my fingers hard."

"What fingers?"

"Oops, sorry. Squeeze your thumbs at the same time. Do they grip strongly, and do they feel the same?"

"Yes and yes."

"Good."

Douglas looked at Suzanne who was mimicking every component of the brief neurological survey on her patient. He whispered into her ear so that Jehanne wouldn't hear. "Are you, your Fin, and your German all finished viewing some hops? I need to get back on track."

"Most certainly. Sorry . . . it's just that—"

"Jehanne, you must return to your captors," Douglas insisted as he cut across Suzanne.

"Why? What good can I do France if I am a slave of the English?"

"That is not for you to decide."

Returning her grip on her ankle, Loni nodded slowly, her shoulders dropped. "I understand. It seems I have made too many impulsive decisions already. I have violated the wishes of all you who have tried to help me. I have listened and acted upon my own rationale over instructions which are divinely given. Saint Catherine, will God ever forgive me?"

"He needs you no longer as a soldier, Jehanne." Suzanne's voice was reassuring and motherly. "Your battlefield has changed. He needs you to go with the English as their prisoner. You are a prisoner of war, and you must be stronger now than ever before. They will try many techniques to discredit your faith and in so doing, they will appear as the heathens they truly are."

"They will kill me. I know they will," Loni's voice shook.

"They will kill themselves. They will kill their claim to all of France. Their deeds upon you will stoke the fire of nationality in all Frenchmen." Mickey nodded to Suzanne, motioning for her to continue. "Jehanne, many Burgundians who are today's enemies will see the injustice done to a flower of France and will then side with the Dauphin. Compiègne, Blois, Soissons, Paris, Rouen, and all the cities in France will come back under the rule of the monarch of France."

"Must I be imprisoned for all this to happen?"

"Your greatest ability to unite France from this point onward is in the dignity you carry while under duress. You will do more for France as the enslaved Maid than you can as the frontline Maid in shining armor. Remember the humility of Jesus our Lord Savior. In his frailty, he gave us victory."

"Will God forgive me?"

"There is nothing more to forgive. God loves you. He still needs you, but in the way you can best serve France. Not by wielding the sword of Charles Martel. Not studded in golden armor at the head of a cavalry charge."

"I will go back into chains and never more try to flee. I will do it because God wills it."

"It will not be easy, Jehanne. The challenges of being a prisoner of war will be many. There will be humiliation heaped upon humiliation. Keep reminding yourself of our Christ and what he had to endure."

"I do not have the strength of Christ . . . but I do have the strength that He imparts to me. I will endure because my God wishes for me to do so."

"Yes, exactly." Suzanne paused. "Goodbye, precious Jehanne."

"What? Are you leaving me?"

"Only for now. There is a time we will meet again."

"When will that be?"

"You will know it when the time comes."

"How will I know it? Please, Saint Catherine, please. . . ."

"Pierrelot," Mickey said, "your brother. He will be your guide."

Suzanne mouthed *Thank you* to Mickey.

"Pierrelot? Why Pierrelot, Saint Michael?"

"Jehanne," reassured Suzanne, "it is enough for you to know that Pierrelot will be there for you." Suzanne looked at Mickey to receive the confirmatory nod. "When we meet again, Jehanne, we will take away your fear. It will leave you like a dove in flight. . . . Hold tightly to your crucifix."

"My crucifix? I don't have it anymore. I gave it and the precious thorns it holds to the Dauphin when I first visited Chinon."

"That's fine, Jehanne. Then seek the cross of Christ for spiritual comfort," iterated Mickey. "Remember, Pierrelot will show you the way."

"I feel weak, Saint Michael. Please don't go."

"Close your eyes, child." Mickey's voice nearly broke but he recovered. "You are stronger than you know."

"I hear the soldiers. They come for me."

Mickey took one of Loni's hands in his own. "I know. They will take you. Be strong."

"I will go forward boldly. I will try to have no fear."

"I know. You must."

"I . . . I . . ." Loni released her hands from their hold on both her right ankle and Mickey's hand. She slumped back into her chair. The three doctors huddled quickly.

"Mickey," said Douglas, tapping his index fingertips together, "do you think these reassurances and encouragements are what Jehanne needed from the connection to Loni?"

"I did, Douglas. I'm not so sure anymore. Now, having arrived at the tower in the Vermandois, frankly it's hard for me to fathom that Loni's lifetime connection to Jehanne boils down to mere reassurances for Jehanne that her captivity is God's will."

"But," added Suzanne, "there was no other way to play that out, right? I mean, we gave Jehanne what she needed. Told her what she needed to hear. Or did I make a mess of it?" Suzanne looked worried, her hands held in prayer before her face.

"No, no," reassured Mickey, "I was tracking with you the whole time. Nothing was out of place as far as I could tell. But it still doesn't match up. What are we missing?"

"I don't know," said Douglas. "Consider that the Jehanne and Loni connection is significant at multiple levels. You know, with both ends needing something from the other?"

"What do you mean, Douglas?" Mickey bounced his gaze between Loni and Douglas.

"Well, can we agree that Loni's and Jehanne's lives needed to intersect so that both parties could receive data that allowed them to fulfil their respective destinies?"

"Yes, that's reasonable." Mickey audibly sighed. "Jehanne has received guidance, spiritual and otherwise, to keep her on track toward what we know is her historical endpoint. However, what has Loni received?"

"That's the part that's hard to see," said Douglas. "Could it be that Jehanne has already given her information? Already given something applicable in solving a problem Loni is, or has been, facing?" Douglas received a blank stare from Mickey. "I don't know . . . some current, real-world concern Loni is struggling with?"

"That's a big net to cast. I could think of a million issues at hand," Mickey said glumly as he picked at the tape on his wrist brace. "If Joan of Arc had given Loni something, anything, wouldn't we know it?"

Suzanne slapped his hand away from his brace as she walked over to Loni. The golden light which had been creeping into the room through the window became tinged with delicate shades of blushing roses and subtle sherbets as the sun bid the Vermandois adieu.

"Gentlemen, have we really tried to look?" She knelt at Loni's side and lifted the pendant crucifix. "The answer is hiding in plain sight."

Suzanne felt the tingling in her fingertips. She held her breath. Using her thumb, she slid the face of the crucifix upward to open the hidden compartment of the pendant. Her face, painted in the peaceful pastels of sunset light, was at odds with her expression of utter shock.

81

Reasons and Beyond Reasons

Maternity hospital
Saint-Quentin, Somme River Valley
Vermandois region, France
Current day

"Oh my God! Oh my God!" Suzanne remained motionless.

"Stop saying that and tell us what you see." Douglas leaned in.

"Nothing. I see nothing. I'm not supposed to see nothing."

"Did you expect to find the thorns, Suzanne?" Douglas asked.

"Yes, I did." Her shoulders slumped and she dropped her head back, speaking to the air above her. "I really did . . . but they're not there. What does that mean?"

"It can only be that this pendant has fulfilled a mission between Jehanne and the Dauphin," said Mickey.

"How's that?"

"Remember, Douglas?" Suzanne said. "Mickey and I told you that the Dauphin needed to see the missing thorns to be convinced that Jehanne was the Maid of Lorraine. Once that happened, the missing thorns need no longer be encased. The Legend of the Missing Thorns came to fruition and the pendant's mission was complete."

"Yet, here it sits, empty, on Loni's neck." Douglas scratched at his chin stubbles.

"Yes, Douglas, that's because there's more," said Mickey.

"Less is more?"

"Yes, because there's some purpose yet to be filled beyond Jehanne, beyond the Dauphin, and beyond the dark that we are stuck in. This pendant has traveled through history to Loni's family and, albeit with some unpleasant family politics, ultimately to Loni herself."

"At least we *know* that is true because I'm holding it in my hand. Proof positive." Suzanne closed the empty pendant and carefully rested it back on Loni's chest.

"Yes, Suzanne, but the question remains why? What is the purpose?" Mickey asked and then went silent.

"Well, what's the answer?" Suzanne stood and stretched her back. "Mickey? Douglas? Anyone?"

"I don't know, but if Mickey is correct and we are at a crossroads with Jehanne and Loni both being in the Vermandois and Jehanne's pendant's mission is complete, then Loni herself should be able to return and tell us . . . after she's rested, of course."

Suzanne looked to Mickey and saw his far-away gaze. She reiterated for him, "Hey, Mickey, Douglas thinks after she has rested, Loni will come back to us. What do you think? Mickey?"

"I dunno. I just want all this to be over. I want Loni back." Impatience gripped Mickey's face.

As a physician he knew Loni needed to rest. *We all need rest,* he thought, *serene peaceful slumber in actual beds, not naps on hospital couches.* He looked at the two other doctors who had been burning their midnight oil with the same fervor he was. Only a smidgen of that oil remained. *I'm so grateful for them—especially Douglas, considering our rocky past. How can I ever repay him?* Mickey's mind shot through multiple versions of expressing gratitude and apologizing for his past instances of disrespect. The very man he had defamed through silence had risen above pettiness and rescued where no one else could. *There must be correct words to capture this moment, but. . . . Loni will know what to say. When it comes to Douglas, she always does. What would Loni say? What would Loni say?*

Suzanne saw the rapid blinking of Mickey's eyes and the trembling of his lips in the prolonged silence. She gripped his left elbow hard and spoke to him slowly and clearly as if speaking to a deaf-mute lip reader.

"Mickey, I think it's time for you boys to clear the air." Suzanne yielded to privacy as she left the room. Mickey moved over to the window where he saw his haggard reflection. *Suzanne's right, but how can Douglas see any sincerity coming from someone who looks like this?* Mickey used the glass as a mirror, preening those hairs which looked more like ruffled feathers. *Oh, well. It is what it is.* Mickey turned and leveled his gaze.

"Douglas, I . . . I—"

"Stow it, Mickey," said Douglas, holding a palm to Mickey's face. "Whatever you feel want to say, just save it." Metaphorically, Douglas pulled his finger out of the dike and let the water go. "Your words can never undo the things that were done and said in the past. Your thoughts of me are what they are. I know it and so do you, though you *think* you feel different about it now. I will be the same Douglas Coletrane that you spit on tomorrow, just like you did yesterday. From my perspective, I don't care. It doesn't define me as much as it does you. It never has. I am proud of the choices I made that have led me here today. Despite the ridicule I have received along the way from you and your contemporaries, the tools that I brought to the table were the tools needed to make the fix. There is only one thing I *do* need from you though. It hasn't changed from the past and it won't change in the future. Listen carefully."

Throughout the emotional deluge, Mickey's eyes had progressed slowly down and away from Douglas's face. *Wow, both barrels at once.* Mickey turned toward the open hospital room door. *Now might be a good time for an ally. Someone? Anyone?* Mickey stared through it to the windows of the hallway and beyond that to the skittering clouds heralding the sunset. *Where are you, Joan, on your horse? In which direction do I go now?*

"Hey! I need your full attention. I mean it, Mickey."

"I'm listening, Douglas." His eyes still scanned the piece of sky in his view. *Nothing?*

"Look at me, Mickey!"

"I said I am listening." He turned, cast a hard stare at Douglas, and held it.

"Take care of Loni like she is gold. You hear me? She is the *only* part of you that has any redeemable value."

"I appreciate your devotion to Loni, but regarding me, don't you think you're being a little harsh?"

"Funny, Mickey, I was thinking that I wasn't being empathetic enough. You have done more to damage to me with your absence of malice. The one who stands by and watches the stoning—but doesn't throw a stone nor stop others from doing so—is just as responsible. Did you actually think that not participating in the Douglas Coletrane slam-fest at the conference in Passau was enough?"

"Well, I. . . ."

"You were wrong. You acted like Peter who denied Christ thrice before the cock crowed."

"You're *not* Christ."

"Apparently, neither are you."

"Okay, I admit it. I should have done what Loni did. I should have stood up for you. But, come on, Douglas. That was 12 years ago. You've got to let that go."

"You don't get it, do you?" Douglas gave a rough, mirthless laugh.

"What?"

"You can't help failing to stand up for me because, Mickey, you don't see me as a true medical professional. You think because you nursed at the breast of an accepted medical degree–producing institution that you are above me. At this moment, you are rattled . . . maybe a bit confused. Right now, because we are on the cusp of Loni's return, you *think* you see me differently. But, no, you don't. It's a passing façade. Once a little time has passed, I'll be the south-end of a north-bound mule once again."

"As I said, I *should have* followed Loni's lead."

"True, she won't ever steer you wrong. She has always been a demonstration of love and kindness. Understanding the lineage within her, I now better understand the basis of her greatness."

Douglas watched Mickey fidget with his cast and shift his stance to maneuver himself into a position to extend a hand in friendship. The light from the room's window was now streaked with scarlet and vivid oranges. The colors were fierce, and Douglas could not help but think that they were painted just for him.

Mickey reached as deep down as he could to present the greatest amount of sincerity. "Douglas, I understand what you are saying to me, and I accept your assessment of the sniveling creep I have been. Nevertheless, I would formally like to say to you that I am truly . . . very—"

"Enough said, Mickey. You're wasting your breath." Douglas pushed away Mickey's extended hand.

"Maybe you're right, Douglas. Maybe I didn't give you credit where credit was due. Maybe I needed to see what you could do before I gave my respect. That doesn't make me the lapdog of Satan. Does it?"

"Lapdog? No, that would be a step up."

"Anyway, Douglas, rather than judge me. Why don't you help me to see you as Loni does . . . did . . . does? Teach me how to use the power of your voice. I would like to help guide Jehanne as Saint Michael."

Forgetting that she had stepped out of the room, Mickey turned where Suzanne should have been. Seeing no trace of her, he shouted out the door, "Would that be okay, Saint Catherine?"

Suzanne came to the door, but before she could answer, she was pushed aside by a stampede of the nursing staff as they rushed into the room. They were yelling and pointing at the monitor displays and Loni.

The three American doctors were confused. Loni was quietly resting. She looked a bit flushed, but normal in every other way. She certainly was not going into labor; not from the data which was showing on the monitors. Nonetheless there was a flurry of nursing activity. All three realized that they had better find out what was going wrong with Loni and begin to lead, follow, or get the heck out of the way.

82

Heating Up the Action

Maternity hospital

Saint-Quentin, Somme River Valley

Vermandois region, France

Current day

"She is thirty-nine. . . ." one nurse, speaking in broken English, addressed Suzanne. The staff moved Loni to the bed and swiftly adjusted the fetal monitor's position.

Any woman in her 50s would love to hear that. Suzanne gritted her teeth. *But not now. Not with the damage an elevated temperature can do to Loni and the unborn twins.*

"No. Thirty-nine point one . . ."

"Point one? What?" Suzanne huffed.

"Thirty-nine point two."

"Oh my God, her core body temperature is climbing," annotated Suzanne in a grave tone. "It's rising fast." Quickly doing the mathematical conversion in her head, Suzanne updated, "She's 102.6 Fahrenheit. There it is on the monitor. Thirty-nine point three." *Where are the French attendings? I'm sure they have been notified. It would be criminal not to.*

"Switch the scale to Fahrenheit, Mickey." Suzanne eased into the acute-care mode for which she, as an internist, was well trained to do. Mickey and Douglas fell into the helper bee roles as best as they could now that Suzanne had taken point.

"One hundred two point seven." Douglas reported the temperature updates.

"Infection?" Mickey posed as he mentally sorted through the etiologies of elevated core body temperature. "What would be the source—hospital acquired? Staph? Pseudomonas?"

"One hundred two point eight." Douglas bounced his gaze between Mickey,

341

Suzanne, Loni, the door where the French obstetrical physicians would arrive, and the monitor.

"Inflammation?" Suzanne mused aloud as the wait for the cavalry of obstetricians continued.

"*Oui*," said a nearby nurse in a heavy French accent, "inflammation."

"One hundred two point nine." Douglas's face grew taut.

"How well can Loni tolerate a rapidly rising temperature?" Mickey knew the answer even as he asked.

"The human adult can tolerate a temperature well above one hundred three. However, the chance of seizing might occur as the brain starts to cook," Suzanne replied.

"One hundred three," said Douglas through clenched teeth.

"What about the twins?" Suzanne posed the question no one else was asking.

"Not good—not good for our babies—" Mickey scowled.

"Mickey!" Suzanne's voice elevated. "Will the twins be harmed?"

Mickey's expertise for the situation had now superseded over Suzanne's in his knowledge of obstetrics and pediatrics. Suzanne's internal medicine practice was essentially adult focused.

"Infants can seize at 100.2," responded Mickey. "There are some studies that even pose that heated whirlpools and hot tubs have been linked to increased miscarriages."

"The baby's monitor looks the same right now. I'm guessing it's okay but that could change any minute," commented Douglas, hoping he was more wrong than right. "One hundred three point one," he added.

One of the French nurses switched back the monitor scale to centigrade. It read thirty-nine point six Celsius. Her face grew stern. As she looked away to the others gathering, arranging, and connecting cooling equipment, Douglas switched it back. Fahrenheit was easier for an American to understand.

"*Ne touchez pas!*" A French nurse scolded switching it back. "No ... to touch!" She repeated in French-accented English. Douglas glowered briefly then redirected to his patient.

"Loni, please listen to me." Douglas watched as the nurses brought in more cooling blankets. Another brought in a chest full of ice. Another applied wet towels to Loni's face and her gravid belly which was now starting to show increased baby movement relative to the rising core body temperature.

"I feel so helpless." Suzanne wrung her hands.

"One hundred three point two." Douglas did a quick switch, read in Fahrenheit, and return to Centigrade. "The babies are kicking. I can see them. Maybe we need to induce labor?" Douglas knew he was treading precariously over his scope of practice.

"We don't have the credentials *to do anything* in the French hospital system," Mickey thundered at the group. The frustration of rising helplessness swelled within him.

"Or in the American system either, guys. None of us are OB-Gynies," Suzanne reminded the guys of the obvious.

"Maybe we won't have to do anything," said Mickey whispering as if to himself. "The body is designed to take care of itself and the babies. It is possible that it will start to release the babies spontaneously."

"But will it do so before permanent harm is done to the tiny developing brains inside?" Suzanne asked. Then, seeing Mickey's face cringe, she hated her own impetuous mouth. "Sorry."

"We all thought it, Suzanne," said Mickey. "It's just hard to hear it out loud."

"One hundred three point three," interjected Douglas after the French nurse flipped the switch for him to quickly read. She returned it to Centigrade. He could feel his own heart rate quicken. The deepening sunset cast an eerie light into the room and what would have felt warm and inviting in any other situation now felt close and oppressive.

"Okay, okay," Mickey pressed his hand against his forehead. "The core body temperature will start to drop showing the shift into labor."

"But what is the cause of the sudden rise?" Douglas asked.

"Nothing good," snarled Mickey in response to the fever as much as to Douglas.

"One hundred three point four." Douglas was relentless and timely with his quick peeks.

"Can you at least give us good news?" Suzanne sniped at him.

"Don't kill the messenger. I am here to help," Douglas defended.

"Well, Douglas, if there was ever a time for you to help, now is the moment." Suzanne placed her hands on her hips for emphasis. Her eyes burned into Douglas. "You need to reconnect with Jehanne—*now!*" Suzanne pointed for emphasis. "Loni and those babies are burning up. We *need* to find out what is going on."

"Douglas, you gotta get Loni back." Mickey grabbed Douglas's shirt collar. He could no longer hide his rising emotion. "You gotta get her back."

Douglas responded to Mickey, simultaneously convincing himself. "I know, Mickey. Loni and the twin's well-being rides on it." He turned to the fitful woman in the bed. "Loni? Jehanne? Talk to me. Jehanne. . . ."

"One hundred three point five," squeaked Suzanne.

83

Maid to Burn

Maternity hospital
Saint-Quentin, Somme River Valley
Vermandois region, France
Current day

"Jehanne, can you hear me?" Douglas's neck veins bulged as he spoke.

"I hear you, Helper Angel." Jehanne's voice was raspy. "I hear you."

The room released an audible, unanimous sigh. But Mickey's brow furrowed.

"It is the thirtieth of May, isn't it?" asked Mickey, leaning over Douglas's shoulder as Suzanne leaned over his. Seamlessly, the nursing staff continued to refresh cooling equipment while the maternity physician reviewed the data.

"Yes, Saint Michael," said Jehanne. Mickey squeezed his good hand into a fist. "They're . . . killing me now."

"Killing you?" Douglas parroted, while wincing at Mickey's bandaged hand boring into his shoulder. Douglas glance up and rearward noting the rigidity of Mickey's and Suzanne's stone-carved features. Surrounding the three American doctors, the nursing staff moved quickly and methodically to the point that cold towels and pads were replaced with colder.

"They've lifted my platform over a smoldering woodpile. It's warm ... and getting warmer. The floor . . . the pole . . . everything here wooden . . . made to burn . . . *maid* to burn. . . ." Loni whipped her head to the side, "No, not that!"

One hundred three point seven glowed on the digital display of the monitor in the rapidly darkening room. It seemed that the French nurses had grown comfortable switching the scale for Douglas to get his Fahrenheit reading before returning to Centigrade.

"*Merci*," said Douglas, nodding his thanks.

"She is on the square at Rouen." Mickey spoke through his clenched teeth.

"I'm barefoot and iron clad," Jehanne whispered. "My white shift and hat have horrible things written on them. I hear the people say the words that I cannot read. 'Liar,' they call me. 'Sorceress, superstitious blasphemer of God,'

344

they say aloud. 'Invoker of devils and heretic.' All these are attached to my name." Jehanne gasped and Loni shuddered.

"They're hateful words, nothing more, Jehanne," Suzanne said consolingly. "Focus instead on God," she added as she pressed her clenched fists against her lips and locked her eyes on the monitor.

"Lies!" Jehanne hissed. "Hateful lies!"

"One hundred three point eight . . . seven . . . eight . . . seven . . . flickering," reported Douglas, trying not to think what these high temperatures were doing to Loni and the twins. *These numbers must soon go down.* He watched the nurse flip back to Centigrade. *Maybe we should keep the temperature reading here on Centigrade. The value 39.8 is an easier read than over 103.8.* Douglas scoffed. *That's absurd. I'm losing my mind. I hope Jehanne is keeping hers.*

"Tell me what you see now, Jehanne," Douglas prompted.

"I see panicked faces . . . thousands of them." Loni swallowed dryly, her tongue sticking to the roof of her mouth. "Clergy, commoners, many, many soldiers. They stare as I am tied to a stake. Blessed saints, there's my brother, Pierrelot!" Her voiced cracked into a whimper. "He's weeping."

Douglas heard a deep murmuring in the room. He turned his head this way and that, craning his neck around. There was nothing his eyes could discern which could be making the sound he heard. *Maybe Suzanne and Mickey haven't noticed; their eyes are fixed on Loni.* Then, as if echoing around the room, he heard the unmistakable clink of metal on metal and the shuffling of feet. *Armor? Soldiers? It cannot be.*

Douglas took the instant to reach out and tap Suzanne's leg. She whipped her head around toward him, and he gave her a look that said, *Do you hear this too?*

She mouthed, *I told you so.*

"They're stacking tinder all around me."

Snapping, creaking, and shuffling echoed off the walls of the hospital room.

"The crowd is shouting for fire. Why? I've done nothing to them." Loni coughed for Jehanne. "Saint Michael, I can't breathe!"

"One hundred three point eight." Hearing the strain in Douglas's voice, Suzanne knuckled away a tear.

"We are right here, child," said Suzanne, glancing over as a nurse hooked up a second temperature monitor with scale dedicated to Fahrenheit. As Douglas thanked the staff, Suzanne reassured Jehanne, "We aren't going anywhere."

"Do you feel it, my saints? The embers below—they shift and tremble. The floor is getting warmer. Am I truly evil? So awful that not even the Church can protect me?" Jehanne sobbed.

"Evil? Nonsense," Suzanne huffed. "Don't believe it, child! They did the same to Christ. Draw on His strength, please, Jehanne. *This* is the time."

"I'm trying," Jehanne cried. "I am. Why is it so hard?"

"It must be. France must be saved."

"As my Lord upon the cross did, so I too ask now: God forgive them. God, please accept the prayers of all who would show me mercy."

"We are all praying for you, even now," Mickey grunted, his throat thick with anguish.

"One hundred three point eight . . . nine . . . eight . . . nine . . . flickering." *I hope this flicking back and forth means it's slowing down and soon dropping.*

"The smoke is seeping through the floor cracks," Jehanne coughed. "It burns my eyes and blinds me." Loni blinked her eyes hard.

The unmistakable smell of fire filled the nostrils of the Americans—and only the Americans. Douglas, wide-eyed, scrutinized the maternity staff. *Even in their focused work with the refreshing and checking of the cooling equipment, blankets, ice packs, they could not ignore this . . . this tumult, this smell. The sounds, the smells, the gritty taste—it must only be for us.*

"Saint Michael!" Loni bellowed, causing all in the room to start. "Are you there!?"

"Yes."

"I'm clutching a cross made of two twigs. A crying, remorseful English soldier gave it to me. The Church will give me no cross . . . is it enough, Saint Michael?" Loni coughed. "Is it enough?"

"The simple cross is enough, child. But there is nothing simple about your sacrifice, Jehanne," said Mickey. Then, gathering his courage, he continued. "There will be another Englishman—a great man named Winston Churchill who has the respect of the whole world, and he will speak of you."

"What will he say?" Jehanne's voice was becoming fainter with every passing moment.

"He will say that in a thousand years, there will be no equal to you. You shine with unconquerable courage, infinite compassion, the virtue of the simple, and the wisdom of the just."

"If so, why?" Loni's head lolled to the side. "Why then should this be done to me?" Jehanne sobbed. "The flames creep ever closer, Michael!"

Above the sound of crackling of flames, the rancor of a restless crowd pressed in upon both Jehanne and the Americans, whose pent-up emotions writhed beneath their skins.

"One hundred three point nine," whimpered Suzanne, glancing rapidly between the monitor and Loni.

A nurse in the room flipped on the overhead bed light, shocking the room with sudden incandescent brightness. Once their eyes adjusted, all could see that Loni's face was getting redder. Sweat beads formed between the streams of cooling water from the cold compresses applied by the nurses.

"Why could I not have been in a Church prison?" Loni sputtered and coughed. "I protest before God, our only judge, the great wrongs and grievances done to me!"

The jeering of the crowd ebbed and flowed around the room.

"One hundred four." The monitor alarm wailed.

"I see my condemner," Jehanne whispered, diverting her comments to the man before her eyes in the market square. Loni too turned her face toward empty space as she spat the martyr's words. "Bishop, I die through you!" Loni drew a ragged breath. "I will complain of your mishandling of me before God!" Her chest heaved. Her fists' knuckles grew white.

From admonishment to adoration, Loni's face shifted instantly. "Angels, my brother is here!" Jehanne whimpered. "Pierrelot, where shall I be tonight?"

"Do you not trust God and the angels?" Her brother's voice resonated around the hospital room.

"I do. I do." Jehanne wept. "Jesus, guide me to paradise."

Amidst the rising smoke and popping of sap, a cruel voice shouted from the crowd, "Priest, are you going to get on with this? Some of us have to be on time for dinner."

"One hundred four point one," Suzanne reported over the sound of the monitor alarm's blaring.

"You, Priest!" Jehanne heaved. "Bring me a cross! I beg you!" Loni's chest convulsed with Jehanne's coughing.

"Saint Catherine! They will not . . . they do not . . .! I have no cross to see!"

"One hundred four point two." Suzanne clutched fistfuls of her hair as the monitor alarm screamed incessantly. *Oh, God! Nothing is keeping Loni's temperature down!*

Bodies rushed in through the door toward the bed.

"Get back, guys!" Suzanne hollered. "The French cavalry is here!" She quickly stood, relinquishing her place but not the monitor. "Finally! It's about time!"

"Who are these guys?" Douglas anchored himself against the bed rail, not giving an inch. He, as well as Mickey and Suzanne, watched as the incoming personnel rolled in adult and pediatric emergency lifesaving equipment as well as an incubator.

"Emergency obstetrical physician team. Hey! Easy with the shoving, fellas!"

As personnel and equipment were pushed forward, Mickey and Suzanne were pushed rearward in the maternity suite. Douglas, however, yielded no ground.

"Wait. . . ." Loni sucked in hard for air. Breathlessly, Jehanne continued, "Pierrelot comes from Saint-Sauveur du Marché! He has a staff . . . a crucifix!" Jehanne coughed, then groaned, "The English mock me. . . ."

"We hear them, Jehanne. Let them laugh," Mickey called out over the sounds in the hospital room. "We are here, Jehanne! We are here!"

Mickey pressed his hand against the cold window, trying to get leverage to raise himself above the crowd. The light outside was all but extinguished.

"One hundred four point three." Suzanne's voice floated through the din of the room.

Loni tossed her head from side to side, grimacing. Her forehead wrinkled and her face sagged as she muttered, "Rouen, Rouen, shall you suffer for being the place of my death?"

An instant later, Loni's head snapped up—her eyes squinting for Jehanne as, together, they peered through the gathering smoke. "My brother climbs the platform," she rasped. "He pushes others away. He holds the crucifix before my eyes." Loni's eyes welled with tears, then grew wide in terror.

"The flames! They are here!" The voice of Jehanne rose in sheer panic. "No, Pierrelot! Get down! Get back! Hold up the cross! Hold it up! I can't see it. Rouen, will you be my end?"

Mickey clawed his way to Loni frantically. "Fight, fight, Loni! Don't die, please baby . . . fight! I need you! Please don't die!"

Just as he arrived, Loni's body convulsed, all her muscles flexing in pain. She arched backward screaming, "Jesus!"

The monitor flatlined. Her body went limp and unconscious. Mickey collapsed onto the floor at Douglas's feet.

84

Death and Beyond

Maternity hospital
Saint-Quentin, Somme River Valley
Vermandois region, France
Current day

From the hallway, Douglas peered in through the door panel of Loni's suite. Suzanne clutched Mickey's arm, forcing him to sit at the L-shaped couch in the waiting area. The hospital's security staff had dragged all the Americans, kicking and fighting, out of the room so the emergency obstetrical team could remain in position to do their lifesaving and resuscitation work.

After a brief silence, Loni's monitor could be heard beeping and along with it, they could discern the fetal monitor's steady rhythm.

"Is she okay?" Mickey bolted up, but Suzanne yanked him back down. "Is she okay?"

"It looks like she's okay. . . ." Douglas stood on his tiptoes. "Yes, I see it. She's okay."

"And the babies?" Mickey lurched forward again, but Suzanne remained a steamship anchor.

"They're good too. The fetal monitor never missed a beat." Douglas exhaled. "We just couldn't hear it in the commotion."

Mickey collapsed back on the couch with Suzanne's nails still dug into his splint. Douglas tipped an imaginary hat brim toward Suzanne.

"Mickey, the core temperature is falling—One hundred four." Douglas edged farther into the doorway.

"Is she birthing?" Suzanne asked.

"Not according to the monitors. Fetal monitors look the same." Douglas came a few paces down the short hallway.

"Whoa, what was that?" Suzanne swatted the air in front of her face. "What just happened, guys?" The men glanced at her, confused. Douglas turned back to the room.

Suzanne shook her head and rose from the couch, tucking her hair behind her ears as she went to the window. "Didn't you see that?" she asked no one in particular. No one answered.

She stared through the glass, searching desperately for an answer in the inky sky. *Some light? Somewhere? Please, just a glimmer.*

Mickey remained reclined, his forearm cast shielding his eyes as he mentally replayed the previous scene.

"Well, she died." Douglas pressed his face against the door pane. "Yes, she's gone."

"Dead?!" Mickey jolted. "What?! That . . . that can't be. You just said. . . ."

"*Jehanne* just died, Mickey," Douglas squatted in place, leaning against the hallway wall. Suzanne rolled her eyes at him and returned her gaze to the window. He continued. "And, I think for a moment, Loni did too."

"But look . . . Loni's back. Right?" Suzanne posited, speaking toward her own dark reflection. "The agony is now over . . . for both of them." Her head rested against the cool, glass window.

"I can only hope." Douglas peeked in again. "Core temperature is still falling—one hundred and three."

"Thank God. The worst has passed," Mickey exhaled. His voice grew heavy. "Jehanne suffered greatly before she died. The executioner had permission to strangle Jehanne or at least cut her throat to spare her the final agony. But it didn't happen. Nothing, and nobody, spared her."

"Oh Jesus, how she must have suffered." Suzanne's forehead pounded rhythmically against the plate-glass window.

"History says that Jehanne cried out the name 'Lord Jesus' at least six times. She implored the aid of the saints of paradise. Finally, she yelled 'Jesus!' loud enough for the ten thousand witnesses to hear her."

"Add the number here to that!" Suzanne rubbed her aching forehead, then wiped the sweat from her face and neck and turned her back to the darkness beyond the glass.

"The Maid had to endure the full brunt of the execution before her head finally fell forward and the flames consumed her body." Mickey drifted into silence.

A cart filled with housekeeping supplies squeaked up the hallway. The person pushing it paused at Loni's doorway, peeked in the room, and looked over at Suzanne and Mickey in the waiting area. The woman edged over to Douglas. Slowly, he stood to meet her.

"Hi, Clarisse," Douglas wearily smiled.

"The pregnant lady . . . she's good?"

"Yes, Loni is better now," said Douglas, glancing at the maternity staff doing some final physical checks on Loni and the babies. Others stood nearby doing some close-out charting. "It was scary for a minute, but she's fine now. What brings you here?"

"I was sent to return the room to order. Though, I think they are not quite finished in there yet."

"No, but soon." Douglas rubbed his temples. "Soon."

"How is the angel and the broken-hand man?"

Doulas chuckled. "Suzanne and Mickey are better now. Tired. Worried. But better."

"And Jehanne?"

Douglas's head cocked, his mouth agape. Clarisse smiled, gently pushing Douglas's jaw shut for him. Her fingers were tender against his rough stubble.

"I told you. I am nobody. I see and hear everything. I saw Jehanne come alive through the skills of three American somebodies—"

"Did you hear all the—" Doulas raised his hands and motioned them about trying to both indicate and describe the other sensations that had surrounded him.

"Like all French people," Clarisse interrupted, "I keep Jehanne close in my heart. It was a blessing to hear her words."

"But what about the—"

"I share your sadness as Jehanne has now died . . . again."

Clarisse quietly slipped into Loni's room as most of the obstetrical staff finally departed, effectively diverting herself from further questioning. Douglas gave up on getting a straight answer out of Clarisse and beckoned to Mickey and Suzanne silently.

Before they entered the room, Douglas whispered briefly, "When the coast is clear, we need to talk about what just happened. About what *we* experienced." He raised his eyebrows meaningfully. "I've never witnessed *anything* like that." The other two nodded their understanding.

Inside the room, Douglas pulled a chair to face Loni. Suzanne and Mickey stood behind him vigilantly at the back corners of the chair. Only the quiet shuffling of room cleaning could be heard until, eventually, those sounds trickled into silence. Removing her gloves, Clarisse walked over to Loni and stroked her hair. Mickey started to intervene, but Douglas put out an arm to stay Mickey's action.

In a soft, soothing tone, Clarisse spoke to everyone and no one at the same time. "Jehanne la Pucelle, perhaps God's most faithful servant and the savior of France's freedom, you now have passed from this life. This dove, this virgin bride of Christ, is now with her beloved Savior." Clarisse withdrew and returned to her tasks.

Pointing to the two temperature monitors, the last remaining staff, a nurse, announced the dropping core temperature before she left the room. "Thirty-eight point eight . . . one hundred two Fahrenheit."

For a while the room sat quietly with Douglas monitoring the core temperature, Suzanne doting on the fetal monitor, and Mickey clutching tenderly the hand of his wife. Clarisse worked quietly in the background.

Then in a calm, steady voice, Mickey spoke. "Can I tell you what happened next? I feel like we owe that to Jehanne. To pay witness, in some small way?"

He received somber nods and so he continued.

"Jehanne was soon dead, and her clothes all burned. Then the fire was raked back. Her naked body was shown to all the people to eliminate any doubts that she might have escaped execution. When enough people had witnessed the dead body of Jehanne still bound to the stake, the executioner got the big bonfire going again until both flesh and bone were cremated to ashes. John Tressart, secretary to the king of England, was alleged to exclaim, 'We are all lost; for it is a good and holy person that was burned.' Some reports said that the name of 'Jesus' leapt written across the flames of her pyre. One English soldier—who had harbored much hatred for the Maid and was witnessed to have said that he would be honored to be the first to add an extra log to the fire—afterward confessed to have seen a strange thing during her burning. He saw something which took away the hate in his heart."

"What could he have seen to mitigate such hate?" Suzanne asked reverently.

"He said that at the moment Jehanne died, he saw a white dove leave her body and fly off toward Paris."

"One hundred point one," Douglas reported to the others.

Clarisse tidied Loni's bed covers, moving silently and serenely.

"The executioner later admitted to Pierrelot that he was afraid that he was damned, having burned a saint. He feared that God would never forgive him. He said that in spite of all the oil, sulfur, and fuel he had used, he could not reduce her heart to ashes. He was told to throw her ashes and heart into the nearby Seine River. Some believe that the river carried its precious cargo to Paris, the city which holds the crown of thorns of Christ."

"One hundred," reported Douglas.

Suzanne sighed. She relinquished her post at the fetal monitor and made her way to the window, secretly hoping for some surreal backup.

"I really hate to bring this up but, now that Jehanne is gone, when will our Loni come back? I mean, we can see that her body survived but what about her consciousness?"

"We'll just have to wait, Suzanne," said Mickey, tracing the lifeline in Loni's palm.

In the glass Suzanne saw only herself. *No Christine. Well, Suzanne, did you really expect her to appear at your leisure?* she scolded herself. Just then she caught sight of the moon as it started to make its grand entrance onto the stage of the velvet sky. *Well, you asked for a glimmer, and you got it, that's something, Suzanne. That's something.*

The team of American doctors didn't have to wait much longer for an answer. Just as Clarisse left the room, Loni opened her eyes, her face dripping with sweat.

Mickey cupped her face in his hands, splint and all. He looked into her eyes, unable to speak, but waiting to hear words indicating she was back from the world of amnesia.

She said nothing—her gaze blank, unknowing, placid. Douglas stepped in to invoke her attention still under hypnosis. "Loni, are you better now?"

"Better than what?" Loni replied, her voice was harsh and unyielding.

"Jehanne?"

"Who is Jehanne?"

"Who is this?"

"Who *am I*? I know myself, who are *you*? Does your voice come from the moon?"

85

Moonlight and Shadows

Maternity hospital
Saint-Quentin, Somme River Valley
Vermandois region, France
Current day

T he Americans stared, bewildered. Each looked from one to the other with shock. Each was afraid to speak for fear of what they were now facing.

Jehanne was clearly gone but Loni had not returned. From her mouth came the tone of someone very different than had been heard thus far.

Douglas was the first to shake off his dismay, quickly taking control of the dialogue and directing the conversation where he needed it to go. "Why did you say that my voice comes from the moon?"

"The moon is larger tonight than I can ever remember. There was a shadow that crossed it just as I heard your voice. Are you that shadow?"

"Yes and no," Douglas evaded. "I am Coletrane, Dr. Douglas Coletrane. I am a shadow, but you need not fear me."

"Fear you?" Loni scoffed. "I fear no one. I am Vlad Tepes." Loni's hands rose as two quivering fists, framing the uncharacteristic sternness of her face.

Douglas looked back over his left shoulder at Suzanne for some clue as to who Vlad Tepes could be. All he saw was astonishment in her face. But he could tell there was something familiar in that name to her too—she just didn't have a bead on it yet.

"Coletrane, my shadowy friend, have you come to help me?"

"I cannot say. I might, indeed, have been sent to help you—or maybe you are the one to help me."

"I am not sure how I can help the shadows," said Vlad Tepes. Douglas chanced a glance at Mickey for help. *Seriously, guys!? Nothing? I'm treading water*

354

here! Douglas was about to turn away when he saw Mickey's eyes go up and left. *Yes! Please, Mickey! Give me something to work with.* Douglas could see him lock in on the thought that was registering in his left-brain synapses.

Mickey's face went from neutral acknowledgement to something which looked like dread.

Oh, God. What now? thought Douglas.

"Mickey, talk to us." Suzanne struck the window glass with her fist, punctuating her desperate plea. "What do you know?"

"God, give me strength, Suzanne. I only have recall of one Vlad Tepes."

Overhearing Mickey, Vlad Tepes responded, "That would be me. I am the one and only. Come out, shadow-people, where I can see you. Come sit with me and dine." Loni smiled welcomingly. She gesticulated as if combing a large mustache.

In anticipation of the invitation, Mickey's face grew ghostly white. *The indisputable Kazikli Voyevoda was indeed Vlad Tepes, a man revered as much as he was feared. Passionately loved and hated. To some he was a god and to others a devil. Not someone I consider a great dinner companion—depending, of course, upon which side of the table I'm seated.*

"I . . . uh . . ." The words hung in Douglas's throat and fell dead in the air.

"Come, dear shadow-friends. Celebrate with me the second swallowing of the moon I have thus far witnessed. Dates, kebabs, and mint tea await you here in Sibiu on this, the twenty-second of May in the twenty-second year of my life. The moon is not a stranger in the sky. Why, then, should its shadows be? It is only appropriate that the moon's shadow-friends should dine with a newfound friend."

Kebabs? Suzanne mouthed silently to the others.

Mickey looked at Douglas and Suzanne with great trepidation and whispered, "If this is the Vlad Tepes that I have in mind, kebabs would be his specialty."

He looked at the face of his beautiful pregnant Loni and wondered how the voice of Vlad Tepes could be emanating from her. *Then again,* he reminded himself, *after everything that has happened so far, how can you be surprised anymore? Whatever the reason for this, this painful journey is far from over.* He shook his head and rolled back his shoulders. *You want your Loni back? Get on task, solve it. Get the date, get the facts, bring back your wife.* Mickey retrieved the notebook and pen from his travel vest pocket.

"Vlad Tepes," Mickey spoke with more confidence than before, his pen poised over the paper, "can you tell me the year of this celebratory feast?"

"The year? It's 1453."

Mickey nodded in acknowledgement to the statuesque Suzanne and Douglas before continuing. "Is there a great battle ongoing now?"

"Yes, I hope that our beautiful Constantinople will survive. What think you, shadow-friends? Have you wisdom from beyond the moon to share with me?"

Mickey was now certain that his hope for Loni's expedited return would be unrealized. Not wanting to reveal the future to this next man in the parade of characters, Mickey played his part well and kept the answer to Vlad's question cloaked within the moon's shadow.

"We must eat well tonight, my Lord Vlad Tepes," Mickey said. "For by sunrise tomorrow, many of us will be found feasted upon by the piercing cold and the breathless."

THE END

Sneak peek of the next book in the series:

*Devil's Order of Dragons (*Novel 3 of 12)

1

Passing of the Prince

Snagov Island
Wallachia
1476

"This body grows heavier with time." Wearing his gauntlets and forearm protecting metal vambraces tied to his belt, the soldier panted, hitching the load up higher in his arms. "How much farther to the church?"

The steady crunching of the forest floor echoed off the haunting wood line as well as the moon-bathed side of the Russian Orthodox monastery.

With all the armor clanking and leaves crunching, surely the enemy must be able to hear us, the soldier thought to himself.

The prince's elite personal guards had many responsibilities. Carrying a dying prince to a priest was least desired but, nonetheless, an important duty.

"I can see the church windows ahead," the younger of the two soldiers whispered hoarsely as he pointed. Sweat matted his forehead locks inviting war grit to stream down into his bright eyes.

"Be strong, boy," the elder of the pair puffed as he clenched tighter his gnarly fist. "We're almost there."

"Why did His Highness want us to bring him to the priest instead of the field surgeon?"

"Surgeon work is for those who might live, not for the soon to be dead."

"How do we know this priest will be the correct clergy?" The young soldier grunted.

"He must, son. He is the only patriarch in the only church on this island. Come on, not much farther."

It wasn't more than a few minutes more before the two Moldavian soldiers stood at the chapel door, holding the sagging prince between them. When the heavy door groaned on its rusted hinges, a warm, bright light backlit the shape of a cowl-covered nun.

"Come in quickly," the sister whispered as she clapped away the cold. "The father is in the back, in the rectory. I bid you step carefully over the planks. We haven't yet finished construction of the entrance way flooring. A trip and fall here could yield yet another casualty tonight."

At the back of the sanctuary, a priest sat quietly reading to a small peasant girl who held an ornate candelabrum. The flame flickered in her green eyes. Scooting the girl toward a side curtained doorway, he rose when he saw the men approach.

"Here, lie him on the draped table," said the priest, quietly praying over the casualty with his one hand raised, two little fingers down and index and middle extended upward. "Careful with his head."

The candle lights cast shadowy likenesses on the walls of the room as the four people huddled around the dying prince.

"Sister, take the little one away," the priest ordered. "She doesn't need to see this."

As the nun escorted the girl from the room, the priest placed his head against the prince's chest. Then he put his ear against the prince's mouth and nose.

"He's gone." The priest scowled. "Sister," he said as the woman returned, "I'm going to need one of the books from behind my desk."

"Which book, Father? There are so many."

"Yes of course, Sister. How unclear of me. How would you know?"

"I know I haven't been here long, but I'll find it . . . just tell me."

"Look on the top shelf. It's the only book wedged between all the stacks of unbound ledgers. The cover is red, and embellished upon it is the shape of a dragon painted in gold. It bears the words *Devil's Order of Dragons*. Please, Sister, hurry."

The priest turned his attention to the soldiers, his eyes searching their faces. "What information did His Highness give you?"

"He said to bring him here." The elder soldier tapped the table.

"Did he say Snagov Monastery?"

"Yes, Father. He said to take him only to a priest."

"Has anyone seen him en route, a doctor maybe?"

"No. The prince said that no one was to examine him," said the elder. "He refused to allow us to remove any of the armor above his waist nor below his chin. He wanted his dagger, sword, and pistol to be brought."

"His Highness trusts you greatly."

"Of course. Why wouldn't he?" The elder watched the sister pass by him with the book, place it on the table, and then disappear into the flickering shadows on the far side of the room.

"Who are you two who have gained the trust of the prince?" The priest bounced his gaze from one soldier to the other.

"Isn't it apparent?" asked the elder.

"Humor me."

"Forgive me, Father. Old age and fatigue have stolen my manners." The elder soldier cleared his throat. "This boy and I are what's left of the prince's personal guard."

"Nothing to forgive," said the priest, with a nod. "I need you now to respond to me as you have your prince. Understood?"

"Yes."

"Give the sister the bloodied dagger."

"Sure." The elder searched the distant shadows. "Where is . . . ?"

"She stands behind you now." The priest wiped the sweat off his upper lip. "Thank you. Now pass that sword to me, hilt first."

"Do you want his pistol?"

"I have no need for the pistol. You can pass it, grip first, to the sister."

The weapon disappeared into the folds of the sister's smock. Her hands reappeared empty.

"Sister, slide over the red book. Now, go get me my reading candle. I need to see His Highness's last requests."

The sister's movements flowed with silent agility. After a few moments of careful reading, the priest closed the book.

"What happens now, Father?" the younger Moldavian soldier asked as he stared at the body. "What does a priest do for m'lord after death?"

"Had he arrived alive, I could have performed the sacrament of final unction. It's too late for last rites."

"Can you do anything to prepare the prince for his journey beyond?"

"Yes, I can. But I need your help." The priest shifted his gaze from the younger to the older soldier.

"Anything, Father," said the elder Moldavian, rolling his shoulders back and standing erect, ready to receive orders. "Just tell us what you need." From the food preparation room located through the curtained doorway beyond the feet of the prince, the nun brought in a large bowl holding a pitcher of steaming water, soap, an alabaster jar, and some cloths. She set all but the alabaster jar on a small table next to the doorway. The jar she brought and handed to the priest before leaving back through the curtained doorway.

"First, go to that wash-up table," said the priest. "Then, using the pitcher and bowl, wipe that war grit off the front of your armor. After that, wash the blood and dirt from your hands and arms, all the way up to your elbows." The priest opened the alabaster jar for the soldiers. "Last, cover your skin completely with this oil so that it coats all the skin of both arms. When you have finished, show me both arms to the elbows." The priest left with the nun, and after several minutes, he returned alone.

"Are you finished?"

Having rolled up and buckled their chain mail sleeves, the Moldavians held up their bared arms. Glinting on the left arm of each man was an identical tattoo—a roaring dragon standing on its tail in front of a Jerusalem cross.

"You have done well," the priest said as he ran his fingers over each tattoo. Then he went to the prince's left arm and revealed the same marking. "You two are of the Devil's Order."

"Yes, of course."

Nodding toward the curtained doorway, the priest spoke. "Sister, you can put the weapons away now." The soldiers heard the nun sheath the dagger and then released the hammer on the pistol. As they turned toward the sounds, they only caught a glimpse of the two weapons as they quickly disappeared into the nun's habit.

"Who did you think we were, Father?" asked the elder soldier, his facial features strained. "Thieves? Enemy soldiers?"

"Just a precautionary measure as requested by your prince, gentlemen." The priest tapped the red book.

"Well, I trust you are satisfied." The elder soldier released the buckles and jerked down his rolled sleeves.

"His Highness's concern was that those who delivered him might be others who looked to gain."

"Gain what?" asked the younger soldier, rolling down his chain mail sleeves as well.

"That which you will both witness shortly. Please forgive the deception. These are your prince's desires, not mine. From this point on, we move together as one."

"What exactly happens from here, Father?" the young soldier asked.

"A great secret. Everything that is seen or heard must be never spoken or shared with anyone outside *our* order." The priest lifted his left sleeve. "Here begins the action which guards a secret greater than our prince, our kingdom of Wallachia, and all Christendom. What we do in the moments soon to come will prepare all Christians for victory at Armageddon itself. Gentlemen, remove your chain mail and armor. Assist the nun with the removal of the prince's breast plate armor and tunic. It is time to save all the tomorrows and the ultimate tomorrow which follows."

About the Author

B. Albertill is the author of the 12-book historical fiction series, the Lost Books of Benjamin (LBoB). Albertill is a retired (2015) U.S. Army physician-scientist, educationalist, science researcher, Christian apologist, historian without portfolio, and modern-day Christian Templar. Having served in the military from Vietnam era (1973) to his last posting in Afghanistan (2014), he has served in clinical, research, and operational military medicine, the field of chemical warfare, and in the history of military medicine. His writing is underpinned by a worldview defined by this professional education, military training, and resulting personal experiences across the globe.

Albertill writes historical fiction supported by a lifetime of travels/residencies throughout Europe, the Mediterranean countries in northern Africa, and the Levant. As LBoB novel protagonists Mickey Peronne, Suzanne Coletrane, Russell Lange and the numerous historical characters move through these regions, Albertill literally strolls shoulder-to-shoulder with them. The gift given to the reader is the palpable flavor of credible historical fiction from novels penned by a thin-soled wanderer who has firsthand imbibed each of those incredible historical settings.

The Lost Books of Benjamin
3 Benjamin 2:1-85
Beyond the d'Arc
Novel 2 of 12 in the 3rd Book of Benjamin
B. Albertill

Publisher: SDP Publishing
Also available in ebook format

 SDP Publishing

www.SDPPublishing.com
Contact us at: info@SDPPublishing.com